THE GEM OF IRELAND'S CROWN

CULLEN'S CELTIC CABARET - BOOK 4

JEAN GRAINGER

Copyright © 2024 by Gold Harp Media

All rights reserved.

No part of this book may be reproduced in any form or by any electronic or mechanical means, including information storage and retrieval systems, without written permission from the author, except for the use of brief quotations in a book review.

❦ Created with Vellum

Then onward sped and I turned my head
    And I looked with a feeling rare
    I said says I to a passer by
    'Who's the maid with the nut brown hair?'
    He smiled at me and he said, said he
    'She's the gem of Ireland's crown.
    Rosie McCann from the banks of the Bann
    She's the Star of the County Down.'

          Cathal MacGarvey 1866-1927

CHAPTER 1

KILKEE, COUNTY CLARE, IRELAND, MARCH 1926

 ETER

Dear Mr Cullen,

I hope this letter finds you well and enjoying continued success with your show. Allow me to introduce myself. My name is Harp Devereaux, and we share an acquaintance with Clive Stephens the ventriloquist. I knew Clive when he performed here in Atlantic City with a vaudeville troupe a few years ago, and he speaks very highly of you. I note you have achieved considerable success, not just in Ireland but in England, Scotland and Wales as well.

Clive and I remained in occasional correspondence when he left America, and he mentioned to me in his last letter that you would be interested in taking your cabaret to America. And so I have a proposition that may interest you.

Currently I and my band, Roaring Liberty, have a residency at the Ocean Diamond hotel here in Atlantic City, New Jersey. We perform six nights a week in the main ballroom to sold-out shows, and we occasionally perform at private functions as well.

My husband, JohnJoe, and I are expecting our first child, and we've decided we would like to spend the summer months back in Ireland with the baby. My mother and stepfather live in Cobh (how wonderful that we no longer call it Queenstown?), and we were wondering if you and your cabaret would be interested in filling our slot here in New Jersey for four months?

Atlantic City is known as the 'try-out town', where all the big shows and acts that aspire to be on Broadway or to tour the country perform first for the summer audiences to see how they are received. It could be a nice platform if coming here on a more permanent basis appeals to you.

If you are interested, please contact me at the above address and we can discuss it further.

Yours faithfully,

Harp Devereaux-O'Dwyer

* * *

SITTING in a soft pool of candlelight at the kitchen end of the beautifully designed Eccles caravan, Peter reread the letter for maybe the fiftieth time. When he'd found an envelope with an American stamp among the pile of bills he picked up from the post office that morning, he hadn't known what to expect. And he still couldn't believe it.

He'd been trying to find a way to break into America for the last five years, writing to theatre after theatre with no success. Now, out of the blue, the opportunity of a lifetime had landed into his lap.

And it was thanks to Clive, of all people.

The ventriloquist was a seriously odd and annoying little man. He drove Aida in particular insane with the way he treated his red-headed puppet like it was a real boy, even insisting on having one of the larger new Eccles caravans all to himself so Timothy could have his own bed. But he'd really pulled the rabbit out of the hat this time.

Peter just wished May had shown a tiny bit more enthusiasm about it.

He glanced towards his wife now, fast asleep in the big double bed at the far end of the luxury caravan, with the curtain drawn half across. He trusted May with his life, and just as importantly, with his business. She was always happy to talk to him about his hopes and dreams and help him with every aspect of Cullen's Celtic Cabaret. Today she'd spent hours dealing with an obstinate farmer who insisted they move the tent once it was almost up, something to do with him being able to see his herd from his house. She had the patience of a saint, she really did.

Yet when he'd shown her Harp Devereaux's letter, offering him a chance at his ultimate dream, maybe a permanent foothold in America, she hadn't looked as thrilled as he'd hoped she might be. Instead she'd said something about having to think it over before anyone else was told, and how they'd have to find out how much it would cost to store the equipment they couldn't take, and that they had to remember that Aisling would soon turn six and though she knew Peter didn't want to send her to boarding school, they would have to sort out some kind of formal education for her, so there was that to consider...

Peter thought that a 'proper' school would crush Aisling's spirit.

He himself had dropped out when he was only seven years old, after the priest beat him for mimicking Brother Constantin, but he'd never stopped learning, had he? And his daughter was like him, a sponge for information. She could already speak Spanish just from listening to Aida and Ramon. And he knew she would jump at the idea of travelling to America; she loved moving from place to place. She was a wild child, full of adventurous spirit.

He stood and tiptoed over to look at his daughter, fast asleep, tucked up in the bunk bed that pulled down from the wall opposite the sofa. The idea that he was not delighted six years ago, when May told him she was expecting a baby, horrified him now. His little girl was the light of his life. He knew May was always hoping to have another child, and was disappointed every month, but if he was honest, he couldn't imagine ever loving another child as much as he loved their precious little girl. Aisling was his whole world.

He stroked the treacle-dark hair fanned out across her pillow. She was dark-haired like his father, though he and May were both fair. Her little nose was pressed into the velvet rabbit Eamonn had given her when May refused to allow Bug, her real pet rabbit, to sleep in the bed with her. Peter would have allowed it – he was putty in Aisling's dimpled hands – but May was not for changing. Bug had to stay outside in a metal cage that Two-Soups had welded for him, and she wouldn't hear Aisling's tearful protests that because Bug was a performer in the cabaret, he deserved to live in a caravan like the rest of them.

It had been Aisling's idea to put Bug on stage. She performed in the weekend matinees now, her own little act with the rabbit and a pram, and Peter almost burst with pride when she bowed to the appreciative audience. She loved it, and everyone loved her, a born performer like her daddy. She squealed with delight when Tiny, the strongman, lifted her over his head and twirled her around. And May nearly had a fit last week when she found out that Enzo, the acrobat, was teaching her trapeze, but she was like a little monkey the way she could climb the tent poles. And the theatre was a drug to her, like it was to her father.

At bedtime she never wanted the usual fairy stories. Instead she wanted him to tell her about the time he saw Harry Houdini in London, at the Alhambra Theatre. She demanded tales of the time when the world's most amazing escapologist defied officers at Scotland Yard and strolled out of their cells despite being chained up. Or how he was buried alive, or sealed in a milk churn filled with water.

May complained that filling her head with such stories was giving their live-wire daughter ideas and that she needed eyes in the back of her head to watch her as it was, but Peter carried on, seeing how the stories lit his daughter's brown eyes with delight. In America he would show her things that would have those eyes out on sticks, and that would be better than any kind of school. Whatever May said, come hell or high water, he was going to make this adventure happen.

There was no way he could sleep now. He was too fired up, too restless. He'd burst if he couldn't tell someone else the exciting news, someone who wouldn't immediately start worrying about the cost of storing all the vans, the tent, the trucks and everything for four months, and how to pay to get all the actors and their props to America. Someone less practical than May. Someone more inclined to dream, like him.

Maybe his old friend Nick would be awake and up for a cuppa and a cigarette. They wouldn't be disturbing anyone because Nick had his caravan to himself now that his wife, Celine, had decided she wanted to live full time with their three sons in Brockleton, the huge stately home of the Shaw family in County Cork, which Nick would inherit when his father died, along with the title of baron de Simpré.

Peter crept out of the caravan and walked across the field, through the still, crisp air, past the looming, shadowy tent. It was a clear starry night, cold for March. He could see his breath and was glad of his woollen coat, cashmere scarf and felt trilby hat covering his blond hair.

The cabaret had another few days here in Kilkee, County Clare, before moving on. Everyone here was delighted to see them back – except the farmer. It had been three years since they were in this part of the country, as the demand for them everywhere was so high. They were doing so well, and financially they were very comfortable. They paid their acts well and expected the best from them. They could easily keep going like this, but America…that was the dream.

Atlantic City, New Jersey… Even the sound of it was glamorous.

And he was going there, with his own show. Him. Peter Cullen. Raised in a rat-infested tenement in Dublin, son of violent, useless drinker Kit Cullen. He would be playing at the Ocean Diamond hotel in Atlantic City. 'Atlantic City.' He whispered the words to make them real. This was the moment he'd been waiting for.

To his disappointment, in the gravel yard behind the farm, Nick's van was in complete darkness.

He carried on to the caravan that Enzo shared with Ramon, the flamenco guitarist from Spain. Like Nick, these two were old friends from the trenches in France. They'd all fought shoulder to shoulder against the Hun and then set up Cullen's Celtic Cabaret to entertain the troops, before bringing it to London at the end of the war. And then to Ireland, after the theatre they played in burnt down.

But no lights were showing in Enzo and Ramon's caravan either. Not that it meant they were tucked up in bed; they were more likely out on the town. Enzo was flirtatious and slippery as an eel in the romantic stakes. Despite several women's best efforts, he was not one to be shackled, and he liked to take Ramon with him on his adventures. A while ago Ramon had been keen on the chorus girl called Rosie, but Enzo was a bad influence on the Spanish lad and wouldn't let him settle.

Two-Soups's caravan was also in darkness. He was certain to be asleep, alone in his bed. The Scottish comedian had once had a mild flirtation going with one of the other girls, Delilah, but she finally realised he was never going to put a ring on her finger, so she took off and married a fishmonger from Castletownbere in West Cork. Peter didn't think Two-Soups would ever get married, to anyone. Years back, he'd been engaged to a girl called Betty who got killed in a car accident, and it seemed he only had one great love story in him.

At the far end of the yard, there was a lamp burning behind the curtain in Aida's caravan.

Peter hesitated, standing with his hands in his pockets.

May was so touchy on the subject of the Spanish dancer. She didn't say anything to his face about it, pretending everything was fine, but he knew by her face how uncomfortable it made her when he and Aida danced the tango together on stage.

At least she'd never tried to stop them doing it; in fact, she complimented them on their performance. The tango was the high point of the show on dance night. The passion of it always brought the audience to their feet, and that meant more money for the cabaret, so he supposed May's business brain could see what a good idea it was.

Besides, she knew by now that he would never do anything to rock their marriage. He was a committed family man, especially since Aisling had been born. He couldn't help what he felt, only what he did, and he'd never done or said anything to Aida that could be construed as being untrue to his wife.

Still…he knew May would go mad if she ever found out he'd gone to see the Spanish dancer at this hour of the night.

He glanced left and right around the silent yard. There was nobody to be seen.

He walked quietly across the gravel, climbed the two small wooden steps and tapped gently on Aida's door.

CHAPTER 2

IDA

SHE'D KNOWN it was him before even opening the door.

Without saying a word, she stood back as he entered, stripping off his coat, hat and cashmere scarf.

He looked more distinguished now than the boy she'd met in London in 1919. Seven years of hard work, miles and miles of travel and the acquisition of a good deal of money had made an astute, shrewd businessman of him. He still had his boyish good looks, a wiry, muscular body, blond hair brushed back off his face, sparkling dark-blue eyes that crinkled when he smiled. But now he was dressed in fine clothes made for him by a tailor in Dublin, he wore handmade Italian shoes, and even at this hour of night, he smelled faintly of a spicy cologne.

'Good evening, Mr Cullen. 'Tis late enough you're rambling?' She often spoke English as the Irish did, sort of inverting sentences, putting the last part first as was the way here. She enjoyed the way it sounded and rolled off the tongue, though she knew it made people laugh to hear it done in a Spanish accent.

He smiled. 'Indeed and it is then, Senorita Gonzalez. But I have news, and I was going to explode if I didn't tell someone aside from May, who wants me to keep it under wraps for a while, and yours was the only light on.'

Neither of them commented on the fact that May would be less than pleased if she knew he was here, and not just because she wanted the news kept quiet. And Aida had an even better idea of May's feelings than Peter did, having a woman's eye.

When Aida had come back from Dublin Castle, almost six years ago now, her body bruised and broken by her English captors, her hair torn out and face swollen and poor feet crushed, May had been nothing but kind. But now that Aida had recovered her beauty, Peter's wife had taken to barely tolerating her again.

'Go on,' Aida said now as she set about making coffee in her little percolator, one of her few precious possessions.

'I'll let you read it for yourself.' He handed her a letter, then moved away and sat down. He always made himself comfortable in the same place, on the seat she'd upholstered in a fanciful fabric with pink orchids. Her van was eclectic and colourful and very tidy, just as she liked it.

She poured the coffee into the tiny china cups she'd had sent from Valencia, brought his over to him, then stood by the tilly lamp hanging on the wall and read the letter quickly, her heart filling with pleasure for him.

'*Si puedes soñarlo, puedes hacerlo*,' she said as she gave it back to him.

'What does that mean?' he asked, his blue eyes begging her to share his delight.

'If you can dream it, you can do it.'

He gave her one of his wide, beautiful smiles. 'It's my dream, all right. What do you think?'

She smiled back at him. He was like a little boy sometimes, so excited, so full of enthusiasm. 'I think it is a wonderful opportunity, and a very lucky break, as you say.'

'It really is. And it's all down to Clive knowing Harp Devereaux. Imagine, this is from *the* Harp Devereaux! Of Roaring Liberty! They played in Dublin last year, and tickets sold out in minutes. Incredible.'

'I know. Even I have heard of Harp Devereaux. She is so famous now, and you can be sure she will not be performing in some second-rate venue. If Roaring Liberty play there, then it will be the best.'

'Ocean Diamond.' Peter said the name with awe. 'Sounds amazing. I remember passing the Ritz in Paris when we were demobbed – wouldn't have dared to go in, as they would have had a heart attack rather than let a scruffy private in the door. But I remember reading that the same man, César Ritz, managed the Carlton Hotel in London, and he was known as the king of hoteliers and hotelier to kings. Nick laughed when I told him that, saying nobody of blue blood would be caught dead in a hotel. Shows how much I know, eh?' He laughed gaily at himself. 'We thought the Shelbourne in Dublin was the height of sophistication when we were nippers.'

One of the things Aida loved about Peter was that despite the way he embraced his newfound wealth – he had a lovely car, and he and May were always dressed to perfection – he never pretended to be anything other than what he was, a poor boy who made a good life for himself by his own efforts.

'And it is lovely.' She smiled. He'd taken her there for afternoon tea one time on her birthday when they were performing near Dollymount Strand. Something else she suspected he hadn't mentioned to May.

'May must be very happy for you?' she asked now, stirring a quarter of a lump of sugar into her black coffee. She was as slim and lithe now as she was when she was a girl, but she had to watch it and so did not allow herself many indulgences.

Peter sighed. 'I hope so. I'm not sure. She's always had a bit of a notion to settle, maybe buy our own bricks-and-mortar theatre, a house, all the rest. She might see this as a step in the wrong direction.'

'And if she says no?' Aida asked quietly.

Peter fixed her with that look, the one that spoke volumes, his head slightly to one side, his blue eyes deeper than the sea. The look that said 'You know I didn't get to where I am by listening to other people.'

Aida remained silent. She could see that no answer was required. The cabaret was going to America, no matter if May's dreams were different from her husband's.

'Do you think everyone else will be happy to come? Is everyone happy with the constant moving around?' Peter asked her, eyeing her over the dainty cup as he sipped his coffee. Aida knew he saw her as his eyes and ears. She kept herself to herself, but by being quiet and discreet, she often noticed things that noisier people overlooked. And she heard things that would never be said in front of Peter or May. Not that either of the Cullens were disliked – it was more out of loyalty and respect.

'Well, yes, I think so. Ramon, certainly, and Two-Soups and Enzo as well – there's nothing to keep them here, no ties or attachments. Enzo split Ramon and Rosie up at the first sign of anything, and Two-Soups doesn't seem to mind that Delilah went off with the fishmonger.'

'We're like the bachelor show here,' he said, looking relieved at the thought. 'Just as well none of them are tied down. Enzo, Ramon, Two-Soups, Clive, Magus…'

'And me,' she interjected.

He looked slightly abashed. 'Ah, Aida, that's not for want of men trying, is it? One day someone will catch your eye.'

She shook her head with a slight smile. Men showed interest, of course they did; she knew she was beautiful. But she could never make herself vulnerable to a man again. Her first experience was with the landlord's son in Valencia when she had to prostitute herself to pay for her mother's funeral, and the only other time was when Harvey Bathhurst tortured and raped her in Dublin Castle. Bathhurst was dead now, thankfully, but her trust in men had been destroyed. Peter Cullen was the only man she would ever open her door to in the dead of night. She trusted Peter, but no other man.

'Why is it all right for your men friends to not want wives but not for me to not seek a husband?'

Peter shrugged and blushed slightly. 'It is all right, it's perfectly all right. You don't need to explain yourself to anyone, Aida, ever.' He added quietly, 'And for the record, there are days when being single would be a hell of a lot easier…'

'You know who will be wild to go?' she said, heading him away from the subject of his marriage. 'Maggie. She'll be on the next bus to Cobh.'

Peter laughed and rolled his eyes. He knew well his sister's wild enthusiasm for everything. Copper Topsie, as she was known, was a star of the show in her own right now, and her bubbly irreverent ways lifted everyone's spirits. Despite his initial reservations about bringing her on board, there was no doubt Peter's little sister was a tremendous asset.

Then he became serious again. 'Will Nick come, do you think?'

'Ah. That's a different matter, because Nick doesn't just have himself to consider.'

The Honourable Nicholas Vivian Shaw, with his wonderful tenor voice, was one of the backbones of Cullen's Celtic Cabaret, and he adored his life on the road. Yet every week, when the tent was struck and the cabaret moved on, Nick took that day or two to head back to the stately home of Brockleton, where his French wife, Celine, lived with their three sons: five-year-old Remy, named for his French grandfather, and four-year-old twins Pierre and Laurent, who were called after their godfathers, Peter and Enzo, only using the French versions of their names.

Nick would become the sixth baron de Simpré when his father died, and then, everyone supposed, he would have to go home for good. But until that day, he and his future baroness had settled on an unconventional but harmonious relationship. Nick travelled with the cabaret, while Celine stayed behind in the family mansion, minding Nick's father, Walter, and his grandmother Alicia, with the help of her best friend, Millie Leybourne. It was an arrangement that had always struck Aida as odd, though she would never comment on it. Everyone deserved their privacy.

'I'm really not sure, Peter. He loves you, but he does feel a responsibility to his family, so four months might feel too long of a gap. He's determined to be a good father to Remy and the twins, and he adores Celine and his father and grandmother. You might have to find someone else to sing with Maggie.'

Maggie had been Nick's singing partner since Celine left, and if anything, they were even more popular than he and Celine had been. Peter's sister was a fine singer and dancer, but she was also a rogue, so she brought a bit of humour to the performance that Celine didn't. And in their love duets, Aida had noticed that Nick sparked off Maggie in a different way – less boyishly sentimental than he had been with Celine, more edgy and knowing somehow – and audiences really liked it. So to Peter's obvious relief, it had all worked out fine.

Peter looked downcast at the thought of his best friend not coming to America with him. Then he cheered up. 'I'll set May on him – she's very persuasive. And if that's not enough, I'll corner him and persuade him more.'

'Clive will definitely come,' Aida said encouragingly. 'He's always been wanting to go back to America after his tour there.'

Peter nodded. 'That's good to hear. I know he annoys you, but the audiences love him. And Magus is American, so I imagine he'll jump at the chance. And I'm sure Tiny will be thrilled – he's never been abroad.'

'Mm.'

'What?' Peter looked at her sharply. 'What do you know that I don't?'

'His wife might not be too taken with the idea.'

'Why on earth not?' Peter was astounded. 'I know he's married, but Tess travels everywhere with him within Ireland. Why not America?'

Aida thought about how to answer him without seeming to complain about Tess.

When Millie had left the cabaret to live at Brockleton with Celine, where she helped Celine with the children and Walter to manage the estate, Tiny had taken her place. It had been a great success. People flocked to see him, and he was a much bigger draw than Millie had been, with her sharp little comedy act as a male impersonator. The huge man bent iron bars and ripped phone books in half and lifted benches with rows of shrieking girls from the audience perched along them. He was also useful when the cabaret moved from place to place, more than making up for the fact that he cost Peter the price of a guest house every night because he was too big to sleep in a caravan bed, even an Eccles caravan.

But his wife was a serious problem. Tess the Tyrant, as everyone called her behind her back because she treated Tiny like a naughty schoolboy, was a small, fat woman from Northern Ireland who hated all foreigners with an equal degree of venom. Peter, being Irish, wouldn't have noticed, but Aida, being Spanish, did. And she suspected Tess was egalitarian in that regard. Spanish, English, Americans – it wouldn't matter to her; she mistrusted and disliked them all.

Eventually Aida said, 'I just don't think she'll want to leave Ireland, and Tiny won't go anywhere without her. He adores her.'

'Well, let's hope you're wrong. Aisling loves it when he picks her up and spins her around.' His face lit up at the thought of his daughter. 'She's learning Cherokee off Magus now, the same way she picked up Spanish from you and Ramon. She has that man wrapped around her little finger.' And he rattled on, as loving parents did of the surprising perfection of their own child. Not that he was wrong about Aisling. Her big brown eyes could melt the hardest of hearts. She was the mascot of the cabaret, adored by everyone, including Aida. It was impossible not to, and her efforts to remain aloof from Peter's family in as much as was possible given how they lived, were thwarted by Aisling's persistence in befriending her.

'I can't believe she's my daughter, Aida. She's so clever and bright and beautiful. She's going to love America. And I think May will like it too, when she gets there.'

Feeling suddenly tired, Aida glanced at the clock. It was just after three in the morning.

Following her gaze, Peter drained his coffee cup and stood. 'I see

I've well overstayed my welcome. Good night, Aida, see you tomorrow. And thanks for letting me know your thoughts.' He gathered his hat and scarf and coat, smiling his farewell.

'Good night, Peter. Take care.' She stood to let him out and watched him for a moment as he walked away, before she shivered in the cold night and closed the door after him.

CHAPTER 3

AY

SHE KNEW HE WAS OUT; through her sleep she just felt it. And as she came awake, she knew where he was too. It burnt her inside, the way it had done since she first saw Aida Gonzalez.

The pain of her jealousy was constant these days, now that the Spanish girl had recovered her looks. Yet even when Peter danced that passionate tango with Aida, May tried her best to hide her feelings. She had no right to them. Peter had not been unfaithful to her, she was sure of it. He might love another woman as well as her, possibly more than her, but he had never acted on it. She, on the other hand, was an adulteress, a woman of such low morals that she had no right to feel anything but shame and guilt.

She had been unfaithful to the man she'd fought so hard to have, and that sin had resulted in the conception of her precious daughter. Because no matter how she longed for it to be otherwise, she was very sure Aisling was not Peter's child, and however much her husband and her daughter loved each other, that fact could never be changed.

Her cheeks burnt, as they did every time she thought of it. To have relations with another man, that was such a betrayal, but when that man was her husband's brother... It was as low as it was possible to go. The weight of the guilt, the shame, the terror that Peter would ever find out, sometimes threatened to suffocate her. And when she felt as she did right this minute, her jealousy of Aida twisting a knife in her heart, she knew she deserved her pain.

She sat up in the bed, and by the bright moonlight streaming through the van window – they always parked their own caravan in the same field as the tent and slept with the curtains open to make sure they weren't robbed in the night – she could see her little daughter, sleeping peacefully, her velvet bunny in her arms, secure in her world.

Aisling adored Peter. She loved May too, looked to her for all her needs and hugged and kissed her fifty times a day, but she worshipped her daddy. She was him; she had the same impetuous, impatient, determined, charming way about her. People could not say no to Aisling Cullen, any more than they could say no to Peter.

For the last five years, May had longed for another child. Not just because she would have loved a sibling for Aisling but to prove to herself that Peter could be Aisling's father. She'd done all she could, counting out the days as Dr de Vries had explained when she'd visited his clinic in Dublin all those years ago – he was Dutch and seemed to find it easier to discuss such things than an Irish doctor – but she never again became pregnant.

Now, after five years of ensuring they made love at the right time – that was sixty times she could have become pregnant but didn't – she was more sure than ever that Eamonn was Aisling's father. And she knew Eamonn was convinced of it as well.

It was obvious in the way he doted on the girl. He did far more for her than he ever did for his sister Kathleen's children, like buying her that gorgeous velvet bunny – it must have cost him a week's wages because he only earned a pittance on the sites.

He took her for treats and allowed her to ride around on his back like a horse. He made her a dollhouse for her fifth birthday, complete with beds and tables and chairs and all sorts of tiny things; it must have taken him ages and ages to do it all. Then for Christmas last year, he arrived with a rocking horse, another handmade gift, with a leather saddle and a bright-red bridle and a beautiful long mane and tail.

She prayed with all her heart that Eamonn would never say anything to anyone. The thought of the truth coming out made her faint with horror. If it ever did, it was all over. Her life, her family, her child, her reputation – everything would be pulled from under her.

The door opened and Peter came in. When he saw she was awake, a brief flash of something passed over his face. Guilt, perhaps. Or fear of her making a scene. He needn't worry; she was too guilty herself to take him to task. She wouldn't even ask where he'd been, though she knew.

And he knew that she knew, because instead of making up some stupid excuse for coming in at three in the morning, he said nothing at all. Instead he went to Aisling's bunk and tucked a stray strand of her dark hair behind her ear, then bent and gently kissed her cheek as she snuggled the bunny closer.

Afterwards he undressed and got into bed beside her. 'How come you're awake?' he whispered.

'I don't know,' she replied with a loving smile. 'Just woke up.'

He kissed her then, his hands moving over her body, and she responded to him as she always did. And as her husband's body joined with hers, as they moved as one, clinging to each other, she prayed that maybe this time, by some miracle that she knew she didn't deserve, she would conceive.

Afterwards, as they lay quietly together, she realised she had to be more supportive about America. She knew Aida would have encouraged Peter's dreams without giving a single thought to the cost and difficulties. That's why he'd gone to her, of course. Because Aida never objected to his plans, however crazy they were. Aida thought she was fiercely independent and cared for no man, but May knew she'd made Peter's dreams her own.

Nobody bothered their head about May having different dreams.

Peter pretended to care, even nodded along, but he constantly brushed them aside.

She knew for sure now that her husband was not remotely interested in buying or building a bricks-and-mortar theatre in Dublin and putting on respectable plays by Shakespeare and things like that so they could settle in a nice middle-class house and become part of Dublin theatre society and so that Aisling could go to an expensive private school. He'd claimed to be interested, but May had taken him to see four different places that could potentially be a theatre, one building – a former Methodist church hall, now closed – and three sites, and he'd looked bored and impatient at each one.

'So, May,' he said now, curled up against her, holding her in his arms. 'Have you thought any more about going to America?'

May fought down feelings of cynicism that the lovemaking was to soften her up, that in the glow of spent passion, she would be more amenable to his mad scheme. Still, she knew what she had to do. Peter was taking them all to America either way, with her support or without it, so she might as well be on the right side of him, and she was determined to be at least as enthusiastic as Aida.

'You know, I have. I was a little taken aback at first, but honestly it sounds like an amazing opportunity. And to go in at the highest level, not start from scratch as you assumed we'd have to, is really wonderful.' She nearly had to laugh at the look of surprised relief on his face.

'So you're on for it?' He smoothed and kissed her hair.

She rested her head on his bare chest. 'Where you go, I go, Peter. Of course I'm on.'

'And we'll earn more in four months than we would in a year here in Ireland.'

'That's true,' she agreed, trying to sound even more pleased.

May knew her husband thought she was all about the money. She knew he believed that's why she never objected to him dancing the tango with Aida, because it was such a crowd-puller and a money-raiser as well; everyone wanted to pay the performers for dance lessons after they'd seen it to learn how to do it for themselves.

'Maybe we can earn enough to build our own theatre in Dublin, the way you've always said we would one day,' she added, unable to resist testing him a little.

'Sure, of course, someday maybe...' His voice trailed off, but then he added with a lot more enthusiasm, 'It's going to be the break I've always dreamed of, May, I just know it is. America is where it's all happening, the jazz bands – the negro musicians and singers have to be seen to be believed apparently. Eamonn saw some when he was in New York that time.'

The mention of Eamonn forced her to slow her breathing, to not react.

'And the acts over there, they'd kill to be headlining at the Ocean Diamond. People spend years in the business and never get there. Harp says it's called the "try-out town", Atlantic City that is, so if we go down well there, who knows where it will take us.'

'So will you write back tomorrow?'

'Wild horses won't stop me,' he said, his voice now heavy with sleep and satiety.

As he slid into darkness and dreams, she eased out of his arms. Sleep would not come for her now, she knew it. She got out of bed, put her nightie back on and went down to the far end of the caravan. She lit the candle that was sitting half-melted on the table, where Peter must have left it before going out to see Aida, and made herself a cup of tea.

As she sat there in the small pool of light, drinking her tea, she found her thoughts drifting towards Eamonn. Was he awake now? Was he thinking about her? That night with him in Doyle's Hotel was a terrible mistake, she knew it and hated herself for it, but sometimes she allowed her mind to go to the memory of him, the adoration he had for her, reverence almost. He was so different from Peter in every way. He was physically big where Peter was slim and lithe. He was dark where Peter was fair. He found expressing emotion hard where Peter was fluent and charming. And yet she couldn't forget the way her body responded to him, the longing she'd had for him. Or waking that morning to find him gone, with just a note, written in Irish, saying how he was sorry for causing her such confusion and pain but how he couldn't bring himself to regret the night they had spent together.

Eamonn felt about her the way she felt about Peter. And she knew it was the delicious feeling of being loved and adored by him above all others that was why she'd allowed him to take her to bed. Peter was mercurial, almost hers but never quite. He loved her, but not the way she craved him. The truth was he would never have married her had she not forced him by sheer will and bribed him with money.

She shook herself mentally. This was not helpful.

She was a lot older and wiser now than that headstrong, romantic girl who'd chased after Peter in Dublin and then London, convinced if she could only make him marry her, then everything would be perfect and he'd realise they were made for each other.

She'd got what she wanted, no question. She'd made him marry her, and that was the way she wanted it to stay, for all their sakes. For herself, for Aisling, for Peter himself – because how would he and the cabaret manage without her? Besides, she still thought he was the most beautiful man she'd ever laid eyes on. She loved him, she desired him, he was her husband, she'd moved mountains to make him hers, and she refused to mess everything up.

Perhaps putting an ocean between herself and Eamonn might be for the best. He needed to forget her and move on. And he needed to stop coming to see Aisling. His visits unsettled May, and it wasn't just that his big, dark presence was a reminder of her guilt – it was the way he had never denied being in love with her. Sometimes she caught him looking at her with undisguised passion, and a shiver would go through her body and she'd find herself longing for him to wrap his arms around her…

Maybe it was the safest thing to do, to go to America, and if things worked out, maybe they would stay, and the potential disaster of Peter ever knowing her secret would surely be averted.

CHAPTER 4

ICK

PETER HAD CALLED everyone to the tent for a meeting at four. There was the usual grumbling. Mornings were for rehearsal, trying out new material and polishing up and refreshing the old stuff, and they were all back by six for the evening performances, so the afternoon was relaxation time. But Peter hardly ever called meetings, so Nick thought it must be something serious.

Nick's friend bounded onstage as he did every night, but his face was cast in a serious frown. It was strange to see him up there in his shirtsleeves, no tie, and informal trousers. He was always in a top hat and scarlet-red tails with gold braiding as he conducted the cabaret as master of ceremonies.

Was something wrong? Surely Peter would have spoken to him first if there was. Peter was Nick's oldest friend, ever since they'd met in the trenches in France during the Great War. They'd sworn a pact back then to be loyal to each other forever.

Though he knew an unspoken gap had opened up between them in the last few weeks.

It was Nick's fault. He'd been avoiding Peter.

He still loved Peter Cullen like a brother, but something had happened recently of which he was ashamed, and it was hard to look his old friend in the eye.

There had been a night five-and-a-half years ago, when Peter's sister Maggie had shown Nick the meaning of passion. But after that he'd tried his best to stay away from her. She deserved better than him; he had nothing to offer her. Divorce was against the law in Ireland. Maybe he and Celine could be separated after his father's death – Celine wouldn't mind, as she was in love with Millie Leybourne – but Maggie could still never be more than his mistress, and any children they had would be illegitimate and unable to inherit anything.

He couldn't rob a young girl of her future like that. And certainly not his best friend's sister.

Maggie had refused to take no for an answer at first, and Nick had found it nearly impossible to resist her when she got him alone; there had been plenty of 'slips' in the first year. But after his wife got pregnant with the twins – Celine had insisted it was her duty to give him another son, and by a miracle there were two – he'd put his foot down. The clandestine affair had to end. It took Maggie a long time to accept he was serious, and she sulked for a whole year. But at last she took up with an old flame of hers, Bill Tully, who had been run out of Ireland during the War of Independence but who had since come home.

Nick did his best to be happy for her, and for the last few years, they'd managed to 'just be friends'. Until a month ago, when she'd come to his caravan to tell him she'd ended her relationship with Tully, something about him being on the wrong side as regards to the Treaty.

Nick had tried to hide his joy…and failed. Thinking of what had happened next, he blushed, and he couldn't help glancing across the tent to where Maggie was sitting beside Aida. As if she sensed him, she turned her head and winked, and he blushed even more. He then realised Peter was looking at him, so he made a big show of peering around at the other members of the cast, as if he was just checking everyone was present and correct.

The ten chorus girls were sitting in the front row. They'd changed over the years, some leaving to get married, like Delilah, while others had joined to replace them, like Rosie.

The roustabouts stood to the right of the stage, two of them leaning against the poles that held up the roof. The cabaret employed four of them on a full-time basis now, strong lads who were responsible for building and striking the set, moving props and scenery during the show and overseeing everything on moving day.

Ramon and Enzo were sprawled in the second row, eyeing up the girls, while Two-Soups, Clive and Magus sat in the same row as Nick. Tiny the strongman took up two chairs a couple of rows behind Nick, with his wife, Tess the Tyrant, beside him. She liked to keep her distance from the rest of the cast, though Nick wasn't sure why; everyone was lovely.

May stood to the left of the stage, holding Aisling by the hand, but Peter beckoned her to come and stand beside him. Everyone exchanged a look. Something was definitely happening if May was behind it or at least supported it.

Peter took her hand with a grateful look and began speaking. 'Thanks for coming, everyone. I know how much ye hate doing anything other than sleeping at this time of the day, but I've...' He turned to May. 'But we, I should say, have a very important announcement.'

There was dead silence. Normally there would be catcalls or some kind of heckling – the chorus girls were cheeky – but everyone was on tenterhooks.

Nick's old friend took a deep breath. 'We've had an invitation to fulfil a summer residency, four months straight, shows six nights of the week...'

There was an audible groan. The usual schedule was five nights, with a couple of nights off as they moved places. The main performers had other nights off on occasion, and each member of the chorus had a week off for every four weeks worked.

'Wait, wait, wait…' Peter raised his hand. 'Before you all have a fit, this residency is in' – he paused, and his serious face burst into an enormous grin – 'Atlantic City, New Jersey!'

There was a stunned silence.

Then Dolly, one of the chorus, piped up. 'Isn't Jersey that island in between England and France?'

Peter smiled even more broadly. 'No, this is New Jersey, and it's in the United States of America.'

Most of the cast and crew burst into excited chatter then, with the chorus girls and Maggie on their feet, jumping around and squealing for joy. Aida looked calmly on, and Enzo and Ramon shook each other's hands. Nick was delighted for Peter – this was his old friend's dream, breaking into America – and most of the actors seemed to feel the same way, though Magus for some reason looked even darker and more brooding than usual.

Nick turned around to see what Tiny thought of it all, only to see the strongman being ordered to his feet by his diminutive wife, who hissed, 'Don't even think about it, Thomas. If this lot want to go and mix with foreigners, it's up to them. Half of them are from God alone knows where themselves. But this is the last straw. You're going to take up that offer from the circus in Fermanagh.'

Ow. That was bad. Tiny was an important part of the show. And there was another problem. Nick himself. He couldn't see leaving Brockleton for four whole months. He loved seeing his sons at the weekends, his father needed him, and on top of all that, Floss was getting very old now, frail and breathless, and if anything happened to his darling grandmother while he was away and he was unable to be at her bedside, he would never forgive himself.

'And it's all thanks to our own Clive, who made the introductions,' Peter explained from the stage as the tent fizzed with excitement. He read out the letter in his hand, which was from the famous Harp Devereaux. Everyone cheered and congratulated Clive, and the ventriloquist went pink in the face, speechless with delight. His 'son', Timothy, wasn't so reticent.

'Actually, folks, this was all my idea,' shouted the carrot-headed, freckle-faced puppet, while Clive vainly tried to restrain him. 'If it wasn't that I was so brilliant on stage when I was in America and made Harp Devereaux fall completely in love with me, none of this would have happened. So don't let my dad or that Peter Cullen try to take the credit. They'd be nothing without me and they know it!'

CHAPTER 5

ETER

He looked down from the stage, trying to judge who was for and who against the idea. Enzo, Ramon and Clive were clearly thrilled, the whole chorus as well. But Tess the Tyrant was marching a crestfallen Tiny out of the tent, so it looked like Aida was right about her not wanting to leave Ireland. That left a serious hole in the line-up. He wondered briefly if Millie Leybourne could be persuaded to fill in; he'd never really understood why she'd disappeared off to Brockleton, and America might be just the thing to get her back again.

Nick didn't look very happy either. Something was going on there – Peter's old friend had been avoiding him for a few weeks now…

And Magus was moving gloomily towards the exit. What was the matter with him? Surely, being American, he of all people should be delighted?

'Looks like Tiny's deserted us,' he said quietly to May. 'Will you see that Nick is OK? Persuade him four months will fly by in a flash, that he'll be home to his boys and Celine in no time. I'm just going after

Magus to find out what's the matter with him. We can't have half the cast abandoning us.'

The magician had already disappeared into his caravan by the time Peter reached the yard behind the farm. Magus, whose real name was Gil Brown, had a caravan to himself, not because he insisted on it but because nobody really wanted to share with him. He wasn't a man who liked to socialise. On stage he held the audiences in rapt attention, but they didn't love him; instead they were intrigued by him. There was something about him that was mesmerising if a little off-putting. Off stage he said little and spent most of his time alone.

Only Aisling really liked the magician. She called him Uncle Magus and he adored her, and she was always getting him to teach her little tricks.

It took Magus a while to answer Peter's knock, and when he did, he looked darker than ever. He was already an unusual-looking man, with a broad face, a defined jawline and a strong nose. His eyes were jade green and deeply set, and now they were sullen and sad and his black brows were tightly knitted.

'You all right, Magus?' Peter asked.

'Yes.' Magus was a man of few words. He stood in the doorway without inviting Peter in.

'I've never really got to see inside your caravan, but Aisling tells me it's full of books and you've taught her lots of stuff. I'm very grateful to you.' He was turning on the full blaze of his charm, without much result. 'Any chance of a cup of hot pond?' he asked hopefully. 'Hot pond' was the name Aida had given tea when she first tasted it, and now it was what everyone in the cabaret called tea, even May.

Magus seemed to take a long time to decide. He didn't make eye contact but gazed over Peter's right shoulder, then eventually said, 'Come in.'

Peter bounded up the steps before Magus could change his mind and stood looking around him. The caravan really was full of books, many torn and tattered, some brand new, piled high on every surface, even the bed. While Magus put on the kettle, Peter ran his hand over the shelf behind the sofa, where the books were stacked on their sides, five or six deep. There were books about magic, but there were also all sorts of other topics – history, anthropology, botany, geography. And there were books written in what looked like funny squiggles, maybe Chinese. Peter had never really been interested in Magus's private life, but the American Indian seemed to be a very learned man.

'So, Magus, I've just realised I don't know much about you, which is odd considering we've worked together for years.'

The magician didn't seem to think that needed a reply; he just raised his eyebrows slightly. This was going to be hard work. One thing Peter did know, though, was that the magician had been a soldier in the American army. Maybe that would be a good way to start the conversation.

'We were all so relieved when you American boys joined the war,' he said, and not just for the sake of saying something but because he meant it. 'Saved our skins, you did.'

'Milk? Sugar?' asked the man, placing the cups on the table.

'Both, thanks. We were in Ypres. Did you see much action yourself?' He cringed as he heard himself. It was such a ridiculous question, as if the carnage and misery they endured daily were an interesting show.

To his surprise, Magus answered him. 'The Somme.' And then even more surprisingly, he added, 'Do you want an iced bun with your tea?' while holding out a cake tin.

Pleased that the man was unbending a little, Peter accepted a currant bun with yellow icing and sat at the table. 'I didn't see you as a cake man, Magus.'

A shadow of a smile crossed the American's gloomy face as he sat opposite Peter and poured milk and heaped sugar into Peter's tea while leaving his own black. 'A certain little girl introduced me to the delights of buns, and she takes milk and sugar in her tea, like her father. I have them for her.'

Peter was delighted. He'd almost forgotten that he and the magician had an obvious, easy point of connection. 'Ah, of course! Aisling loves coming here. She says you teach her all sorts. She spoke some Cherokee to me the other day, or that's what she said it was.'

Magus didn't react, just sipped his tea. There was a strange kind of stillness to him; he didn't appear to move at all, any part of him. His dark hair was shiny and still, his breath barely perceptible. He didn't even seem to blink much. There was a set to his jaw, a strength to the man that was impossible to define.

Peter decided to drop the niceties and speak directly; it seemed Magus preferred that type of communication. 'Are you coming to America with us?'

After what felt like a fortnight, the man spoke again. 'No.'

All right, Peter thought. A silence fell between them as he ate his bun, which even though it was fresh and sweet now tasted like ashes in his mouth. It was going to be next to impossible to replace Magus.

He decided to turn on the charm again. 'This bun is delicious. Magus, I honestly thought you'd be delighted about Atlantic City. I mean, you're American, so it would be a trip home...' He hoped he wasn't crossing a line.

'Do you know what I am?' Magus asked, his green eyes penetrating and unfathomable.

'Well...' Peter felt himself get flustered, an unusual sensation for him. 'I know you are an Indian. Cherokee, Aisling says...'

Magus smiled then, and Peter realised he'd never seen him do that before. 'Indians. That's what they called us, the white men, because they didn't even know my homeland existed – when they got there, they thought they were in India. But we are not Indians. We are Cherokee.'

He stopped then, and Peter wondered if that was all he was going to get. If so, he wouldn't push it.

But then Magus went on. 'We welcomed them. We did not believe that a man can own a forest or a river or a mountain, something that has been there before us and will be there long after us. That makes no sense to us. There was a time when the Cherokee inhabited Appalachia, Tennessee, down to Alabama, all the way out to the ocean. We lived in what they call Georgia, the Carolinas...' He looked at Peter closely. 'Have you heard of the Trail of Tears?'

Peter shook his head, listening closely now.

'Many, many of us were wiped out by white man's disease, their cannons, their rifles. Then one hundred years ago, the government of the United States forcibly removed what remained of the Cherokee, and all the other Indian tribes as well, from their ancestral homelands and sent us to what they called Indian Territory. We walked and died, walked and died.'

'I'm sorry. I didn't know.' He felt so ignorant. 'I wish I'd stayed in school a bit longer.'

Another slight smile. 'I don't think they teach our history in your schools. But the Irish are no strangers to tragedy, injustice forced upon you by a foreign invader, one generation after the next, so perhaps you understand in a way others don't.'

'I suppose we do.' He did feel a profound empathy for the man. 'So why did you, and people like you, Indians, Cherokees, I mean, join the American army? After all you endured?'

Magus shrugged, a spark of something in his emerald eyes – sadness? 'The same reason you joined yourself, Peter, though the British had been oppressing you for your whole life. Money. Adventure. To get away from it all, the life of my ancestors. I was restless. I wanted something different. And there was also the idea that by fighting, we would achieve citizenship for all Native peoples, the same as the way the Irish thought the British would grant them Home Rule after the war.'

Peter nodded. The Cherokee was right. 'It wasn't what we thought it was going to be, though, was it, the Western Front?'

'No. Indeed not.'

'May I?' He extracted a packet of cigarettes from his pocket.

'Of course.' Magus took down an ashtray from a shelf beside him.

Peter offered a cigarette to the Cherokee, who took it, and both men lit up and inhaled deeply. 'So what was it like for you in the army, Magus? The English soldiers could be pretty unpleasant to us Irish, though some of them were all right. Like Enzo. He's half-Italian, though – maybe that makes a difference.'

Magus picked a piece of tobacco from his tongue. 'The Allies found us invaluable because they could use us as code talkers.'

'Code talkers?'

'Yes. Do you really want to know all this history I am telling you?'

'I really do.' He also wanted to keep Magus talking; he wanted the Cherokee to see him as a friend, and not just because he wanted him to come to America. Magus was an oddball, no doubt about it, but there was something decent about him too. He'd had no concerns about Aisling befriending him; he was strange but not sinister or menacing in any way.

'Very well. The Allies on the Western Front had a serious problem with their communications being intercepted by the Germans. I was in the 105th Field Artillery Battalion, 30th Infantry Division, with a group of Eastern Band Cherokee, and they heard us communicate in our own language. They imagined, correctly, that the Germans would not be able to interpret us.'

'And you ran messages that they couldn't intercept?' This was extraordinary.

Magus gave another smile then, a full one that lit up his dour face. 'Well, interception was possible. Interpretation wasn't.' He took a long draw of his cigarette, exhaling slowly. 'And it wasn't just Cherokee men they used. There were Choctaw, Cheyenne, Comanche, Sioux… and others, I believe.'

'Because you could all understand each other?'

Another long inhale, exhale. 'Can you understand Russian, Peter? Or Greek? Or Turkish?'

'Well, no, but…'

'We are different nations, as the countries in Europe here are different, so no, all the languages are distinct and unique. And that made it even harder for the Germans.' He rested his cigarette in the ashtray. 'Also, unlike European languages, we all speak many dialects, and only a few are written. They are mostly oral. Cherokee is very unusual. A great man called Sequoyah developed our alphabet.' He pointed to one of the books on the shelf above the sofa.

'That's Cherokee? I thought it might be Chinese.'

Magus took the book from the shelf and handed it to Peter, who leafed through it.

'It is a similar system,' Magus explained. 'A character for every syllable, and they mean different things said in different ways. Your daughter is quite the expert now – you should get her to show you.'

Peter laughed, amazed. 'I will. This is amazing, Magus. So you lot won the war for us. I hope you got a medal for what you did.'

'Victory Medal, Citation Star and the Croix de Guerre.' He said it with no pride or patriotism. Just another fact.

'You were awarded all of those?' Peter tried to take this in. He'd lived and worked with this man for seven years now and clearly knew almost nothing about him. 'You're an American hero! They'll put on a parade in the streets when you go home!'

Magus did that thing again, thinking for a long time, gazing into the middle distance, then shook his head. 'No, I won't be going back there.'

'But you must have some family there, people you'd like to visit.'

Magus inhaled slowly, shut his eyes for a fraction longer than a blink, seemed to hold his breath for a moment, as if trying to curtail some emotion that was bursting to be released, then exhaled. 'Yes.' His voice was gravelly and deep. 'But in the eyes of my family, I am a traitor. My father did not approve of my going to war for the United States government. My father is a very well-respected member of the tribe of Eastern Band of Cherokee in North Carolina, the brother of the chief, and he instructed my family to shun me if I insisted on it.'

'And they did?' This was so sad, Peter thought.

'I wrote to my mother, my sister, once or twice, but never heard anything. I'm dead to them.'

'But maybe not forever?' suggested Peter hopefully. 'My brother, Eamonn, he was in the IRA when I joined up. I thought he'd never speak to me again, but he did. Blood is thicker than water, Magus. Family counts for a lot.'

Magus shrugged again. 'My father is a powerful influence. And there is also the magic. Even if they forgave, they would want me to stop the magic. My people are spiritual. The physical world and that of spirit are one and the same, and they would not approve of what I do.'

'So where did you learn to do magic, Magus?' This had become more and more fascinating. He'd always assumed the magic was some kind of mysterious Indian – *Cherokee*, he mentally corrected himself – thing.

'I met a woman in New York, one night before I was shipped out. She was...unusual.'

'In what way?' He was intrigued.

'She was a conjurer. She performed a certain type of...shall we say...parlour tricks.'

'Where did you meet her?'

Magus took his cigarette up again and smoked it. 'In a brothel on Mercer Street in Manhattan. She was famous for her...well, certain erotic dexterities. I paid for two hours with her, and she taught me magic, both of us fully dressed the entire time. Then she sold me a copy of *The Secrets of Ancient and Modern Magic, the Art of Conjuring Unveiled*.'

Peter laughed incredulously. 'You learnt magic from a prostitute and a book?'

Magus took one last drag and crushed the cigarette in the ashtray, then shrugged. 'Well, Libertina and I continue to correspond, so the lessons are ongoing, and as for the book, well, there wasn't much else to do on the Western Front, apart from getting your head shot off.'

'True enough. Hours of boredom, interspersed with moments of sheer terror.'

Magus nodded.

'Wouldn't you like to see Libertina again?'

A glint of something appeared in his eyes. 'No.'

Peter made one last effort. 'This cabaret is your family as well, Magus. If the one you've got doesn't want you, we'll always be here for you.'

'The answer is still no.'

Sighing, Peter gave up and got to his feet. 'Well, thank you for the tea.'

'You're welcome, Peter.'

'What will you do when we're gone?'

'I have money saved. I will take a room in Dublin for a while, then travel around. I hope you will take me back if you return.'

'If?' He looked at the Cherokee man in surprise.

Magus looked straight back at him, again giving that faint smile. 'Is it not your dream to stay?'

The man really was very perceptive. Peter hesitated...

There was a rush of little feet across the gravel outside, and Aisling burst into the caravan. 'Magus, Magus!' she cried, rushing to throw her arms around him, sobbing pitifully. 'Help me! Help me, Magus!'

'What is it?' cried the magician in alarm.

'Mammy said they're going to send me to boarding school because I'm not learning anything, but I said you were teaching me loads of stuff from books, and she said, well, if you were coming to America and promised to teach me all about the strange American animals and birds and flowers and everything else you know, then I can come to America too, but if not I have to go to that horrible school in Dublin and sleep there and wear horrible clothes and keep my hair in plaits all the time and wear a skirt right down to my ankles, and the nuns beat you with sticks if you get the smallest thing wrong!' The speech came out in one long stream, the child barely pausing to take a breath.

Magus looked horrified. 'Oh, I'm sure that won't happen. Your father would never allow it.'

'Yes he would, because Mammy always gets her own way!'

Peter was ready to say, very firmly, that his wife would not be getting her own way on this one, but then Aisling turned to look at him and gave him a huge smile and a big wink without Magus seeing, and suddenly he knew what to do. His brilliant wife and amazing daughter had set this up for him, and all he had to do was play along.

'I'm afraid Aisling is right.' He sighed heavily. 'May is very keen for Aisling to start her formal education, and May's parents have already offered to pay for boarding school. We had said no, but now that we're going abroad...'

'Please help me, Magus, help me!' Aisling set up another helpless wail. 'If you're my teacher, I don't have to go to the horrible place.'

The magician was crumbling. 'Maybe I could teach you until then and they could get a tutor?'

'No, that won't work!' Her little voice rose in hysterical despair. 'No, I can only learn from you. Please be my teacher, Uncle Magus. Please, please!'

'Aisling, you know I can't go there…'

'Don't let the nuns take me! Please, Magus, please!' A fat tear rolled down her apple cheek, and Peter watched in amazed awe. She was some performer.

'We'd have so much fun, and I can't go if you don't.'

She flung herself into his arms again then, and catching Peter's eye as his daughter clung to him, the stern, strong, silent Cherokee, who Peter had not been able to budge one inch, gave in completely.

CHAPTER 6

ICK

NICK GROANED in ecstasy as Maggie Cullen worked her erotic magic on his body. It was so unfair of her to do this to him...and so bloody wonderful.

After the meeting in the tent, he had told her he didn't think he could come to America. Her revenge had been to tap on his door at midnight. He'd been getting ready for bed but had answered the knock, thinking it was Peter. May had already spent ages trying to persuade Nick to change his mind, but he was still undecided, and she had said she was going to send Peter over to talk to him.

Instead it was Maggie who burst into the caravan in her nightdress, in all her wild red-haired magnificence, eyes shining with merriment, quickly closing the door behind her. 'Make love to me,' she growled, in such a seductive way.

'Oh, Maggie... What if Peter –'

'If my brother was on the prowl at this time of night, then I'd tell him I'm going to the lavatory.'

At the girls' insistence, an outhouse tent was now part of the equipment. The boys could do their business outside, but enough was enough for the ladies. It wasn't a flush, but it was better than carrying chamber pots around the site in the morning.

'Besides,' she added naughtily, 'if he was out and about, it would only be to do with Aida, so he wouldn't have a leg to stand on.'

'Don't say that, Maggie. He's never been unfaithful to May,' protested Nick in alarm. Years ago he'd had a conversation with Peter about Aida, and warned him things were being said. Peter had assured him he had never and would never do anything to wrong his wife.

'There's more than one way of being unfaithful, Nicholas Shaw, and you know it.' She shook her finger at him meaningfully, then laughed. 'Ah, I'm only messin' with ya. Stop lookin' like ya smothered me mother. Now stop worrying, will ya, and make love to me in real life instead of just in yer mind. If I'm not going to even see you for four months, it's the least you can do.'

And like in the old days, she wouldn't take no for an answer, and it was as glorious as ever. As hard as he tried, he'd never been able to stop himself longing for her, and to have her once more in his arms… Such bliss…

He groaned again, even louder.

'Shh…' she whispered.

'I can't,' he moaned, but she kissed him to quieten him, giggling as she did so.

Afterwards, the guilt swept over him again. 'Oh God, I shouldn't have…'

'Do not say it again,' she murmured, spooning her delicious curves against him.

'This is so wrong of me.'

She rolled over and leant up on one elbow. 'Listen to me, Nick. I don't care. How many more ways can I show you I want you whether you're married or not?'

'But…'

She got out of bed and went to the sink, where she lit a candle. 'Nick, I mean it. I can't be doin' with this codswallop every time, right? And I'm sick of you brushin' me off. You want me, I know you do…so stop fightin' it, for God's sake, before we both go mad.'

'I know what you say, and of course I want you – I love you, you know I do – but it d-d-doesn't stop me feeling like a cad.'

'A cad, ja hear him?' She laughed quietly. Unlike her brother, she'd never lost her working-class Dublin accent, and he loved it about her. 'Nick Shaw, how many more times do I havta say this? You're my man and I'm your girl. You happen to be married to someone else. That's unfortunate, no doubt about it, but it is what it is. Celine's happy with Millie in Brockleton, so seriously, who're we hurtin'?'

Nick, who'd been raised in a cold, austere manner, could never in his wildest dreams have conceived that his life would turn out this way. His wife in a romantic relationship with another woman, and that woman ran his estate, and he hopelessly in love with his best friend's sister, the woman who was at that moment shamelessly extracting a piece of rubber from her body before his very eyes, the device she used to prevent pregnancy. It needed vinegar for a sponge or something – she didn't go into details. She popped it in a special pouch she kept in her bag and washed her hands in the basin.

It saddened him that she had to take precautions. He would have loved a gaggle of red-haired daughters, all of them just like her, but they could never be married, so children were out of the question.

'It's not that we're hurting anyone else,' he said. 'It's that I'm hurting you, no matter what you say. I shouldn't be d-d-doing this… We shouldn't… It's wrong of me, a married man, and you a beautiful young girl, who should have the option to marry and have children.'

'Aargh.' She gritted her teeth in frustration. 'How many more times? You're who I want, and I don't care that I can't be your wife, so long as you love me. And as for nippers, are ya mad? And ruin me lovely figure?' She laughed and pulled one of his white dress shirts over her beautiful body. It swamped her. Her copper curls hung down her back, and her alabaster skin was flawless, smooth and soft. She had the physique of a dancer, taut and strong but curvy too, and he was intoxicated by her beauty.

'Oh, I want you too, Maggie, you need never d-d-doubt that…'

'You only stammer on "D" now, did you notice that?'

'I suppose I d-d-do. With you, anyway.' She was right; when he was around her, his stammer was much improved. If only he could live with her all the time.

She opened her arms to him. 'Come here to me, Baron, before I have to sneak off like a bad thing.'

'Oh, Maggie...' He wrapped his arms around her and buried his face in her wonderful hair. 'Oh, Maggie, I could eat you.'

'I saw your light on... What the hell is going on here?'

The two of them sprang apart, and Nick nearly threw up with shock. Peter was standing in the doorway of the caravan, glaring at the two of them in outright fury. 'You... You... You...' He stepped forwards, pointing his finger at Nick's bare chest. 'Nick, she's my sister...and you're a married man! How could you... You're supposed to be my mate...'

'Peter, for God's sake, calm down. You'll wake everybody,' hissed Maggie, pulling Nick's shirt closed around her as Nick worked desperately to get his trousers on, nearly tearing them as he thrust his leg into them.

'Calm down? Calm down, is it?' Peter ranted. But he didn't look at her. His navy-blue eyes blazed directly at Nick, every syllable he uttered dripping with contempt. 'Calm down when my best friend... my best friend, the person I trusted most in the world is' – he stopped himself using a crude term – 'sleeping with my sister. My married best friend, that is, taking an innocent young girl into his bed, my little sister. And...after all I did for you, all we've been through. How often I confided in you, told you my deepest secrets. And this is what you do?'

Nick stood, crushed by shame and despair, as he fumbled to button his trousers. He knew that to try to explain himself was pointless. Peter was right. He deserved all this venom being heaped on his bowed head.

'And to think I came to your caravan to beg you to come with me to America, to say I couldn't manage without you, couldn't imagine the cabaret without you. How could you do this to me? You better leave this place right now, Nick, before I kill you with my bare hands. You're out of the cabaret – gone. I want you gone, right now!'

'Don't you dare speak to Nick like that!' snarled Maggie, her eyes flashing, her hands on her hips.

'Get out, Maggie, go to bed,' spat Peter, turning to her, his blond mop on end, his mouth twisting. 'I'll deal with you in the morning.'

'Deal with me in the mornin'?' She was furious, as angry now as he was. 'Who the hell do you think ya are? Deal with me, you will, in my arse! I'll deal with you, comin' in, roarin' at us, callin' Nick names –'

'Oh, it's not just Nick I'm angry with. Look at you. I'm ashamed of you, behaving like a common slut.'

The crack of the slap rang out in the night air. Peter's face was white where she'd connected with it. Then she leant forwards, her face inches from his, her red curls wild around her face, barefoot in Nick's huge shirt, incandescent with rage. 'Don't you dare speak to me like that, ya jumped-up little nobody,' she spat through gritted teeth. 'Nick's worth ten of you, and he's goin' nowhere. I love him and he loves me –'

With a grunt of fury, Peter grabbed Maggie by the shoulders and shook her roughly. 'He's a married man, you stupid cow. Ya think he's in love with ya, do ya? God, Maggie, you're as thick as the roads. He's after what all men are after, and he's getting it too. Get out of my sight. I'm ashamed of you.'

'You're ashamed of me?' She poked her finger into her brother's chest. 'You're pathetic, just pathetic. Who do you think you are, comin' into here without even knockin'?'

'I'll tell you exactly who I am!' Peter's eyes were wild. 'I'm your boss and I'm his boss, and as of now, you're both sacked. He can go back to his wife, and you can go home to Ma – maybe she can put manners on ya.' He was breathing heavily, his knuckles white as he clenched his fists by his sides.

Nick got hastily between them. 'Peter, stop. This is not Maggie's fault.' He was sure Peter wouldn't hurt his sister – he was not that kind of man – but he had never seen his friend out of control like this. 'Hit me if you like, if it makes you feel better. I deserve it. I won't hit back. But don't sack Maggie. She's your sister, you love her, she loves you – don't fight each other on my account. I'm not worth it. Please.'

'You'd better go back to Brockleton tomorrow,' snarled Peter, his eyes burning, his nostrils flaring with every breath. 'Or I'll never speak to her again.'

'You will not make Nick leave!' Maggie's voice was screechy now as her indignation and rage combined to send her into orbit. 'Having the cheek to judge him, and you makin' calf eyes at Aida since the day you laid eyes on her. Everyone notices it when you dance the tango together – it's disgustin'. And your poor wife there, having to make out she don't notice…'

Peter opened his mouth to yell back at her…then closed it as her words sunk in. He fell back a step, looking dazed; it was as if she'd slapped him again.

'Peter, she didn't mean it,' Nick jumped in quickly. The idea of the Cullens falling out forever and it all being his fault was unbearable. 'Maggie, tell Peter you don't mean it.'

'I will not say any such thing. You're pathetic, Peter, sniffin' around her but afraid to do anything about it.' She jabbed her finger at the open door. 'Or have you? I saw ya sneakin' out of her caravan at three in the morning last night.'

'You… What…' White as a sheet, clearly sick to death, Peter glanced helplessly in the direction of her accusing finger. Aida's caravan was in darkness, but lights were coming on all around, in the chorus girls' vans, in Enzo and Ramon's too.

'Now you go home to your wife, Peter Cullen,' screamed Maggie. She pushed her stunned brother out into the cold night and slammed the door so hard behind him that everything inside rattled. And then bursting into tears, she threw herself into Nick's trembling, guilty arms.

CHAPTER 7

IDA

Peter stood before her on the gravel, helpless, his hands by his sides, his eyes full of pain and sorrow. 'I'm so sorry about my sister. She is a brat and an embarrassment. I'm going to send her home to Ma tomorrow as soon as I can bring myself to look at her.'

Aida glanced around the yard from the door of her caravan. The curtains in the other vans were twitching, rays of candlelight escaping. She knew they were being watched, but she needed to speak to him, right now. This did not need to be escalated – it would tear down everything he'd worked for.

She spoke to him from the top of the steps in a low, soothing voice. 'I think it is best for everyone to stay apart for a while, to calm down. No hasty decisions. No sackings and sending people away. And also I think you need to speak to May now. Everybody heard that, or if not, they will hear it by tomorrow. May should hear it from you.'

Peter stared up at her, and the combination of hurt and fury and incomprehension in his face was new to her. Usually he kept his emotions closely guarded and gave the impression of being in control at all times.

'But how can I let him stay after this? How could he even do this? To Celine, to Maggie, to me?'

Aida shook her head. 'I don't know, but the answer is not this fury. Nick was wrong not to tell you, but perhaps your reacting the way you have is why he did not.'

'So you think I'm overreacting too, do you?' His eyes flashed angrily in the moonlight.

It hurt her, how his rage spilled over to include her, but she stayed calm. Someone in this situation had to keep their head.

'I'm only saying you need to stop and think before you hurt everyone in your shock and anger. You need Maggie. You need Nick. They are a great combination – audiences love them.'

'So you think for the good of the cabaret, I should let my little sister be seduced by a married man for his own amusement? You approve of a rich man making my sister his…mistress, like some common brasser on the street?'

Aida closed her eyes for a moment and inhaled. She told herself this wasn't the Peter she knew who was speaking; it was a different Peter, a man so lost in his troubles, he didn't realise what a cruel thing he'd just said to her.

Gabriella Gonzalez hadn't been married to Aida's father, who was an admiral in the Spanish navy. Rafael Narro's wife and children lived in a fine villa in Madrid, while Gabriella and Aida lived in a tiny rented apartment. When Gabriella got sick, there was no money for medicine, and if Aida hadn't agreed to sleep with the landlord's disgusting son, there would have been no money to bury her when she died.

Of course Aida didn't approve of a rich man taking a mistress. But at the same time, she wasn't going to let her emotions blind her. Nick was a kind and honourable man and surely meant no harm to Maggie, and he seemed to really care for Celine, even though they lived almost apart. There was something deeper going on there, she was sure of it. She'd been sure of it for a long time. Some secret underpinning it all.

'Nick is not the sort of man to exploit Maggie and cast her aside, Peter. You know that. I am very sure this would not be happening if he didn't have deep feelings for her, and she for him.'

He snorted with disgust. 'Maggie's too young and stupid for deep feelings.'

'She is not – she's twenty-four years old. She's not your little sister any more. She's an adult, and she won't be told what to do – by you anyway.'

'She will if she wants to keep her job,' he said darkly, and with that he was gone into the night, storming away across the gravel.

Sighing, Aida retreated into her caravan, shooting the bolt on her door. She did not want to see anyone else tonight. Not that anyone else in the troupe would dream of disturbing her. She'd managed, entirely on purpose, to make herself separate, aloof. She knew most of the others liked her a great deal, loved her even in the case of Ramon, her childhood friend, and in a strange way Peter – not in the way Maggie described it, though, only from a distance.

When the shouting and yelling woke her, Aida had been sleeping peacefully in her silk pyjamas, and before opening her door, she'd pulled on the pale-pink kimono she'd treated herself to when they were in London last year. She retied her belt, lit a candle and put on the kettle. She would never sleep now.

No doubt the whole cabaret would be buzzing with this juicy gossip tomorrow, and she didn't look forward to having to face it all. That stuff that Maggie said about how Peter looked at her, how he felt about her, was out there now, and they could either address it or ignore it.

She took down a caddy of camomile tea. She had never developed a taste for the black tea – hot pond, as they all called it now – that everyone drank here with milk and sugar, except for Magus who drank his black.

That was what it was like in the cabaret. They were a family, they had in-jokes, special words they shared, they knew each other's flaws and had arguments and fell out and then fell back in again, or at the very least agreed to tolerate each other, in the way Aida tolerated Clive despite him driving her mad with that stupid puppet of his.

The way May just about tolerated Aida for the sake of the show.

Aida knew Peter's wife didn't like her, despite the veneer of friendliness and the compliments on her performances or her appearance, and she'd always told herself it was because May misunderstood the friendship Aida and Peter shared. But maybe if she was honest with herself – and this was a thought she'd shied away from – Maggie was right, and there was more than friendship in Peter's feelings for her.

Was it true? she asked herself as she sat at the table, sipping the soothing tea. And did she have feelings for him that went beyond professional friendliness?

She wasn't pining for him; she didn't want to take him from May. She would never become a married man's mistress. And it wasn't just that – she didn't want the touch of any man.

Peter was attractive, undoubtedly. And she knew he found her attractive too. But what was between them went deeper than surface attraction. It wasn't Aida's beauty that mattered to Peter.

When she'd been abused in every way imaginable in Dublin Castle by Harvey Bathhurst, and thrown onto the street, broken and bleeding, it was Peter who came and cared for her. He bathed her, he tended to her injuries, he washed dried blood from her hair. May was wrong about their connection being about Aida's beauty, because Peter hadn't changed a bit towards her when she was ugly and swollen and half bald.

Then, when she was afraid to dance, it was he who coaxed her back onto the stage.

With others, Peter Cullen was almost always self-assured, but he showed Aida a vulnerability that he hid from the rest. And she was the same with him; he was the only one she allowed to see her at her weakest.

She thought and made a decision. This wasn't right. Peter was a married man, and it was wrong of her to have that closeness with him when it was upsetting his wife and clearly they were the talk of the place. She was surprised, shocked really, that Maggie said what she did, and that everyone noticed it. She'd had no idea, but it stopped now.

Maybe she would leave for a while, visit her father.

When Rafael Narro had first written to her more than five years ago, she'd very nearly written back telling him never to contact her again. But slowly her resentment ebbed away and she began to feel, if not love, then a sort of affection for the man who finished every letter he sent her with 'One day, my dear daughter, we will meet, and you will see in my eyes how sorry I am. I long to make amends.'

Rafael had been cruel and thoughtless to Gabriella, but he seemed remorseful now for the way he'd abandoned her. He wrote of a brush with death at sea that left him thinking he wouldn't survive, and how on that long, dark night, he made a pact with God that if he was spared, he would be a better man and atone for his sins. He had begun by confessing Aida's existence to his wife and telling his children they had another sister.

And he'd asked Aida's permission to replace the wooden cross and cheap brass plate, which was all she'd been able to afford for her mother's grave, with a beautiful polished-marble headstone. He had a Mass offered for the repose of Gabriella Gonzalez's sweet soul in the Catedral de la Almudena every year on the anniversary of her death, celebrated by an archbishop no less, and each month he paid Aida an allowance, almost as much as her wages for the show.

She'd said she didn't want or need it, but he said that was irrelevant. She could donate it, she could save it – it was hers to do with as she so wished.

As well as these grand gestures, he wrote once a month, telling her news of her three brothers and two sisters. Maria-Lucia was the eldest, ten years older than Aida, then Raul, then Katarina, then Alberto, who was her age, and finally Luis, the youngest. He sent photographs of Maria-Lucia and her husband and two little girls; the eldest child looked a little like herself, she thought. Her brother Raul was following in his father's footsteps in the Spanish navy, as was Luis. Katarina was a nun, something that astonished her when she found out, though she couldn't say why, and Alberto was, as far as she could make out, a bit of a rebel.

He'd asked her to address him as Papa in her letters, as his other children did, but that she could not do. Papas were like Peter was with Aisling, or Nick with his sons, cradling them as infants, telling them stories, Peter bearing Aisling around the site on his shoulders, with her issuing instructions. Rafael Narro may have been that to his other children, but not with her. She agreed to call him Rafael rather than Senor Narro, and then his nickname Rafa, as his friends did, but that was as far as she would go.

He had asked her several times to come and visit her family. He said his wife had agreed to meet her and wished him to assure her that Senora Narro felt no animosity towards her. Aida wondered if that was true. So far she'd declined, because she already had a family. Her friends in the cabaret were much dearer to her than those distant, unknown brothers and sisters in Spain.

Still, if what had happened tonight couldn't be fixed, if May wanted her gone, she would move back to Spain.

And even if May decided to pretend this disaster had never happened, Aida would tell Peter no more visits to her van late at night, no more chats backstage, none of it. It was harmless – there had never once been an untoward touch or word – but that was not the point. Perception was reality, and she would not play a part in the destruction of his marriage or his business.

There would be no more dancing the tango either. From now on she would partner with Enzo. He was a fine dancer, and even if he couldn't quite manage to be serious, it would be nearly as good.

She hoped Peter and Nick could work things out. The show needed the solid, gentle presence of Nick. He was the anchor while Peter was the sail, and this ship needed both.

She smiled at the nautical analogy. Her father would like that. She would write a long letter to him tomorrow.

She blew out the candle and got into bed, hoping sleep would come and trying not to think about the turbulence all around their little world.

CHAPTER 8

ICK

THE SCENE with Peter and everything afterwards kept going around and around in his head like a horrible film. He'd left for Brockleton at first light, even though Maggie had tried to make him stay.

'No, Maggie, I can't. I've ruined everything. You have to make things right with your brother. Talk to May, tell her everything, get her on your side. Apologise to her, tell her you just lost your head, that you know none of it's true.'

'Don't let him put the run on you, Nick,' she pleaded. 'If you go now, he'll win, he'll know he can get between us. And me sayin' we love each other won't mean much now, will it?'

'I do love you, you know that. That's why I'm going. Peter will be far quicker to forgive you if I'm not there. You said all those things to d-d-defend me, and if he has another go at me, you'll d-d-do it again. I won't come between you and your brother, so I have to go.'

Though she huffed and pouted, he could tell she knew he was right.

But what was going to happen now? Nick remembered that sinking feeling he always got as he returned to Brockleton at the end of the school year, and he had it again now. He was going to have to tell Celine about Maggie, and the awful row. Maybe his grandmother would have some wise advice; she usually did.

'Hello, Armitage,' he said as the ancient butler came to the front door.

'Your Lordship, how did you get here so fast? I only sent the telegram this morning?'

'Telegram?' asked Nick, bewildered.

Armitage looked devastated; there were tears in his rheumy eyes. 'The dowager, sir, she's very unwell. Dr Holmes thought it best to call you. It's her heart, he thinks.' The old man adored Floss, not that he would ever say so; the boundaries of propriety were very important to Armitage. But he'd served and advised Nick's grandmother for over fifty years, from when she was a young American bride and he a mere second footman, and theirs was a firm if unspoken friendship that had stood the test of decades.

Speechless, Nick handed Armitage his hat and coat and bounded up the stairs to Floss's rooms on the third floor, taking the stairs two at a time. He went in and found her resting against her pillows, her face, her hair, her nightgown and the bed linens all white. Celine sat beside her, holding her hand.

He dropped a kiss on Celine's cheek, then bent over the bed, blinking back his tears. 'Oh, Floss, how are you?'

'Ah, Nicholas, my dear boy.' Floss's voice was weak, but she smiled and released Celine's hand and patted the coverlet. When he was little, she would do that so he would climb into her bed and cuddle her. She was the only one who ever showed him affection as a child. His father wouldn't dream of it, and his mother was never there.

'I'll leave you two alone,' said Celine with a sweet smile as she stood. 'I'll bring up some tea in a while.'

As she left the room, Nick kicked off his shoes and lay on the bed beside his grandmother, cradling her thin body in his arms as if she were the child now and he the adult. 'I'm so sorry you're ill. I didn't know. Armitage just told me.'

'Then why are you here, sweet boy, if you didn't know? You never come during the week. What is wrong?'

'Nothing. I'm fine.'

'Tell me.' Her voice might have been weak, but she was still her old self, able to catch him out just as she did when he was a little boy and pretending everything was fine at school, or that his older brothers didn't bully or bother him.

He felt a pang of guilt. Here was poor Floss on her deathbed and she was asking him about his own worries. 'No, it's fine. You have enough to think about. You need to rest and get well.'

She laughed then, a small, throaty sound, and the effort of it seemed to drain her. 'I'm not just ill, Nicholas. This is it, the end of a long road. I always promised I wouldn't leave you until you were old enough to cope, and I kept my promise.'

'I suppose if I told you I wasn't ready, it wouldn't make a difference?' he asked through a blur of tears. He knew he was a man now; he should be managing his own life, not running to his grandmother with his troubles. But the idea that this would never again be an option was one that caught his breath in grief.

'Ah, but you are ready, my love, you are.' She patted his chest with her thin, delicate hand, like an autumn leaf. 'But tell me what is wrong. Perhaps the wisdom of all my years will help you one last time.'

Nick sighed and gave in to his grandmother, as he'd always done as a child. The story came out of him, about Maggie and Peter, and his worries about the boys, and how he longed to marry Maggie but he couldn't be divorced, and how wrong it was to tie her to him when he had nothing to give her.

'Well, let me see.' As always Floss seemed utterly unfazed by the strangeness of her grandson's life. 'Why don't you explain this all to Celine? I don't see why she shouldn't agree to a divorce after your father dies and the property is yours to dispose of, and then –'

'No, Floss. I can't put her and the boys out of Brockleton. I couldn't do that – it's their home.'

She held her hand up to stop him, and he fell silent and waited for her verdict. Floss was the most intelligent person he knew, and here she was planning his life, even now, at this late stage.

'Old Jock McArthur is looking to retire from your Scottish estate, Clochriach. He wrote last month. Since Janie died he's lost his love of the place – it's too lonely without her – and he wants to go to Dundee to live with his daughter. Celine, Millie and the boys could easily move there. It's beautiful and magnificent. And then the boys can attend Castlebruin as day pupils so they won't have to board – we talked about how much you would hate that for them – and Millie can take over from Jock. You can see them often. And in England you will be a lord, a powerful man in Westminster, and you can divorce Celine through Parliament with a minimum of scandal.'

Nick allowed himself a tiny glimmer of hope, but then it died. 'But even if Celine was happy with that, I would want to marry Maggie, and how can I do that? There's no divorce here in Ireland – it wouldn't be recognised here.'

'What would that matter? Maggie is a British citizen.'

Nick laughed, wondering if Floss was in fact going a bit vague in the head. 'You do know she was in Cumann na mBan, her brother was an IRA man and we hid Volunteers in the cabaret, so she's a proud Irishwoman, and a Catholic to boot –'

Floss raised her hand again and cut across him. 'Whether your Maggie likes it or not, she was born under the British flag, so she *is* British and I'd imagine be perfectly content with an English divorce. Seeing how that girl dotes on you, I should think she couldn't care less if she had to ask the king himself for it.'

Still chuckling, he held her close. It was a crazy idea, but he wasn't going to argue. 'Floss, you're amazing.' She'd always made plans for him; she was the mother he'd never had. She didn't always get it right, but he trusted her to have his best interests at heart. And maybe it could work? Who knew? Stranger things had happened. 'So you've sorted all of this part. What about the Catholic part?'

Floss gave a short wheezy laugh. 'Oh, she'll have to quarrel with the pope herself. That's not my problem to solve.' Her voice was growing weak, and she leant against his shoulder; he could feel her slipping into rest.

'Can I get you anything, Floss? Water, a cup of tea?'

'No...Just...sleep.'

'Will I go?' he whispered, hoping she would say no.

She gave a slight shake of her head. She turned slowly and lay close to him.

For hours, he cradled her. The doctor called and said she would probably pass that night, that she was quite comfortable and he should just continue to do as he was doing.

She woke intermittently, and they had small exchanges, mainly him reassuring her that all was well.

Celine and Millie took turns helping Nick keep watch, allowing him time to eat and see his father and sons before returning to his position on the bed, holding Floss in his arms, the old woman peacefully sleeping.

Staff came and all left in tears, and Armitage wept openly as Celine hugged him and kissed his old cheek. The formality of the divide between upstairs and downstairs had been softened, and the house was so much more relaxed now. Nick wondered at how things had changed at the hands of his sweet French wife, who had injected a bit of humanity and human frailty into it.

Late in the evening, Remy, Laurent and Pierre came in with their mother. Celine had told them that Floss would die soon, and Nick was glad she had done it that way, keeping the children informed, allowing them to feel the sadness and not have to put on a stiff upper lip as he had been taught to do; it was all so much better.

One after the other, Nick's small sons kissed their beloved great-grandmother on the cheek and said their goodbyes, and Floss gave the smallest smile each time, barely audibly breathing, 'Goodbye, my darling.'

'She knows it's you,' he whispered to each of them.

'Will I arrange to bring your father up?' Millie asked him as the clock struck eleven and Celine took the boys off to bed.

Nick nodded. Walter was confined to the ground floor since his stroke, but the footmen could carry him up in his wheelchair to say goodbye to his mother.

As Millie went to give the orders, he sat alone with Floss, his arms still around her, his lips on her head, and waited. There was a scuffling outside as the footmen carried the dead weight of Walter and his wheelchair up onto the landing, and then Millie brought him in and pushed the chair up to the bed.

'Good you got here, Nick,' Walter growled. The stroke had slackened the left side of his face and body, and he was hard to understand when he spoke, but Nick had learnt to do so over the past few years. 'Shame 'bout Mama.'

Walter had softened with age but would never become demonstrative. Old dogs and new tricks. There had been a time when Nick would have felt embarrassed to let his father see him be so affectionate with Floss, lying on the bed holding her, but he was past caring about that now. With Celine as their mother, his sons would grow up differently from the men who came before them. Alicia Eugenia Catherine Fenchurch Shaw, Dowager Baroness de Simpré, was leaving a much better world than the one she'd entered.

His father reached over and placed his gnarled, withered hand on Floss's back, patting her gently as if she were an old horse. 'Godspeed, Mama,' he muttered. 'I shan't be long behind.' It was as much as he could bring himself to do. He nodded at Millie then, and she took him away. The footmen would lift him back downstairs, and his valet would see him to bed.

Floss's breathing was laboured, but she wasn't in distress, the doctor had assured him of that. The rattle on the exhale was the only sound in the room. An oil light glowed on the dresser, but other than that, the room was in darkness.

Celine and Millie dozed on the small striped sofa, Celine resting her head on Millie's shoulder. He could just see the face of the clock on the mantelpiece; it was almost four in the morning.

He felt his grandmother fight for her next breath and tightened his arm around her frail shoulders. 'Goodbye, Floss, and thank you for all you did. I can't imagine my life if I didn't have you, and you made me the man I am. For years and years, nobody but you loved me. I will miss you so much, but I'll be all right. I'll take your advice, and I'll look after this place too, and everyone in it. They love you as much as I do.' He sniffed and wiped his eyes with the sleeve of his free hand. 'Your work here is done, and we'll never, ever forget you. I love you, Floss…'

His tears flowed. He kissed the top of her head, and she stirred in his arms ever so slightly. Moments later she took a deeper breath, and exhaled. Then there was nothing. She was gone.

CHAPTER 9

AY

She knew exactly what had happened; the dogs in the street knew what had been said. Peter had come back to the caravan ranting and raving and saying he was going to sack both Nick and Maggie, and in between he'd tried to let her know that Maggie had said something shameful and awful about Aida that wasn't true.

'I don't want to know,' she'd said sharply, though she could easily guess.

When he'd persisted in trying to talk to her about it, she shut the conversation down, blowing out the candle and pretending to sleep.

The day after the 'big bust-up', as she heard it being called, she made sure to walk around the camp with a bright smile on her face, and she was especially lovely to Aida. She was not going to allow any of what had happened into her life. She would not give them anything else to gossip about. She had to live with the situation between Peter and Aida – that was her cross – and she would do so on her own terms. The pity, the glances, the efforts at confidences from cast members were all rebuffed. She was fine, Peter was fine, Aida was changing over to dancing the tango with Enzo because Peter had got too much else to do, Nick had to go back to Brockleton because his grandmother had died, and Maggie was in a bad temper but there was nothing new about that. The less said on the subject, the better, as far as she was concerned.

Maggie had appeared on May's doorstep on the second day after the big bust-up, saying she had come to apologise.

May cut her off. 'I don't want to know what you said, Maggie. It's water under the bridge. All I care about is you and Peter making it up. You need to talk to him about America. Just give him a few days to calm down.'

At the mention of her brother's name, Maggie set her jaw in the stubborn way May had seen Peter do, and also Eamonn. They were all cut from the same cloth, as pig-headed as they came. 'Why should I go crawling to him? He doesn't want us to come, and I can't even look at him. The way he spoke to us, May, the names he called us…'

'Fine, I'll talk to him about it myself when he's calmed down.' She started to close the caravan door, but Maggie stopped it with her hand.

'Did he tell me ma?' she asked, quieter now. And May saw a glimmer of hurt under the indignation on her sister-in-law's face. Maggie adored Peter really and hated that he was disappointed in her and threatening to send her home.

'I don't think so,' May said, a touch more kindly, and Maggie looked like that was a weight off anyway.

May took her own advice to give Peter a few days' space before broaching the topic on her own terms.

Nick was away in Brockleton. Just as well, as it gave Peter a chance to cool off. He'd sent a letter to May about his grandmother's funeral, which was going to be a huge affair taking a couple of weeks to organise. Of course there was no pressure on anyone to attend – he just wanted to let them know. Peter and Maggie had been such heroes on that awful day Harvey Bathhurst had taken Floss and Walter hostage. But of course he understood if Peter didn't want to come, or Maggie.

May was sure a tear or two had dripped onto the paper as Nick was writing; the ink was a little smudged in places.

He'd added a postscript with his own apology.

It's my fault Peter and Maggie had such a dreadful fight. Maggie didn't even know what she was saying. She just wanted to hurt him. And I know Peter loves you more than anyone and wouldn't be able to manage without you.

The last part was true, thought May grimly, if not the first part. She made a note of the arrangements for Floss's funeral before putting Nick's letter into the stove. She would insist everyone went to the funeral, even though Nick said they didn't have to. She hated to be businesslike about Nick losing his beloved Floss, but in some ways, it was a stroke of luck – it meant Peter would have to make up with Nick. She wanted the men to be friends for their own sakes, but first and foremost, she was a businesswoman, and Cullen's Celtic Cabaret needed Nick's beautiful tenor voice, and piano playing, in order to succeed in America.

She'd been having a hard time persuading Nick to come as it was; that's why she'd sent Peter over to see him that night. What a disaster that had turned out to be. Maybe the big bust-up could be turned to the cabaret's advantage, though. Nick would be very upset right now, and racked with guilt and remorse, and likely to say yes to anything Peter wanted.

Then there was Maggie to sort out. The cabaret needed her too; she was a wonderful singer and dancer. But she was absolutely livid with her brother still and refusing to engage, and equally Peter refused to talk to her.

Four nights after the big bust-up, May was sitting at the caravan table totting up everything that had to go into storage. As part of her coping strategy, she'd gone into full organisational mode, arranging everything for the trip. Aisling was in Dublin with May's parents, who were clinging to their grandchild as if she was going to Africa forever, not America for four months, and who didn't at all approve of Aisling having lessons from an Indian man and felt she should be in school. If they had their way, it would be the one May herself attended, just down the road from them.

It was all so wearisome.

Peter stood at the door of the caravan, moodily smoking, and she called him over to ask him a question, then closed her ledger and pointed at the seat opposite. 'Peter, we need to talk.'

He stubbed out his cigarette. 'So you're finally ready to hear my side of the story?'

'I don't want to hear any side of any story, Peter. Maggie came to apologise two days ago, and I wouldn't hear her side of it either. And Nick wrote to me, but I put his letter on the fire. As I see it, it's a personal matter between you three, and I'm not getting involved with it. But I am involved in this cabaret. This is our business, and we've worked too hard to let something stupid like this cloud our professional judgement.'

He sat down, looking mulish.

She went on. 'This is how I see it. Correct me if I'm wrong, but we both know the show is better with Nick and Maggie in it. We're losing Tiny as it is. We were lucky to keep Magus – thank goodness Aisling's as persuasive as you. Aida has mentioned going back to Spain, and I've had to tell her I personally wanted her to stay.'

He looked up at that point, shock mixed with gratitude in his navy-blue eyes.

She continued to keep her tone very businesslike. 'We can't afford to let this...incident...keep affecting things, Peter. I know you're angry, but you'll have to try to work it out. For now I'm working all hours trying to get this cabaret to America, and so I need to know if you are in or not?'

'Of course I'm in, but if you heard what Maggie said...'

Briefly she dropped her mask of practicality and glared at him. 'I'm sure I know very well what Maggie said, but despite all of that, I asked

Aida to stay because I put the show before everything, and I thought you did too, Peter. So stop sulking like a typical obstinate Cullen and go and talk to your sister. And be nice. I swear to God, if you mess this up, Peter, you'll be going to America by yourself.'

CHAPTER 10

ETER

Rosie, who shared Maggie's caravan, opened the door to Peter when he knocked, then said instantly, 'Oh, I have to go and see…um…' And she jumped down and ran off across the field without finishing her sentence.

He stepped in. Maggie was at the kitchen table, buttering a piece of bread.

She shot him a dirty look. 'What do you want?'

'To talk, not fight. Talk,' he answered calmly. May was right. This needed to be fixed for all their sakes.

'At least you knocked this time, I suppose,' she said grudgingly.

'I knocked the last time too,' he said, trying to fight back a surge of irritation, 'but nobody answered.'

She shoved the slice of bread away from her. 'Right, spit it out, whatever you came to say.'

'Can't I have a cup of hot pond with my sister?'

'You can, but you never do, and never have done, so with all due respect, I'm not thick, Peter. You want to say somethin', so get on with it.' There was a weariness in her voice that saddened him.

'All right. I will.' He inhaled and tried to compose the words in a way that wouldn't upset her more. 'It's about you and Nick.'

'You don't say.' She could do the sarcasm thing every bit as well as he could.

'I don't want to fight with you, Maggie.' This was costing him an enormous effort, but May's threat rang in his ears – it was make it up with his sister or doom the cabaret. 'I came here to talk to you about it like adults. I'm not going to make a scene, Maggie. Please just let me have my say.'

'Fine.' There was belligerence in her one-word reply.

'First, I want to say I shouldn't have reacted like I did –'

'Yeah, you shouldn't 'ave,' Maggie answered, though a touch less aggressively than before.

Peter held his hands up in surrender. 'I'm apologising here, all right. You could be a bit more gracious about it.'

'Ya called me a brasser, and a slut, and I forget all the other names, so forgive me if I'm not cock-a-hoop with your apology.' She was not going to let him off the hook that easily.

'I said I was sorry.' Peter was getting indignant now, though he tried his best to keep his voice calm. Another fight might finish the relationship forever.

'No, ya bleedin' didn't. Ya said you shouldn'ta reacted like ya did. That's not the same thing.'

'Yeah, well, what you said about Aida, where's my apology for that?'

She snorted. 'I tried to apologise to May, but she wouldn't listen. I went to Aida as well, but she didn't want to hear me either.'

'That's because they're both sensible women.'

Her eyes, so like his, flashed angrily. 'Not like me, you mean?'

He came further into the caravan. She didn't invite him to sit. He did anyway. 'No, Maggie, that's not what I mean. It's just you're wrong. Me and Aida…we're not…you know…'

'Well, I'm sorry for saying it then,' she fired at him angrily. It was a very poor apology, but he decided to accept it.

'And I'm sorry for treating you like you're a child. I know you're not. You're a grown woman who knows her own mind.'

'That's right. And I know me heart too, and it's set on Nick and that's tha'.' She stuck out her chin stubbornly.

He stopped and took a deep breath. 'I just need you to be aware of what you're getting yourself into. I swear the very last thing I want to do is lecture you. I just want you to understand how this works. Nick has *nothing* to offer you. Maybe he has the best of intentions – I actually think he does – but the fact of it is he's a married man and the road to hell is paved with good intentions. You go down that road, and you'll just end up as his mistress, with no standing, no family of your own. You'll give up your good name, all for a man who can't give you what you deserve.'

She flipped her hand carelessly, though there were tears in her eyes. 'You men are all the same, so worried about women "having a good name". It's such rubbish.'

'It's not rubbish, Maggie, even if Nick says different.'

'He doesn't say different. He says exactly the same as you! You're like a broken record, the pair of ye!' Her voice rose with pain and frustration, and the tears spilled. 'He gets all guilty, he only comes near me when we're singing, he begs me to stay away from him, not to torment him, and I *do* try, for a while, and then I can't help myself and I go back to him and badger him. It's all my fault… I can't be without him, Peter, I just can't. I've tried, God knows I have…'

Peter knew she was telling him the truth. He reached over and held her hand, something he'd never done before. She was his little sister. He'd hugged her and punched her a few times when they were kids, but they were not normally demonstrative. 'So how did this doomed love affair start?' he asked gently.

She looked down but didn't withdraw her hand. 'It was me who started it. I've always wanted him, and I've made him love me too. But Peter, we've hardly ever… See…he does his best to stay away from me –

that's why I went off with Bill for so long. But I couldn't keep going with it, Peter. Bill wanted to get married, and he was so nice. He was my first boyfriend, so he was special that way. I nearly said yes, but then I realised I couldn't marry the poor man when I was in love with someone else. You can't imagine how that feels, to be in love with the wrong man!'

Tears were running down her face now, and Peter gripped her hand more tightly. He knew exactly how it felt, and Maggie had done a braver thing than he had done when May asked him to marry her. But at what cost to herself?

'Maggie, listen to me. If you live with Nick out of wedlock, which you're saying he won't allow because he knows it would be wrong, it would be you, not him, who would face all the scandal, the gossip. You'll be drummed out of your religion.'

She nodded then, her eyes bright with tears. 'If that's the speech, Peter, I'll save you the bother. No woman alive thinks the same rules apply to us as to ye.'

'No, that's not what I was going to say, but you're right.' The frustration with her stubbornness dissipated, and all he felt was a strong need to protect this flighty, brave girl. 'It *is* different for men. It's not fair or right, but it's how it is. But I was going to say, well, to explain or something, I don't know… You're my sister and I love you and I want to look out for you, and… Look, I want you to know, I'm going to talk to Nick. I need to see what he has to say.'

'I know what he has to say. He'll agree with you and send me away again, for good this time, and my life will be over.' And she broke out into big wet sobs.

His heart went out to her, and he forgot all his stern, reasonable speeches. He stood, pulled her to her feet, put his arms around her and hugged her tight. 'Poor Maggie,' he whispered into her hair. 'Poor little Maggie. Life is hard, isn't it? So hard.'

CHAPTER 11

ICK

THE CHAPEL of Brockleton was full to capacity, and the crowds spilled out into the churchyard all the way to the gate. Nick stood as chief mourner, his father beside him in his wheelchair and Celine to his right; their three little boys dressed in dark suits filled the remainder of the pew.

One by one their neighbours, tenants, friends and staff came to sympathise in the Irish way. Nick accepted their condolences and found it comforting. He was a shy man when not on stage, and he hadn't been looking forward to having hundreds of people coming to shake his hand, to say what a wonderful woman his grandmother was, but quite the opposite turned out to be true. He got strength and satisfaction from it. She *was* marvellous, she was loved, and everyone for miles around, from the wealthiest to the poorest, knew it. She had friends of all ages and from all walks of life.

To his delight – he'd thought Peter wouldn't allow it – the whole of the cabaret came, and the sight of them entering the chapel lifted his heart. A flock of peacocks among pigeons was how his grandmother had described them at his and Celine's wedding, and even now, dressed in black, it was true. They were dramatic-looking. Their hair, their clothing, the men with long hair and gold earrings, women with elaborate make-up – they were all eccentric and quirky, and he loved them for it. This was his family beside him, but they were his family too, every last oddball one of them, and he loved them dearly.

Peter shook his hand, then patted him on the shoulder, his eyes meeting Nick's, and the compassion and, yes, love there was plain to see. Nick was so grateful. Whatever about the fight and Maggie; it seemed Floss's death transcended that.

Everyone else in turn came up and hugged him, May and Aida as well. And then there was Maggie, her face white and drawn, her copper curls tamed beneath a black-lace mantilla, her slender frame dressed in a black coat with fur cuffs and collar. He had never seen her look so beautiful.

She kissed his cheek, and whispered, 'I love you,' as she paid her respects. Celine and Millie too greeted her warmly, and four-year-old Pierre, who thought the whole funeral was a bit of a lark, called 'Copper Topsie!' in delight when he saw her.

They buried Floss in the graveyard at Brockleton, a beautiful place of flowers and shrubs, many of which she had planted, and afterwards a reception was held in the great hall of the big house. Hours of meeting and greeting everyone, thanking them for coming, listening to so many stories of Floss – these things were joyful rather than exhausting. Learning of how she stuck up for the tenants with the Black and Tans, how she downfaced a bullying husband who was three times her size, how she arranged for one of the maids who got in trouble to have the baby and have it adopted and kept her job open for her. How she outfoxed a man who was trying to cheat her on a horse, or how she pretended to play the trombone when a visiting bishop came to visit the slightly alcoholic vicar. On and on the stories went, and for all the sadness at her loss, it was a very jolly affair.

But finally the moment Nick had been dreading came. He noticed May say something to Peter, with a glance in Nick's direction, and then Peter stood and came over to him and asked if he fancied a smoke on the terrace.

Outside in the moonlight, they stood looking over the pale gardens and the fields beyond, neither wanting to start. Eventually Peter broke the silence.

'We can't go on this way. If we want to make a proper go of it over there, we can't have this' – he waved his hand – 'between us.'

'I agree,' Nick managed. He swallowed and felt like the gauche boy he was when he and Peter met that night on the Western Front, Peter so worldly-wise and he without a clue.

'Do you want to come to America?'

Two weeks ago Nick hadn't known the answer to that question, but now he grabbed at the offer. 'I do. I've been talking to Celine about how to organise things.'

'I'm glad to hear it.' Peter blew out a silvery cloud of smoke. 'So I take it your wife will be travelling with you?'

Nick heard the slight emphasis on the word 'wife'.

'No, she won't.'

Peter turned and looked straight at him, unsmiling. 'Why not, Nick? She's your wife, the woman you're supposed to be committed to. But for some reason you're not any more?'

'I... I...' This was excruciating, but it wasn't his secret to tell. It was dangerous and could ruin both women if it was known. He'd never told anyone apart from his grandmother, in the first shock of finding out, and Maggie, in a weak moment, though he knew she would never betray Celine.

A sweet French female voice said, 'He is not because I am a lesbian, Peter, and always have been.'

Peter turned in shock towards Celine, who had just stepped out onto the terrace, a cocktail in her hand. 'What do you mean?'

'What I said, Peter. I'm not interested in men. I love Millie. If she were a man, I would marry her, but that's never, ever going to be allowed, so we and our darling Nick here have come to an arrangement.'

'But...' Peter looked in horror from one to the other. 'I don't understand. I thought you and Nick... I mean, you're married.'

'Is it so hard to understand?' Celine took Nick's arm and leant against him. 'Why do so many people get married? Especially in the aristocracy. Nick is my best friend, I really love him, I wanted children. Nick loves me, and I thought we could all be happy. But poor Nick...' This time she pronounced his name in that long drawn-out French way of hers. 'He's not happy. He wants a woman who gives herself to him with her body as well as her heart, and not just for children. And Maggie sensed this need in him. And so, voila!'

She patted Nick's arm fondly, then went to lean on the stone balustrade, beautiful in her straight black dress and long black-lace gloves. Floss had always insisted Celine dress stylishly, as became her rank and position as Nick's wife, and Celine was a fast learner and hadn't let Floss down, not even at her funeral. She was smoking a Gauloises cigarette, using a long tortoiseshell holder.

'So...what... God...I...' Peter's voice dried up as he absorbed this information.

Nick fought back a smile. His erudite, charming friend was never normally speechless.

Celine flicked ash onto the roses that were just beginning to leaf below. 'Tell him Floss's plan, Nick.'

Peter looked at Nick in shock. 'Your grandmother knew about this?'

Nick nodded solemnly. 'Yes, and we talked about it before she died – well, Floss talked to me. She suggested a plan, and Celine and Millie are happy with it. Wait, I should fetch Maggie – this affects her more than anyone. In fact, it's all about her. And let's go somewhere warm.' He had an elegant black jacket on, but he was beginning to shiver. 'Let me help my father see out the last of the guests, and then we'll meet in the small library – there's a fire lit in there.'

* * *

IT WAS midnight before they were all gathered in the library, Maggie and Peter, Celine and Millie. And Nick.

Everyone else was finally gone, the boys and Walter put in bed, and the staff had retired, red-eyed and exhausted. The cabaret had headed back to Ballybunion where they were performing the next night, and May had gone with them, leaving her husband to 'make things right', as she put it.

Nick stood with his back to the ornate fireplace, a log sparking where he'd just thrown it on. His wife and her lover were sipping brandy on the sofa, and Maggie was in the armchair, knees up and legs crossed at the ankles, nursing a glass of port. Peter was perched neatly on the arm of his sister's chair, a glass of soda water in his hand.

Nick told them, there and then, openly and with no hiding, what Floss had suggested. About Celine and Millie taking the Scottish estate, where the boys could be day pupils at a fine school instead of having to board in England as all other children of the aristocracy had to do. Nick would become a lord when his father died and would be important enough to get a parliamentary divorce, and then as a British citizen, Maggie could marry him in England, in a registry office.

'You mean...we can really be seriously and properly married?' asked Maggie in shock.

'And you can live here in Brockleton and hold up your head, and be Remy, Pierre and Laurent's lovely stepmother in the holidays.' Millie smiled; she was very happy with the plan. The Brockleton estate ran like clockwork now, and she was looking forward to getting her hands on the land in Scotland.

But Peter jumped up and walked around the room, shaking his head angrily. 'No, no, no, this won't do at all. Your marriage won't be recognised in Ireland, Maggie. You'll be excommunicated from the Church for marrying a divorced man. People will shun you. This is a very serious thing that's being planned for you, giving up everything for him. Nick, Celine, Millie, I understand why you all think it's such a great idea, but you don't understand – the Church in Ireland is totally against divorce, as well as the law of the land. There was an act passed only this year...'

Maggie had also jumped to her feet, her eyes narrow and temper rising. 'But other people who marry in England are recognised as married here, aren't they? Like if Mrs Juddy and her husband came to Ireland, nobody would think they weren't married, would they?'

'But they're actually British.' Peter was clearly trying to be reasonable but going a bit red in the face.

'And so am I. Nick said so. And so are you –'

'I am no such thing!' Peter exploded. The two Cullens were squaring up to each other now, and neither was going to back down.

'Yes, I am. I was born as a British citizen. Of course in my heart, I'm Irish, and I fought for our country to be free of England, but –'

'But you're willing to run with the hares and hunt with the hounds on this one?' Peter was scandalised. 'It will kill Ma and Eamonn. You'll break up the family!'

'Not if you back me!'

'Why would I back such a terrible plan?'

'It's not terrible, and I'm willing to do what it takes to be with the man I love! And yes, maybe it's going to be a scandal, but we don't care. We want to be together, and you can't stop me. You're always trying to stop me. You didn't want me in the cabaret in the first place, and now you're trying to ruin my life and make me choose between Nick and you and my family and the cabaret and everything –'

Nick had to end this now. 'I choose you both!' he roared, blushing to the roots of his hair, stretching out his arms.

Maggie choked off mid-rant and turned towards him in surprise, as did Peter. 'What?'

'I said I choose you both. And I want you to choose each other as well. So can we stop this fighting...please?'

They both glowered, but mercifully his outburst had shocked them into silence.

'Look, Peter,' he said in a lower voice, 'I understand you're upset, but nothing is broken beyond repair. We can fix this. Maybe it won't be perfect, maybe it won't follow all the usual rules. But everything's changing. The big houses are crumbling, in Ireland the aristocracy is leaving, everything's up in the air, and we're about to have this amazing adventure together, something we could never have even d-d-dreamed of. And I want to share it with my best friend, and my girl, the great love of my life. But I can't d-d-do that if you two are at each other's throats every d-d-day.'

'It's not going to be easy...' Peter was wavering, Nick could feel it. He knew also that if he could get Peter's approval for his plan, the other Cullens would come around eventually.

'I know, but P-Peter, we saw so much waste. So many lads l-like us that should have wives and children are buried beneath the clay in France. We're lucky to be here, to be alive at all, and yet here we are, living and loving and having this incredible life. I love Maggie, and I know there are rules, but as Enzo always says, the rules d-d-don't apply to us. We have our own code of conduct – be d-d-decent, be honest, be loyal. And I swear I'm all of those things, and I swear that if you let me, I'll love and honour her for the rest of my life.'

Peter paused and gazed first at his friend and then his sister. Then he sighed and shrugged. 'I suppose ye're not for changing anyway...'

'I think you are forgetting something, Nick.' Millie laughed.

'What?' Nick said, smiling, looking from her to Celine.

'Yes, isn't there one special person in this room you're ready to choose beyond everyone else?' prompted Celine with a huge grin.

'Oh...what?' For a horrible moment, he wasn't sure what Millie and Celine were talking about. He was so focused on getting everyone to calm down.

'For goodness' sake, Nick Shaw,' the two women chorused, 'are you asking Maggie to marry you or not?'

The penny dropped. 'Oh...oh...yes! Wait here.' He bolted out the door then and up the stairs to Floss's bedroom.

It was empty, and the pang of pain made him catch his breath, but he crossed to her dresser and opened her jewellery box, a gift for her sixteenth birthday from John D. Rockefeller himself, she often said proudly. There were lots of beautiful rings in there, but he knew the one he was looking for. His grandmother loved jewellery and had a lot of it, but this ring was special.

Nick's great-grandmother had never been in favour of Floss's marriage to Nick's grandfather, so she gave this ring to her daughter on her wedding day. It was called her 'running away ring' in case she ever needed a lot of money quickly.

It was an emerald-cut diamond, five-carat weight, accented by two trapezoid diamonds of one-and-a-half carats each, all on a platinum band.

He took it and ran back down. Maggie was now sitting by the fire. Celine and Millie were sitting forwards on the sofa, excited, and Peter was at the window, looking out at the moonlit night.

As Nick came in, everyone turned. Maggie stood up, and he made a beeline for her and got down on one knee.

'Maggie Cullen, this ring is worth a fortune. It's called the "running away ring" in the family. So if you ever want to run away, and I don't blame you if you do, this will see you right.'

He looked up at her hopefully, and there was a long pause while she stood over him in silence with her hands on her hips, her toe tapping on the floor.

Nick's heart sank. He'd got it all wrong. He should have proposed to Maggie alone, made a proper romantic gesture instead of this board meeting with her brother and Celine, his current wife, and Millie, where they thrashed out all the details. But now everyone was watching them, Peter serious and the women smiling. And then he realised he'd not said one word of love.

'Come on then, if we're doin' this?' said Maggie, looking exasperated.

He blinked up at her worriedly.

'Ask me to marry you, ya big eejit!'

He blushed as everyone, even Peter, laughed.

'Oh, I see... Of course. Right. Sorry. What I meant to say was, if after all this messing about, you still don't want to run away, at least not for a few years, then I would love nothing in this whole world so much as for you to agree to marry me some time in the future when we can get it all sorted out – which we will, I promise – to everyone's satisfaction.' He took a big breath after blurting it all out in one go.

Maggie rolled her eyes. 'Well, that's the worst proposal I've ever heard, Mr Shaw, and I've heard a few, I can tell ya. But it will have to do.' She held out her hand, and he slipped the ring on her finger. There was a loud pop of a cork because Millie had fetched a bottle of cold Dom Pérignon, and she filled four glasses.

'To Nick and Maggie. We are so happy for you both, we love you both, and we wish you the happiest of futures.' The Englishwoman raised her glass in a toast, and after everyone drank, she refilled their glasses.

'To Floss, who helped me find a way,' said Nick, wishing his grandmother could have been there to see this happen.

'To Floss,' they chorused.

After a few more toasts to love and friendship, another bottle was produced, and Celine clinked her glass off Nick's and drained it. '*Felicitations, ma chère Nick, et bonne chance.* Now Millie, let's head for bed. I'm exhausted after the day. *Au revoir, au revoir, bonne nuit…*'

'Is this really gonna happen?' marvelled Maggie, standing by the dying fire, admiring the sparkle on her hand. 'No more sneaking or lying or any of that?'

'We will, as soon as I can, I promise,' Nick said huskily.

'We'll get married one day, and then anyone, bishop or beggar, who has an objection will get a clatter of this massive rock.' She laughed.

'We'll face some opposition, and it will take time to get it done properly, but I honestly think we'll get there.' He threw an anxious glance towards Peter, who was still with them, sitting in the armchair. 'Don't you think, Peter?'

'I don't know what I think, to be honest,' said Peter, his voice quiet and his face a bit grim. 'I want to be happy for ye, of course I do, but I'm fearful this is all just a big fantasy ye're tellin' yourselves, which will never come to pass, just to make yourselves feel better about' – he stopped himself from saying what Nick assumed would have been 'living in sin' – 'not being married.'

'Oh, Peter.' Maggie's face fell, and she stamped her foot. 'I'm so happy. Please don't spoil things. Don't be always so disappointed in me – I can't bear it.'

Nick put his arm around her hastily, stroking her shoulder, soothing her, looking pleadingly at Peter over her head.

Long seconds ticked by. Then Peter stood, took a step towards his sister and opened his arms, his eyebrows raised in question.

With a sigh, she left Nick's embrace and walked into them.

'I'm never disappointed in you, Mag,' he murmured, kissing her copper curls. 'I love you.'

'I love you too.' Tears streamed down her face.

Then she reached out with her other hand, beckoning Nick over, and there they stood, the three of them, in the light of the fire, arms around each other.

And Nick heard Peter say in Maggie's ear, in a low voice meant for her only, 'Look, whatever happens, I'll stand behind you, Maggie. You might lose everything if you go after what you want, but I can promise you, you won't lose me.'

CHAPTER 12

ETER

AISLING and the Gallaghers were engaged in an intense match of the Landlord's Game at the kitchen table. Aisling was winning by buying up all the property from under her grandparents' noses and cackling with glee when their counter landed on one of her houses and they had to pay her rent.

She'd been staying with them for a few days before the troupe left for America, but now it was time to go. Peter and May had arrived half an hour ago, but apparently the game could not be stopped. They observed from the doorway, reluctant to break up the happy scene.

Peter noticed his daughter was dressed much more properly than usual. She kind of ran a bit wild around the cabaret, with her hair in a tangle and dressed in hand-me-downs, but Olive had her in a lovely white dress with broderie anglaise over skirts, and her dark nut-brown hair was brushed till it shone and tied back with two white ribbons. He could only imagine the cajoling and bribery it took to get her to sit still for that operation. Even her ankle socks had a trim of lace, and her black patent shoes were polished.

She had her own room, David's old room, and they'd decorated it so beautifully for her, with dolls and books and even a big stuffed bear. It was mutual adoration in both directions.

Peter grinned as Michael moaned that Aisling had taken all of his money and his properties were all mortgaged.

'Did they play this with you?' he murmured to May as they watched.

'Are you mad? They did not,' May whispered back. 'They never played anything with us – this is a new thing. Father bought that game especially for Aisling a few weeks ago.'

'She told me your father bought her a chess set too, thinking he could teach her, but he didn't realise she is a master chess player from Two-Soups. He played chess all day, every day in the trenches. Nobody would play against him by the finish because he kept winning all their smokes.'

He glanced at May, who watched their daughter with a look of sheer love. Aisling was the best thing to ever happen to them. 'She's had a quirky education so far, that's for sure,' May said.

She leant against him, and he put his arm around her shoulders. Despite everything, the fight with Maggie and Nick, Floss dying, the preparation for going to America, she had remained stoic and in full-steam-ahead mode. He sometimes wondered what she was thinking, whether Maggie's accusations about Aida had really hurt her, but he didn't dare raise it. To do so would be to face some questioning that would deserve some honest answers, and he just couldn't.

He glanced at her again now, her blond hair perfectly set as always, dressed in a beautiful silvery-grey coat and dress, the pearls he'd bought her for her birthday at her ears and throat. She always dressed up to see her parents, as if trying to reassure them that whatever Peter lacked in breeding, he made up for in wealth.

'Righto, young lady.' May broke up the game. 'Poor Granny and Granda are poor as church mice now – you've cleaned them out – so we'd best be going.'

They were taking the tram into town; all their luggage had been sent ahead. They had yet to say goodbye to Peter's family, so they'd go there next, and then they would take a train to Cork, then another to Cobh, where they would spend the night with Harp Devereaux, who was now at home, and then board the ship tomorrow. Aisling was beside herself with excitement.

'Bye-bye, Granny, bye-bye, Granda,' she said as she hugged them both. Olive was trying not to cry, and Michael was not far behind her, Peter could tell.

Goodbyes were hard for them, and since their son, David, had reappeared after the war and then disappeared again from their lives, they were terrified of losing May and Aisling.

Between himself and May, they'd managed to convince her parents that David was living in Germany, that he must have had a woman there and that he was living his life there. It broke their hearts to think their son had chosen to live his life without them in it, but the alternative was a good deal worse. Peter and May had decided that it would help nobody for the Gallaghers to know the truth, that David had been shot and killed that night in Brockleton, and his body, along with that of Harvey Bathhurst, was burnt in a fire at Harvey's home.

David Gallagher was now one of the many, after the upheaval of the Great War, of whom there was no account, and never would be.

May hugged her parents, and Peter kissed Olive's cheek and shook hands with Michael.

'You'll look after them, won't you, Peter? You hear such terrible things… And *America*…I mean…' Olive sobbed, all pretence at a stiff upper lip dissipated.

Peter fought the urge to say America was full of perfectly nice people, just like here, and there was no reason to behave like they'd got a one-way ticket to Sodom and Gomorrah, but he understood her pain, May and Aisling were the only family the Gallaghers had left and that they hated them to go.

'He will, Mother, and we'll be back before you know it.' May smiled.

But Michael caught Peter's eye. They were both men of the world, and Peter suspected his father-in-law knew that if Peter was given the opportunity to stay in America, he would certainly consider it.

One last round of hugs, Aisling jigging about from foot to foot, wearing her red hat and coat, dying to go. 'Bye-bye, and kiss Bug every day, and he should have one quarter of an apple and a half a carrot as well as his food every day, and let him sleep in the bed with you if he gets too sad. He's going to miss me so much.'

The Gallaghers had kindly agreed to keep the rabbit, who wouldn't be able to cope with a sea voyage. May laughed at how they bowed to Aisling's every wish and told Peter she could well imagine the rabbit in between the two of them in the bed because Aisling told them to do it.

'Goodbye, my darling. Be very safe now, won't you? And hold Mummy's hand crossing the road, and don't talk to strangers, and be careful in the sea, and don't wander off...' Olive was clearly imagining all sorts of horrors that might befall her precious grandchild.

'I will, Granny.' Aisling grinned. 'Look, Daddy, Granda gave me a silver dollar.' Her eyes were bright as she showed the coin to her parents. 'It has the goddess Liberty on one side and a bald eagle standing on an olive branch on the other. Isn't it lovely?'

'I had them order it at the bank,' Michael said, colouring a little at his own sentimentality.

'Aw, Father, that's so kind of you. You'll have to keep that now, Aisling,' May instructed. 'Not waste it on silly things.'

But Aisling and Michael shared a conspiratorial glance, and the little girl giggled. 'Granda got two – one for me to keep here as a souvenir and another one for ice cream. This is the ice cream one.'

'Ha!' May laughed. 'He didn't give me any silver dollars for ice cream, let me tell you, Aisling. You're going soft in your old age, Father.' She kissed his cheek affectionately.

'But Mammy, you never went to America, so why would he?' Aisling asked reasonably.

'An excellent point, pet.'

Michael hugged his granddaughter, and then at the last minute, May's parents decided to accompany them to the tram stop instead of waving goodbye from the front door. There was much finding of suitable hats and scarves, and Peter and his little family nearly ended up missing the tram, but finally he got them all aboard.

As they pulled away, Olive and Michael stood on the pavement, looking as forlorn as it was possible for two people to be, and Peter felt a rush of affection for his in-laws. He picked up Aisling so she could wave to them until the last possible moment.

* * *

PETER'S OWN MOTHER, Bridie, had lit every candle in the church according to his little sister Connie, and was doing the nine-day prayer as well as a special novena to St Christopher, patron saint of travellers. Peter would never tease his mother about her deep faith, but he did find her belt-and-braces approach to intentions hilarious. She would cover all eventualities and leave no saint undisturbed with her pleas for help. He could never tell her that he didn't believe any of it. There was no God – how could there be? After all he'd seen during the war in the trenches, he was sure.

As soon as they arrived to the little house in Iveagh cottages, which had been built by the Guinness factory for their workers, Bridie told them she'd had the priest say five Masses for their safe return.

'Ma, we'll be grand, I keep telling ya. Stop worryin'.' Peter placed his hands on his mother's thin shoulders and tried to ease her fears. 'It's just the same as here, only it's America.'

'It is not. There's gangsters over there and all sorts,' she said ominously. 'And what about Sacco and Vanzetti and Leo Frank? Supposing they kidnap Aisling?' Some helpful soul had given his mother some kind of magazine of all the high-profile court cases in America, which had her up all night with terror.

'Ma, after what we've seen here in the last few years, America has nothing on us in terms of terrifying people and bad things happening. But anyway, where we're going is a seaside place, like Rush or Portmarnock, just a beach and a few shops. It's a sleepy little place.'

He was stretching the truth a bit there. Whatever he'd heard about

Atlantic City, New Jersey, sleepy was not a word anyone would use. Eamonn had been in America for a short while, after he'd escaped from the English in the War of Independence, and according to him, Atlantic City was a place for people to relax and get up to all sorts of mischief, despite Prohibition. In fact, apparently Prohibition made things worse, with gangsters running illegal booze. But Peter wasn't worried. Harp Devereaux had assured him that the Ocean Diamond was run by a really respectable woman, Maud Flynn, who stuck strictly to the no-drink, no-shenanigans rule.

'Can I come with you, Peter? I'm seventeen now, the same as Maggie was when she joined the cabaret.' His sister Connie was green with envy and made no secret of it.

'You stick to your studies, Connie,' he said fondly, ruffling her hair. He was so proud of his youngest sister. She was studious in a way that none of her siblings were. She even had a plan to go to university, though she hadn't told their mother yet; she knew she would face opposition. 'You're going to be the making of this family yet.'

'Don't be putting notions into your sister's head. She'll have no need of all that book learning once she's properly settled,' said their mother crossly.

Bridie was a nice woman who couldn't believe how wonderfully her life had turned out after such a rocky marriage, and couldn't for the life of her see why her daughters would not be over the moon with marriage to an abstemious hard-working man and a rug covered in babies.

Kathleen, who was busy showing Aisling the lovely story book she had bought her for America, was living that exact life. Her husband, Sean, was a shoemaker and had inherited his father's cobbler shop in the city centre. They were living with Sean's elderly father; his mother died years ago. As far as Bridie was concerned, Kathleen had done well. She'd given up her job in Arnotts, as it wasn't the done thing for a married woman to work, and she had two children now, four-year-old Eamonn, named for his uncle, and a two-year-old girl called Martha.

Maggie living as she did was a mystery and a source of concern to

Bridie, and it would be worse when she found out the truth about her and Nick, so Peter knew his mother would want to keep Connie close. She would set her sights on marrying her off to a local boy, who would set her up in a nice, modest home; that would be enough for her youngest child, more than enough actually. And once the first baby came, there would be another and another, and that would be how life was.

'Ah, I'm not putting any notions into anyone's head, Ma,' said Peter, with a wink at Connie. When his youngest sister had come to him a few months ago with her dreams of going to university, he'd advised her to hold her fire until she finished school and did her exams, and when the time came, he would support her and offer to pay for her to continue her studies. He knew Bridie would accept it because it came from him, and his mother believed every word out of his mouth as if it were taken directly from the Bible itself. It made him feel bad sometimes, conspiring with Connie behind their mother's back.

Bridie was on about Maggie now. 'Are ya sure she'll be safe in America, Peter? A single woman? You'll have to mind her. Supposin' she catches the eye of one of them mobsters? She's daft enough to go with one. I wish she'd married poor Bill – he was mad about her.'

'I'll take good care of her, Mam,' he said, feeling guilty as sin.

Maggie had already been to say her goodbyes to her family. She was gone to Cobh already to stay with Nick in a hotel for a couple of nights, and though she'd said they'd be in separate rooms, he knew that was just a lie to make him feel better.

'But you won't be sayin' anythin' to Ma about me and Nick, will ya, Peter?' she'd asked him anxiously.

'Don't worry, I've no notion of it,' he'd replied. 'I don't need any more wailing out of her any more than you do.'

He could only imagine the horror from Bridie at her daughter's ruination if she found out Maggie was living in sin with a married man and a Protestant, and the blame that would be heaped on his head for allowing it to happen. And Eamonn would be fit to kill Nick. Eamonn had never trusted Nick as it was, Nick being part of the

Anglo-Irish aristocracy and a cousin of Harvey Bathhurst. Even though that was the connection Nick had used to get Aida and Eamonn out of Dublin Castle.

Eamonn had arrived, big strong man that he was, and he lifted Aisling and swirled her around.

'Can I go for a spin on your back, Uncle Eamonn?' she squealed. She loved playing 'horsies' with Eamonn, and the patience his older brother showed towards Aisling always amazed Peter. Eamonn was much more interested in her than in Kathleen's two, even though the boy was named for him.

'You cannot, and ruin your lovely dress and break your poor uncle's back into the bargain,' May admonished.

'Nice to see her priorities, eh, Eamonn,' Peter joked. 'The dress before your back. And I thought my wife cared for you.'

To his amusement, May coloured. 'I didn't mean I didn't care…'

'Only joking, May. Right, we really have to go now.' He'd just checked his watch and was anxious to get going. There followed hugging and kissing and tears from his mother and sisters, until he protested, 'Enough of this weeping, like we were going to our graves and not on the adventure of a lifetime. Now good luck to ye all and mind yerselves.'

Eamonn had stood aside during the leave-taking, looking oddly despondent, Aisling in his arms, her little arms wrapped around his strong, thick neck.

'Come here to me, Aisling, we're off…' Peter gently extracted his daughter from his brother's embrace and handed her off to his mother to get her coat. He pulled Eamonn in gruffly for a one-armed hug. 'See ya, Eamonn. Stay out of trouble now, do you hear me? In fact…' He'd been thinking of this for a while, ever since Harp Devereaux's offer. 'Why don't you join us in America for a while, after we're settled?'

He had often wondered at his brother's adamant refusal to emigrate. Eamonn had plenty of connections in America from the time he was over during the Troubles; he could make a great life there.

And he hated his job here. He got passed over every time a promotion came up because of the way he went over the Treaty.

Eamonn had been against the Treaty and had for a time fought against the Free State Army who supported Collins, and the legacy of that divide was still an open wound in Irish society. People were divided into those who supported Mick Collins and those who didn't. Those who did seemed to prosper, and those who didn't were marginalised. Eamonn was passed over for promotion at the building site, over and over, and he was sure it was because of his political convictions. The boss was a Free Stater.

It happened to all the men who took against the new government. People were taking revenge, Peter supposed. Frank McCoy, the owner of the construction firm for which Eamonn worked, was a rich Protestant whose parents were English, and he despised all rebels but reserved particular hatred for those who went against the Treaty. So many of Eamonn's friends who disagreed with the Free State had ended up just leaving, going to America for good.

'Don't be luring him to America! Isn't it enough losing you and Maggie?' protested Bridie as she helped Aisling on with her little red coat.

'Ah, we'll only be gone for a short time.' Peter smiled. 'But Eamonn could make some good money there on the sites, Ma. It wouldn't be right to hold him back.'

'Not at all. Eamonn has to stay here, doesn't he, Bridie?' said May, fixing Aisling's red hat onto her dark hair. 'To look after you all? Kathleen and Connie and yourself…'

'Sure, they're grand altogether,' said Peter. 'It would be a great opportunity, Eamonn, and you've said it yourself – you'll never get ahead here now.' He looked at Eamonn with an encouraging smile, but for some reason, his brother looked away.

Kathleen chimed in as she tried to stop little Eamonn from climbing up the dresser to get at Bridie's lovely little china ornaments. 'Eamonn needs to meet a girl. God knows he's handsome enough, and the girls all have an eye for him.'

'Would ye all give over with the advice? I'll do as I please, and the only one I listen to is Aisling, isn't that right, pet?' He twirled her around again, and she giggled.

May smiled stiffly, and said, 'Either way, we need to get going. Come on, Aisling.' She took her daughter from Eamonn's arms. 'Stay out of trouble, you hear me?' she said to Eamonn quietly.

'I think the only thing that might get me in trouble is going to America, so I won't be doing that,' said Eamonn, quite seriously. Peter laughed and clapped him on the shoulder, and then there were a flurry of waves, entreaties to be safe, prayers and more hugs. And they were gone.

* * *

ON THE TRAIN TO CORK, they had a private compartment. Aisling was sleepy, so May tucked her up under Peter's coat for warmth on one set of seats, then sat down opposite, next to Peter.

As the green countryside chugged by, Peter studied his daughter, her long, dark, silky hair falling around her cheeks, and he thought about Eamonn not being married, and how dark and gruff he was becoming as he got older, the dancing light gone out of his eyes. A man could be too long without a woman. A man needed a family.

He still felt terrible about what Maggie had yelled the night of the fight, that he was in love with Aida and May had no choice but to watch and say nothing, but every time he'd tried to reassure his wife, she didn't want to discuss it. He thought maybe he should have one more try.

'May, I know you don't want to talk about –'

'You're right, I don't.'

'Fair enough, but I do want to say this. I do not regret marrying you, and if I had my time over again, I'd change nothing, I promise.'

And it was true. Aida and he had a connection, he wasn't denying it, but May was the reason – well, he and May together were the reason they were here, in this position, going to America. Aida with her abrasive personality would never have been able to smooth their way as May had.

It was pure genius, the way she'd sent Aisling to pull that stunt with Magus. She'd been right to persuade him to make it up with Nick and Maggie. She'd organised for the cabaret to be paid in advance for the first month by an agent called Frederick Tibbet, based in America, and she'd got all the necessary paperwork in order for this trip. His wife's astute management of money, her ability to see exactly what a problem was and how to solve it, her skill at getting the best out of people without getting anyone's back up, those were priceless gifts.

He smiled at her fondly, the capable girl he'd known since she was seventeen years old. 'Well, go on then, May. Don't leave me hanging here. You don't regret it either, do you?'

His wife didn't say anything in reply, but she looked pleased and took his hand, and as the train rattled on, they settled into an easy silence. He held her hand all the way to Cork.

CHAPTER 13

May

THEIR CABIN WAS MAGNIFICENT, like a hotel room only even more luxurious, with a chandelier and mahogany furniture and oil paintings, and a shelf of leather-bound books and a writing desk – though how one posted letters on a ship, she'd no idea.

She'd booked them on the *Corinthian*, which sailed from Bremen in Germany via Southampton and then Cobh in Cork, where the whole cabaret had embarked, their vast luggage stored in newly purchased shipping chests.

She, Peter and Aisling were travelling first class.

Peter had been against it, said it looked bad, but May called a logistics meeting in the big tent and said the cabaret was paying for second-class passage for everyone and anyone who wanted to pay the difference to upgrade to first was free to do so out of their own pockets. The performers, used to caravans and muddy fields, all decided the money could be better spent in America.

Except for Nick, who also booked himself a large first-class cabin, much too big for one person. May guessed why but didn't comment. Quite enough had been said on that particular subject.

She and Peter had had a lovely two days together in the charming seaside town of Cobh, staying with the famous Harp Devereaux and her husband, JohnJoe, in the Cliff House, a magnificent place overlooking the harbour, which had been all but destroyed in a fire but was renovated and restored and was now home to Harp's mother, Rose, and Rose's husband and a menagerie of cats and dogs and even a goat called Lloyd George.

Harp was as everyone said, nice if a bit odd, very direct, beautiful in a quirky way. She seemed kind of otherworldly to May, but being in the end stages of pregnancy, she was also probably just tired. JohnJoe was an Irish American, funny and practical, and he clearly was besotted with his wife.

You could tell the couple were famous and had lots of money, but they weren't ostentatious. Harp was a staunch Irish republican and a personal friend of the late Michael Collins, and Rose's husband, a very charming man called Matt Quinn, was a famous IRA commander, so there was no doubting the colours of that house.

Matt's days with the IRA were behind him, but there had been great bitterness and division after Collins signed the Treaty with England, then when the Big Fella, as he was called, was shot dead in his native county of Cork, it had soured whatever victory might have been felt by those who'd finally freed this part of Ireland. They may have known of Eamonn's rejection of the Treaty, so they avoided the topic; instead they'd talked of America and music.

Harp had explained to them about the sort of tunes that Irish Americans related to, and she gifted Peter a stack of sheet music. JohnJoe had also given them all sorts of sensible advice, the main one being to stay on the right side of Maud Flynn, the highly respectable owner of the Ocean Diamond.

Miss Flynn was a very important person in Atlantic City, as was her cousin, the chief of police there, Bartie Flynn. Maud Flynn had risen to the top of the ladder in terms of business, no easy task for a single woman. She had never married but had a niece, the daughter of her late brother who had died of liver failure at thirty-five, so she was dead set against alcohol, and if you wanted to work for her, you needed to live a clean life as well as do your job well.

But that was all ahead of them, and now here they were, on the high seas, on a beautiful ship. They had striped canvas chairs on the first-class deck, rented for the entire voyage, food and drinks brought to them at the lift of a finger. The sea glittered as the sunlight bounced off the gently rippling waves. Elegant, beautifully dressed people strolled past along the polished deck. Everything was so spotless and shining. The crew, in their immaculate uniforms, worked round the clock ensuring standards were maintained as the huge liner cut through the ocean, bearing them ever closer to America.

It was blissful – apart from one thing. So far she and Peter had dined alone in the first-class restaurant, even though his best friend, Nick, was living on the same deck. They always went to the second sitting in the dining room, after putting Aisling to bed after the children's supper, so she guessed Nick – and presumably Maggie, as his 'wife' – were going to the earlier sitting to avoid Peter, who was only grudgingly accepting of the situation still.

She looked across at her husband now.

Aisling was playing in a sandpit set up for the children of first-class passengers. There was a dollhouse and buckets and spades, and a set of monkey bars for climbing. She'd made friends with two little German girls, and they were totally occupied. Peter was leaning on the railing surrounding the play area, watching the children play.

She put down her book and went to join him. 'I know you don't want to talk about the situation with Nick and Maggie, but can I just say one thing,' she began.

'Depends what it is.' He never turned to her, just stayed focused on the three little girls.

'This is your big break, the thing you've been dreaming of since you were a boy. It's actually happening, and you are letting this thing between Nick and Maggie ruin it for you.'

His gaze never left Aisling and the others. He gave no indication he'd heard her.

'Peter?' she nudged eventually. 'Please talk to me. Tell me what's on your mind.'

He turned to her with a sigh. 'What's on my mind is, I don't think I should have gone along with what happened in Brockleton. I got bounced into it, that's what, because of the day that was in it, Nick burying his grandmother and everything. I wouldn't have agreed otherwise.'

May knew he was right. In fact she'd banked on it. That's why she'd insisted on him going to the funeral. 'OK, you had a soft moment, but you did agree, so why don't you just put a good face on it?'

He went silent for a while longer, but she could see him psyching himself up to say something more. Eventually he growled, 'Nick booked a double cabin, here in first class.'

'Yes, I know.' She pretended to look puzzled. 'What's wrong with that?'

'You know what's wrong with it, May. He might have put a ring on her finger, but there's nothing official about it, no marriage vows taken, and yet here they are...' He gripped the railing of the playground till his knuckles went white. 'I'm so angry, May, so furious with him more than her, though she's such a headstrong female that there's no dealing with her, never has been...'

'Peter, stop this,' said May firmly. 'You know they have to wait until Nick's father dies, and who knows how many years he might live. What were you expecting, them to sleep in separate rooms for the next ten years?'

'That's what unmarried people are supposed to do.'

'But *we* didn't, Peter, did we?' she said, a little sharply.

His mouth opened and shut, and he blushed slightly without answering.

She pressed home her advantage with brutal honesty. 'You wouldn't have dared, but I seduced you, Peter. And I wouldn't be at all surprised if it was the same way around with Maggie. And look at her – how could any man resist?'

He reddened further. 'Don't talk about my sister like that.'

'You have to stop thinking of her as your little sister. She's twenty-four, and you can't expect her to live like a nun until she's maybe in her thirties. And put your business hat on. She's a wonderful part of the act. She and Nick are a delight together on stage, far more so than he and Celine ever were, and I hate to say it and I don't want to offend you, but now we know why, don't we? There's a reason for that spark between them, so stop trying to put it out and make them ashamed of themselves or they won't be able to perform properly, and then bang goes your big break, and not just yours – everyone's. You're allowing your emotions to come before the show, Peter, and that's not like you.'

She stopped then and licked her lips nervously, worried she had gone too far, that she was going to make a bad situation even worse. But something had to be done or the cabaret would fail.

'Look at me, Daddy!' Aisling hung upside down on the bars, her dark hair dangling, watched by the two little German girls with their mouths wide open.

'You're like a monkey,' Peter said, grinning.

'No, I'm like Enzo!'

'Same thing.' He chuckled, and May was relieved to see the smile on his face.

He might be a bit conservative around Maggie, but at least he wasn't a stuffy parent. May's mother would never have allowed her to dangle upside down, showing her drawers to the world, but Aisling was being raised differently. May knew it worried her mother. Olive Gallagher was very respectable, and she had been very upset when she'd overheard her arch nemesis Mrs Cuddihy, from the church flower committee, remark that Aisling was 'half wild'.

That's why Olive had offered to keep Aisling in Dublin for the four months they were gone, so the little girl could start school, but Peter had turned that plan down flat, saying he couldn't stand the idea of not seeing his daughter every day.

She knew Aisling would have to have some formal schooling eventually, whatever Peter wanted, but they would consider that when they got back. Meanwhile she was learning plenty, because everyone had agreed to teach her something. Magus was her main tutor, but all the cabaret were happy to step up.

Clive showed her maths – well, Timothy did – and Aisling found the whole experience hilarious. But despite the high jinks, she could already do long multiplication in her head, so she was learning. Carpentry and chess she got from Two-Soups; he also taught her the poems of Robert Burns. She could perform them in a broad Glaswegian accent, and everyone loved to hear her recite the one about the 'little wee beasties'.

Enzo was forever encouraging her to climb and tumble and jump, and he spoke to her in Italian, because although he was a Londoner, his father was an Italian ice cream maker. And Ramon taught her the guitar and also how to swear very proficiently in Catalan, which May wouldn't have realised except she'd overheard Aida scolding him about it. Ramon had shown no remorse whatsoever; he seemed to think it was hilarious.

It fell to May to teach Aisling Irish. Peter couldn't remember any of it, so traumatised was he by the brutality of the Christian brothers during his short experience of schooling. Together she and her daughter studied the aisling poems, written in that beautiful expressive language.

There were things to learn on the ship as well. A drawing class was offered for the first-class children, which Aisling loved, and the ship had an indoor heated swimming pool where the children were given lessons.

While May and her husband stood at the railing, admiring Aisling's gymnastics, the two little German girls were collected by their nanny, and Aisling, instantly bored without an audience, dropped off the bars and came bouncing over.

'Can we have ice cream?' she asked. May had promised her a trip to the café on board as a treat for not screaming the ship down as May washed her hair. Aisling hated washing of any kind and kicked up blue murder every time.

'We can, come on.' Peter picked her up and put her on his shoulders – she was small for a five-year-old – and they walked to the other end of the deck.

May gave their order to the liveried waiter, and they sat out on the sunny deck to wait for him, at a wooden table with a yellow sunshade.

'Daddy,' Aisling asked, 'do you know the story of the two wolves?'

'I don't think so. Is it an old Irish story?'

Aisling beamed, delighted to know something he didn't. 'No, it's a story of the Cherokee. Uncle Magus told me.'

'Really? Does he teach you all that stuff as well as all about the animals and flowers and birds?' May knew Peter was constantly amused at his daughter's vast knowledge on such diverse topics.

'He does. He teaches me about the Unetlanvhi and the Jistu – that's the Great Spirit and the rabbit – and the Uktena – they're like dragon-headed snakes – and the Tlanuwa, big birds with wings like metal.'

'My goodness, they sound like very scary lads altogether,' said Peter earnestly as their ice cream arrived in cut-glass bowls, a rich yellow vanilla with real strawberries in it for Peter, dark chocolate for May and a lemon ice for Aisling, which the little girl tucked into with gusto.

'Well, some of the stories are, but I like the wolf story the best,' she replied, coming up for air after she'd demolished the first few spoonfuls.

'Tell it to us,' encouraged May. She could listen to her little daughter's chatter forever.

'Well, a boy is talking to his grandfather after doing a bold thing. I don't know what it was, but he felt very bad about it. He was ashamed and sad that he'd made his parents so angry. He thought he was a very bad little boy. But the granda explained that the boy was neither all good nor all bad. The granda was a wise man in the tribe, and he told the boy this story. He said that there are two wolves, and they fight inside of everyone. One is a good wolf, and he thinks good thoughts and is kind and nice, and the other wolf is bad, and he thinks mean things and wants to hurt people.'

May shot Peter a smiling glance, and he smiled back at her. She loved it when they were together like this, sharing the familiar feelings of pride in their bright little girl. Aisling delighted them both.

'Go on,' Peter urged their daughter, fascinated.

'And the little boy asked his granda which wolf would win inside of him.' She paused to scoop up a big dollop of the ice cream. 'Can you guess which one wins?'

Peter considered it. 'I don't know. The good wolf wins in some people and the bad one in other people?'

Aisling's little brow furrowed in thought. 'That's true, but the one that wins in each person is the one you feed,' she said solemnly. 'I didn't really understand it, so Uncle Magus explained. It means if you think bad thoughts and do bad things, then the bad wolf gets stronger, so if you're angry with someone and want them to be sad, then that's how you feed the bad wolf. But if you forgive someone and try not to think bad thoughts about them, that feeds the good wolf, and that one wins.'

Peter didn't speak for a long moment, pushing his lower lip to one side in that way he did when he was thinking. 'That's one way of looking at life, I suppose. But it's not easy to have kind thoughts when you're angry with someone.'

She shrugged nonchalantly. 'I know. But Uncle Magus says that it's always that way, for everyone. We're only human, so we can just try.'

'Well, aren't you the wise old owl?' Peter said thoughtfully, digging his spoon into his ice cream.

And May smiled to herself as she savoured her smooth darkchocolate dessert. Had Aisling succeeded where she had failed? Time would tell.

CHAPTER 14

ICK

ENZO, Ramon and the others were having a party in the second-class bar. Everyone was in flying form, embarking on the trip of a lifetime; no wonder they wanted to sing and dance and drink the night away. They'd wanted Nick to come, but he wasn't in the mood.

He'd overheard three young ladies who were travelling with their mothers discussing how to give the elders the slip and go to the party in the second-class lounge. He feared for their virtue, but they weren't his to worry about.

He'd seen Peter, May and Aisling having ice cream on the deck earlier. They'd all been laughing, and he'd just felt such a pang of misery and despair that he'd decided to have an early night.

He convinced Maggie to go without him, though. He knew she loved a party, and he didn't want to drag her down. She was so happy-go-lucky, so full of fun and joie de vivre, though when he'd said that to her, she laughed at him.

'Joy da what?' she'd asked.

'The joy of life, Maggie.'

'Oh, I'm all for that. We're here for a good time, not a long time, Nicky-boy.' It was her favourite catchphrase. She eschewed all responsibility; she regarded life as a bit of a lark, to be enjoyed, and hang the consequences. It was so refreshing, and he didn't want to be a wet blanket.

'Go to the party and have fun,' he'd urged her.

'But I don't like the idea of you being alone…' She'd hesitated in her lovely royal-blue and polka-dot dress. She was so gorgeous with her creamy skin and curvy figure.

'I'm just tired, Maggie, that's all.' He didn't like to say it to her, but alone was exactly what he wanted. Even in the normal course of events, he was quieter than most of the rest of the troupe, and now with things as they were, he couldn't face seeing everyone all together.

Maggie didn't want her mother or Eamonn to find out about her and Nick, and she agreed Nick's aristocratic social circle had to be kept in the quiet as well for the sake of his father and the boys, and for Celine as well, who mixed in that society. But she'd put her foot down when it came to the cabaret. She wasn't prepared to keep 'sneaking or lying', as she put it, around her closest friends, the ones she spent night and day with.

'Sure we're like family, and what happens inside the cabaret stays there. None of the rest of them are exactly nuns or monks either now, are they?' she'd argued when Nick suggested Peter might prefer it if they were discreet. 'Look at the way Enzo carried on with Lady Florence Gamminston, and still does when she can track him down, and she's married. And Ramon, he's as bad. Two-Soups and Delilah were at it for a while, and the girls have a different fella in every town, not that May realises it, of course. And besides, if Peter wanted us to be discreet, maybe he shouldn't have bawled it all over the campsite that I was a brasser.'

When she'd first kissed him in public, though, even Enzo and Ramon had looked shocked, and Nick didn't blame them. His friends had put up with him mooning around Celine for years, always going on about her, and they'd seen how happy he was at his wedding. And then there were the boys. And though Celine lived at Brockleton with Millie while Nick stayed on the road, he'd kept on acting like everything was fine, and everyone assumed they were a happy couple.

And now this, with Maggie, Peter's little sister.

Nick knew he'd never struck anyone as the kind of man who cheated on his wife, but to explain would be to tell about Celine and Millie, and how shortly after their wedding, he'd discovered them in bed together. But he couldn't do that to Celine, so he would just have to live with the reputation of being a cad and a bounder and a thoroughly despicable person, and though no one said anything to him, it was hard to take.

Especially with Peter openly ignoring him in front of everyone.

After Maggie had finally gone, he kicked off his shoes and lay on the bed.

Maggie had insisted they get a double cabin, and she didn't care that it was on the same deck as Peter. It was palatial compared to the perfectly functionary second-class cabins, and he was glad they had a double bed and not a bunk and that his feet didn't hang out the bottom. Being six foot four was tricky in small spaces.

Even so, for Peter's sake, they should have booked two single cabins and pretended not to be together.

He gazed at the mahogany ceiling, wondering if agreeing to come to America had been a terrible idea. Maggie for all her bravado and her 'to hell with him' attitude was heartbroken underneath it all that Peter was still unhappy, despite the conversation in Brockleton. Perhaps it would have been best if they'd stayed at home.

Two more days and they'd be docking in New York. To take his mind off his misery, he thought of Floss, and her deep love of the country of her birth.

'I married an Anglo-Irish lord and live in Ireland, which I love, but in my bones, in the essence of who I am, I'm an American, and nothing, no amount of time or distance, can ever change it,' he often remembered her saying.

That was her mantra of life and the lens through which she saw everything, though she had left the United States as a girl of twenty.

She had kept her New England accent – her family came from Rhode Island and had made a fortune in mining, hence the prestigious marriage to a peer of the British realm – she drank coffee not tea, and she insisted on saying sidewalk and faucet and other words that used to drive her son, Nick's father, to distraction. Nick smiled at the memory.

A knock on the door interrupted his thoughts, but he didn't answer it. He knew it was only someone trying to convince him to come to the party – not Maggie, as she would have walked straight in – and he really didn't want to go. There was another knock, more insistent. He continued to ignore it; they'd go away eventually.

Then a voice. 'Nick, it's me.'

He sprang from the bed, his mouth dry, and opened the door.

'Can I come in?' Peter was in his shirtsleeves, open-necked, no tie or blazer.

'Of c-c-course.'

THERE WAS a small round table by a porthole with a seat either side, and he offered Peter to sit. A small table lamp illuminated it, and wall lamps lit up the rest of the cabin. Outside, the dark ocean pitched and tossed gently. A book lay face down on the table, and Peter picked it up and turned it over. An Agatha Christie.

'Who did it?' he asked.

Nick didn't know; it was Maggie who had been reading the book. 'The butler, at a guess.'

Peter smiled slightly. 'Isn't it always?' In the trenches, Peter had slowly taught himself to read properly, running his fingers along under the words, and Nick had kept him supplied with books that his grandmother sent him from home, plenty of Agatha Christie's among them, and had helped him with the words he couldn't make out. They had such a long, close friendship, forged in the flames of war.

Nick braced himself. 'Look, Peter, I'm sorry. I shouldn't have –'

Peter raised his hand sharply. 'Stop. Don't say anything. I'm thinking.'

Nick fell silent. A full minute passed. At last, unable to stand it any longer, he asked nervously, 'What are you thinking?'

Again the hand stopping him. 'Kind thoughts. I'm feeding the good wolf. Give me more time.'

Nick began to worry that the strain of moving the whole cabaret to America, and the shock over Maggie, had affected Peter's mind, but after another minute, Peter sighed and ran his hand through his hair, a gesture Nick had been familiar with for years now.

'Right, I'm ready. Now, I know you've said you'll marry her, and I'm going to believe you mean that. But what about her reputation in the meantime, Nick?'

'I know. I'm sorry. You're right. We should have booked separate cabins, but...' His voice trailed off.

'But Maggie insisted,' finished Peter with a wry smile.

'No, it was all me. It's not Maggie's fault – it was my suggestion –'

Peter slapped his hand on the table, making Nick jump. 'Stop right there.'

'I'm sorry –'

'Stop!'

Nick stopped and sat in miserable silence, his stomach churning.

'Now,' said Peter firmly, 'I've been thinking about this all evening, in the kindest way I can. I've been feeding the good wolf for hours, so don't spoil it by telling me lies – we've always been straight with each other. And there's no point – I know my own sister, and no one but no one can make her do what she doesn't want to do, and no one but no one can stand in her way when she wants something. So I know well whose idea this was, and –'

'But it was only because she hates the sneaking and lying,' protested Nick, determined to defend Maggie in one way or another.

There was a long pause as Peter absorbed what he'd said, his elbows on the table and his head in his hands. 'I wish this had never happened,' he said finally, in a quiet, defeated voice.

'I know. I understand, but I don't feel the same, truthfully. I'm glad it did.' Nick would apologise for the lies, the sneaking around, the indiscretion, but he could never apologise for loving Maggie.

'Where is she?' Peter asked then.

'At a party in the second-class bar.'

Peter stood. 'I'll be back.'

'Peter...'

'Don't worry. There's not going to be a scene.'

Five minutes later he was back, with Maggie in tow, bristling yet always beautiful.

'What do ya want?' she angrily demanded of her brother as he closed the door behind them.

'I wanted to talk to both of ye together,' Peter began.

'If this is another parish priest performance, Peter, you can forget it. I'm not listenin' to ya. Nothin' you can say will make us give each other up, so you can just –'

'If you'd shut up for one bleedin' second, I'd tell ya what I'm goin' to say,' Peter snapped, and Nick heard the rare Dublin accent. Peter spoke in a very cultured way compared to when he first met him, but when he was very worked up, it crept back in.

'Let him speak, Maggie,' he said gently.

She glared at him, then at Peter. 'Fine. Say whatever you have to say,' she snapped.

'What I want is...' Peter took a deep breath. 'Look, I love ya, Maggie. And I love Nick too. And I know it's unreasonable of me to say ye could be together and then go around acting like I hate it, and I know it can't be said aloud about Celine and Millie...'

Maggie tossed her copper curls. 'Yeah, it is. You pretended you were fine and then this.'

Peter glanced at Nick. 'Nick has a reputation as a good, loyal man, and it's hurting him that everyone thinks he's a...well, not the man he was.'

'And what about my reputation?' demanded his sister, eyes flashing dangerously.

Nick tensed, expecting the worst, but Peter took a deep breath and restrained himself from saying she had no reputation to worry about. Instead he offered Maggie his arm. 'Come on, let's go.'

'Go where?' she asked suspiciously, not taking the arm.

'Back to the party.' He offered it to her again, and his other arm to Nick.

'What, so ya can bawl us out in front of all our friends?' she said scathingly. 'Well, I'm not –'

'Maggie, we're going back to the party where everyone is, and you two are going to dance together, and I'm going to be there, not a care in the world on me. Ye're right. This isn't fair. Nick is a gentleman and you're a lady, and the circumstances are not exactly ideal, but I want to go down there and show them all that you two have my blessing, if that's something you want.'

'And no more scandalised monsignor act?'

He smiled. 'No.'

'It was so hypocritical, by the way. Everyone knew May was sleeping with you in Mrs Juddy's long before ye got married, smart an' all as you thought you were,' she said, with a toss of those copper curls, but her navy-blue eyes, Peter's eyes, were gleaming with merriment.

'Well, there's no fear I'd get away with anything, is there, with you watching my every move.'

'I'm really sorry for what I said about Aida and all of that. It was wrong and very disloyal…'

'Forgotten.' He put his arm around her and gave her a hug. 'Right, let's go and show everyone that we've kissed and made up, will we?'

That night the second-class bar was treated to the sight of Nick and Peter doing the tango with Ramon on guitar, to the endangerment of a lot of cocktail glasses and catcalling and screams of joy from the assembled crowd, with Maggie leading the rhythmic clapping and Aida rolling her eyes in disgust at seeing her precious flamenco being mangled just for the fun of it.

CHAPTER 15

ETER

THE BALLROOM of the Ritz-Carlton in Atlantic City was like nowhere Peter had ever seen, even in his wildest dreams. Scantily clad waitresses weaved through the glamorous crowd seated at the tables, bearing aloft trays of what looked like soft drinks, but judging by the merriment all around, he had his suspicions that something stronger was on offer.

He had decided to bring the cabaret to watch the show here before beginning their residency next week at the rival hotel at the other end of the Boardwalk, just to see what the opposition offered, and he was very impressed at the sumptuous surroundings.

The men were all wearing beautifully cut suits, with silver and gold collar studs on dazzling-white shirts, and on their wrists were expensive-looking watches. He looked down at his two-tone shoes. Thank goodness May had convinced them all that it was the fashion in America. She'd done a lot of research, insisting they wouldn't arrive looking like muck savages. He hadn't been sure, but as usual she was right.

May herself was dressed in a dropped-waist pink silk dress with no sleeves and had set her hair in waves, pinned back by a clip with a silk flower on it. She turned heads, she was so pretty, and she blended in perfectly with the chic crowd. He and she looked the perfect couple, there was no doubt about it; May had made sure of it.

Peter sometimes had to pinch himself to make sure he wasn't dreaming. He was in America, he had his own company of players, they were going to perform for four months at the Ocean Diamond in Atlantic City, New Jersey, to American audiences. Could this really be happening? To him? A boy who grew up in depravity and abject poverty, who had pulled himself up by his bootstraps? He didn't normally allow himself too much self-congratulation, but surely this was worth acknowledging?

On the ship their fellow first-class passengers had been the wealthy of both sides of the Atlantic, most of whom he imagined were born to that kind of privilege and accepted it as their right.

He'd already changed his accent from working-class Dublin to a more genteel middle-class Irish one, but while crossing the Atlantic, he'd heard a lot of upper-class people and he'd softened his Rs further to suggest he might be from anywhere in the United Kingdom. It served him well; he blended in perfectly. Maggie should do the same, he thought. Unlike him, she sounded like she never left Henrietta Street. Before this he might have thought it didn't matter, but now it did. He didn't think Nick's world would ever accept his sister, no matter how much Nick loved her. But she could help herself a little, he thought, if she fixed her 'ings' and her 'ths'.

The Black jazz band had just come off stage to rapturous applause. They were mesmerising, so it was well deserved. And now the stage had been taken by a bizarre man, his face painted white, with arched black eyebrows painted on and red lips, a boater hat on his head, wearing a blue-and-black striped blazer with gold trim.

He was a comedian, and Peter gave a glance at Two-Soups, who looked like he might be sick with nerves now that the reality of what they were facing was before them all. Playing in a tent in rural Ireland, or even England, was one thing, but here, well, this was light years away.

The comedian began his set with a song, apparently about his girlfriend, called 'The Dumber They Come, the Better I Like 'Em'. And the audience, men and women, seemed to be lapping it up. This was followed by rapid-fire jokes, all beginning with 'my girl is so dumb...', and giving examples, which sent the audience into paroxysms of laughter.

'Peter glanced around and could tell that none of the girls of the cabaret were impressed, and the men of the troupe were a bit nonplussed by it all. Aida's face was stony. He caught her eye, but she hastily looked away. She'd been avoiding him like the plague since the big bust-up, and he couldn't blame her, though it hurt, especially her decision to dance the tango with Enzo instead.

That night in the second-class bar, after Nick and he had made an amusing show of prancing around like two elephants, Enzo had pulled Aida to her feet and announced they were going to 'show them how it's done'.

And Peter, watching Enzo and Aida dance together, had to accept that his mate was quite good at faking the passion needed for the tango. He supposed he had plenty of practice pretending every woman he pursued was 'the one for him'. All Enzo's women seemed to believe it anyway. Florence Gamminston was loudly convinced that if only her husband died, Enzo would be delighted to step up.

May touched his arm, and he realised he was staring in Aida's direction and pulled his eyes away. Hopefully May would come to trust him enough, and Aida too, so things could go back to normal soon. Then he could be friends with the Spanish girl again and go back to chatting and dancing with her.

His wife had twisted in her seat, staring towards the back of the hall. The comedian's set had been interrupted by some sort of commotion; a group of respectably dressed women were trying to force their way in. They were bearing banners with the name 'American Temperance League', and they were shouting and demanding to be admitted.

'What's going on?' May asked him.

'No idea.' He stood up to see better. All around them, people were emptying glasses onto the carpet. Behind the women were uniformed police. There seemed to be a general feeling of panic as patrons, who were only minutes earlier socialising and laughing, were now making to leave.

'Everyone remain seated please,' boomed a tall, forbidding man in a long trench coat and a grey suit. 'I am Federal Agent Joel Kopeck, this is my assistant Agent Ernest Barnes, and we are Prohibition agents of the Federal Bureau of Investigation. Remain in your seat please.'

The police and plain-clothes agents were checking glasses, and some went behind the bar. Contrary to the instruction, the doors at the opposite end of the ballroom near the stage had been opened and people were streaming out.

'Should we go?' Enzo asked.

Everyone looked to Peter, and he glanced at May. She nodded, and they all stood, joining the teeming crowds out onto a side street. They followed the wave of people and arrived onto the Boardwalk, which despite the lateness of the hour, was as busy as during the day.

Huge electric searchlights lit up the sky over the ocean, and the warm evening air smelled of the famous saltwater taffy, a kind of sweet they discovered was a delicacy of the area. The shops and attractions were all still open, and music filled the air. Families, couples and groups of young people perambulated up and down, and several people were being pushed in wicker chairs with wheels. He'd assumed when he first saw them, on the way here, that the people in the chairs couldn't walk, but when he saw a big fat man get out of one, pay the person pushing him and walk away, he realised they were just a tourist attraction.

The front of the Ritz-Carlton was blocked with more of the women from the American Temperance League, and one lady pushed a flyer at Peter, which read 'Prohibition Is Progress'. May looked amused as she read the banner two of the women were holding up, which declared 'Lips That Touch Liquor Will Never Touch Mine'.

'That's why I love you, Peter, your lips never touch alcohol,' she teased him. 'Now I think we better get out of here before we get ourselves arrested, because there's others among us who aren't as abstemious.'

Peter agreed and called everyone together, and the performers set off back to their lodgings. It was only their second night here. There would be plenty of time to explore this amazing place.

They passed signs for supper clubs, where jazz music poured out through saloon-style doors, a clam shack, whatever that might be, and so many taffy and gelato vendors. He could hear Enzo explaining to Aida that gelato was a kind of Italian ice cream, much better than ordinary ice cream apparently.

'Our landlady at the boarding house said they built the Boardwalk to keep the sand outta the hotels,' Maggie was saying to Nick. 'Imagine that in Bray or Dollymount?'

'It's amazing, isn't it?' Nick's eyes were lit up with the wonder of it all.

'And this is only a part of it,' Ramon said. 'There are all different piers with amusements and all sorts going on. They apparently have a show where horses gallop off one of them into the sea, and they swim around and come back and do it the next hour.'

'Poor horses,' Magus muttered, not as impressed as all the others. He clearly looked at Atlantic City with distaste. 'Everyone is out to make a buck.'

'Aren't we all at that, though, Magus, to be fair?' Peter asked reasonably, as they tried to stay together, stepping aside to allow several boys in bow ties and soft caps to chase each other up the Boardwalk. 'Trying to make a few bob?'

Magus fixed his green eyes on Peter. 'We have scruples, though, things we won't do, lines below which we will not sink. Here…it's different.'

May said kindly, 'Well, where we're playing is very different to this end of town, I think, Magus. It's a place more suited to families, so we'll be keeping it all very clean and wholesome, like we always do, so don't worry.'

Just then a girl in a backless dress with a flowered headband ran up and offered them some picture postcards for sale. They depicted the beach or the Boardwalk, but all featured scantily clad girls.

'No thank you,' May said firmly, waving the girl away.

Peter didn't think that was just May putting on a show of good morals for Magus; he remembered how she had objected to the playing cards he'd had made up with pictures on the back of Aida and Celine in their costumes. He'd thought they were lovely and would make them lots of money selling them after the show, but May had said they were smutty and would get them in trouble with the Church.

They passed signs advertising 'midget boxing', which Ramon, Two-Soups and Enzo had been curious enough to go and see last night, and they had reported back that it was exactly what it said on the poster. Small men, most under four feet tall, beating seven bells out of each other, and people paid to watch and put bets on.

Peter was glad to have missed it, it was so degrading to those people and even the boys, who were often oblivious to the sensibilities were appalled at the gross exploitation.

HE AND NICK had taken Maggie and May out to dinner at Dock's Oyster House on Harp Devereaux's recommendation. It was owned by an Irish family, the Doughertys, and they'd had a wonderful night. The peace between him and Nick had taken such a weight off his mind, and he felt he could really enjoy this amazing experience now.

The crowds on the Boardwalk made it difficult for everyone to stay walking together, and he and May got separated from the rest. He looked over his shoulder and saw that everyone else, even Magus, had stopped to get a gelato. Enzo ordered, and Peter watched him hand Aida her ice cream first, with a flamenco-style bow.

'Come on, Peter…' May pulled him on.

His wife was keen to get back to Aisling, who was being watched over by the landlady's daughter at their boarding house. A little boy Remy's age ran by, chasing a small dog, and Peter wondered if Nick was missing his sons. He and Nick regularly marvelled at the intense feelings they had for their children, and it made their own fathers even more unfathomable. He couldn't have left Aisling behind in Ireland, and he was grateful for May standing up to her mother despite Olive Gallagher's fears over their Bohemian lifestyle.

The little boy came back past them, the dog now on a lead, his hand held by an elderly lady who was berating him.

'Matthew, I will not tell you again, if I have to go looking for the ridiculous animal one more time...'

Matthew clearly was just delighted to be reunited with his dog and wasn't duly concerned at his grandmother's admonishments.

May watched the scene with a smile, then said, like she had read his mind, 'I wonder if Nick would like Remy to visit? Aisling gets on well with him – it might be a treat for her too. And I don't think Nick's ever gone without seeing him for more than a month. Maybe Celine could bring him.' Then she frowned. 'No, too awkward. The landlady thinks Maggie is his wife. Maybe Millie could bring Remy. I might suggest it to Nick.'

'Remy would love it,' agreed Peter. 'And I still think Eamonn should come over, so if Millie is too tied up with the estate, maybe Eamonn could bring him.'

May flushed slightly, as if the idea annoyed her slightly. 'But Eamonn said he didn't want to come to America.'

Peter had long been mystified by May's attitude to his brother. There was a time when the two of them had been very fond of each other and could talk for hours on any topic. Yet around the time she'd had Aisling, May had gone very cold towards him, even though he was such a generous and doting uncle to their daughter. Maybe it was a political thing. May was a passionate supporter of Michael Collins, while Peter's older brother had taken the anti-Treaty side.

It often surprised Peter how seriously his wife took her politics. She was interested in the women's movement here, and she was already talking about going to some meeting next month where a leading light of the New Jersey Woman Suffrage Association would be speaking.

He was in favour of women voting, of course he was, but she wasn't American. Most women had the vote now, here and at home in Ireland, and he was mystified as to why she felt the need to involve herself with this. He personally never involved himself in politics unless it affected him directly, as it had done during the War of Independence.

'He did say that, I know,' he agreed. 'But if we asked him to bring Remy, it would be a good excuse to get him here. I still think America could be the making of him, May. Why don't you write to him? He listens to you, when you bother to speak to him.'

She frowned and shook her head. 'I don't think so. It would break your mother's heart if she lost both of her sons to America, Peter.'

'Both?' He turned to her in surprise. 'Sure we're only gone for four months, aren't we?'

But she gave him a look from under her eyelashes that told him she knew what he was at, even if he didn't, that his dream was for the cabaret to do so well, they would get another theatre in America, and then another.

With a vague sort of gratitude for the way she knew him better than he knew himself, he squeezed her hand gently and felt her squeeze his back.

PETER HOPED his nervousness wasn't betrayed in his demeanour as he was shown into the well-appointed office of Miss Maud Flynn. It was his first face-to-face appointment; she was very busy. Evidently the Ocean Diamond was only one of Miss Flynn's concerns.

The lady was a leading light of the American women's temperance movement and a devout Catholic who did a lot for the Church, as well as owned several boarding houses and the huge Ocean Diamond hotel and ballroom, which was, according to Harp, one of the few genuinely dry establishments in the country.

THE GEM OF IRELAND'S CROWN

The shows put on at the Ocean Diamond ballroom were popular with families and God-fearing folk, and Peter knew his show was going to be perfect for it. Nothing smutty or racy, just good, clean family fun. Maud Flynn was going to love it.

The carpeted office was located in the hotel itself, on the seventh floor, overlooking the Boardwalk. Maud Flynn had her rooms on the same floor; it was where she lived and worked.

An elderly Black manservant had shown Peter in to wait, and he'd taken a seat where the man indicated at one side of a large polished wood desk with a leather inlay. There were files and papers in neat piles all over the desk. He found the seat very low but didn't dare move. On the other side of the desk was a leather chair, higher, and he wondered why.

The walls were decorated in oil paintings of what looked like Ireland, lots of green fields and stone cottages and fishing boats. There was a large green embroidered wall hanging over the desk, weighted either end by a carved wooden pole that read 'Erin go Bragh'. It was decorated all around the outside with golden harps and shamrocks.

He suppressed a smile. That was not how that phrase was spelled; even with his poor Irish, he knew it should read 'Éirinn go Brách'. Maud Flynn was an Irishwoman, or at least of Irish stock, and Peter hoped that would work in their favour, but he was coming to realise that Irish America had some very different customs and habits from Ireland itself.

In Cobh, Harp had given him a stack of sheet music and explained they would be expected to perform songs such as 'Mother Machree' and 'Danny Boy' as standard, and he knew Nick had also gone to great effort in the last few weeks to find and learn songs made famous over here that were supposed to be Irish but that nobody at home had ever heard of.

Nick and Maggie practised all of that, as well as all their own favourites; a beautiful rendition of 'Star of the County Down' was one everyone at home loved.

They were used to the audiences knowing the chorus and singing along, but May had had the idea to print the words on little booklets that were collected at the end of the night so everyone could learn them.

He recalled the lyrics and knew they'd soon have everybody lilting away.

> Near Banbridge Town *in the County Down,*
> *one morning last July,*
> *down a bóithrín green came a sweet cailín,*
> *and she smiled as she passed me by.*
> *She looked so sweet from her two bare feet*
> *to the sheen of her nut-brown hair.*
> *Such a winsome elf, I'm ashamed of myself,*
> *for to see I was staring there.*
> *From Bantry Bay up to Derry's quay,*
> *from Galway to Dublin Town,*
> *no maid I've seen like the fair cailín*
> *that I met in the County Down.*
> *As she onward sped, sure I scratched me head,*
> *and I looked with a feelin' rare.*
> *And I says, says I, to a passer-by,*
> *'Who's the maid with the nut-brown hair?'*
> *Well, he looked at me and he said to me,*
> *'That's the gem of Ireland's crown.*
> *Young Rosie McCann from the banks of the Bann,*
> *she's the star of the County Down.'*

Maggie Cullen was, as far as everyone was concerned, the gem of Ireland's crown.

Clive had told him before about how some Americans saw the Irish, and how one show he was in years ago even had dwarfs dressed as leprechauns and they were paid five dollars a week to dance around in green and gold costumes. Americans loved Ireland, said Clive, and everything about it, but sometimes their version of it was a little off, making out everyone was drunk and fighting all the time. He hoped that wasn't what Maud Flynn was looking for; he would not be doing any of that nonsense, just giving them first-class entertainment.

The brass plaque on her desk read, in copperplate engraving, 'Miss M Flynn', and it looked impressive. In fact, everything about this room was impressive: the huge sash windows overlooking the Boardwalk and the beach, the heavy gold brocade curtains, held back by thick silk swags, the paintings, the glass cabinet, the mahogany furniture. On a lovely rosewood side table with barley-twist legs sat a quarter-veneered teak–cased gramophone with shiny brass fixings. It was open, so he could see the His Master's Voice brand and logo on the porcelain plaque. He had delighted Aisling by telling her the original dog in the picture was a fox terrier called Nipper. He also told her the story of how he 'liberated' a gramophone from an officers' dugout during the war by pretending to pull the pin on a grenade; she had him tell her it over and over.

The twelve-inch turntable was the one with the internal horn. He'd wanted one for himself, but May had vetoed the purchase, saying the Deccaphone Grippa in its plain oak case was fine and did the job very well. It was scuffed and a bit battered from all the moving from place to place, but it worked. She was right of course, but he loved this one.

On the wall was a gold-faced clock that looked expensive as well, and it told him that Miss Flynn was now twenty minutes late for their meeting.

He stood – this was ridiculous, crouching in the small chair, his knees higher than his hips – and stretched, took a closer look at the gramophone, then walked to the window. He caught his reflection in the oval gilt mirror that hung over an ornate fireplace. He smiled. Was that really Peter Cullen from the tenements of Henrietta Street? He hardly recognised himself.

His blond hair was longer than most men wore it, but May said it added to what she called his Bohemian allure, and he'd always resisted the trend towards moustaches. His dark-blue eyes were the same as ever, but he'd filled out from the whip of a lad he'd been. Years of pulling and dragging that blasted tent and the props and the sets had bulked him up. His jacket and trousers were Prussian-blue linen, the jacket lined with ivory silk and more fitted than he normally wore, showing his natural waist. Under it he wore a coordinated cream waistcoat with a thin blue stripe, a cream shirt and a blue and gold tie and pocket square. Of course the two-tone shoes finished the outfit. May had spent forty minutes this morning ensuring every single thing was correct. She was a big believer in making a good first impression. The entire outfit had cost a small fortune – his poor ma would have had to lie in the dark if she knew what they'd spent on clothes for this trip – but it was their big break. They had to get it right.

Thirty-one minutes after the appointed time, the door opened and a large woman in her fifties entered. She was dressed conservatively, in a long dress of an indeterminate colour, something between brown and green, and her salt-and-pepper hair was set in an austere style. She exuded a businesslike efficiency, and as she marched towards him, hand outstretched, any surprise he'd harboured that a lone woman could achieve so much in business dissipated. Maud Flynn was a force to be reckoned with, and anyone who thought otherwise would, he realised, be making a huge mistake. She had an air of a Reverend Mother about her. Around her neck was a gold crucifix, but she wore no other adornment or make-up.

'Mr Cullen, my deepest apologies. I was held up. I'm so sorry. It's very nice to meet you. Mrs Devereaux-O'Dwyer has told me all about you and your wonderful performers.' Her accent was American, clipped and perfectly elocuted.

Peter took her hand and shook it. 'That's no problem, Ms Flynn. I'm admiring the wonderful view you have here.'

'It is beautiful, though you are no stranger to the splendour of God's creation being from the old country, I am sure.' Her smile seemed genuine, and she was charming, no doubt about it. 'Might I offer you tea? Or a cold drink? You must find it warm here after the gentle breeze of Ireland.'

'A cold drink would be very nice, thank you.'

She rang a bell and the Black man appeared.

'Clay, fetch us a jug of lemonade please, plenty of ice, thank you.'

The man withdrew.

'Now then, Mr Cullen.' She smiled and he relaxed.

She was nice, even though he was sure she had to be tough to make it in business. 'Mrs Devereaux-O'Dwyer assures me that you are a teetotaller?'

'Yes, I have never had an interest in alcohol. My father drank enough for the whole family and I saw the destructive power of it, so I decided to steer clear.'

She beamed with approval. 'Very wise. Ah, it is a trial indeed. My own brother, may the Lord have mercy on him, died as a result of the demon liquor. There's scarce a family unscathed. His daughter, Beatrice, lives here with me now, as she had nowhere to go. He swallowed every penny. Tragic.'

Peter wasn't sure how to respond, but said, 'Indeed there's a weakness there among the Irish, sure enough.'

'But together, Mr Cullen' – her pale-grey eyes blazed now with intensity – 'you and I, and your troupe of performers, will do our best to undo the terrible damage that reputation has done to besmirch the good name of our country. We will show the people of this town that not all Irish are drunkards and layabouts. We will show them that there is a way to be entertained without the poisonous effects of alcohol and all its associated depravities.'

Though her words were delivered in gentle feminine tones, she could have taken her speech from those of the Redemptorist priests who would descend every few months to each parish in Ireland to identify and vilify the habits of the locals when it came to drink, gambling or, worse, sex.

'Our show is, I can assure you, Miss Flynn, entirely free from anything that would be considered distasteful or crude. And as for alcohol, my wife, May, and I run a very tight ship, so you need have no concerns on that score.' An image of that night in the second-class bar, with himself and Nick being cheered on by somewhat inebriated friends, flashed through his mind, but he hastily pushed it away.

'Wonderful.' She clapped her hands as Clay appeared with a jug and two highball glasses on a silver tray, which he placed on her desk. From a silver bucket, using matching clawed tongs, he clinked three ice cubes in each glass before pouring lemonade from a pitcher. It was so hot, Peter could feel the sweat running down his neck, and the cracking of the ice as the liquid hit it made his mouth feel even drier.

'We must remain ever vigilant, Mr Cullen, for I know it may shock you to know that certain establishments in this city flout the Volstead Act and all it tries to do. The Federal Bureau of Investigation do their best, and God knows they have to deal with some very unsavoury types in the process, but they are brave and upstanding men who know the misery caused by alcohol, so we as citizens must do all we can to help. The struggle is ongoing and very much alive.'

Peter assumed she was referring to the raid last night and prayed nothing had reached her about him and the rest being there. Although she could have no proof of any of them having been drinking – thank God they'd escaped out the back and gone home early.

He looked longingly at the lemonade. Condensation had clouded the outside of the glass and was now running down in rivulets.

'So, Mr Cullen,' she went on.

The glass was tantalisingly within reach, but he wouldn't take it until he was offered.

'Tell me about your show.' She paused. ' And please, help yourself…' She gestured at the glass, and he reached over with what might have been described as indecent haste. He brought it to his lips, and the sharp sweetness of the lemonade was possibly the most delicious thing he'd ever tasted. It was mildly carbonated, which added to its thirst-quenching properties, and it was an effort not to swallow the entire glass in one go. He forced himself to replace it on the tray after a long sip.

'Well, we can adapt to whatever is needed here,' he said. 'We have singers, dancers, a comedian, a magician, a ventriloquist, an acrobat… But as I say, we're flexible.'

'Have you seen any of the other acts on offer here – Bobby Kane, for example?' Ms Flynn asked, and her face gave no indication of her own opinions. Peter thought quickly. Kane was the comedian they'd seen last night at the Ritz-Carlton. Did Maud Flynn know he had been there after all? Her cousin was the chief of police. Maybe the Flynn family knew everything.

'I did. I was anxious to check out the opposition, so to speak. But his act was interrupted by some very concerned ladies who had discovered there was alcohol being served. It came as a great shock to me and my wife, I must say. We all left at once, so if the show continued after that, we weren't there to see it.'

'And what was your verdict, Mr Cullen?' She seemed quite unperturbed.

'My verdict?' For a moment he thought maybe she was asking his opinions on temperance.

'Of Kane,' she said, a touch impatiently.

'The crowd seemed to enjoy him,' Peter replied diplomatically. The strange man in the boater and striped jacket was singularly unfunny in his opinion.

Maud Flynn gave a slightly dismissive eyeroll, only barely perceptible. 'They do. Is your man like him?'

Peter didn't like to be rude about other performers, but he had been honest his entire career in a business rife with charlatans and swindlers. It had served him well, so no reason to stop now.

'Not even a bit, except for the part where people laugh – he can do that all right,' he answered honestly. 'Our main comedian is Scottish, and he tells funny stories as well as jokes, but it's all in the best taste. Back in Ireland families come to see us, the local clergy and the sisters from the convent as well, and there is never a complaint about the content of the performance.'

'That is most reassuring to hear, because let me be very clear – I will not tolerate any smuttiness or lewd behaviour in my hotel from anyone. Now tell me about the others.'

Peter explained the various other parts of the show, Aida and Ramon, Enzo's acrobatics, Nick and Maggie, the dancing girls – all very tasteful, he assured her – Clive and Timothy, and when he came to Magus Magicus, he explained about escapology being part of the act.

'We had Houdini here last year, drew a huge crowd. Goodness knows how he does it.' She shook her head. 'There's something kind of…I don't know…dark about him, I think. We won't have him back. He's a little disconcerting.'

'Must go with the territory – our magician is not exactly a cheery chap either, to be honest, but he intrigues the crowds with his tricks. He's from here actually.'

'Atlantic City?' She looked surprised.

Peter laughed. 'No, America. I'm not sure where exactly.'

'You're not in Ireland now, where everyone knows everyone else. This is the United States.'

'It's a big country, all right –'

'And a very different one from what you are used to. Many of the people here lack any type of religion, and you need to keep your wits about you. Opportunities for immorality lurk everywhere.' She pointed her finger at him to emphasise her point.

'Now I know you are all staying at the Beachside Boarding House these last three nights, but you will be more comfortable here on this side of town, away from the less savoury elements. There are a block of three lodgings very near this hotel that I own myself, with enough room for the entire troupe. They will cost you less than where you are now, and I'm sure the rooms will meet with your approval. Then you'll have four more days to settle in and rehearse before beginning the residency here on Saturday night. Now, if there's nothing else, I'll bid you good day, and I look forward to seeing the show.'

Maud Flynn stood, and there was no doubt about it – Peter had been given his orders and now he was being dismissed. She followed him to the door as the telephone on her desk began to peal.

'Good day to you. I shall say a prayer that you and your family enjoy the summer here and that the good Lord keeps you all safe.' She smiled and offered her hand again, which he took and shook.

'Good day, Ms Flynn, and thank you for the warm welcome.' He felt slightly like he'd been run over by a truck, but the offer of the three lodging houses at a cheaper rate than they were paying sounded good; he would see what May thought about it.

Outside, the tall Black man, Clay, was waiting. The man's hair was cut tight to his head to appear almost shorn, and his big brown eyes were soft and gentle.

'The keys for your new accommodation, Mr Cullen, sir,' he said, his voice sonorous and gravelly. He held out a ring with three keys on it. 'A fleet of taxis will pick you up from your present lodgings at nine tomorrow morning. The kitchens will be stocked and the beds made. There will be a housekeeper to meet you all – she is in charge of the properties – and she can arrange for laundry and cleaning at a very low cost because Mrs Flynn also owns a domestic agency. If you wish to engage a nanny, the housekeeper will arrange it immediately. If you need anything else, please let me know.'

Peter was taken aback by everything being organised for them without so much as a by-your-leave, but still, it sounded like a good arrangement, so after a moment's surprise, he smiled and accepted the keys. 'Thank you very much, Clay, and I'm Peter.'

'You're very welcome, sir,' the manservant replied, not using Peter's first name. He pressed the button for the lift, then stood aside.

Peter could see the cage far below in the deep metal shaft and watched it lurch its way up towards him. It stopped on the floor below for nearly a minute. Just as he'd decided to take the stairs – it was only seven floors – it started again, so he waited. When the bell-hop, a teenage boy in an orange uniform, pushed open the metal door, a thick-set young lady in an old-fashioned pale-blue floor-length dress with lots of frills on it and a ribboned bonnet got out. She wore spectacles and was, by every standard, plain.

As she swept past, she glanced at Peter but did not introduce herself or enquire who he might be. 'Hello, Clay,' she said in a haughty tone. 'Is my aunt here?'

'She is, Miss Beatrice. She's expecting you.'

May was outside waiting for him, eager for news. He took her arm and walked her down the street, wanting to be a bit further away before he told her how it all went. It had discomforted him, how Maud Flynn seemed to know he'd been at the Ritz-Carlton the night before.

'Well?' she asked again, once they were fifty yards down the Boardwalk.

'I don't know if you're going to like this, but she didn't give me a chance to say no, so…' And he told her about the houses and the housekeeper, and the cleaning and laundry, and the nanny they could have if they wanted her.

May looked a little annoyed. 'I don't know, Peter. It's a bit of a liberty. Moving again is such a big upheaval, even if there are taxis arranged. And I've paid the Beachside Boarding House a week in advance, so we'll lose that money, and I don't like letting the landlady there down either about the rest of the four months – she's a nice woman and her daughter is lovely with Aisling. I hope this nanny Miss Flynn has in mind for us is suitable. I hate being bounced into things.'

'Still, it does sound like a good value,' he said persuasively. 'And she is our employer, and JohnJoe said to stay on her good side.'

'I suppose…'

'And she loved the sound of the show.'

'Did she?' May began to unbend. 'And she liked you, do you think?'

'Sure, why wouldn't she? I'm very likeable, aren't I?'

With a laugh, she linked him and patted his arm as they walked on. 'You're that certainly.'

'So apparently we will have to pack up tonight, because the taxis are coming in the morning, but it sounds like everything is ready for us. And we can take the nanny for Aisling, and then, Mrs Cullen, I suggest you take a well-earned rest.'

'Yes, I think I might climb into bed and sleep for two days,' she agreed, resting her head against his shoulder briefly.

'Do you want an ice cream first?'

'I'd love one.'

He went to a vendor selling out of his shop directly onto the Boardwalk. The sun was hot and the beach full of people splashing and sunbathing. He got two cones, but when he came back to where he'd left May, he couldn't see her.

Then he caught a glimpse of the dove-grey silk shawl with the silver tassels draped around her white shoulders; she used it to keep the sun off her pale skin. She was gazing in the window of some sort of establishment.

Peter joined her and handed her the ice cream cone, then turned to see what she was looking at. At first he thought it was a doll in the lighted glass case, but then he realised it was a real child, a tiny infant. The sign over the establishment said 'Infant Incubators' and asked for a donation of whatever a person could afford, and the infant was displayed like goods in a shop. The card under the baby said he was only two pounds, nine ounces, born three months early, but his 'scientific mother' was helping him to survive and thrive.

'He's so tiny,' May breathed, her nose up to the glass.

'Poor little man.' Peter put his hand on her shoulder. He knew the fact that they had never had another child after Aisling was a source of deep pain to his wife, though she never said it out loud; it was just in the way she looked at babies.

He didn't much mind himself. He could never say this to May, but he was happy to have just Aisling. She was enough for him, and she fitted so well into the life of the cabaret, even as an infant, that the disruption to their lives he'd imagined had never happened.

Seeing May now, though, looking at this little tot, made him sad for her.

'It will happen yet, May,' he whispered in her ear. 'Sure we had one once, so why wouldn't we have another? Just give it time.'

And she looked around at him and smiled, her eyes bright with tears, uneaten gelato melting onto her fingers.

CHAPTER 16

ETER

PETER CALLED an after-breakfast meeting of everyone in the drawing room of Number Nine, Atlantic Terrace.

Miss Flynn's houses had turned out to be magnificent, three in a row in a beautiful crescent overlooking the sea, only five minutes' walk from the Ocean Diamond, with so many gadgets as yet unseen in Ireland. May had spent an hour wondering what a device in the drawer of their bedroom was until the housekeeper told her it was an electric machine for drying hair.

Each house had four bedrooms, except the dancers' house which had eight, so he and May shared Number Nine with Nick and Maggie. For Aisling's sake, Nick and Maggie had a room each, while he and May were in another and Aisling slept in the smallest room.

The after-breakfast meeting was in the drawing room downstairs, which spanned the width of the house and easily accommodated the entire troupe, including the ten dancing girls. The four roustabouts had come as well. They were in digs further down the street. They weren't really needed, but May had whispered to Peter that work had to be found for them or they'd lose four of the ten chorus girls overnight. That would be a disaster, so the roustabouts were going to turn their hands to selling programmes and changing sets and things like that.

Peter clapped to draw the room to attention, and everyone settled down, facing him and May, who was standing next to him.

'OK, folks. You were at the Ocean Diamond rehearsing all day for the last three days, so today everyone is going to take the morning off, then have a rest in the afternoon so you are fresh for the opening show tonight.'

'And come early. I think we should rehearse the salsa number one more time,' said Aida, to groans from the girls.

'Nah, Aida, pack it in, it's fine,' Enzo piped up, to cheers and applause from the chorus. 'If you had your way all the time, the poor things wouldn't even stop to sleep or eat.'

'But they are not yet perfect...'

Peter hesitated, torn. He didn't like to undermine Aida's authority with the girls, and he wished he'd had the chance to discuss this with her first. But Aida was avoiding him these days and he never got the chance to talk to her alone, and so he'd taken May's advice, which was to give the girls the day off.

'The whole set looks wonderful to me, Aida,' May said smoothly from beside him. 'Your tango with Enzo will bring the house down – it's better than ever. And that number you dance alone will have everyone talking.'

Peter threw his wife a grateful look. It was wonderful what good work May was doing, keeping everyone on side, even though it stung a bit to hear her compliment Aida and Enzo on the tango.

'Thank you,' said Aida politely, inclining her head. 'It was the first time I tried it here. I used to dance something like it in Spain, called El Soleo. It was a dance to represent the, em...*corrido de torres*' – she tried to think of the word – 'the running of bulls, ah yes, bullfight. Now it is called paso doble. It should have two, a man and a woman, but nobody can do this, it's too difficult, so I adapted it to a single-person dance.'

May smiled but didn't otherwise react. He knew it drove May mad, what she saw as Aida's arrogance. But Peter knew it wasn't pride – it was honesty. She was so far superior to any other dancer in the cabaret. Something like the paso doble would be beyond Enzo, as it would be beyond Peter. No one else in the troupe could dance like her; no one had that sort of discipline.

'Right, try to relax, eat some of that mysterious taffy stuff, go for a swim, but stay out of trouble, do ye hear me, girls? Rent your bathing costumes. No arms or legs showing.'

There was a ripple of laughter. Yesterday Maggie and the chorus had decided to go to the beach for a quick dip before the afternoon rehearsal, and they'd worn the swimming costumes they always wore in Ireland, one-pieces with short legs and bare arms. To their astonishment they were approached by a beach censor, a man in uniform armed with a tape measure, who proceeded to measure the length of the costume and berate them all for showing too much flesh. He told them they could rent costumes that complied with the rules on the Boardwalk but that they were not to parade all that flesh on the public beach.

As the censor turned his back, Maggie started singing the popular music-hall song, and all the other girls joined in. '*Au revoir* but not goodbye, soldier boy. Wipe that teardrop from your eye, soldier boy. When you're on the deep blue sea, will you think sometimes of me? When you've won your victory, God will bring you back to me. *Au revoir* but not goodbye, soldier boy...'

Nick, who had gone with the girls to mind their belongings, had had to intervene to stop the scandalised official calling the police, though what the charge might be was anyone's guess.

'No, seriously, girls,' Peter said sternly as the gathered cabaret laughed. 'And lads as well. We have to follow the rules. Maud Flynn runs a very tight ship. It's not enough for us to be good at what we do – we have to be squeaky clean as well.'

'If we are good enough at what we do.' Two-Soups sighed. Since

Betty died he had never quite gone back to being his old devil-may-care self, at least off stage. A worried murmur went around the room, and Peter could see it wasn't just Two-Soups who was nervous. He straightened his shoulders and smiled at the gathered troupe, trying to project a confidence he was far from feeling himself.

'So before ye go, I just want to say, well…how proud of everyone I am. And I know this is daunting and a bit nerve-racking. It's bound to be – the surrounds are different. But they are just an audience the same as we've played every night of the week for eight years, give or take.

'I know with certainty that when myself and Nick and Enzo' – he made a point of making eye contact with Nick, who blushed with pleasure – 'stood up in the corner of the Aigle d'Or in France and sang a few songs, bombs and bullets flying in every direction, and were acting the eejit, we never in our wildest imaginings thought we would ever come to this, but life is strange. We've had our ups and downs over the years, and God knows a few bust-ups too –'

More laughter.

'But despite it all, we've stuck together. Whatever our internal squabbles, we look out for each other, we're a family. And as we always say, we have no room for divas, male or female. Everyone in this troupe pulls together for the common good, and that's why we've come so far. So I think we should give ourselves a big round of applause for that.'

With much joking, they did.

'And so after you're rested, we'll go on stage tonight, and we'll give it our all as we do in Ireland. And we know audiences there love us.'

'Except in Mullingar!' Ramon yelled, and everyone rolled their eyes and groaned.

The last time they played in the town of Mullingar, in County Westmeath, a woman had set up a protest outside, claiming they were the work of Satan and that anyone who crossed the threshold of the tent was condemned to burn in hell for all eternity. The local parish priest, a nice old man called Father Dunne, heard about it and trooped himself and the two curates and several nuns in past her and her placards that very same night as a show of support.

Everyone thought it very funny, but nobody knew that the previous time they were in the town, May had made sure to make a significant donation to the church roof fund. She was so clever like that, always thinking ahead. She greased the wheels wherever they went, quietly and with no fuss.

Peter waited for the amusement to die down. That comment brought him back to his main point. 'Well, I think the decency police here are too busy worrying about ladies' bathing costumes to worry about the mortal souls of those in the Ocean Diamond. But there is one thing I want to say, and this is really important.'

He paused and looked hard at Enzo, Ramon, the dancers, the roustabouts, all usual suspects for blackguarding. 'Booze is available here for some people, as you've seen, despite the law. I've no idea how it works, nor do I care, but the point is, it is illegal. The woman that invited us here, Miss Maud Flynn, is a strict teetotaller, and she runs a very clean house with absolutely no boozing. The very last thing we need is any run-in with the police or anything like that, so I'm asking – well, no, and I don't often do this, but I'm instructing, telling, ordering, whatever you want to call it – everyone to have nothing to do with alcohol of any kind. When we go home, ye can drink yerselves into oblivion if ye want, but here you don't touch it. We don't want the hassle, and we need to make a good impression.'

'Lips that touch liquor will never touch mine...' Enzo did a dramatic swoon as he spoke, and Peter smiled, but he needed them to understand this.

'I mean it. She's not messing. She's part of that bunch of women who raided the place we were the other night. If she gets even a whisper that we're flouting the law, we're all out on our ears, so to reiterate, I couldn't care less what ye do in terms of drink back at home, so long as you can do your job and not cause me any headaches.'

'You care what *we* do,' called Dolly. The double standard of May's oversight of the behaviour of the chorus girls was a source of much debate among them, but May was resolute. Even the affairs with the roustabouts were only allowed to be minor flirtations.

'Yes, well, in that case it won't be a problem for you to be the perfect pioneer of total abstinence since you're so accustomed to it,' he replied smartly. Dolly was a mouthy one, always had been, but she was a great dancer. 'But for the rest of you, I need your word that you'll stay away from it, and any other carry-on that might get us into trouble. We're not in Ireland now, and things are very different here, I'm sure, so let's just do our shows, have a good time, but stay out of trouble, right?'

There were reluctant murmurs of agreement.

'Everyone?' Peter raised an eyebrow. 'Agreed?'

'Agreed.' A chorus of voices, like kids in school.

'Right.' He hoped he'd got through. 'All the props, costumes and make-up are already there. We did the balance call yesterday afternoon, so the sound is fine – the electric microphones aren't distorting the voices. We're fine as regards blocking. This is a much bigger stage than we're used to, but we've worked that out – don't forget to use it. So see you all backstage at five to start prep. May will liaise between us and the front-of-house team, who will give us the cue for clearance. It's going to have to be seamless from the beginning. So, any questions?'

He looked around at his troupe. 'No?'

There were murmurs and shakes of heads.

'Class dismissed!' Enzo called, causing everyone to laugh again, and soon they were all gone, off to the seaside.

CHAPTER 17

THREE WEEKS LATER

*M*AY

THE CABARET WAS GOING down a storm. They were a huge hit; tickets were sold out night after night. More people were behind the Volstead Act than May would have imagined, and families liked to go somewhere wholesome.

Though the show had changed a bit over the first couple of weeks, on the orders of Tibbet and Maud Flynn.

Peter was gloomy about it. 'Tibbet says the show needs to be more "Irish", by which he means "Oirish" of course,' he'd grumbled to May. 'He's got some dwarfs dressed up as leprechauns to show the audience to their seats, and Maud Flynn called me in as well – she wants the whole show full of shamrocks and shillelaghs.'

May was half-amused, half-horrified. 'Oh dear. Well, she's the boss. Could we get the girls doing some Irish dancing?'

'I doubt Aida knows any…'

'But Rosie comes from a background in Irish dancing – apparently she was really good. She could show them a few steps.'

He'd sighed. 'Fine.'

May could see he hated the thought of Rosie taking over from his precious Aida, but she rose above it. 'Nick and Maggie have those songs Harp Devereaux gave them, so that's OK. But I wonder how Magus can make his act a bit more Irish?'

'Ha! I suppose we could dress him in green and stick a shamrock in his ear. Clive is all for it. He knows the drill – he's played America before. He's gone and dressed Timothy up as a leprechaun already. It's shameful, and I promised myself we'd never do this, but I suppose we better had if we're going to…' He stopped himself before he said anything about Tibbet getting them another gig in some other theatre, but May had known what he was going to say.

But despite Peter's initial disgust, it all worked out for the best. The crowds loved the 'Irish' nonsense and kept on coming. Only yesterday the agent, Frederick Tibbet, had handed her the next month's payment in advance. Everything was going well with the management of the Ocean Diamond ballroom.

Maud Flynn had made quite a pet of Peter, and May had made it her business to befriend the niece, Beatrice Flynn, often taking the girl out to tea. She was a bit dreary and very religious, even more than her aunt. At the same time, she longed to get married, if only she could find a man 'good enough for her'. She had a massive crush on some famous dancer called Carlos Pérez, who she'd seen in New York. She showed May a theatre bill with a picture of him on it, and he was stunningly handsome in that Latin way. 'I just feel if I could only meet him, May, he'd see we were made for each other.'

Even though she was clearly deluded – this heartthrob wouldn't look twice at the dowdy Beatrice – May felt sorry for her. She was almost the same age as May, but her innocence reminded May of her much younger self, when she was seventeen and developed an instant crush on Peter when she saw him playing the comic porter in Macbeth in the Gaiety, back in the day when his ambition was to be a 'real' actor. Like Beatrice, she'd been convinced that if she could only get to meet that beautiful man…

In her case, of course, it had worked, but she very much doubted Beatrice would have the same success. *If bullying and bribing someone into marrying you can be considered a success*, said a little voice in the back of her mind.

There had to be someone out there for Beatrice, though. May had bucked her up and offered to go shopping with her to get her a few more modern outfits. She was inclined to do it anyway, out of sympathy, but also it could do no harm to be friendly with Maud's niece. And Beatrice took her advice and started dressing more like a girl her age.

Looking back over the last three weeks, May was amazed to think they'd been here so long already.

Life in Atlantic City was a revelation. The inhabitants were a mixture of people on their holidays, though they called it 'vacation', and those who attended to the holidaymakers' every need. The actors were enjoying themselves tremendously. They had taken to sporting new sunglasses, something May had never seen before, wonderful against the bright light of the shore, and were constantly stuffing themselves with cheeseburgers, something she'd never heard of either. The delights of the New Jersey resort were a million miles from anything any of them had seen at home. It was all so different from Ireland, even though the language was the same. Well, almost.

May was reminded daily of Oscar Wilde's line in his short story 'The Canterville Ghost': 'We have really everything in common with America nowadays, except, of course, language.'

Every day there was a new misunderstanding. Faucets instead of taps, sidewalks for footpaths, diapers not nappies, bangs instead of a fringe, fall for autumn – the list went on and on. There had been some hilarious crossed wires between Enzo and some woman who assumed he meant Christmas when he said he was there for his holidays.

Aisling was loving it here as well. There were swings and a climbing frame at the end of the street, and she'd made friends with some other children who lived in what they called the neighbour-

THE GEM OF IRELAND'S CROWN

hood. At first they'd told her that she talked funny, but Aisling had made May laugh by announcing very firmly that it was she who talked normally and they who were funny-sounding.

Her daughter was out now at the beach with her rather stiff German nanny, Gertrude Müller, provided by Miss Flynn. The woman wasn't much fun and never smiled, but at least the sponge-like Aisling was picking up a lot of German, and Gertrude seemed very conscientious – she watched over Aisling like a hawk.

May settled in the chair by the window that looked out onto Atlantic Terrace, a handsome street where there was no end of activity. Delivery horses with wagons bearing groceries, milk, bread, meat, flowers even. The postman, whom they called a mailman, and any number of uniformed governesses and nannies pushing prams, most of them Black women.

She loved the permanency of living in this luxurious house, taking baths when she wished to, having a housekeeper. It was a life she could get used to.

She'd just made herself a pot of tea in the beautifully appointed kitchen. Electricity was everywhere here, even in private houses, and she was really enjoying it. Hot water, electric light, a big comfortable bed, no damp, no muddy fields, sunshine every single day. It was wonderful. She was even coming around to the idea of staying, if Peter's dreams worked out. Just for a few years, before they went home and built her theatre in Dublin. Maybe they were young enough to pursue both sets of dreams, hers and Peter's, one after the other.

She poured herself a cup of tea and took up the letter that had arrived for her and Peter this morning from Kathleen; she recognised the handwriting.

Peter had had no time to open the letter; he'd been rushing out to meet Maud Flynn, who had summoned him to her rooms once more. This happened often, at least once a week, and Peter never seemed to emerge any the wiser about the purpose of the meeting, except that Maud liked to talk about the 'old country', which she'd visited for a month when she was fifteen, long ago, in 1890, the time when Ireland's great hope and leader of the Irish Parliamentary Party,

Charles Stewart Parnell, fell in love with a married woman, Katharine O'Shea, nicknamed Kitty disrespectfully in the press. Katharine divorced her husband and married Parnell in a registry office because the Church wouldn't have them, but the scandal destroyed the great man and set back the cause of Irish freedom. Maud was scathing about Parnell and his affair with a married woman and affairs and divorce in general, and Peter had said it made him very twitchy in case she found out about Nick and Maggie.

Now, since the letter was addressed to them both, May opened it.

DEAR PETER *and May and of course our little Aisling,*

I hope this letter finds you both well and continuing to enjoy your time in New Jersey. Even as I write this, I find it hard to believe that ye are all the way over there, so far from home.

I read your last letter out to Ma and Connie yesterday, and we were all agog at the things you described. Ma said it sounded like something out of a story, not real. The Boardwalk and all the food and the music and the picture houses and all of it.

Connie is finished with school for the summer and driving Ma mad, around the house all day, saying she's bored! Imagine us at her age being bored, Peter, and there are so many jobs to do? She's having a very different childhood to us, that's for sure. Not that I'd wish the way things were for us on her, but it is funny to see.

In other news, well...I'm expecting another baby. We're very excited, and please God, the baby will come in time for Santie. That's what Sean hopes anyway. He's like a child himself, he's so up in a hoop about being a daddy again.

MAY SMILED. She was delighted for Sean and Kathleen; they were wonderful parents.

She went back to the letter.

. . .

I'm worried about Eamonn, to be truthful. He is gone into himself of late, no more messing or laughing out of him, as was his way. He's easily vexed now, and it's hard to know what ails him.

I don't know what will become of him, but I hope he finds some way to be happy. What you said about him coming to America, that he could make a fine life for himself there away from all the bitterness and begrudgery here, Peter, I think is true, but there's no budging him.

God bless ye all and much love,
Kathleen

MAY SAT FOR A WHILE, with the letter in her hands, trying to tell herself that Eamonn and his life were not her concern. She'd been selfishly glad to leave him behind in Ireland. She was tired of being reminded of her own deceit. What better way to escape her guilt than to put an ocean between her and the cause of it?

And it wasn't her fault he was miserable. She refused to believe he was pining for her, despite the way he'd clung to Aisling and the look he'd given her when she kissed him goodbye on the cheek. She preferred to believe his misery was the fault of the Civil War, and his failure to get up and sort himself out. It was tough for him, constantly being passed over at work, but he'd made his choice regarding the Treaty. And maybe he and the people like him had a point, but it was all over and done with now, and it wouldn't do anyone any good to be dwelling on things that were best left in the past.

Yet the idea of Eamonn, once so big and strong and full of mischief and sincerity, now brought so low, hurt her heart. There was no point in denying it.

Her mind went back to Peter's suggestion, on their second night here, that she should write to Eamonn and ask him to accompany Remy to America, using that as an excuse to get him here. The twins were too small to be parted that long from Celine, but Remy was one age to Aisling and he'd be fine. Maybe it had been wrong for her to refuse to do it, to hold out her hand to save Eamonn from himself, just because she feared the sight of him.

Nick had just said last night how he'd love to have Remy here, to take him riding on a donkey on the beach, and Aisling had got really excited. She had spent a lot of weekends in Brockleton, and she would love to see her little friend.

May folded the letter and replaced it in the envelope.

A very possible scenario unfolded in her mind: Nick and Maggie would come in with Peter tonight after the show. May would make tea and show Peter the letter, and Maggie would ask to read it as well, and then she and Peter would worry about Eamonn. Maybe Peter would repeat the idea to Nick about Eamonn bringing Remy to visit, and Nick would get excited about that, and somehow the whole thing would snowball. And then Peter would ask May to write to Eamonn about it, and it would look really strange if she said no, so she would have to do it.

Not that she would want to do it. Of course not.

CHAPTER 18

THREE WEEKS LATER

ETER

He sat watching the early morning rehearsal he'd insisted on calling after last night's very haphazard performance. Groans and complaints at being dragged out of bed so early were what met him, but he didn't care. This was ridiculous.

The cabaret had started magnificently, creating a huge splash. Maud was delighted with the sales of tickets, and they were the talk of the town. They were six weeks into their residency, nearly halfway through, and though Maud Flynn and Frederick Tibbet were still raking in the cash and May was happy with the finances, he knew standards were slipping, and he was not going to allow it.

Partly he blamed the Oirish thing. It encouraged the performers to ham it up and act silly instead of working to make everything perfect.

But the biggest problem was all the temptations with which they were surrounded.

The town never slept as far as he could see, with speakeasies, parties and clubs of all kinds going till the early hours every night of the week, and most of the troupe were burning the candle at both ends. Even those who didn't overindulge, like Aida, were having their sleep disturbed by those who did, like Enzo and Ramon, crashing home at all hours, often fleeing disgruntled mothers or husbands.

Maud Flynn had not noticed the troupe's bad behaviour yet, or if she had, she hadn't mentioned it, but he knew this carry-on wouldn't go down well with her and that if they were caught, they'd be out on their ear.

Last week, when he and Maud had their weekly lemonade and a chat, she had invited him and May to attend Mass with her the following Sunday and to hear a leading light of the sobriety movement, some woman he'd never heard of, speak afterwards at a potluck, whatever that might be. He'd agreed to go, even managed to sound enthusiastic, as they had no choice, but luckily Aisling had been awake with a toothache all of Saturday night and so they were able to cry off. Maud had been most sympathetic and instructed them to go and visit a dentist of her acquaintance, who even on a Sunday was willing to pull the bad baby tooth. Aisling was brave as a lion about it, and he had been going to take her for gelato once it was over, but May put the kibosh on that idea, claiming it was all the treats she was eating that caused the rotten tooth in the first place.

Aisling's teeth were not the only thing going bad out here.

Maintaining discipline had been easy in rural Ireland, he realised, because opportunities for diversion were few and far between. And for the first two or three weeks in Atlantic City, his actors had behaved at least as well as they would in Ireland, especially after his initial lecture. But here was a whole other world, and his troupe had embraced the American way of life and all it had to offer in a way he hadn't anticipated.

Even May, who was normally so sensible, had been affected. She'd undressed for bed last night, and he'd seen she was wearing a totally new arrangement of underwear. Not that he was complaining, but it was much more racy than he'd ever seen before. She assured him with no blushing whatsoever that the days of bloomers and chemises with corsets over them were gone – they were horribly uncomfortable – and the new styles of dresses, which she had taken to with alacrity, it would seem needed a different style of thing. Brassieres and matching frilly shorts were all the rage now as far as he could see. No doubt all the women of his troupe were attired similarly under their dresses.

He looked different himself, he knew that. He was dressing every day now like an American gentleman, with his two-tone shoes, attached-collar shirts and pinstriped suits. He'd taken to slicking back his hair with Brylantine and wearing a trilby hat he'd bought at a very fancy gentleman's outfitters on the West Jersey pier.

He was still the same person inside, though, and he wished he could say the same for his performers. They were creative, talented people, but also impetuous and fiery. It took a lot to manage the many big personalities, and now they were like dogs off a lead.

Enough was enough. Even if the audiences hadn't noticed the collapse in standards, he had, and he wasn't having it.

Last night Maggie had rushed on stage in a hurry from a cocktail party and started her song in the wrong key, and for some reason, she seemed to find it hilarious. Luckily the audience did too; they assumed she was doing it on purpose.

Clive Stephens insisted he was being squeaky clean as Peter demanded, but Timothy was downing an alarming amount of hooch backstage, and it had to be going somewhere. As lifelike as the red-haired puppet was, Peter refused to believe Clive's 'son' had a working digestive system under that ridiculous leprechaun outfit.

Two-Soups had a great head for whiskey, being reared to it as a Scotsman, unlike Timothy, who got so loud and belligerent that the normally mild-mannered Nick had threatened to wring his neck, but even the Scotsman forgot a punchline the other night. He got away with it by switching jokes, but they couldn't go on flying by the seat of their pants like this.

Ramon's ankle was in a bandage after doing some drunken

Charleston moves three nights ago in Jezebel's, a nightclub of ill renown, and the chorus girls were dishevelled and so unprofessional, he could scream.

For that, he blamed Enzo. The acrobat had been getting sillier and sillier, throwing himself around so carelessly on the trapeze, he'd actually dropped his partner, Eliza, a few nights ago. It was as well Two-Soups had made them a trampoline for safety, so when Eliza fell, to screams from the audience, she bounced clean back up again and Enzo caught her on his returning swing, which led to massive applause; everyone thought it was part of the act. But it could have been a tragedy, and Eliza had been really upset, and it had taken all May's powers of persuasion to get the poor girl to go up again on the next night.

And worse, Enzo was annoying Aida. He'd begun to dance the tango for laughs, dressing in a bright-green costume covered in shamrocks, with a green rose clenched in his teeth and a huge cheesy grin, encouraging the audience to laugh instead of reducing them to awestruck silence with the passion of the dance.

His antics had led to a screaming match between him and Aida, part of it in rapid Catalan (her) and furious Italian (him). Aisling helpfully translated all the swear words for Peter, which had him clutching his head in despair.

The flamenco section of the show should have been about perfection and discipline, and by undermining Aida and making a joke of it all, Enzo's lack of discipline was infecting the chorus girls as well. And the Irish dancing section was a total shambles. Rosie had done her best, but she didn't have Aida's fierce uncompromising teaching skills, and the chorus weren't scared of her the way they were of the fiery senorita.

Peter would have spoken to Aida about it, but she was still avoiding him, and May as well. She hadn't even come to him about Enzo, which made things very hard to sort out. Until now, even Peter hadn't realised how important it was to the show that Aida was always at his side. The performers liked and respected May. But they were in awe of Aida, her relentless professionalism, her attention to detail.

May was good at finances and keeping people happy. Aida was about the beauty of a perfect performance – and that was what made everything else possible.

He sat in the empty darkened auditorium, watching the rehearsal sourly. The cleaners would be here in an hour or so to get it ready for another night. The whole show was going very badly, even worse than the night before; nobody had their cues correct.

'Wrong,' he snapped at his sister. 'Again. For God's sake, Maggie, can you just get it right! This is ridiculous. You've done this correctly hundreds of times, but now, all of a sudden, it's beyond ye…' She was still drunk from last night, he supposed. Plus she looked like she'd been dragged backwards through a hedge and Nick not much better; clearly Maggie had dragged him through the hedge with her.

Enzo must have made some lewd comment, because there was a guffaw of raucous laughter from the wings. Peter felt his blood boil but inhaled and exhaled slowly several times. Blowing his top wasn't going to help fix the show.

'Right, that's enough. Next!'

Magus calmly appeared on stage, pulling all the equipment he needed for his act on a wheeled trolley. He was wearing a dark-emerald suit, which Maud Flynn had insisted on, but at least he was reliable. His act was always perfect, and he changed it up sufficiently so that people weren't bored if they came several nights.

But then a massive racket came from backstage, followed by a crashing of something falling over, no doubt due to horseplay, another complete disregard of the normal rules. Peter was honestly beginning to regret bringing them here. The temptations, the lifestyle were just too alluring, and they seemed to have entirely forgotten they were there to work.

'Right, the finale.' He sighed wearily.

This number was a funny take on the post-war hit 'How Ya Gonna Keep 'Em Down on the Farm (After They've Seen Paree)?'

The chorus were supposed to be the Parisian temptresses, and the boys were the American soldiers, overawed by it all. Nick and Maggie were dressed as old folks, Reuben and his wife, bemoaning the fact that their sons would have no interest in making hay or milking cows when such delights existed.

'"Reuben, Reuben, I've been thinking," said his wifey dear. "Now that all is peaceful and calm, soon our boys will be back on the farm."

'Mister Reuben started winking, and slowly rubbed his chin. He pulled his chair up close to Mother, asked her with a grin, "How ya gonna keep 'em down, oh no? How ya gonna keep 'em down, oh no, oh no? How ya gonna keep 'em away from Broadway? Jazzin' around, and painting the town? How ya gonna keep 'em away from harm? That's the mystery. They'll never want to see a rake or a plough, and who the deuce can parley-vous a cow? And how ya gonna keep 'em down on the farm after they've seen Paree?"

'"Reuben, Reuben, you're mistaken…"'

Peter knew how the old couple felt. His world, the one he'd so carefully constructed out of nothing, the future he was planning for, it was falling apart at the seams.

The performance was scrappy, the dancers kept turning the wrong way, the choreography was all over the place, Aida wouldn't meet his eyes, the group singing was raspy and discordant, and overall it was a total shambles.

'Right, stop everything. Everyone on stage, and I mean everyone,' he bellowed.

He rarely lost his temper, but it was necessary now. He'd worked so hard for this. This was their big chance – any night of the week, a talent agent could be in the audience and it might be the big break, the invitation to Broadway or to tour the country. Harp Devereaux had said Atlantic City was the try-out town, and these people were just not trying.

Two-Soups lifted the needle off the recording; they used a gramophone record of the music for rehearsal, though when they performed live, the house orchestra accompanied them for this one. Everyone huddled together in awkward silence; some had the grace to look sheepish at least.

Peter climbed up on stage, trying to compose himself. 'Nine

months to worry, three months to hurry,' he began. 'Do any of ye know what that means?'

Nobody said a word.

'It means' – he paused – 'that this is a seasonal business, it's a fickle business, and nothing, absolutely nothing, is guaranteed or owed to us. We worked very, very hard to get here. We were relentless, practicing, rehearsing, finding new material all the time, and we did that for audiences in fields in rural Ireland.'

One could hear a pin drop now.

'But for some reason that I simply cannot fathom, you've all decided that the level of effort required now, here, at the biggest opportunity we are ever likely to get, is no longer needed. Apparently we can turn up to the show, with minutes to spare, looking like something the cat dragged in.'

Again, deathly silence. From the corner of the stage, Aida was watching him, but when he caught her eye, she looked away. He felt a pang of regret for not saying 'except for Aida', because in her own act, she was as professional as ever. At the same time, she wasn't keeping the chorus up to scratch.

'Magus is the only one who is pulling his weight,' he said. 'You girls out all night, the men too, not getting enough sleep, drinking, though this is supposed to be a dry town, and giving lacklustre performances *at best* every night, of the same old rubbish you've been doing for six weeks. No new numbers, no new routines, same old stuff, over and over. Why? Because you are tired and hung over and can't be bothered to spend any energy on the reason you're even here in the first place.'

He paused, not caring how awkward the silence was. He knew he sounded like the parish priest now, but it was preposterous and he wasn't having it any more. He wanted them to cringe, to be mortified. He mentally dared one of them to challenge him, but they wouldn't, because they knew perfectly well he was telling the truth.

'We have just over two-and-a-half more months left to run here. I need you to take better care of yourselves and each other.'

His voice softened ever so slightly, and he glanced at Ramon, whose foot was elevated to reduce swelling. 'Not to get stupid injuries acting the eejit.' He glared at Maggie and Nick. 'To know your cues, to instinctively know the notes you are to come in on.' He moved closer to the gathering of chorus girls, who suddenly found the floorboards absolutely fascinating. 'To dance as you have been taught but seem to have entirely forgotten, in unison, on time. Enzo is not your leader – it is Senorita Gonzalez. I hope she hasn't forgotten that, and I hope you haven't either.'

He hated calling Aida out. He didn't look in her direction, but he eyeballed every other member of the troupe. 'For the rest of the run, no going out after the show. For anyone. It was never an option in Ballybunion or Salthill, but as you know, you can stay out till the dawn here if you like, but it's not working. So if you want to socialise, do it in your hours off in the afternoon.'

They wouldn't be happy about that, but nobody would dare object. Going on the batter at four o'clock in the afternoon for two hours when they had to work that evening was not as appealing as a speakeasy at midnight, undoubtedly. He didn't care.

'And I asked at the start of our time here that you respect the laws regarding alcohol. And you assured me you would. I think I'm safe to say that promise was not kept by a great many of you. That stops as of now. No booze. Anyone, and I mean anyone, found drinking will be sacked on the spot, and I don't care who you are. You might think it's a stupid law, but it *is* the law here.'

He felt sanctimonious, but he had to do it. 'From now on, we rehearse every morning, every single member of the troupe, nine sharp. Work till 1 p.m., as we did at home, working on new material, polishing up old stuff. We need to get back to where we were, and we need to do it now. Am I clear?'

Nods and murmurs of 'Yes, clear.'

'Right. Take a coffee break and come back after the cleaners. We'll go from the top again.'

They filed off, and as they did, Nick and Enzo approached him.

'I wish we 'ad a billycan full of tea that tasted of petrol and was stone cold.' Enzo smiled, recalling their many cups of tea at the front. 'Life was simpler then, eh?'

'It was, Enzo.' He sighed. 'In lots of ways, it really was.'

But then the three of them laughed at the notion of the daily terror of being at the wrong end of a landmine or sniper's bullet being better than this luxury.

Enzo flung his sinewy arm around Peter's shoulders. 'You 'ad to give us a rollickin', mate. It was gettin' out of 'and.'

'We d-d-deserved it,' Nick agreed. 'But things will change now, and Enzo and I will take more responsibility. We weren't exactly a good example. We got carried away, I suppose, with the place and everything, but we'll d-d-do better from now on.'

'I'll take things more seriously, I promise ya, mate, no more muckin' about,' Enzo added. 'You're right, it's not on, even if you have dressed us all in bloody green and Timothy has a leprechaun hat on and is drunk all the time.'

Peter felt a wave of love for his two best friends. They had never let him being the boss interfere with their friendship, and here they were supporting him now, even after he'd torn strips off everyone, including them.

May wasn't being much use about this. She hadn't come with him today, and she seemed to not grasp how much things had gone downhill. When he complained about the Oirish business, she'd just laughed, and when he'd told her how Enzo was destroying the tango and floated the idea of maybe going back to the way it was, himself dancing with Aida, she'd said the set looked fine to her and that if Enzo made the audiences laugh, no harm. Keep the butts on seats, as the agent Tibbet was fond of saying.

Sometimes he thought May didn't care what the cabaret performances were like providing the money came in, that to her it was just a commercial exercise, not like the 'proper' theatre she dreamed of owning sometime in the future.

Usually if he had different ideas from his wife, he made a confidante of Aida, but now Aida seemed paralysed to back him in any way in case people started gossiping about them again.

It made him feel bone-weary.

Still, at least he had Nick and Enzo.

***

As he approached Number Nine, Atlantic Terrace, he saw Magus had got there ahead of him; he was sitting on the steps of Number Seven, with Aisling on his knee, teaching her a trick with a coin, and she was totally absorbed.

Yesterday he'd taught her how to pick a lock with a hairpin, and Gertrude the German nanny had not been pleased when Aisling came in on top of her when she was in the bathroom. Which reminded him, he must ask May to warn Nick and Maggie that if they were going to 'sneak around', then they needed to push a piece of furniture against their door, not just lock it.

'Look, Daddy.' Aisling climbed off Magus's knee and ran over to Peter with a coin. 'It's a Buffalo nickel, see?' She showed him the silver coin. 'It has an Indian chief on one side, and that's a bison on the other side, and it says United States of America and five cents.'

'Well, isn't that just beautiful.' He crouched down to see it, examining it with her.

'The picture is meant to represent two Indian men. One was called Iron Tail of the Lakota Sioux, and the other man is called Two Moons – he was a chief of the Cheyenne, and he fought at the Battle of the Little Bighorn. The Cheyenne and the Sioux are different tribes to Magus – he's Cherokee.'

'And the animal is a bison, is he?' Peter asked, as always amazed and proud at how bright his daughter was.

She nodded. 'Lewis and Clark, you know them?' she asked seriously. 'They were explorers. Anyway, they saw loads of them, so they drew pictures when they were exploring in America. The bison is very special to the Indians. People call them buffalo, but that's wrong – they are really bison.'

Peter winked playfully at Magus. 'Well, aren't you a font of information?' He looked at Aisling again. 'I hope you say thanks to Uncle Magus for all the teaching.'

'I do.' She said, balancing the coin between her fingers again and concentrating fiercely.

'It's my pleasure. She's a clever girl,' Magus said, his deep voice rumbling.

'Magus knows everything, Daddy,' Aisling said matter-of-factly, rolling the coin through her small fingers, trying to make it disappear but with no luck.

'I'm sure he does.' Peter smiled at the man. 'What's it like being back in America?'

The magician shrugged. Nobody could accuse him of being sullen or rude, but unlike most people, he seemed to prefer communicating with the fewest number of words necessary.

'Changed much?' Peter probed.

'I was never in this city before.' Magus watched Aisling as she struggled to make the coin disappear.

'It's called a French drop, Daddy, but I can't do it.'

'You can.' Magus got down on his hunkers on the pavement. 'Look.' He took the coin and slowly performed the action. 'Like this.' The coin was there in his hand one moment; the next it was gone.

'I can't see how you do it.' Aisling was frustrated.

'You must keep the coin in the first hand, use the fingers from your other hand to hide it, and in this movement, make it look like it's gone to your other hand, see?' He opened his empty hand. 'Then make some magical gestures with this hand, distract the audience, have their eyes on this empty hand, and then drop the coin in your pocket, open both, no coin.'

Aisling tried again. 'I can't do it.'

'Practice,' he said calmly.

She looked up at him. 'For how long?'

He gave her one of his rare smiles. 'Until you can do it.' He got to his feet again and headed up the steps into Number Seven, which he shared with Enzo, Two-Soups, Ramon, Clive and Aida. Magus and Aida were the only ones to have a separate bedroom. '*Stiyu*, Aisling.'

She waved. '*Stiyu*, Magus.'

'What does that mean, sweetheart?' Peter asked as he took his daughter's hand to bring her home.

'It's Cherokee. They use that word as goodbye, but it means be strong. Magus and I always talk in Cherokee to each other,' she added, as if a child of two Dublin parents would naturally be able to converse fluently in Cherokee. 'And you have to say it the right way. In Cherokee, words that sound the same can mean different things. Like kamama means butterfly, but if you say kamama' – this time she put a different inflection on the word – 'it means elephant, so you have to be careful.'

'I can see that, or you'd end up trying to catch an elephant with a butterfly net.'

She nodded solemnly. 'Yes, you're right, that would be very dangerous. The Great Spirit gave the Cherokee language, but it has to be used wisely.'

He could just imagine his mother's and his mother-in-law's faces if they heard their precious granddaughter explaining about the Great Spirit.

Peter's world as a child had barely moved outside the bounds of the Dublin inner city, ruled by wealthy business owners and landlords on one side and the Catholic Church on the other. But his daughter, just one generation on, was having a totally different experience of life growing up, and he was so grateful for it.

CHAPTER 19

IDA

A<small>IDA KNEW</small> May Cullen was up to something, she just wasn't sure what. Not long after Peter's excruciating dressing-down of the troupe, his wife had organised this visit to a nightclub for everyone to 'cheer them all up'. Apparently the acts were amazing. And she had insisted Aida come as well. Like everything with May, there would be a reason, and Aida suspected it was to shock them out of complacency.

Aida didn't want to go. Her feet ached; they had never entirely healed from being tortured by Harvey Bathhurst. She wanted to slip away, get to bed with her book. She had absolutely no interest whatsoever in going out and didn't understand why May wanted her to come.

It wasn't that May even liked her. For the last few months, ever since the big bust-up, Aida had done everything to make May feel more secure about her husband. She'd changed dancing partners and she'd avoided Peter at every opportunity, to the detriment of the show. But still May gave her the evil eye when she thought Aida wasn't looking.

Yet now May was practically throwing her in Peter's way, saying Aida had to come with them to the nightclub to see a show with two performers 'fresh off Broadway'. They were going to be interviewed onstage for the radio apparently, because everyone wanted to know how to be a star.

'Please come, Aida,' May had said. 'You know Peter longs to really break into the American scene, so he has to see what calibre of performance is needed to get to Broadway. And I think we should all support him, and you know how he values your opinion.'

'I don't think he does, May.'

'He does, Aida. Please. It's for the sake of the show.'

And Aida, puzzled and troubled, had felt obliged to say yes.

The nightclub was crowded, the air crackling with excitement. The 'fresh off Broadway' acts were being interviewed on stage, the gathered crowd hanging on their every word. The first to be interviewed was a singer, the crooning kind, Jack McNamara. He had a big name and was handsome, but when he sang after the interview, Aida felt bored; she didn't think he could hold a candle to Nick's rich emotional tenor, and if Peter wanted her opinion on that, she would give it to him.

She glanced across at Peter. He looked bored as well. May was sitting next to her husband, with Enzo on her left, and she caught Aida's eye and sent her a bright smile. She was wearing brilliant red lipstick.

The second man to be interviewed was a dancer called Carlos Pérez, from Cuba. He had his own band, brass players mostly and a man with a tumbadora, the tall, narrow, single-headed drum.

Carlos Pérez wasn't just handsome, he was gorgeous, and he knew it. He had black hair, black as her own, that was swept back from a high forehead and curled around his collar, but his eyes were light brown flecked with gold. His bone structure reminded her of those Greek statues, perfect in every particular. He was tall and muscular but lithe too, an athletic body.

'So, Carlos, you dance alone on stage, is that right?' the smooth-talking radio interviewer asked, speaking into the round mike set on a stand between them.

'Yes, always solo. I don't dance with anyone,' Carlos drawled in a cultured American accent with hints of his Cuban background, and Aida had to force herself not to roll her eyes at the way the women in the audience swooned as he spoke, including Maud Flynn's plain little niece, Beatrice, who was sitting right at the front, her eyes shining like stars.

'Why is that?' the radio host asked. 'Good-looking lad like you, I'd imagine the ladies would be lining up.'

'They are,' said Pérez dismissively. He ran a hand over his oiled curls, full of his own self-worth. If he had a spoon, he'd eat himself, as Peter might say. 'But there is nobody good enough. I am, well, something of a master in the Terpsichorean sphere – it makes finding a partner of equal skill impossible.'

Terpsichorean? Please. This man was a conceited braggart, and while his attitude might inspire awe in other women, she was impervious. Finding him nothing short of ridiculous, Aida longed again for her bed and her book.

She couldn't help glancing across at Peter again; he was also looking irritated. But May was whispering to Enzo, and suddenly the acrobat called out towards the stage, 'You ain't danced with our Aida, mate!'

A ripple of interest went around the audience, and people craned to peer at her across the softly lit nightclub.

A middle-aged man piped up. 'That's Aida. I've seen her dance with that all-Irish cabaret – she's amazing!'

'Yes, dance with Aida, and let's see what you're made of!' another man from behind her bellowed.

'Let's have Aida!' shouted several more men, while their wives shot Aida venomous glances, and Beatrice as well, as if she thought Carlos belonged to her.

Aida cringed. She suspected May had put Enzo up to this. Maybe it had been the plan all along. This was the last thing on earth she wanted. She knew she was exceptional, but unlike that eejit – in her mind, she used the Irish word – on the stage, she didn't choose to show off at every opportunity.

Carlos Pérez leant back in his chair, his long legs crossed, and cast a glance over at her, a sultry up-and-down look, and she felt herself redden. She was not an animal in a marketplace to be appraised – who did these men think they were?

'I have not had the pleasure of seeing you dance, senorita.' He addressed her directly from the stage. 'And I am sure you are a good dancer, as far as Irish cabaret dancers go' – a sneer crept into his voice – 'but with respect, I'm from Cuba, not from Ireland. I have been dancing since I was a child, it is in my blood, and there is no possibility that we are in the same league.'

The arrogance. Aida would not react – it was what he wanted – but it took every modicum of self-control. Without deigning to even look at him, she took a sip of her water.

The interviewer looked uncertain, but the master of ceremonies stepped forwards from the wings in his bow tie and tails. 'What do you think, ladies and gentlemen?' he asked the crowd. 'Should the great Carlos Pérez from Cuba dance with Aida from the Emerald Isle, and we can judge who is better?' He seemed delighted at the idea of someone challenging the haughty young man.

The crowd clearly wanted that as well, judging by the hollering and clapping and stamping of feet. Aida was inclined to just get up and walk out; she was not a slave to do their bidding.

Carlos Pérez shrugged and gave a small smile. 'If you wish it, but I can tell you in advance who will win such a challenge.'

He rose to his feet, stepped down off the stage and shimmied through the tables towards her. He had the snakelike hips of a dancer, and she could tell he was athletic, but as to whether he could actually dance, well, that was a whole other matter, one that didn't concern her in the slightest.

Reaching her table, he stood before her, bowing from the waist, an outstretched hand ready to take hers. 'I apologise for this. It is not a fair competition, but if these good people here wish me to dance with you, then of course it would be an honour.'

Aida remained seated. She was furious now, absolutely livid – the cheek of this man – but she kept her face utterly calm.

'Aida! Aida! Aida!' roared the crowd.

She ignored them. She would not be treated like this, for anyone.

'Are you coming, senorita?' He still held out his hand. 'I promise we will dance something very simple.'

'No thank you,' she replied coldly.

Carlos Pérez registered a split second of surprise. She doubted many women had ever refused him anything. But then he smiled, revealing straight white teeth. 'You are a wise woman. Nobody wishes to be humiliated.' He bowed once more and returned to the stage.

A murmur of disappointment ran through the audience, and then to Aida's shock, May stood up from her seat. 'Not only is Senorita Aida your equal, Mr Pérez, she is your superior, so I would suggest a little humility might not go astray.' Her arched eyebrow and dismissive tone caused a titter of amusement among the gathering. 'And in fact I have anticipated just such a thing as this. Aida, I took the liberty of bringing your *sandalos* – I have them here with me.' She lifted up the small leather bag that Aida kept her spare pair of dancing shoes in, along with the other props, behind the ballroom stage at the Ocean Diamond. 'I and my husband, Peter Cullen, the proprietor of Cullen's Celtic Cabaret, would take it as an honour if you were to represent our show on stage tonight.'

So it had all been planned in advance. Aida shot Peter a furious glance. He was looking at her with a pleading expression on his face, but whether he was trying to tell her he was innocent or begging her not to let the cabaret down, she couldn't say.

She was cornered, and there seemed to be only one thing to do. Impatiently she exhaled, kicked off her low heels and, to a round of applause, strutted in stockinged feet across the floor towards May, who met her between the tables, smiling her bright-red smile. 'Thank you, Aida,' she said sweetly, handing over the shoes. 'We mustn't let the side down.'

Without a word Aida bent and strapped on the *sandalos*. Then she straightened and followed Carlos up onto the stage, standing proudly opposite him in her knee-length black dress with the flared skirt.

'So, you dance with an Irish cabaret? I won't suggest the flamenco in this case, though you are Spanish. You dance ballroom, I assume?' Carlos asked, with a bored expression, as the master of ceremonies hurried to remove the chairs and radio microphone from the stage and the interviewer stepped down and took his seat among the audience.

Aida looked coolly at him. 'Naturally.'

'The waltz, perhaps?'

'The samba?' The freer but no less technical styles of the Latin samba were what she used to warm up with before a show.

A flicker of respect crossed his face. 'Ah, you are very confident.' Her choice was the most difficult and intricate of all Latin dances. The syncopated rhythms, bouncing actions and rolling hip movements required grace and stamina as well as perfect timing.

Aida jerked her chin towards the band. 'Can they play "Pelo Telefone"?'

'Certainly, they can.' He nodded at the band leader, and samba music filled the hall. All eyes were on the dancers as she placed her hand in his.

They began slowly, their outer hands held aloft as their hips swayed in time to the music, beginning in perfect synchronicity without missing a beat. Aida felt a sudden shiver of surprise and recognition. The man's boasting was not idle. He did indeed know how to dance.

On they danced, feet in unison, bodies moving as one. Round and round the stage they went, each anticipating what the other was going to do a split second before each move, so they were ready for each of the turns, twists and twirls. The appreciative audience were clapping wildly, uttering shouts and whoops of encouragement.

As she spun into his arms, her back to his chest, he ran a hand along her ribcage, and though it could not be seen – he looked as cool as a summer breeze – she could feel his heart pounding in his chest.

Again a thrill ran through her – this man was good, very good. Not as good as her, but good enough to dance with her. Maybe even the paso doble.

More spins, the three fast-step weight changes, with a slight knee lift on alternating feet. The rhythm of quick, quick, slow, repeat was etched in her body without any need for her mind to interfere. Over and over they danced perfect *voltas* and *boto fogos*, while all the time maintaining exact kick changes.

They side-stepped and strutted, and finally to rapturous applause, the dance came to a distinctive, dramatic climax, executed flawlessly, as she and Pérez threw back their heads, arms extended by their sides. They were both breathing heavily now.

The audience rose to their feet, roaring their approval, and the master of ceremonies called from the side of the stage, 'I think we can safely say you have met your match, Senor Pérez.'

'She is more than my match,' gasped Pérez, his chest heaving, and before she knew what was happening, he was on his knees before her, her hand in his. 'I have never danced with someone of your calibre, ever in my life. I can say this with certainty. I was arrogant – it is how I am – but before you I lay my foolish arrogance aside forever.' He was speaking loud enough for everyone to hear. 'I am overwhelmed. I have been bested. My humblest apologies. I am your servant, senorita.' Then, as the crowd applauded his humility, he dropped his voice and spoke his next words only for her. 'I mean it. I am yours, to do with as you wish. Lead and I will follow. *Hoy es un buen día para sonreir.* Today is a good day to smile.'

The Spanish phrase was one her mother often used.

'*A veces tienes que caer antes de volar*,' she replied in Spanish, more loudly, and he laughed.

'What did she just say to you?' called the interviewer from the front. Beatrice beside him was glaring at Aida jealously.

'She said, some days you may fall before flying,' Carlos responded, rising to his feet. 'Senorita Aida has graciously taught me a lesson in humility, and I deserved it. I can only strive to be as good as she is.'

Aida descended the stage steps to rapturous applause and went back to her table to take off her *sandalos* and retrieve her shoes. In moments the whole cabaret were clustered around her, congratulating her, bursting with pride. They clearly felt she'd fought on their behalf and won. Her heart lifted, and she was overwhelmed by a warm feeling of belonging.

May wasn't among the others, but Peter was there, and he shook her hand. This time she didn't pull hers away but let him hold it for a moment.

'Was this your idea?' she asked, with the ghost of a smile, her eyebrows raised cynically.

'No, I had no idea. It was all May,' he said. 'And you were magnificent. As always.'

'Thank you.' She inclined her head and then, seeing May approaching, drew her hand away.

But for once May beamed at her without a trace of malice. 'Maud Flynn's niece, Beatrice, she told me about Carlos Pérez. She saw him in New York and was crazy about him like all the women are – he's a huge draw. And when I heard he was coming here to Atlantic City, I just knew I had to put the two of you together, and that if he danced with you, he wouldn't be able to resist the offer I've just made him,' she announced happily.

'You've made Carlos Pérez an offer?' Peter was clearly startled, glancing towards the stage. Carlos had disappeared from view.

'I did!' She beamed at him. 'He had to rush off. He and his band are playing in another venue tonight, so I couldn't bring him over, but he gave me his word and I'm sure he'll keep it. And now, if you agree, Peter – of course I said it had to be with your agreement – Cullen's Celtic Cabaret has a new act with Broadway connections!'

'Oh... I...' It was painfully obvious he hated the idea.

May didn't notice, or didn't care. 'But of course you'll agree – it's what's best for the show,' she said cheerfully, then gave Aida a sudden, surprising hug. 'You two will make the perfect pair, won't you, Aida?'

CHAPTER 20

TWO WEEKS LATER

IDA

CARLOS WALKED beside her as they approached Atlantic Terrace, his bare arm occasionally brushing hers. It was after two in the morning, and nobody else was about. She and Carlos had had a peaceful, enjoyable evening, their third date in the three weeks since he'd joined the show, a meal followed by a movie, a fruit sundae in a seafront ice cream parlour and then a long walk on the beach, admiring the moonlight on the sea.

And they'd practised a few steps of flamenco, a new move that he'd asked her to show him. And then he'd gone to kiss her, but only chastely, on the cheek. And for the first time, she'd allowed it to happen.

There was something so conducive to romance about this holiday city.

The smell of the salt on the air, the gentle lap of the waves on the shore. It was like Ireland, but the way it was still warm enough after midnight to be out in the dark in short sleeves reminded her of her childhood in Valencia. And talking to Carlos in Spanish was very comfortable. Even Ramon, who had an English father, tended to speak English unless he was swearing, so it was relaxing to express herself fully for the first time in years. She loved dancing with him; he could do everything she could do. Only the most knowledgeable judge of flamenco could have seen the skill gap between them, and Carlos was determined to close the gap. He spent hours rehearsing with her and learning from her.

It even flattered her a little, that this gorgeous man looked up to her and wanted to be closer to her.

She knew the other dancers and all the women in the audience – including Beatrice, who came every night – swooned over him. He was very attractive, no doubt about that, and there was a kind of passion to him that both intrigued and scared the ladies. She had the same quality herself, and she knew it. In that way they were a perfect match. He was tough, arrogant almost, on the outside, as was she. Yet as with her, there was a wounded vulnerability to him that he liked to hide. Or that's what he said to her. And she assumed he was telling the truth, because when they were alone, he put aside his usual swagger and confidence and was not at all sure of himself.

He'd told her about growing up in Havana, how his uncle was Raul Alvarez, a racketeer and pimp during the Cuban War of Independence, fought against Spain. His uncle was his mother's brother, and in the absence of a father, Raul had stepped in. He was not a good man, and though to many Cubans he was a hero, to young Carlos he was a terrifying figure. He insisted his nephew was fluent in English as well as Spanish, and when Carlos was fourteen, he sent him to one of the women in his luxurious brothel in the red-light district of old Havana, to 'make a man of him' so he could be trained up in the family business.

Carlos told Aida how he ran from the woman, how she terrified him, that he had no clue nor desire to do as she assumed he would. He became a laughingstock, and the other men who worked with his uncle teased him. His uncle laughed along, but that night he dragged Carlos from his bed and, in the full sight of Carlos's mother, beat him senseless.

He woke in the hospital, and as soon as he was able to walk, he took the money his mother gave him and ran away. There was no future for him in Cuba.

He got a job waiting tables in a small bar and *cocina* in Miami, serving mojitos and learning to dance. It wasn't true, what he'd told the radio interviewer about having been dancing since he was a child, but that was just part of his arrogant act – and in fact it made it even more impressive to her that he was so good. Once he'd started to dance, he progressed, his talent undeniable. He was spotted by a Broadway producer on vacation in Miami, and he was lifted from Florida and dropped right into the beating heart of New York performing arts. He had danced at Carnegie Hall, in the Royal Albert Hall in London, even saw 'La Argentina' dance in Madrid, the Buenos Aires woman famous for her dancing but also for writing musical notation for castanets. His life was in some ways very different from hers, and in other ways so very similar.

She resisted his advances at first, but then she had agreed to one date. And then another, when she allowed him to hold her hand. And then tonight, a peck on the cheek. But that was all. She knew he would like to go further, but she wasn't ready. And despite his confiding everything about his life to her, she couldn't yet reciprocate. She had told him of her mother and shown him one of her father's letters, but she said nothing of the landlord's son and nothing of Harvey Bathhurst.

They were approaching Number Seven now, the house she shared with Enzo, Two-Soups, Ramon, Magus and Clive. When they'd moved here, she had thought of going in with the dancers, in Number Eight, but she would have had to share a room and bathroom, and the girls would drive her mad with their chattering and dates and all the rest of their silliness. In Number Seven she had her own room on the second floor and exclusive use of one of the bathrooms, while the men shared the other bathroom on the third floor.

Aida loved her bathroom. Hot and cold running water, a flush toilet. These houses were so luxurious, centrally heated, electricity in every room. How they would ever return to damp caravans in wet fields in Ireland, she had no idea. Only Nick had ever known such luxury before, and even he was quick to point out that though Brockleton was big and grand, it was also freezing and had no modern conveniences at all.

They reached the front steps, and she turned to smile at Carlos. 'Good night, Carlos, and thank you for walking me home. I'll see you tomorrow.'

'Aida, wait,' he said gently, catching her hand as she turned. 'Tell me, please, what am I doing wrong?'

She frowned but allowed him to keep hold of her hand. 'Wrong?' she asked.

'Aida, you know what I mean. Please don't pretend you don't.'

Of course she did. A brief hold of her hand, a chaste kiss on the cheek; she knew it wasn't enough, even if it was all she was willing to give.

She looked at him in the streetlights, his slanted brown eyes, his dark hair, his angular face with the dark stubble on his jaw, his strong arms and sinewy body. She should want him, she knew she should – almost every other woman would jump at him – but she didn't. It was like seeing a beautiful painting in a gallery. You could admire it, like it, but not want to take it home and hang it on your living room wall.

Maybe she was just afraid? Maybe, after being so violently raped and used, she could not imagine being intimate with any man in a loving way? Maybe she should try?

'I do know... I just...' She failed to find the words.

'I want you, Aida. Don't you want me?'

'It's not that... I... Well, you're very attractive.'

He moved closer then; she could feel his breath on her face. His hands went to her hips, but he didn't try anything. They just stood there, and deciding she should at least try, she did as she imagined she should and allowed her arms to creep up to his shoulders, around his neck. Gently she drew his head to hers and felt their lips touch. Tentatively at first, he pressed his lips more firmly to hers, then his kiss became more urgent and his arms encircled her waist, softly bringing her body closer. On and on they kissed, the hibiscus-scented air all around them.

'Can I come in?' he whispered as they broke apart. 'No pressure, nothing you don't want, I swear to you...'

She was about to refuse when she saw the outline of May at the bedroom window upstairs in the third house. She was silhouetted in her negligee, opening the window. Only yesterday Aida had heard Peter warning her against opening the windows at night because of the mosquitos, but May said she couldn't bear the heat and would take her chances with the bugs. She must be following through on her word now; she was always so headstrong. And then she would go back to bed with her husband. Maybe even the movement would wake him, and they would make love sleepily, before dropping off, naked in each other's arms, as they should.

Aida knew what she must do.

'Yes,' she said, taking him by the hand and leading him into the house, up the stairs and into her bedroom.

* * *

THE FOLLOWING morning she woke to the sensation of a body in the bed beside her; it was one she had not had since she was a child, sleeping beside her mother. It took a moment, but then it was there, he was there, lying fast asleep on his front, completely naked, his toned and perfect body not covered by a sheet, his beautiful face turned towards her.

Making love with Carlos had been a revelation to her. He was warm, gentle and passionate. He whispered that he loved her, and she told herself to trust him, to believe him. Their bodies had moved in perfect harmony, as when they danced that samba that first night. It had been good, nice even. She felt no passion of her own, but no revulsion either, and maybe one day the passion would come. It was impossible for her to know. She had never done this before.

He stirred but didn't wake as she crept out of bed. She put on her silk robe before going to the bathroom, then she went downstairs in her bare feet to make coffee. The house was in silence. She thought everyone must still be sleeping, which was good. She wanted Carlos up and out before anyone else woke up.

As she reached the bottom of the stairs, the front door opened and there was Two-Soups. And Peter.

'Morning, Aida,' said the Scotsman cheerfully. 'I was out walking on the beach, and look who I found having a wee early morning dip?'

Peter smiled at her. 'I've been awake since the dawn. May opened the window last night. The mosquitoes don't seem to bother her, but I got eaten alive. I had to get up and go for a swim in the saltwater because the itch was driving me mad. Join us for a cup of hot pond?'

She forced herself to smile back. 'Thank you, but I've just come down to make myself a coffee.'

'Well, join us for that anyway,' he said.

She would drink one coffee in the kitchen, then take another upstairs with her when she left, letting Peter think the second cup was also for her.

As they turned towards the kitchen, a door opened above. 'Aida?' And there he was, Carlos, bare-chested, bare feet, just his trousers on, standing above them on the landing. 'Aida, I thought you'd run off and left me.'

Aida could feel her face was on fire; she dared not meet Peter's or Two-Soups's eyes. 'No, I was just getting some coffee.'

'That sounds great. Will I come down?'

'Don't, I'll bring it up.' This was terrible enough. She couldn't face the thought of the four of them in the kitchen together, Carlos being loving and Peter looking at Aida the way he was now, like she'd stabbed him in the heart. As if he had some kind of right to her and she'd betrayed him.

'I'll go back to bed then. Good morning, gentlemen.' His grin was not one of conquest, or a 'you know what went on here', but he *was* delighted, that much was clear.

'Let's get that kettle on, eh?' said Two-Soups, trying kindly to act like everything was normal, and he disappeared into the kitchen, followed by Peter.

While the Scotsman made tea, prattling on about nothing, Peter's face was a mask. He was a performer first and foremost and rarely betrayed his true feelings. She could usually see through the façade, however, but not today. Aida waited for her coffee percolator to boil, and it seemed to take hours and hours. She was torn by a storm of conflicting emotions.

Shame.

Rage.

Shame, as if she had been caught being unfaithful. Shame because this was not how nice women behaved, taking lovers without a ring on their finger. Rage, because how dare he judge her? She was a free woman, he was a married man with a child, he slept with his wife every night – he had no right whatsoever to have an opinion. The gossip about their nonexistent relationship had taken weeks to subside after the night of the big bust-up.

She made her coffee and decided she would take it upstairs after all – the atmosphere in the kitchen was unbearable.

CHAPTER 21

ETER

It was the most stupid mismatch he'd ever seen in his life. The man was like a peacock, all that smouldering and wiggling his hips and the women swooning, even that plain little niece of Maud Flynn's. It was pathetic, and he was surprised and horrified at Aida for falling for it like the rest. The man was a gigolo, that's what he was.

And it was May's fault. She'd actually encouraged this foolishness, recommending places to Carlos for Aida and him to go, and offering to do Aida's hair for her so-called dates. Aida didn't need to do anything. Her dark hair was like silk and poker straight, and it was always in a bun, but May had her in all sorts of ridiculous hairstyles that did nothing for her.

Not that it had bothered him in the beginning. He was sure the dates were just a chat and a meal. He could see that Aida liked Carlos as a friend and thought he was a decent dancer, but he saw no passion in her eyes when she looked at him. They sparked off each other on stage, that was true, but it was only acting.

Or so he'd told himself.

How long had they been sleeping together?

It was none of his business, of course, and God knew the morals of the cabaret left a lot to be desired at the best of times – he could only imagine the reactions of the clergy, or his mother, if the full extent of it was ever revealed – but Aida? She wasn't like that. And if she was going to find a man, it surely wouldn't be Carlos Pérez. He was so… well, so obvious. It was pathetic.

He tried to switch off the voice in his head. He had no right whatsoever to tell her who she could or couldn't see.

'Penny for them.' May slid into the plush red-velvet seat beside him; she'd decided to join him at the rehearsal for a change.

'I'm thinking the whole show is rubbish,' he growled.

Up on stage the dancers were working through a new number. Aida was nowhere to be found – mortified, he assumed. Rosie stumbled over the new girl, a Cuban called Benita who was cagey about her past and had yet to learn all the right steps for the Irish dancing slot. He hit the arm of his chair with the flat of his hand and shouted angrily at the stage, 'Do it again, Benita! You're as graceful as Lucy the Elephant!'

Lucy the Elephant was a huge construction in the shape of an elephant – the size of a building – with an elaborate box on her back, advertising something; he'd never noticed what. They'd passed her on their way into the city.

'But the others are dancing perfectly. They're working so much harder now, and Benita has only just joined – don't frighten her,' murmured May in his ear.

Next up was Clive with that irritating puppet Timothy dressed up as a leprechaun, and his Oirish accent was so atrocious, it made Peter's ears bleed. 'Oh shut up, Clive,' he yelled at him. 'Just talk like a normal Irishman, not like a bloody fool.'

'Sodem and begorrah, ya big potata!' roared Timothy over Clive's shoulder as the ventriloquist stalked off in a huff.

'It's not his fault, Peter. You know Maud Flynn likes it – it's the way the audiences think we talk,' whispered May. 'Maybe to them that's how we sound?' She smiled, but he wasn't in the mood for jokes.

He shrugged her off irritably. 'To hell with Maud Flynn and what she wants. This is my cabaret.'

May glanced at him in surprise. 'You're not regretting America, are you?'

He'd hadn't regretted it for a moment until Carlos turned up on the scene. But he could hardly say that. 'Of course not. I love it.'

'But you seem so down.'

He shrugged and came up with an excuse. 'It's just I miss being the boss. Here, Maud Flynn says jump and I have to ask how high. It doesn't suit me.'

Two-Soups was up next and had worked out a whole new set with lots of Oirish jokes, which Tibbet had insisted on.

'Paddy walked into a pub and ordered seven shots of whiskey, two glasses of port wine, twelve pints of Guinness and a bottle of cider. And downed them all in five minutes, to the barman's astonishment.

"You got through those very fast," the barman remarked.

"You would too if you had what I have," says Paddy seriously.

"What's that?" asks the barman, concerned.

"Only a shilling," Paddy replies.'

A ripple of laughter emerged from the cleaners and waitstaff who were setting up for the evening's show.

He went on with another.

'Two Irish lads are working, one diggin' holes in the street, the other fillin' them in right away. Nobody knew what they were doing…diggin' and fillin', diggin' and fillin', until eventually someone asked, "What's this all about, digging and filling?"

"Oh, sir," says the Irishman, "we're normally a three-man team, do you see, but the fella that plants the trees is off sick."'

There were more giggles in the background, although the Irish members of the chorus rolled their eyes and only the new girl, Benita, who was Cuban American, laughed out loud.

'Do you know the Irish secret to a happy marriage?' Two-Soups asked. 'Every week Seamus and the wife go dancing…'

This elicited an 'aww' from the chorus girls, who were lounging around on the stage, before he delivered the punchline. 'He goes Tuesdays and she goes Thursdays.'

May nudged him. 'For goodness' sake, Peter, smile.'

'Painful, not one bit funny,' he muttered.

'It's what Tibbet wants, and he knows what he's doing. Two-Soups goes down a storm, and it's harmless, you know it is.'

'Well, I hate it.'

Magus followed Two-Soups. He was capitalising on the Houdini obsession that was sweeping the nation. He had perfected being chained up by Ramon in a tea chest and a coffin, and he'd even done a version of Houdini's famous Chinese Water Torture Cell trick, where he was suspended by his feet from stocks and lowered into a cube of water, chained and locked into it. From there he could escape in a matter of minutes as the audience held their breath. Nobody knew how he did it; he refused to be drawn on it.

Peter stayed quiet. It was impossible to fault Magus, yet even that fact irritated him today. If only the man was more…collegial or something, instead of stalking off alone all the time.

Next up were Maggie and Nick, who had been updating their repertoire to include a few more modern pieces that they hoped the audience would enjoy.

'You're Gonna Miss Me When I'm Far Away' as a duet was really popular at the moment, and they'd also added 'By the Light of the Silvery Moon'. Maggie was wearing an emerald backless dress with a bright-green fringe and pearls around her neck. She had done her hair in the popular finger wave, though it was so curly naturally, Peter had no idea how she'd managed to make her lovely wild curls look so fixed. But she did, and he thought it looked stupid. Nick was wearing a green cravat and a green top hat for the number, and he carried an emerald-tipped cane, and suddenly they started on a simple dance routine.

'God's sake, Nick,' snapped Peter, jerking forwards in his seat. 'You're as nimble as a billiard table. And Maggie, are ya deaf? You're a quarter tone off. Sing it again.'

'Peter, don't yell at them,' said May sharply, loudly enough now for everyone to hear.

'Shh!'

'I will not "shh".' May was indignant. He never spoke to her like that, even in private, and definitely never in front of anyone, so she was not going to let it go. She was fiery and clearly past caring who heard her now. 'What on earth has you so ratty?' she snapped. 'You're either glowering or biting everyone's heads off. Your sister is singing beautifully, and I don't appreciate being silenced either, just so you know –'

He held his hand up to her mid-sentence. 'Well, maybe if you ran a tighter ship and didn't allow everyone out till all hours running amuck, we wouldn't be in such a bloody shambles,' he hissed back at her.

'We are not a shambles! Everyone is doing exactly as you ask. They're not drinking or going to parties – they're behaving perfectly.' May was close to shouting now.

The other performers were hastily absenting themselves. They'd all done their acts, and they were getting out of there as fast as they could, escaping from Peter's scowl to their cheeseburgers and ice creams.

'The shows are selling out every night. It's only you bringing everyone down.'

'Somebody has to care whether we get things right or not. The star dancers can't even be bothered to turn up to rehearsals.' He knew he shouldn't say this, but it was bubbling up inside of him, the pain and the... *Jealousy*. The word crept into his consciousness, unbidden, but as true as the daylight.

May looked at him with her eyebrows sharply raised. 'Don't be ridiculous, Peter. Aida never misses a step, nor does Carlos. They practice for hours on their own, every single day, and thanks to them, we're making more money than ever before. They're perfect together.'

'Well, they're setting a terrible example to the rest of the troupe, and they need to stop thinking the rules don't apply to them just because they think they're so vastly superior to the rest of us,' he snarled, then roared at the stage, 'Maggie, you're a disgrace! Do it again!'

Peter's sister threw down her sheet music in a fury. 'God, Peter, you're like a briar these days. I'm sick to death of you.' She stormed off, and Nick, who had been standing there looking miserable, went after her.

'Well done, Peter,' said May sarcastically. 'How many more of our top stars do you want to insult today?' And she got up and went backstage herself, presumably to try and smooth things over.

Everyone else was gone, and the theatre was empty except for Two-Soups, who was sitting on the edge of the stage, swinging his long legs and looking at Peter with his head to one side.

'Do you want a wee chat, just between us?' asked the lanky Scotsman.

'No thanks.' It was the last thing on earth he wanted.

The Scotsman came down off the stage and stood before him. 'Och, I ken what this is about, mate. I reckon you need a cuppa and a cake,' he said firmly. 'Come on.' He clearly wasn't going to take no for an answer.

With an irritated sigh, Peter stood and followed him out to the lobby of the Ocean Diamond hotel, which served as a tea room, and they took a couple of high-backed upholstered chairs at a polished teak table with brass legs. Uniformed waiters scurried about, and soon a young Black man arrived to their table.

'What can I get you, gentlemen?' he asked politely.

'Two teas, please,' said Two-Soups, 'and a couple of wee buns or something as well.'

'Excuse me, sir?' The lad, who was no more than fourteen or fifteen, looked confused. Two-Soups had never lost his strong Scottish accent, and he left most people here totally bewildered.

'A pot of English breakfast tea for two, and some cake or pastries or whatever you have, please.' The Scotsman enunciated very slowly, and this time the waiter understood what he meant.

'Sure, sir. We've got a nice pineapple upside-down cake just out of the oven – would that suffice?'

'I have absolutely no idea what that might be,' said Two-Soups, still very slowly. 'Is it good?'

The lad nodded enthusiastically. 'Delicious, sir, I promise you.'

'Then we would love some, thank you.'

The waiter left, and Two-Soups leant back in his chair and gave Peter a look that spoke volumes. 'Do you want to talk about it, Peter?' He was treading softly.

'Talk about what?' Peter snapped.

Two-Soups kept looking at him steadily, his bright-red hair in its usual mess from running his fingers through it. 'Peter, this morning's rehearsal wasnae like you. It's one thing dressin' us down when we deserve it, like when everyone was going off, whoopin' it up, wi' booze and that, but everyone's behaving perfectly now, May's right, and you should nae be taking things out on them. It'll throw them off their game.' He dropped his voice a little. 'It's nae their fault about Carlos.'

'Carlos? Why are you talking about Carlos? I've no feelings on him whatsoever,' lied Peter furiously. 'He's nothing to do with me.'

'And besides' – Two-Soups carried straight on, as if Peter hadn't said anything – 'Aida's a lonely wee lass. She deserves someone of her own. Like you have May. You should be happy for her. Unless…' The Scotsman paused and gave him a look of great pity.

Peter knew where this was going and fought the panic. He could never admit it. He had never really even admitted it to himself, not properly. He slowly exhaled through his nose. 'Unless what?'

'I dinnae ken much, but I ken this. When you love someone wi' all of your heart, like I did with Betty, there's nae room for anything else. Since she died I've never felt that way about another woman, and I dinnae ken I ever will. But I'm glad I had that brief happiness, Peter. Do you want to deny Aida the chance to be happy? Do you want to sulk and scowl until she leaves Carlos, 'cause that's nae fair, mate. You have nothin' to offer her.'

Peter shook his head. This was not a conversation he wanted to have.

'Ye cannae expect Aida to sit on a shelf where no one will touch her, while you continue to act the family man with May.'

Peter swallowed, and it felt like a cold, hard lump of ice was stuck in his throat; it wouldn't go up or down.

Since that first day, when Aida arrived to the YMCA in London, her dresses in her bag, his heart was hers; it could never be anyone else's. He should never have married May. He shouldn't have taken her money, lied to her, promised her something he couldn't give her.

He recalled a conversation he'd had with Eamonn the morning of his wedding, when his brother cross-examined him on his feelings for May, asked if they were genuine. He'd laughed him off, told him he was being stupid, but the truth was Eamonn was right then, and Two-Soups was right now.

It was such a mess, one of his own creating. But he had made his bed, and now he would have to lie in it. May was a good wife, a kind person, a capable person, and she was the mother of his child. He'd made a promise, a commitment to his family, her and Aisling, and he would honour it, no matter the cost to himself. Aida had made it easy over the years, being available for him to confide in, to talk to. She was never with anyone; she lived life as solitary as an oyster. So he could bear it, leaving her alone in her van to go to his marital bed. But now she was no longer alone. She and Carlos Pérez were a formidable pair, both handsome, sharing a language, a love of dance, a magnetic allure that he could never have. And he had no right whatsoever to object or deny her the right to be happy. But witnessing it was like a serrated saw to his guts.

He could find no words, so he just shook his head.

'So what's to be done?' Two-Soups asked gently. 'Are you going to keep on rantin' and sulkin', or are you going to smile and wish the wee lass well?'

'I *do* wish her well.'

'Then show it. Let her go, man. She's not yours and she never can be. Focus on loving your own wife.'

'I do love my wife,' snapped Peter, and he glared at the Scotsman, who said nothing but looked at him patiently.

After a moment or two, Peter dropped his eyes.

Two-Soups was right. He was in love with Aida; he had been for years. And he had done nothing about it, he'd just let things drift, and now she was Carlos Pérez's woman and it was too late; he could do absolutely nothing about it. So he had to let her go.

CHAPTER 22

May

MAY TOOK Millie's letter out of her handbag and handed it to Peter. She was sure her husband would be pleased with Millie's news.

Over the last two weeks, Peter had been making more of an effort, being complimentary to the performers, to her as well. Today he'd even agreed to get out of bed at nine and come to breakfast with her. The idea of dining out for breakfast had seemed so decadent to May when they first arrived, but she had soon adapted, and now they were having eggs and bagels – another revelation – at a place called the Solitary Oyster, run by a charming old Jewish man called Albie Fierstein.

'So listen, Millie brought Remy to Cobh, and they stayed in the Cliff House with Harp Devereaux, and Eamonn joined them there. Don't worry, no one talked about the Treaty!' She laughed as Peter visibly winced. 'They just talked about the new baby, and what JohnJoe is going to do now that Harp has decided to take the year off.'

This was not the big news; Maud Flynn had already told Peter that Harp wasn't coming back at the end of the four months.

'So if I have the dates worked out right, Eamonn and Remy set sail two days ago and they'll be here in three days' time.'

She waited for him to be delighted. Surely he would be happy that Eamonn was coming; it was his idea after all. She knew Peter loved his older brother, even if they were so different. Both of them were dreamers, though Eamonn was an idealist who never changed his mind; that's why he'd taken the anti-Treaty side. Eamonn was headstrong like May; he liked to smash his way through obstacles. Whereas Peter was urbane and charming and preferred to work around them. Peter had dreams, but he was a realist who usually accepted it when he couldn't have what he wanted and just changed tack.

It would be unfair to say Peter was shallow – he wasn't – but he was not emotionally charged the way his brother was. They were like chalk and cheese, and yet they were very close. Peter looked up to Eamonn, sought his approval, even now, even when Peter was the successful, wealthy one.

That was why, even if she could ever admit to herself that Aisling might not be his child, she would never, ever, while there was breath in her body, tell Peter that Eamonn could be Aisling's father. It wouldn't just destroy her marriage, it would destroy Peter, Eamonn, the Cullen family who'd endured so much, her little precious girl, the cabaret... Everything would be blown to smithereens by such a revelation, and so it would have to remain forever locked away in her heart. A dark, poisonous little secret.

Peter said nothing, just nodded, handed her the letter back and started on his breakfast.

She felt a surge of irritation. 'I thought you'd be pleased. I can't wait to tell Nick – he's dying to see Remy. And Aisling's going to be so thrilled. I'm keeping it as a big surprise for her, that's why I left her to have breakfast with Gertrude while we talked about it. What's the matter?'

This time Peter looked up and smiled at her. 'There was a time when his navy-blue eyes would crinkle at the sides when he smiled at her, but now she felt he was smiling with his mouth only.

'Sure, May, of course I'm delighted. It's just I won't have much time to be entertaining him. But you'll be around, and Aisling will be thrilled to see her Uncle Eamonn, and I know poor Nick is missing Remy something wicked. I'd be the same if I was away from Aisling this long.'

'Oh, I know, you're such a good father,' she said, genuinely admiring him for it. So few men were as good with their children.

'I just wish I had more time to spend with her. There's such a lot of work in putting the show on in the hotel. I didn't realise how hard it would be. I thought it would be easier than all the putting up and striking the tent.'

She reached across the table, taking his hand in hers. 'You said you'd be a success, and now you are – us being here at all is the proof of it. You did it, Peter.'

He smiled slightly. 'We did it, May, the two of us, not just me.'

'We're a good team, all right,' she said, and she meant it, they were. They had it so much better than a lot of couples, much better. She felt it was enough for her; she hoped it was enough for him.

'What's next, though?' he asked, and there was a weariness to his voice that was new. 'For so long I was focused on getting us here, to America. I even thought we might make it really big here. Or at least have our contract renewed after Harp wrote to tell Maud she was staying on in Ireland for a while longer after having the baby. But that hasn't happened, and I suppose it won't now. So what do we do next, May?'

May hesitated. There was something she knew that Peter didn't. She'd had coffee and cake with Beatrice Flynn a few days ago, and the girl was in fantasyland, thinking she was absolutely gorgeous now that May had dressed her in a few decent clothes and brought her to the hairdresser for a fashionable cut. She kept saying that if only Aida was out of the way back in Ireland, then Carlos would fall into her arms.

Beatrice hadn't actually spelled it out, but May was now convinced that the girl had put pressure on her aunt to not renew the cabaret's contract in order to get rid of Aida. Carlos was part of the cabaret here, but she couldn't see him in Ireland somehow.

She wondered if there was any point in warning Peter about this. But what was he going to do, get rid of Carlos? That would hardly be fair on Aida.

'Would you have liked that, to stay here, maybe renew our contract, then move on to Broadway, get even bigger?' she asked. 'Now that you're here, you've seen it?'

He sighed, and it sounded like it came from his feet, the weight of the world on him. 'Maybe.'

'That's not very enthusiastic.' She gave his hand a squeeze.

He laughed, just a single breath that had more resignation in it than humour. 'We aren't getting the chance anyway, so it's all a moot point. I'm a bit disappointed, I think. I thought once the people here saw what we have, what we do, that we'd be...well, they'd think it was special, unique. But there are so many shows, so many acts, all scrambling for that small market.' He shrugged. 'Tibbet told me he has another fifty acts on his books, that he can't get a gig for anywhere, and they're good too.'

'So at the end of the four months, we go back and put up our tent and get on the road again?' she asked, keeping her voice neutral.

'I suppose so.' He took a bite of the hot bagel dripping with butter. 'What else can we do?' Yet he didn't sound happy about that either, and she knew why. He feared Aida would stay in America with Carlos.

'Peter, you have your whole life ahead of you. What about your dreams?'

He paused. His eyes rested on hers, and there was something new there – and it wasn't good.

'I'm twenty-seven years old, and I'm tired, May. I feel like I've been hustling all my life, as they say here, always on the lookout for the next opportunity to get ahead, to turn a few quid, to improve myself.'

'And look how far you've come,' she pointed out.

'I know. I could never have imagined this. But I suppose it doesn't feel like I thought it would.'

She was beginning to get fed up of reassuring him and bit back the retort that this malaise only began when Aida started courting Carlos Pérez; before that he'd been bouncing on air.

Instead she went into business mode, thinking maybe that would snap him out of it. 'Well, we've plenty of money saved. Maybe it's time to think about that bricks-and-mortar theatre in Dublin. Settle down and buy a house there, send Aisling to a good school.'

He smiled again, but it still didn't reach his eyes. 'Maybe you're right. Maybe we can just go home and become leading lights of the Dublin theatrical world, rub shoulders with the great and the good of Irish literature. Have drinks with Yeats and Lady Gregory or John Millington Synge, become the sort of people who know people.'

He made it sound ridiculous, like none of it was possible.

'There's worse things we could do, Peter,' she said, still trying to keep her temper. 'And there are things about Dublin that are better than America. Aisling wanted that little girl she met on the street – her mother lives a few doors up – to come to the beach with her, but she said she couldn't, that she had to go to the Missouri Avenue Beach, which is for the coloured people.'

May had been surprised and then shocked at the segregation she saw everywhere in Atlantic City, but Americans of all colours just seemed to accept it. The only Black people she'd met were the domestic servants, the shoeshine man on the Boardwalk or some of the barmen and waiters at the hotels. She'd never seen a Black person enjoy a drink or a meal in a restaurant. She'd soon realised it wasn't allowed. Even the jazz musicians who were so popular had to use the back door of the theatres.

'That's terrible,' said Peter, a bit vaguely. He'd never had the same level of interest in politics as she had, another difference between him and Eamonn.

'I went to hear a woman last week – I've heard her speak a few times actually. Florence Spearing Randolph is her name. She's actually a preacher in one of the churches here, and she was a suffragette, and now she speaks about advancing the cause of coloured people. It was interesting, Peter.'

He shrugged. 'Well, we don't really know the full story, like people coming to Ireland during the war and thinking they had the answer to our problems. Nobody really knows another country. It's complicated.'

'Well, people being mistreated just because they have black skin is not complicated, Peter,' May said, irritated by his lack of interest. 'It's just plain wrong. The same way as the English occupying the land of Ireland was wrong. No complication there either.'

'You're right, completely right,' he said, in that new tired way of his.

She sighed. This wasn't what she'd brought him out to breakfast for. They were supposed to be having a happy conversation about his brother coming over, but even Eamonn's imminent arrival seemed to be of no interest to him. She made a fresh effort. 'I'm sorry, Peter, I don't mean to be cross with you…'

This time it was he who took her hand and pressed. 'No, I'm the one who should be sorry, May. Oh look, ignore me – I'm like a bag of cats today. I don't know what's wrong – there's no pleasing me. I just feel a bit flat or something lately. I *am* pleased about Eamonn coming, and thanks for arranging it. This trip is wonderful, all I ever dreamed of, and I don't know why, but it's not making me as happy as I thought it might.'

May felt another wave of frustration. He was miserable because the great love of his life was involved with someone else. Suddenly it burst out of her. 'And this newfound depression has nothing to do with Carlos Pérez sharing Aida's bed, I suppose?'

She regretted it the moment the words were out, the words themselves and the acidic tone too, but they'd come unbidden, not thought out.

She waited for him to be angry and tell her she was paranoid, but to her hurt astonishment, he did something far worse than get angry. He didn't say anything at all. He just threw some coins on the table for the bill, stood up and left her sitting there alone.

For a while May remained sitting at the table, in shock, staring at the remains of his bagel, discarded, and his undrunk coffee. The lovely breakfast she had planned had descended into this.

How much plainer could her husband have made it? He was not hers. He never was. Not really. What was she going to do about it? A flare of self-righteous indignation coursed through her veins.

Maybe she should just let him go.

She could get divorced here in America. She'd been shocked to discover that Maud Flynn's late alcoholic brother, despite being Catholic, had been married twice, both women divorcing him on the grounds of adultery. Beatrice was the only child of either union and had not seen sight nor sound of her mother, his first wife, in years.

She was entitled to a divorce; she was the adulteress. She could march into the offices of Parker J Bligh, Attorney-at-Law – she'd seen his offices three blocks from the Ocean Diamond – announce she had been unfaithful to her husband, that in fact she had borne another man's child, and so could she please have a divorce? It was so ridiculous, even the thought of it made her smile. She might as well be considering having tea with the man on the moon.

Nick could get his fancy parliamentary divorce when he became a lord, but he had money and land, and what was allowed for the aristocracy was not realistic for Catholic middle-class girls from Dublin. Divorce and all of that was not for people like her and Peter. Nick had the money to ride out a thousand scandals. She and Peter would be ruined by just one.

Under her pain May was nothing if not pragmatic and practical.

She would let her anger subside. She would carry on. With her encouragement, Aida was likely to stay behind with Carlos, and then back in Ireland, Peter's pain would fade. If he lost his hunger for the cabaret for a while, if he wanted to lie in bed and sulk, then she would take the reins. She would build them a bricks-and-mortar theatre, the one she'd always dreamed of.

Peter might have sounded cynical when he talked of May becoming a doyenne of the Dublin theatre scene, but she knew there was a strong part of him – the part that had led him to shed his working-class accent, something Eamonn would never do – that aspired to being middle class in the new Ireland. He would enjoy it in the end.

There was too much water under the bridge in their marriage now. Somewhere deep in her heart's core, she knew that she'd been foolish and headstrong and too determined for her own good, and that she had more or less manoeuvred Peter into marriage. He'd married her for her money certainly, but there was more to it than that. He was fond of her and thought her beautiful, even if he didn't love her as she loved him.

Though it was hard to keep loving a man who barely denied his love for another. May was headstrong, but she was no Eamonn, pinning her colours to the one mast, determined to love no other if she couldn't get the one she wanted.

May was the one Eamonn wanted, she never doubted it, even though he expected nothing in return.

Unbidden came the look Eamonn had given her when she was leaving Dublin, when he had hugged Aisling that last time. After all these years of playing second fiddle to Aida, the lure of being the one a man desired with all of his heart and mind and body was intoxicating; she could allow herself a moment to imagine it.

She had fought it. She had pushed Eamonn from her heart. She had played the dutiful wife and mother and business partner and all the other practical things that Peter needed and loved her for. And her husband did love her in his own way; she was sure of that even now. And Aisling was the centre of his universe; he would never leave May if it meant he risked leaving his daughter.

Sitting abandoned in the Solitary Oyster, she yearned for that time she had sunk into Eamonn's muscular embrace. That golden moment of being utterly worshipped, as if she were a princess, a goddess even. That moment she had experienced just once in her life, in Doyle's Hotel in Dublin one winter night, almost seven years ago. The night her daughter was conceived.

She'd told herself how much she regretted that night, but did she? Really? Hadn't she deserved to spend one night of her life with a man who adored her, body and soul?

CHAPTER 23

ICK

HE AND MAGGIE watched from deckchairs as Aisling and Remy played in the sand.

The two children had fallen on each other with whoops of joy when Nick and Maggie had met Eamonn and Remy off the ship three days ago, and they had hardly been out of each other's company since. Even that rather stiff nanny, Gertrude, who Maud Flynn had provided for them, seemed taken with his son, who was a gregarious and charming child, not unlike Nick's oldest brother, Roger, he thought, who had died in the war.

Remy would make an ideal baron when his time came, but for now his son was delighted to be spending time with the cabaret. He'd always been jealous of Aisling. He thought she was so lucky living in a caravan when he had to make do with his massive stately home, which was so boring apart from the horses.

Like Roger, Remy had a dominant personality, and when Nick took the two children donkey riding on the beach, the boy managed to make his poor donkey gallop. Aisling, well used to horses from all the camping she did on farms, galloped after him, and the poor donkey owner nearly had a fit. Nick had had to hand over a lot of money to calm him down.

Now the two of them were building two separate sand castles and striving to outdo each other. Nick had bought Remy a bucket and spade the exact same size as Aisling's, to save arguments, and they were running to and from the surf to collect more water to mix with the sand. Aisling's dark hair was wet, but her curls were just like Maggie's and sprang up immediately. They were being quiet and focused, and were giving him and Maggie, and the German nanny, who was watching the children from her deckchair, some peace.

Maggie yawned and pulled the brim of her hat over her face. She had such fair skin being red-haired, and she took no chances with the strong New Jersey sun. All the Cullens were fair and freckled. Well, except Eamonn, who was dark and swarthy. Aisling seemed to take after her uncle, because she tanned well, and as for Remy, thanks to his French ancestry, he'd already gone as brown as a berry in the sun.

'Is Eamonn having a good time, d-d-do you think?' Nick asked.

'Eamonn is happier than he's been for a good while. I've not seen him smile in years, but he's full of life since they landed. He's mad about Aisling.'

'She loves him too.' He watched Aisling and Remy chasing each other with bits of seaweed and smiled at their antics. 'The kids fight a lot, but I think they like each other.'

'If it comes to a standoff between a baron and a Cullen, who will win, I wonder?' Maggie asked, and Nick laughed.

'A Cullen every time. Though when we're married, you won't be a Cullen any more, you'll just be a baroness, so it will be a fairer fight.'

Maggie pealed with laughter then, a raucous, loud sound more suitable to a chorus girl than a member of the aristocracy. 'Maggie Cullen, a baroness. Ah here, will ya give over? What nonsense.'

Nick twisted in his deckchair to look at her, surprised. 'It's not nonsense. When I'm the baron, and I and Celine d-d-divorce through the House of Lords, I'm going to marry you, like I said, and then of course you'll be the baroness.'

Maggie turned her head to stare at him; she opened her mouth and for once shut it without saying a word. And Nick realised that what had always been obvious to him had come as a total surprise to her.

She must have been paying no attention at all to the financial discussions with Celine and Millie about the Scottish estate and Brockleton, and where Remy and the twins would go to school, and the holidays they'd spend in Ireland, because it had clearly never crossed her mind that she would be getting a title and wealth along with Nick.

With a pang of fondness, he reached over and tucked a copper curl behind her ear. He loved her for this, that she didn't care a hoot about him being a baron. Nonetheless she needed to know that that was what he was going to be.

'I want so much to show the whole world you're my girl, I'm your man. So much, Maggie, sometimes I feel like I'll explode.' He swallowed. 'It's been nice here, just with the cabaret and other people who d-d-don't know us, being able to act like a normal couple. I know Eamonn is here now, and we're back to pretending there's nothing between us again, but this won't be forever, I promise. One day we'll be able to tell your family.'

'And I'll have to pay for the new heart for me poor ma,' Maggie said, with a look of horror. Nick had been fully up for explaining everything to Eamonn, but Maggie wasn't ready yet to tell her older brother. Or her mother. Bridie Cullen was a devout Catholic, and the idea of telling her mother that she was marrying a Protestant, aristocrat, divorced father... Well, it was not a thought she relished.

'But we'll have to tell her one day, you know, that is if you're still happy to be my wife. When I'm a baron, I'll have a lot of responsibilities. We'd have to give up the cabaret – it would mean us returning full time to Brockleton. You d-d-don't have any objection to that, do you?'

Maggie removed her sunglasses and continued to stare at him.

Nick's heart sank. Had she imagined their life would continue as it was? Like Remy, did she think of Brockleton as 'an awful bore'?

'I think you'd make a wonderful baroness, if you agree to it,' he said anxiously. 'You are kind and you know hardship, so you'd be a great advocate for the tenants and the staff.'

Maggie shook her head so fiercely, she nearly lost her hat. 'There was a time when I couldn't even have dreamed of being a chambermaid at Brockleton, you do know that? And now you're suggestin' I be the lady of the house? Ah, will ya cop on, Nick. I'd make a total show of ya in front of all them toffs and meetin' all the posh people you know. You'd be scarleh!'

He smiled at her use of the Dublin slang for red with embarrassment. 'I would not be scarlet, as you say. I would be so proud...' He heard the catch in his voice but carried on. 'So very proud to call you my baroness, Maggie, and if you can still agree to marry me one day, and put up with the bother of having a title and being called "My Lady" and having staff to look after and more rooms than you can count and tenants who need you and... Well, if after all that, you d-d-decide not to go using your runaway ring just yet, I'll count myself the luckiest man in the world.'

'You're serious.' The penny had finally dropped. She went pale. 'I know we talked about it back in Ireland, but I never really thought... Well, I thought you and me might be able to be together somehow, but I hadn't really believed the whole...title thing...'

'I am, d-d-deadly,' Nick responded, with more certainty than he'd ever felt about anything. His divorce would be a scandal, he knew it, and the marriage to Maggie as soon as possible afterwards an even bigger one, but he didn't care.

As soon as it became possible, he would marry Maggie Cullen and return to Brockleton with his beautiful flame-haired baroness to live happily ever after. If she would just agree to be his baroness, that was. And take that expression of horror off her lovely face.

CHAPTER 24

AY

SHE AND EAMONN had only had the most cursory of conversations since he arrived three days ago. It was as if they were skirting around each other, she keeping him at arm's length and he watching from afar. Though the way he looked at her...well, after years of marriage to Peter, having to witness daily the way he looked at Aida when he thought no one was watching, it was balm for her battered soul.

He was living two doors away from her, sharing a room with Magus at Number Seven. Eamonn was one of the few people who found the Cherokee's dark, brooding mystery a pleasure to be around. He was like Aisling in that way, May realised, able to see through the surface to the depths beneath.

She had got him a ticket for the show, of course, and meant to sit him beside Beatrice. But Beatrice was gone away somewhere for a few days, and so she had to sit beside him herself. But she slipped away before the little afterparty Maggie had arranged for him, saying she had to check on Aisling and Remy, who was sharing

Aisling's room in Number Nine. Of course she hadn't really needed to check; Gertrude didn't mind how late they were back. And the next day, Peter had invited his brother to breakfast in the Solitary Oyster, but May, who loved her eggs and bagels, stayed in bed with a headache.

On the third day, Eamonn came to find her. She was alone in the house. Nick and Maggie had taken the children to the beach, along with Gertrude, and Peter was at the theatre. When she opened the door, there he was on the doorstep, tall, black-haired, broad-shouldered. She should have got her coat and offered to bring him out to the café, where they could have chatted innocuously in public. Instead she let him in, her heart thumping. She prayed he didn't notice the flush on her face. She knew she was playing with fire, that it was insanity, but she did it.

'Eamonn, won't you come in? Peter is out, if he's who you're after, and Aisling is gone to the beach…' Her mouth was dry and her voice overly bright. She went into the sitting room, a big bright salon with large bay windows giving a view of the ocean.

'So what is going on, May?' he said quietly, closing the door behind him even though the house was empty. She always pulled the blinds half down during the afternoons to keep the house cool, so despite it being only 4 p.m., the room was in the glow of twilight.

'Nothing's going on,' May responded, trying to inject some nonchalance she didn't feel into her voice.

'Talk to me,' he said, his deep voice rumbling.

She went to the window, pulled the blind up a little and looked out down the street towards the sea. Though the ocean in Ireland had a myriad of colours in it too, here she was fascinated by how it changed so often and so rapidly. Today the sea was a pale-aqua pastel, but other days it could be inky blue. There was no breeze, which made people tetchy, and the sea was almost mirror flat, but more frequently there were frothy white tops to the waves.

'Hard to believe it's the other side of the same ocean we see at home,' he said, and she realised he'd moved to stand behind her. Still two or three feet behind her, but it felt closer. 'It looks different here.'

'I was thinking the same thing,' she said quietly. She turned then. 'How have you been?'

He shrugged and gave that half smile that was only his. 'All right.'

'Really?' she asked. 'Kathleen wrote to me that she's worried about you.'

He sighed and plunged his hands into his trouser pockets. For the entire duration of the Troubles at home, when he was in the IRA, he turned up at the cabaret each time looking more dishevelled than the last. She realised she was used to seeing him with three or four days of stubble, his dark, wavy hair too long, wearing clothes that had seen a great many better days. Seeing him now, dressed nicely, shaved, his hair cut, she had to admit how powerfully she was attracted to him. She couldn't help it. Maybe it was knowing that he always had and always would love her with an intensity that her husband just never had, maybe that was some of it, but she didn't know.

'Is that why you sent for me then?' he asked, fixing his blue eyes on her.

'I didn't send for you,' she said earnestly. This was getting too close to the bone. She knew she couldn't play with people like this, and Eamonn more than anyone else would be nobody's toy. 'Peter asked me to write. He thought America might be an opportunity for you.'

She'd written to him in Irish, as she always had. She'd been taught it at school, but he'd learnt it in the ditches and farmers' barns when he was an IRA fighter, waging war on the Black and Tans.

Eamonn shook his head. 'You never do anything you don't want to do, May.'

'But I like to do what Peter wants me to do. And Nick is my friend, and it was convenient for you to bring Remy as well. That's all.'

'Nick could have paid a servant to accompany his son. So why did you go along with this, May? Why summon me in the Irish language across the Atlantic? To torture me more? To see if anythin' had changed, to test your own resolve?'

She tried to pull the ragged edges of her thoughts into something coherent, something believable, something safe to say, but words, phrases, slipped from her grasp. He took a step towards her. He was still an arm's length away, but she could feel the heat of him, smell the spicy scent she recalled from all that time ago, soap and tobacco and hair oil.

He made her feel physically small, unlike Peter, who was barely taller than she, and she found she longed to be enveloped in his arms and held to his broad chest. Memories of that night flooded her mind, rendering her incapable of speech.

'No… I…'

'What, May?'

'I wanted to see you,' she said, the honesty forcing itself out of her mouth. 'I missed you.'

He dropped his head, so she had no idea what he was thinking. Then he ran his hand through his thick dark hair, running it down his face and rubbing his jaw. He covered his mouth, his fingers splayed out on his cheek that was already showing dark shadow despite him having clearly shaved this morning.

On and on he looked at her, his eyes raking her face, and though she knew she should say something, change the subject, move away, do something, she couldn't. It was as if she were rooted to this spot, in the direct gaze of a man who was not her husband, a man who was her brother-in-law, and though it was wrong, so wrong, it felt right.

He held his hand out to her, and she reached forwards, placing her hand in his.

'Will we tell each other the truth, maybe for the first time ever?' he asked.

She nodded.

'Right. I'll go first.' He inhaled and blew the air out slowly, as if steadying his nerves. 'I don't know about you, May, but I'm tired. I feel like an old man. I'm twenty-nine, but I feel seventy-nine, and I know that's mainly due to the life I've lived, living in ditches, being arrested more times than I can count, getting seven bells knocked outta me regularly, fightin', always fightin'.' He shook his head sadly, and May longed to hold him. 'I just want some peace in me life now. Peace in me country, and in me city, and – here's the hardest bit – I need peace in me heart.' He paused and looked at her, his face open and honest and questioning. 'D'ya understand that?'

She gave another nod. She didn't trust herself to speak.

'And I can't...' He exhaled again, through his teeth, as if he too had trouble finding the words. 'I know I can't live me life this way, half livin', workin' for nothin' 'cause the fella that owns the company hates me for the stance I took on the Treaty. Most of the lads I knew came over here – there's nothin' for us at home. After all we did, it's a bitter pill to swallow, but it's true.'

She heard the pain. He'd sacrificed so much, fought so bravely for his country – it was so dispiriting to see how he was being treated. If it wasn't for people like Eamonn, willing to risk it all, there would be no free Ireland, but people had short memories when it suited them.

'But I couldn't do it, leave Ireland, and you're the only one who really knows why. Nobody understands why I don't go. They say I could earn better money here, maybe make a new start...'

'So you're thinking of staying?' She heard the raw emotion in her question.

'That depends.'

'On what?' she asked, knowing the answer.

He looked at her then, a slight smile at the corners of his lips, an eyebrow raised. 'On you.'

Long seconds ticked by. Neither spoke.

'What do you want me to do?'

His smile almost broke her heart. 'Honestly?'

'Honestly.'

'I want us to go to Peter, tell him the truth, that we love each other and always have. That you and he should never have married, and that I told him so the morning of yer weddin', and that you want to be free. And that once you are, he can, with your blessin', tell that Spanish woman for once and for all that he feels for her what I feel for you and see if she'll have him.'

Her heart throbbed painfully. 'You know about Aida?'

He nodded and stroked the back of her hand with his thumb. 'It was when the English came for you and Peter that day, and Aida pretended to be you to save you. In the prison van, on the way to Dublin Castle, we were shackled to each other. The Tans that picked us up were half drunk, and we talked, and she didn't say it openly, but it was plain as day – she'd sacrificed her life for Peter's happiness. She'd stepped in to save you because you were carrying his child.'

May bowed her head, her hand still in his. She'd always known the truth.

'And I told her something in return, May.'

'What?' She glanced up fearfully.

'Oh, don't worry,' he said a little harshly. 'I didn't tell her that I hoped you were carrying my child. I just said that if she were to survive this and I did not...well, she was to tell you I died with your name upon my lips and my love for you in my heart.'

May withdrew her hand, turned away and sank silently into the armchair by the empty fireplace. He took the other chair, and his bulk filled it. He leant forwards, resting his forearms on his strong muscular legs.

'I haven't much to offer you, May.' He glanced around the living room of the lovely townhouse. 'Nothin', if I'm to be honest. But maybe over here, I could get a better life goin' and make a few bob to set us up. I had a friend in Dublin who's in New Jersey now – he said there's work can be found for me down the coast from here, in the sweetcorn fields or driving trucks or something like that. There's money to be made, and the houses are cheap. But maybe that's not what you want at all, May, and if it's not, then I'll stay here by myself and you go back and I'll figure out me own life. So I suppose I'm askin' ya, what do you want?'

'And you love me that much?' She needed to hear him say it, to hear his worship.

'More than I've ever loved anyone in me whole life, May. I fought and nearly died for Ireland many times, and I want you more than I wanted a free Ireland.'

'And what about your mother, and the girls? And Peter...and my parents...the scandal...' She couldn't believe she was even entertaining the idea, but she couldn't stop herself.

He inhaled through his nose, puffed his cheeks and exhaled slowly. 'I know. There's no point in sayin' it would be all right, 'cause it probably wouldn't be, but I'd sacrifice them for you. It would be hard, and it might break me ma's heart, and God knows I've put that woman through enough, but what's the alternative? Live half a life? Heart breakin' in me chest every day, thinkin' about you and Aisling, imaginin' him with you, touchin' you. I... It is enough to drive me out of me mind, so it is.'

His head dropped then, and he gazed at the floor between his knees.

'I've tried to make it work with Peter,' she heard herself say. It was her turn to be honest. 'I really have. I tried too hard from the start is the truth. I wanted him so much, I assumed that would be enough, but he was never mine, not really.'

Eamonn didn't reply.

'And the moment he set eyes on Aida, I should have walked away, but I was a stupid, impulsive, spoiled girl, and I thought I could make it as I wanted it to be, bend everything to my will.'

She sighed deeply. 'But he's been a good husband, you know? He never was unfaithful...and he is kind and good. And I know you might not want to hear this, but we have a good marriage in every sense, except that I've always loved him more than he loved me. And I suppose that wears you down over the years, that and always having her around, wanting to hate her, but she never did anything to me to warrant that. And then when she sacrificed herself for me when I was expecting Aisling, and Peter was so worried, and how he nursed her back to health, got her to dance again... And all that time, I just had to stand by and say nothing, because I'd done far worse to him than he'd ever done to me.'

The unanswered question hung between them. Where did that leave Eamonn?

Did she love Eamonn? She honestly couldn't answer that. She was attracted to him, and she hungered for how he wanted her, that was certainly true – that night in Doyle's was like nothing she'd ever experienced before in her life – but did she love him? The truth was she didn't even know him, not really. A shadowy figure for all the years of the war, dipping in and out of their lives, and they never knew when it would be the last time they would see him. Something about him seemed almost mythical, as if any time he could fade away like a cat into the night.

'The past is done and can't be undone May,' he said.

'Do you regret it?'

He shook his head. 'No. I should, but I don't.'

She suddenly felt so weary of it all. These games were for romance novels, not for real life, not for real, substantial, ordinary, practical people. How could she do as he suggested? Destroy her precious child by either leaving her behind or taking her from the only father she knew? It was impossible. She'd been too selfish as a young woman, caring only for what she wanted. It was time to grow up and live with the consequences of her actions.

And one of those actions was the way she'd brought Carlos into the troupe and pushed him at Aida. It had worked; she'd destroyed Peter's hopes, put Aida beyond his reach. She could hardly abandon her husband now.

'Well, I regret it,' she said firmly. 'And we have no future, Eamonn, none at all. I'm Peter's wife, and that's how it will stay. Aida is with Carlos now, and I'm going to make my marriage work. We're going back to Ireland. Maybe I'll build a theatre. You should stay here after we leave, make a life, marry, have children. Some woman would be lucky to call you her husband.'

'You're telling me that you want to put an ocean between us? That you never want to see me again?' His blue eyes bored into hers.

May held his gaze, not flinching. Eamonn had to believe she meant this, for once and for all. 'I'm his wife. I'm so sorry for hurting you, Eamonn, more sorry than I can ever say, but the best thing for you to do would be to forget about me.'

'Fine.' He stood, and the pain on his face reached into her heart and squeezed so hard she felt almost breathless. 'Goodbye, May.'

CHAPTER 25

*E*AMONN

THE WELCOME INN in the coastal town of Strathmere, a train ride south from Atlantic City, seemed to be a respectable enough establishment, overlooking the sea. He'd been told to ask for the gentlemen's toilets and then go in by a small door there marked STOREROOM, STAFF ONLY. He did as instructed and found himself first in a long corridor and then in a thronged speakeasy.

'Well, if it isn't the famous Eamonn Cullen,' the barman said. Eamonn recognised him as an annoying fella from Kerry he'd met the last time he was in America, those two months after he'd escaped from Dublin Castle. The Kerryman had got out long before there was any trouble, though he let on he was a hero of course. 'Watch out, lads! IRA chief sniper is in the house now – mind yer manners.'

'A pint of Guinness please, Tim,' Eamonn said quietly.

It was full, and Eamonn was soon surrounded by men, all wanting to hear of his exploits during the fight against the British. They knew exactly who he was. He was not one for glorifying what was a gruesome and miserable war, but these men really wanted the guts-and-glory version of events. He feared he was less than they were hoping for.

'How many d'ya kill?' a kid in a soft cap and a tartan suit asked, a cigarette hanging from his lips, gangster style.

'No idea,' Eamonn said, taking a sip of his stout.

'Not enough, I'd say!'

This was met with a cheer from his gang, not one of them over eighteen and not one of them had ever seen a day's hardship in their lives.

There was a look men got, Eamonn realised, whether it was from the Irish War, the Great War – any war, it probably didn't matter which one. But there was a look in the eyes of a man who'd seen war for what it really was, not medals and stories and all that rubbish, but the actual bloody, torturous grind. The fear of wondering, every morning that you woke up, if this would be your last day on earth, that feeling you got in the pit of your stomach when you said goodbye to your ma or your sweetheart or your child and prayed it wasn't forever.

That look couldn't be manufactured. Only those who had seen what he'd seen could wear it. And they recognised it in each other. Over here even, Eamonn could tell at a glance men who'd been in combat and those who hadn't.

'What d'ya call a ship full of Englishmen, sunk to the bottom of the sea?' another boy called, a baby-faced lad who was desperately trying to grow a moustache and making a very poor fist of it.

'A good start.' A chorus of voices, the clinking of glasses.

They hadn't a clue. Those soldiers, Tans, police, they were just lads like himself, doing their jobs, trying to not get killed and to get home to their loved ones. He'd seen young Tommies bleeding and crying for their mothers. He'd posted letters for stoic prisoners before they were executed in retaliation for the killing of IRA men. He'd even sat and drunk tea with a few, talked of farms in Lancashire and shops in Newcastle, sweethearts and football teams and mates down the pub. Whoever was to blame for the sorry state of the world, it wasn't a lad in a uniform with a gun on his back. They were just pawns. That truth would fall on deaf ears here, though, so he didn't bother.

To his right a man shouldered his way to the bar. 'I heard you were here,' he said with a grin, and then he and Eamonn hugged.

Charlie Horgan had seen plenty of action, as much if not more than Eamonn himself had, and he'd had to be snuck out by the Capuchin monks down in Cork, a bounty on his head. It was Charlie he'd come to when he was in a similar pickle himself after he and Aida were arrested and tortured in Dublin Castle.

'Good to see you again, Charlie. How are things?' Eamonn smiled, glad to see his old friend.

'Grand, and you?' Charlie nodded at Tim, who delivered a pint of stout with a smirk. 'Will we sit down?'

Eamonn was glad to escape the bravado of the young crowd at the bar. He'd known too many lads like them at home, all guff, with loose tongues that got them in trouble, sometimes even killed.

'*Is minic a bhris bhéal duinne a shrón*,' Charlie murmured, and Eamonn laughed. The old Irish adage that "twas often a fella got his nose broken by his mouth' was particularly true here.

Charlie Horgan had a tight crew cut, and under it he could see his scalp had more than one scar. He was missing a front tooth, lost in a fight with an Auxie in County Meath in the summer of 1920. He was a low-sized but sturdy man of thirty-five or forty, born and reared in the Liberties of Dublin and hard as nails.

'All talk. They love the stories, but they'd wet their pants if they saw a fraction of what we did.' Charlie took a long slug of his pint. 'So what has you here, Mr Cullen? Not that I'm not happy to see you of course.'

'Looking for work, a start,' Eamonn replied. 'Someplace to live.'

'I thought you were stayin' at home – you told me you'd never leave?' Charlie cast him a strange glance.

'I was, but…now I'm not.'

'Fair enough, I don't blame you. Things are bad for us back there now, I hear?'

Eamonn nodded. 'Anyone who went against the Treaty can forget it if he thinks he can get ahead. I wish it wasn't so, but it is, so 'tis time to accept it.' He raised his pint in salute. '*Sláinte.*'

'And the married woman you had a thing for? That's over, is it?'

Eamonn had confided in him one night, full of whiskey, that he loved a married woman. He was still in such pain after the repeated hidings in Dublin Castle; drink was the only thing that numbed it, and it had loosened his tongue.

'Yeah, that's not the case any more.' The words were like acid in his mouth, but he needed to get them out, to purge.

'You don't care for her?' Charlie asked, then took another slug.

'Nah.' That sound, spat out as if it was nothing, when in fact it was everything. Absolutely everything.

'Did her husband guess, is that it?'

He laughed grimly. 'No.' He knew Peter would never guess. It would be a betrayal beyond comprehension to his brother. It was all so wrong. Every last bit of it. He felt sick to his stomach with guilt. But he could not regret it – Peter didn't love her and he did.

'Look, best forget about her, Eamonn. She's made her bed. And sure, look, there's a pile of women here who go weak at the knees for the accent.' Charlie winked at him.

'I've forgotten her already, Charlie.' He hadn't, but if he could, he would. Going back to Atlantic City, after all that happened with May, was impossible. The situation at home was never going to improve either. 'Can you get me a start, Charlie, put a word in? I'm good with timber and anything in the building line. Or driving a truck, or picking sweetcorn, whatever they do around here.'

Charlie sat back and observed him. 'I can get you a job, if you're interested.'

'Go on.'

'Well, the fella I work for, I kind of run a crew for him. Dick Carney's his name. His people came from Donegal originally but over here for generations now, all stuck in the Ancient Order of Hibernians, that sort of thing. But he's done well for himself, and he might have something for ye.'

'Driving a truck or construction or what?'

'Well, he has all kinds of businesses on the go, and one is sort of import-export.'

Something in Charlie's face made Eamonn realise this might not be exactly above board. 'Oh yeah?' He was dubious. The last thing he needed was more brushes with the authorities. He'd had enough of that in Ireland to last a lifetime.

Charlie lowered his voice. 'Look, it's booze, all right. They're all at it. The place has more booze than it ever had, places like this, speakeasies all over the place. The cops know it, everyone knows it, and so if you get caught, it's just a slap on the wrist, no big deal as they say over here.'

Eamonn shook his head. 'Nah, Charlie, I'd rather go straight.'

'And you can, but this would set you up. It's a run – it will be in a few days, just from Cape May up the coast to Atlantic City. The shipment is on its way already. There's a small island near Newfoundland called Saint Pierre. It was French, and France never agreed to cooperate with US Prohibition, so the booze comes in through there. And the smugglers get false registration papers, claiming the cargo is bound for the Caribbean, and there's loads of inlets in Cape May, and we just have to make sure it gets from there to Atlantic City safely. No risk, I swear. And I could use a strong man like yourself, someone I know who can handle himself.'

'For a job that has no risk?' Eamonn raised an eyebrow.

'Almost no risk.' Charlie shrugged. 'And 'tis three hundred dollars a man, one night's work. It would take you six weeks to make that on a building site. It's easy money. And I've another one next week. By the end of the month, you'd have enough for a place of your own and to get set up here. You can go straight then if you want.'

'If we don't get caught,' Eamonn said, still sceptical.

'Look, it's a stupid law anyway, and it's not like anyone is getting hurt. We're not the villains here, Eamonn. This whole Volstead Act is just a way of the government screwing more money out of people with fines and keeping the women from carpin' in the bigwigs' ears all day about drunkenness.'

Eamonn pondered the idea. Three hundred dollars was a lot of money, and if it was just as Charlie said, making sure a lorry got from here to Atlantic City, he supposed he could do that.

'We take a farmer's road through the sweetcorn fields from Cape May to Winslow. It's bumpy and rutted, and no Fed is going to risk his wheels driving through there. Besides, they hate the night and the rain, and it's going to be cats and dogs all week. And once we're on the main road to AC, no one will stop us then – the Feds will leave us to the AC police, and the AC police are paid off. It'll be grand, I swear. I've done it loads of times already.'

'What would I have to do?' Eamonn asked.

'Nothing, just come with me and three other lads. We'll make sure you have a piece...' Seeing Eamonn's lack of understanding, he explained. 'A gun. Not that you'll need it. You ride up front with the driver of the first truck, and me and the boys will be in the other two. It will be crates of sweetcorn and blueberries – they're used to that coming and going – and the booze hid beneath. We drop to a depot in AC and away we go, simple.'

'And you've definitely done this before?'

'More times than I can count. I wouldn't steer you wrong, Eamonn. We're old comrades, been through some hairy times together, but you took more risks in an hour with the Tans and Auxies than you'll do with this in a year.'

'And it's cash in my hand after?'

'A hundred up front. I get paid when we drop off, and I'll divvy up the rest of your share there and then.'

Eamonn thought. It probably wasn't entirely without risk, but as Charlie said, it was not like anyone was getting hurt. It was a few cases of whiskey, getting around a ridiculous law anyway, and that amount of money would set him up. And he needed to get his life on track; he'd wasted enough of it.

He thought of May advising him to get set up here, get married, have a family. As if he could just shake off his love for her. There had been no one else, not for seven years. Before that there had been plenty, but since that night with May, no one.

'Are you in?' Charlie asked.

'I'm in, I suppose.' Eamonn drained his beer.

'Right, now let's get some chop suey in you.'

'What the hell is that?' This country was full of weird food.

'The grub the Chinese eat. Looks dire but tastes better than a Burdock's fish and chips.' Charlie laughed and led him out of the speakeasy, through the hotel, along the windswept seafront, then left down an alleyway to where there was a small clapboard shack with red lanterns hanging outside.

Five minutes later they were sitting in a tiny restaurant, its walls and furniture painted in red and gold. Charlie ordered, and a bowl came out a few minutes later full of vegetables and meat and some kind of white long things that looked like worms, the whole thing floating in some kind of soup.

Eamonn looked down in horror. 'I'm not eatin' that…'

'Try it, trust me,' Charlie said, then tucked into his own bowl of the same stuff. Very reluctantly Eamonn did as he said, and to his surprise, it was actually delicious.

'See? I told ya. Trust me.' Charlie winked. 'I presume you're sleeping at my place tonight?'

'Well, considering how many times I put you up in my brother's tent, it's the least you can do.'

'Fair enough. How are they, Peter and…May, isn't it?'

Eamonn forced a smile. 'Grand. They're here actually, in Atlantic City, for the summer season. They're the show at the Ocean Diamond.'

Charlie let out a low whistle. 'The Ocean Diamond, is it? Very fancy. That's Fraud Flynn's place? That's a long way from a field in Portmarnock.'

'*Fraud* Flynn?'

Charlie chuckled. 'Maud. She's not all she seems, but best not get into that now. Watch her, though. She's as slippery as an eel, that one. And her niece is notorious.'

Eamonn shrugged. He hadn't met either of the Flynn women, but Peter had told him they were proper Holy Marys, and he knew people loved to cut other people down who had done well while still managing to stay on the right side of the law. 'Whatever you say. But yeah, it's a fine hotel, and Peter and May are doing great, brought all the troupe over. There was an Irish band called Roaring Liberty booked there –'

'Roaring Liberty?' Charlie perked up. 'Isn't your one in that band Harp Devereaux? She's one of us, ran guns, information. She's Matt Quinn's daughter, or stepdaughter or something. Knew Collins personally and all.'

'I know, I stayed with them in Cobh.' May had arranged for him to meet Millie and Remy there. He'd been dreading meeting Matt Quinn, a staunch supporter of Collins, but he'd found him to be a tough but fair man who offered the warmest of welcomes. 'She never said about the gun-running, but then we didn't talk politics at all.'

'Well, you know the ones that do be shootin' their mouths off did nothing.'

Eamonn nodded. That was true. The real IRA men and women had been properly trained; they knew that discretion was the single most critical trait of a successful operative. He wished Charlie was a bit more discreet himself. 'So tell me about life here in Strathmere. Is it a good spot to set myself up?'

'As good as anywhere else.' Charlie nodded. 'This is the land of opportunity *a chara*.' He winked.

CHAPTER 26

AMONN

THE NIGHT WAS wet and warm. Sheets of rain obscured the view of anything from the three trucks parked on the flat sand, their backs open to the wind and rain. Small boats kept pulling up on the beach, and men in waterproofs rushed through the dark, carrying crates.

He and Charlie stood in the open back of one of the trucks, soaked to the skin, the rain relentless, receiving the sealed crates and stacking them under open ones of sweetcorn and blueberries.

Eamonn made sure he didn't make eye contact with anyone who handed a crate up to him; this, like a lot of his business during the Troubles, was on a need-to-know basis, and he most certainly did not need, nor care, to know.

In less than twenty minutes, all the trucks were fully loaded and ready to go, with several hundred bottles of Canadian whiskey concealed under the fruit and vegetable produce, and Eamonn was slick with sweat as well as rain due to the weight of the crates and the speed with which they had needed to be stacked inside.

'Sweeney?' Charlie called to the ferocious-looking man in charge who stood in the rain on the beach, his collar pulled up and his hat pulled down, exuding threat, not helping with the movement of the cargo but eyeing everything.

'Sweeney will take delivery,' growled the man. 'But this one's going north.'

Charlie had explained that the booze business was run by families, Irish and Italians mainly, some Jews as well, and they allowed men like Charlie's boss, Doherty, to take all the risk in bringing the alcohol into the country, but he in turn charged a high price for it.

Charlie was ambitious to be a Doherty one day. The risk was high, but he didn't care. There were fortunes to be made in this business, and Charlie had an eye for nice things.

Once everything was loaded, they pulled the tarpaulin down and secured the tailgate with a pin that shot through two steel eyes.

'OK, boys, let's go,' Charlie called, banging his hand on the side of the truck. 'You go in this one, Eamonn.'

Eamonn climbed into the sodden cab beside the driver, the seat squelching as he sat on it. The cab was open, no roof or windows, and though the night was warm, he shivered as he felt the water soak deeper into his clothes. It was only fifty miles to Atlantic City, but a lot of the way was over rough farm tracks in the middle of the night, so it was going to take them a couple of hours at least.

He nodded a greeting to the driver, a bearded man who smelled of porter, but got no response so didn't attempt any further communication. Niall Barrett was a taciturn fellow who still seemed to resent Eamonn's presence, though Charlie had introduced him as his friend from the old country. He hadn't got any friendlier either, even though this was Eamonn's fourth mission.

He'd only meant to try the one run at first, and that would be it. He had no interest in criminality – it was a mug's game. But the first one had been so smooth and easy; there'd been no sign of the FBI, and it was like the police of Atlantic City didn't even care. The second, and then the third, had also passed without incident.

A few days ago, near Strathmere, he'd seen a couple of new houses for sale, not expensive, and he'd had a thought that maybe, if he was set up someplace around here, had a home and a proper job, then he could have a new life. Maybe Charlie was right – he could find an American girl, someone who knew nothing about his past, make a whole new start. Meet someone who would love him and make him happy, and he'd make her happy too.

He'd need a few bob for that, because nice, innocent girls didn't marry penniless wasters. Maybe a couple of thousand to buy a place, and furnish it, and some land around it that he could farm, maybe some grazing stock, and then he'd stop. He already had nine hundred dollars in a sealskin wallet that he kept in a pocket he'd sewn into his undershirt. He was living in Charlie's digs in Strathmere. They were run-down, and he didn't trust the management or the other clientele, so he kept his valuables on his person, always, the same way he kept his money when he was in the IRA.

Leading the short convoy, his truck pulled out onto the dark farm road, bouncing over potholes and slushing through deep puddles. There were huge swathes of sweetcorn fields between here and Winslow, and that was the route they would take. As the truck bounced over the rutted roads, Eamonn kept his eyes peeled. He was conscious of the Smith & Wesson tucked into his belt and the short-handled knife attached to his lower leg with a leather strap.

Being armed was only a precaution, of course. As Charlie said, these operations were really simple. The FBI were incompetent, and the local police clearly turned a blind eye – Eamonn thought they must be in somebody's pocket, maybe this man Sweeney.

The first half hour went by without a word between him and the driver. The night air was heavily scented by the sweet smell of the ripe corn that was all around them, as high as a man's head, brushing against the side of the lorry. The other man smoked incessantly, his eyes fixed firmly on the road.

Then, out of nowhere, there was something up ahead.

'Look out,' Eamonn said, instinctively reaching for his gun. But it was only a girl. She was standing in the middle of the road, and a car sat at an angle, blocking the single track. She was drenched.

The driver slowed, cursing to himself at the stupidity of women drivers and how it shouldn't be allowed, and the other trucks behind them slowed too. The girl, a plain thing in thick spectacles and a summer dress, with no coat or hat, approached the passenger's side. Rain ran in rivulets down her face and into the valley between her breasts. Her mousy hair hung in wet tendrils around her face, and she looked in despair.

'Oh, thank goodness,' she said, gazing up at Eamonn. 'I broke down and I was –'

Suddenly she was grabbed from behind and pulled away, screaming and kicking. Before Eamonn had time to register what was happening, the gunfire began from all sides. He ducked down, taking refuge in the stepwell of the truck while giving return fire. He felt a bullet whizz past his ear and saw that Niall had been hit, a single shot, fatal; he was slumped over the wheel.

It sounded like Charlie and the others had their own weapons; he could hear machine-gun fire coming from the trucks behind. He got out of the truck and, under the cover of their fire, ran down the side of the field, his intention being to get to Charlie, to consolidate their return fire. But he couldn't get a clear run. The track was being rutted by gunfire, and the familiar smell of cordite filled his nostrils. He bent at the waist and ran in among the sweetcorn, the sharp leaves catching at his sleeves, shadows all around. He found a deep rut, filled with water, and he lay in it. His clothes were black, and he smeared mud over his face, camouflaging himself as much as was possible. He could see the trucks just about, through the stalks.

Another hail of gunfire erupted from the cornfield on the opposite side of the track, with no response from any of their three trucks. Silence, then rustling as the assailants emerged from the field. Eamonn heard a match being struck, saw a flare of light and then caught the smell of tobacco being burnt. Then heavy feet and male voices. 'All dead. What'll we do with the bodies, take them into the fields?'

'Dump them out where they are,' a female voice said. It was the girl, and she seemed to have got over her fright, if she'd ever been frightened in the first place. 'Make sure you keep their weapons. Paul, you take the first truck, Willie and Cosh in the second, and Ted, you take the third. I'll follow in the car. Give me the car keys.'

'Here…' A jangle as they flew through the air, and a cry of annoyance from the girl.

'What d'ya throw them for, Ted, you idiot? They've gone in the dirt now.'

'Ya ever hear of catchin' something, sweetheart?'

'Watch it, Ted, or this'll be your last tango,' said the girl fiercely. 'Now find those keys, all of you.'

There was silence, then a scuffling as the men looked for the keys. Someone shone a torch, and Eamonn held his breath; they were so close to where he was lying in the deep, water-filled rut.

'Dumb broad,' muttered one of the men under his breath.

'She couldn't catch the clap.'

A third voice hissed, 'Enough, boys. Let's show a bit of respect, eh? Remember who's paying you. Is that them?'

After the keys were found, there was more heaving and shoving as the bodies were pushed out of the trucks. Niall Barrett landed with a thump, his pale face staring up into the rain.

If anyone shone a torch his way, Eamonn would be exposed. He took a deep breath and dipped his face into the water. His heart was beating a tattoo against his ribs. He was used to the sound of rats in the corn, but the sensation of one or more running over the back of his legs was the least of his problems now.

Moments later there was the roar of all three trucks being driven away, followed by the car.

Once he was sure the attackers were gone, the last sound of the engines fading away into the damp night air, he stood up, dripping. He walked over to Niall Barrett, then knelt and whispered an act of contrition in his ear, followed by, 'Eternal rest grant unto him, oh Lord, and may perpetual light shine on him forever, may he rest in peace.'

Moving back to the farm track, he took a box of matches from his pocket. It took five goes to make one light, as the box was sodden, but eventually it did and he held it aloft. Further back, the bodies of Charlie and the two others were lying at the edges of the corn fields. The match burnt down to his fingers and he had to drop it, but the rain had slowed and a sliver of moon appeared, giving a faint silver light.

He went first to Charlie Horgan, a bullet clean through his forehead, his blue eyes open, silver-white in the moonlight.

It struck Eamonn as so sad, this bright, cheerful lad from the heart of working-class Dublin, who had survived the British Army, the Black and Tans and the Auxiliaries, survived sleeping out on the Irish countryside for months on end, only to die here, surrounded by acres of American sweetcorn, thousands of miles from his home.

'Eternal rest grant unto Charlie, oh Lord, and may perpetual light shine on him forever, may he rest in peace.'

He slapped the back of his neck as something bit him, and again another. Mosquitos. He'd been eaten alive by midges on summer evenings living in the gorse and heather at home, but these savage things they had here were in a whole other league.

Still slapping at his neck, he did the same for the other two men.

Then he considered what to do next. Nobody knew he was involved, nobody who was still alive. Apart from Doherty, who would assume he was dead as well and would distance himself as far as he could anyway. It would be a while before these bodies were spotted and the police started poking around. He needed to get himself out of here as fast as he could and disappear for a while. His digs wouldn't miss him, and he'd left nothing there they could trace him by, only a spare change of clothing in a leather bag without even the maker's labels. He'd learnt to travel light and anonymously, from his time in the IRA. They would just think he'd moved on and be happy to steal his clothes.

Everything he needed was in the waterproof sealskin wallet, his money and his passport. He just needed to dry out.

He washed the mud off his face in a puddle, then started walking up towards the main road, beating off the mosquitos. He reached a firmer road and walked for another two or three hours, his feet squelching in his boots, his body weary and cold. Every time he heard an engine, he stepped off the road into the head-high corn, and then, when it had passed, walked on, his way lit by the thin light of the moon.

Later, as the sun came up, he found himself on the crest of a hill, a small town in the valley below him, and by the time he passed a sign that said 'Welcome to Corncrake' and the occasional house had become a street of houses, the sun was hot and his clothes were steaming.

Stepping behind a tree, he unbuttoned his coat and pulled up his shirt to get at the wallet in his undershirt. He took out a few notes, still dry, pocketed them, then tucked his shirt into his trousers again and rebuttoned his coat.

Half a mile further ahead was another sign pointing up a sideroad, for the Corncrake Hotel. That would do.

CHAPTER 27

AMONN

THE PAIR of old ladies who ran the tiny Corncrake Hotel started fussing as soon as he walked in.

'Oh, I'm sorry, sir, we're full...' They'd taken one look at him in his mud-caked clothes and with no luggage and had decided he was not the kind of clientele they were interested in. He glanced at the wall clock, a plain wooden circle – it was only seven in the morning.

'I know, ladies. It's early, and I look a little dishevelled, but my car broke down and I've had to walk for hours. I had to leave the encyclopaedias in the car – I'm a travelling salesman, you see.' He wasn't as good as his brother at accents, but he could flatten his own enough not to mystify them entirely.

As the ladies continued to flap, he sized up his surroundings. Like the clock, everything around him was modest and plain, all the furniture simple and rather small, and behind the counter there was a framed piece of embroidery that read 'The stranger who resides with you shall be to you as one of your citizens; you shall love him as yourself, for you were strangers in the land of Egypt. Leviticus 19:34.'

'I am far from home, ladies, a friendless stranger, in desperate need of a bath and a sleep,' he said, in a gentle, respectable voice.

The ladies hesitated and twitched like a pair of little birds. They wore lace caps on their flurry of grey ringlets, and their dresses were as modest and plain as the furniture. They were clearly women of faith, though not of the Roman Catholic variety, because there were no Sacred Hearts nor Virgin Marys in sight.

The Catholic Church did not trust its flock to read the Bible for themselves, choosing to interpret it for the faithful instead. But he remembered one Protestant vicar's wife in County Westmeath who took pity on him and his men one night, a filthy, dirty night like the one just gone but freezing cold as well, and she brought them into the vicarage and fed them and dried them off. When he asked her why she did it, given that her husband was the minister for the local British barracks and both she and he hailed from Northumberland in England, she'd quoted a verse from the Bible.

He was far from a biblical scholar, but he'd remembered that good lady's words and he repeated them now. 'Does the Bible not say "Come unto me, all ye that labour and are heavy laden, and I will give you rest"?'

That was the sum total of his knowledge, but he hoped it would do enough to secure him a bed and a basin of warm water. Maybe even a meal.

'Matthew 11:28.' The old ladies nodded approvingly.

'That embroidery is beautiful. My mother would love something like it. Where might I ask did you buy it?'

They flushed bright pink then. 'Oh, we made it, sir. We do them in the evenings, my sister and I. And our darling niece Dorothea – she is like a daughter to us since our sister died – she sells them at the Quaker bazaar to raise funds for the local hospital.'

'Well, it's very lovely and so perfect. I'm afraid my big hands would fail miserably at anything like that, but maybe I could buy one from you, for my mother?'

He wouldn't say anything to give his affiliation to the Church of Rome away. He'd learnt from Peter there was a certain degree of mistrust in Catholics, given that the Irish and the Italians had terrible reputations as gangsters.

He took one of the notes out of his pocket, and seeing it, the two ladies seemed to make a decision.

'We'd be delighted, but let's get you checked in first, Mr...?'

'Ed,' he said easily, giving the shortened English version of Eamonn to sound less Catholic. 'Ed Cullen.'

It struck him, not for the first time, how adept at bending the truth he had become over the years. He didn't consider himself a liar, and he tried to be straight in his dealings with people, but years of a life in the shadows had taught him to think on his feet.

'You are welcome here, Mr Cullen. You just take a seat there, and we'll get the room ready.'

He did as they bid him and sat on a small wooden stool, very low but sturdy; everything in this place seemed to be designed for miniature people. He was reminded of the book he'd bought Aisling, *Gulliver's Travels* by the great Irishman Jonathan Swift, the story of a sailor who visits the land of Lilliput, where everyone is tiny and he is huge by comparison.

He could hear female voices upstairs as feet shuffled about, getting things ready for 'poor Mr Cullen'. And he felt a pang of shame. They were really sweet ladies, and he didn't like lying to them about being a salesman. His mother didn't rear him to tell lies, and he liked to justify his actions in his own head. All through the last years, he could tell himself he was fighting for his country, or he loved May. But now? He was a criminal running illegal alcohol, and that had resulted in four men being killed in cold blood.

Was he really honest? A man of principle? Of course he wasn't. He had got his brother's wife pregnant, he'd killed more men than he could count – boys, if he was honest, who had mothers and sweethearts – and he was just last night committing another crime. He might be fooling others that he was a decent person, but if he'd been the one to get that bullet last night, not the man sitting beside him, and he was meeting his Maker, could he really stand over his actions? He doubted it. He hoped he was right and God did not exist.

One of the ladies appeared, her cheeks pink with the exertion. 'Please, Mr Cullen, follow me.'

He walked behind her, climbing the tiny staircase and filling the entire space with his bulk. On the top landing there were four doors, one open into a small white room.

Inside was the other old lady and a much younger woman, presumably the niece; they were making the last adjustments to his room, puffing up the pillows and arranging a cushion on a chair with another Bible verse embroidered on it.

'The bathroom is the second door there, and I hope you'll be comfortable,' trilled the one who'd brought him upstairs. 'Will you be down for breakfast, Mr Cullen? It starts at eight.'

He smiled. 'I'd love that, but I'm afraid I've got no other clothes – I left my suitcase in the car as well – and I wouldn't like to put your guests off their meals by appearing looking so wet and dirty.'

'Aunt Elsie, I think Mr Cullen might be around the size of Uncle Thaddeus, what do you think?' murmured the younger woman. She was barely more than a teenager, fluffy blond hair tied back and large grey eyes that flicked shyly in his direction.

Elsie looked at her niece as if she had just invented the wheel. 'Dorothea, do you know, I think he just might be.' She clapped her hands gleefully. 'What do you say, Constance?'

'Our dear departed brother, Thaddeus, was killed at the Somme. He was an officer,' Constance explained to Eamonn, with such pride and love; the naked raw pain of his loss was written on every line of her face.

Eamonn felt a wave of guilt. These were good people, trying their best. How many sisters, mothers, wives and daughters had his own actions left bereaved?

Before he could say anything, they were all three gone, leaving him standing by the bed. It had a light-blue embroidered counterpane, and over it hung another embroidered sampler, this time warning that 'For the wages of sin is death, but the gift of God is eternal life.

Romans 6:23.' By the window, which overlooked the front of the house, was a plain wooden dressing table with a white pitcher and ewer. The floorboards were waxed pine and partially covered by a small blue rag rug.

Eamonn thought it was the nicest room he'd ever seen. Simple, sunny, clean, and like a place he could sleep for years.

The women bustled back in, Elsie carrying a waistcoat and jacket, a shirt, a tie and a pair of trousers over her arm, and Constance with a pair of socks, suspenders and some underwear. Amazingly the old woman didn't seem at all embarrassed at handing over the undergarments; her innocence was total and her mind was clean. Dorothea stood behind her aunts, holding a pair of men's brogues, her grey eyes regarding him cautiously.

'Now then, Thaddeus was a little more rotund than you are, Mr Cullen,' Elsie said, appraising his body, 'but we found a belt and suspenders, so you should be fine. We'll have Jim take up some hot water for you to wash in the bathroom, and when you are ready, please come down to the dining room. We have steel-cut oats, boiled eggs from our own hens and hot coffee.'

'Thank you both so much, Mrs...?' He knew they were unlikely to be married women, but best to assume they were.

'Miss – misses actually. We are the Misses Harticoote.' Elsie blushed, and he got a glimpse of what they must have been like as girls, pretty and innocent, just like their niece.

'Well, I want to thank you both – you've been so kind. I'll take my clothes to be laundered once I've cleaned up, and I'll ensure your brother's things are returned in perfect condition.'

'Don't mind that. Dorothea will take care of your laundry for you, Mr Cullen,' Constance fussed around him. 'And I was thinking Jim's brother has a car repair shop – he might be able to go check on your vehicle for you?'

Eamonn made sure his face gave nothing away. 'Wonderful. If you tell me where that is, I can go there after breakfast and take him to where the car is and please God no one has stolen it in the meantime.'

'Marvellous. Now we must let you freshen up. Breakfast begins at eight and we serve till nine, so if you'd like to take a nap first, then you'll still have time. Dorothea can wake you at a quarter to nine.'

A wave of exhaustion almost floored him. All he could think about was crawling into that bed. He couldn't do it without washing, though; he'd destroy the lovely clean linen.

'Thank you, ladies. I'll take a wash, and maybe I will rest a bit. I can't thank you enough.'

'Our pleasure, Mr Cullen. You are very welcome.'

He washed and shaved in the large functional bathroom – they'd even supplied a razor and some shaving soap – and dressed in the clothes of poor old Thaddeus. He smiled as he saw how his initials, TRH, were neatly embroidered into everything, even his underwear.

When he returned to the room, he found his old clothing gone. The grey-eyed niece must have taken them to launder them. His wallet, gun and knife he'd brought to the bathroom with him, and now he looked for somewhere to hide them. A plain polished writing box sat on a small desk facing the window, with a key in the brass lock. He put his belongings in there and pocketed the key.

It felt like turning the key on his past life.

CHAPTER 28

ETER

THE CONTRACT WAS DRAWING to a close, and there had been no offer yet either from Maud Flynn to renew it or from Tibbet to find them another show in America.

'Talk to Carlos,' May had suggested. 'He's got contacts.'

Peter hadn't been able to bring himself to do it, not even for the good of the show, not even for his dreams.

So May had taken it upon herself and came back with the news that if the cabaret wasn't going to get its contract renewed, then Carlos would probably stay in America with his band, but he wasn't interested in bringing the whole show along with him. Only Aida Gonzalez, as lead dancer, maybe in an off-Broadway show. And perhaps he'd bring Benita, who, being Cuban, had a good grasp of flamenco.

'It's an awful nuisance losing them,' she said to Peter gently. 'They're so popular with the crowds, and Benita is turning out to be a lovely dancer. But I suppose we can't stand in their way.'

Peter couldn't say anything. He just stood, looking out of the window of Number Nine, staring down the road at the sea, the endless sea.

'I'm surprised he wants to bring Benita, to be honest,' said May, moving around the room, tidying up some tea things. 'I always thought they didn't like each other. They've barely exchanged a word since she joined the show – if one comes into the room, the other gets up and goes out.'

He shrugged. He didn't give two hoots about the mysterious relationship between Carlos and Benita, or why they avoided each other but were somehow in cahoots.

'I'm going down to the post office.' He picked up his hat and left the house, leaving May sighing very loudly and pointedly behind him.

'Peter?' Aida was standing on the step of Number Seven. 'Peter, can we talk?'

He walked on past her.

'Peter!'

He turned and looked at her. She was in bare feet, wearing a thin red dress thrown on carelessly, as if she'd just hurried out of bed. 'Peter, I wanted to say –'

'You don't need to say anything,' he responded coldly. 'I've heard all about it already, and if you want to abandon the cabaret for something else, I won't stop…'

The Spanish woman's eyes flashed fire, and she stormed back into the house before he could finish the sentence.

Going to the post office was just his excuse to get out of the house – Kathleen's weekly letter had arrived yesterday – but there was an envelope there waiting for him after all, with a Winslow stamp. Eamonn had finally got in touch after having been gone for weeks without a word.

It was a long letter, written in Irish as usual. Eamonn never could get his head around the fact that Peter was hopeless at his own country's language.

After a turn up and down the seafront, cursing himself for being so bad-tempered with Aida, who didn't deserve it, he brought Eamonn's letter back to Number Nine and asked May to read it out to him. Maybe it would contain some good news for a change.

'Dear Peter,' read May. She sat in the armchair by the empty fireplace, while Peter stood looking out of the window again, his hands clasped behind his back.

'I'm sorry I wasn't in touch before, but time got away from me. I know I left in a hurry, and I apologise for that, but I suppose you're used to me coming and going. Anyway, I had an appointment to keep in Strathmere for a job as an encyclopaedia salesman. I didn't mention it to you in case it fell through, but I got it all right, and it was going very well, very good money, until I broke down on the road and had to walk miles in the rain to this little place called Corncrake. I was soaked to the skin, but two ladies, the Misses Harticoote, they have a small hotel and they took me in and fed me, may God be good to them.

'I had to leave the books in the car, but their man Jim had a brother with a repair shop, and we set off in his van to find the car, but could we find it? No. Someone had spirited it away, encyclopaedias and all. Bad cess to whoever it was.'

'Oh, poor Eamonn.' May sighed.

'So I rang my boss from the phone in the hotel, and he said don't come back again. He was raging, said I should never have left the books unattended, but I don't know – in Ireland who would steal a car and load of encyclopaedias? They'd never get away with it. But then of course Ireland is a small place and everyone knows everyone, and America is a continent and thieves can move from one state to the other and never get recognised, no more than if an Irishman ran off to Timbuktu.

'So there I was, stuck, no car, no job, a bit of money but that's all, and the ladies were so kind to me. They gave me a job as the hotel gardener and keeping the grounds of the local church. It's a Quaker establishment, very plain, no gold or incense or anything, but it's peaceful, Peter, and it's nice to have a bit of peace. Sometimes I think Corncrake is the most peaceful place I've ever been in my life.

'And talking of peace, there's a girl here' – May stopped for a moment, then cleared her throat and carried on – 'a girl here who is very peaceful as well. Her name is Dorothea, and she's the niece of the Misses Harticootes, but more like a daughter to them because her mother is dead. She's a shy thing and rather young but pretty enough, and the way it came about was there was a dance at the village hall and there was no one to take her, and her aunts sort of pushed me to take her. I owed them so much, I couldn't say no, so I did and that started it.'

Again May stopped to clear her throat, then returned to reading, her voice still a bit hoarse. 'And like I said, Peter, she's a peaceful girl and it got me thinking, maybe that's what I need. There's a little clapboard house for sale not far from the hotel. It's small, but it has a tyre tied with a rope to a tree in the garden – or the yard as they call it here – and a swing set, and it got me thinking about a family of my own.'

Here May stopped again and swallowed. It was probably the pollen, Peter thought; she sometimes got hay fever.

'And the long and the short of it is, we're engaged to be married, Peter. And while you're still in Atlantic City, I'd like to bring Dorothea to meet you, and get your blessing, and May's too, of course.'

May's eyes were watering and her voice sounded hoarse, and Peter, who was keen to hear the rest of the letter, went to fetch her a glass of lemonade from the kitchen. When he came back, she gulped down the lemonade and blew her nose.

'I'm sorry. Reading this much has made my throat dry. It's coming to an end now.'

'Constance and Elsie, they're the two Misses Harticootes – we're on first-name terms now – are delighted and say they might retire early – they're both in their seventies! – and leave the hotel to me and Dorothea and move into the clapboard house themselves to not be in our way, and we might do it that way for a while. I never thought of myself as a hotel manager, but of course Dorothea was brought up to it.

'Now talking of first-name terms, I have a confession to make. When I saw the place was a Quaker place and I was still trying to get them to take in a poor man with no luggage at seven in the morning, I told them my name was Edward, not Eamonn, so to seem more East Coast and less… Well, you know Catholics have a bad reputation for fighting and stuff, so… Anyway, don't be surprised if Dorothea calls me Edward. You don't have to follow suit. She knows now ye're all a bunch of wild Irishmen and will call me the Irish way. Poor Dorothea. She is very nervous about the idea of Atlantic City and Catholics and actors and things – like I said, she's a quiet little Quaker bird with grey feathers – but I assured her your act is as clean as anything, and she's heard of Maud Flynn and that she's a devout woman even if she's a Catholic, so that was a consolation to her.

'Anyway, I hope you like her…'

'Et cetera, et cetera,' said May, throwing the letter aside onto the table with a sour expression.

'What's wrong, May? I thought you'd be happy for him?'

'I am, but it's just so typical of him – nothing for ages and then this madness, marrying a girl he barely knows.'

'Ah, don't be cross with him. I suppose it crept up on him.' Peter smiled.

Eamonn's news had really lifted his spirits. He couldn't understand why May wasn't delighted as well; she was always saying how his brother needed to sort himself out, get a girl and settle down.

'I don't know. She sounds a bit milk and watery, doesn't she?'

'Give her a chance. We haven't even met her yet.'

'And calling himself Edward. I mean, for goodness' sake…'

'It's hard when people are used to calling you one thing to ask them suddenly to call you another. When she hears all his family and friends calling him Eamonn, that will change things. But come on, May, never mind the English name – Eamonn's not suddenly forgotten he's Irish. He just wants a quiet life, so why not be pleased for him?'

He picked up the letter from the table and folded it into its envelope, which May had also discarded in her annoyance. 'And I'm sure he is very serious about this girl,' he added. 'He's certainly never gone as far as getting engaged before. I was beginning to think he never would.'

He hoped he was right about that. Eamonn would have to love this girl a lot. It was hard to imagine his brother being settled for very long; he'd need a strong rope to hold him.

CHAPTER 29

AMONN

'She doesn't like me, Edward.'

'Of course she likes you, Dorothea. How could anyone not like you? You're a dote,' said Eamonn firmly. 'And May is very respectable herself, so she likes how respectable you are as well.'

They were walking along the Boardwalk towards the Ocean Diamond, his fiancé's hand tucked into his arm, and she was glancing nervously around at the holiday crowds. It was mainly older people now as the children had returned to school, but still bustling and busy. It was as far from Corncrake as anyone could imagine, the very opposite of peace.

That morning Aisling and Remy had terrified the life out of her. They had rushed up with a big bucket of crabs they'd caught off the pier using bacon rinds from breakfast. The creatures kept trying to climb out, making Dorothea squeal in terror. Gertrude had panted up behind them very crossly and apologised, with a particularly hard look at Aisling. Remy she seemed to excuse for bad behaviour because he was a boy, but she clearly felt that Aisling should behave better because she was a girl. The nanny told her off in German about the crabs. Aisling seemed to understand her perfectly well but answered her in Irish…and then, with a glance at her uncle, switched into what sounded to his ears like Spanish.

'What's she saying?' Dorothea had whispered in terror. 'Is she speaking in tongues?' She seemed to think Aisling was an imp from hell.

'No, Irish, and she's saying she'll try to be better.' Eamonn grinned as Remy and Aisling rushed off again, pursued by Gertrude. Judging by what Aisling had said in Irish, though, before she'd remembered Eamonn could understand her and switched to the language Ramon had taught her, the whole thing was just swear words.

Dorothea was also frightened by the smutty postcards on sale and the general Sodom and Gomorrah feel to the whole place. He was beginning to regret bringing her here, though she was comforted by the beach police who made the lady bathers wear swimsuits with long sleeves and leggings, and she was looking forward to meeting the famously upright Maud Flynn and her niece, Beatrice, who had invited them to tea along with May and Peter to 'celebrate the end of the season'.

The end of the season for Cullen's Celtic Cabaret, anyway, because the cabaret had only another week to run.

In the foyer of the hotel, Peter came to greet them. Eamonn found his brother very subdued these days, though he had been very welcoming to Dorothea. May not so much – Eamonn had caught her rolling her eyes a few times when Dorothea flinched or squawked at anything unusual.

'Hello, Dorothea. Hello, Eamonn. May is in the hotel lounge –'

'Oh!' Dorothea gave a frightened scream at the sight of a dwarf dressed as a leprechaun wandering across the foyer. It was a sight that made Eamonn want to quietly scream himself, but it was hardly scary.

Being with the Harticootes had made Eamonn realise something about May. He was a working-class Dublin man, and she was a middle-class Dublin woman. He'd always thought it was just respectability that kept her glued to her marriage, the fear of scandal. But now he could see she wasn't 'respectable' at all, not in the way Dorothea was, too afraid to take risks. May was a risk-taker. She was as brave as he himself, it's just she was determined to do what was right. And she was practical too. She wasn't a woman to faint at a mouse. She would stand up to a lion if it got her what she wanted, and what she wanted was the best for everyone, not just May Cullen.

Though it had to be done her way, of course.

May was seated in the lounge when Peter brought them in, and she had already ordered coffee and a silver tiered platter of little iced cakes. She greeted Dorothea with a kiss on the cheek and didn't quite meet Eamonn's eyes. When Dorothea told her about the crabs, she covered her mouth with her hand and said, 'How terrifying for you – crabs are notoriously dangerous. I'll have strong words with her later, I promise.' But this time her eyes did meet Eamonn's, over Dorothea's head, and they danced with amusement.

There followed some awkward chat, in which Dorothea told Peter and May all about the hotel in Corncrake and how she and Eamonn were going to be running it together. 'It's a nice, quiet, family hotel, like this one. Like Miss Flynn we are very in favour of Prohibition,' she twittered away softly, and once more May caught Eamonn's eye with a flicker of amusement.

Eamonn looked around him as he listened. He'd been in such a whirl on his last brief sojourn here that he hadn't taken the place in. The Ocean Diamond might be a family hotel like the Corncrake, but there the comparison ended. This family hotel was only for very well-heeled families. It was the fanciest place Eamonn had ever seen in his life.

After half an hour, the ever-busy Maud Flynn finally appeared.

Somehow the rich, powerful woman looked nothing like Eamonn had imagined. No pearls or diamonds to display her wealth, only a crucifix around her neck that exuded propriety. She was plainly dressed in a brown and mustard tweed suit, a skirt and a jacket buttoned to the neck, with the collar of a cream blouse showing underneath. She had a sensible hairdo, pinned back, no frivolous dye, just the natural greying of her once-mousy hair, and a broad, open face that must have been plain even when she was young.

Before she had quite reached their table, she was waylaid by a venerable matronly type who congratulated her on her work for the Temperance League. As Maud accepted her good wishes, the younger woman who had been walking with her came towards them by herself; Peter whispered to him that this was Maud Flynn's niece.

The poor girl, God love her, took after her aunt, meaty more than fat, and plain too, in spectacles, though her mousy hair was nicely cut and she was dressed in a frock suited to her age. Peter had mentioned that May had taken her in hand.

'Good afternoon, May, Peter. Good afternoon...?'

'Miss Beatrice Flynn, may I introduce my brother, Eamonn Cullen?' Peter said, standing. 'And his fiancé, Dorothea Harticoote.'

'A pleasure.' She shook hands with them both. 'Nice to meet you.' The spectacles she wore made her eyes look enormous, and she looked at Eamonn for a fraction too long, as if trying to place him.

A vision suddenly came to him of that moment in the sweetcorn fields, when the girl had come to the side of the truck and looked up at him...

No. What a ridiculous thought. It couldn't possibly be her; he was imagining things. He hadn't even got a good look at that other girl. It was dark, the rain had been torrential, she'd barely said a word to him before the shooting had started... After sitting down again, he picked up his coffee, his mind racing.

Charlie had called Maud 'Fraud Flynn'. But that was just a joke about her being a very devout woman, one of those who sat up in front at Mass but was running such a profitable establishment.

Did he seriously think for one second it was possible that Maud Flynn's niece had arranged the ambush? Murdered his old friend Charlie Horgan? Defrauded Doherty? Stolen hundreds of bottles of whiskey for herself?

Absurd. Of course it was a different girl.

'Oh, excuse me. That skirting board has a mark – I must mention it to my aunt.'

Beatrice Flynn went back to her aunt and pointed something out. They went over to inspect the dirty skirting board, shaking their heads, then called over a passing waiter, who nodded and hurried away, presumably to fetch a cloth. Eamonn couldn't see anything wrong with the skirting from where he was sitting, but maybe it was a very small smudge. Standards were very high in the Ocean Diamond, the whole place so spotless, you could eat your dinner off the floor. As the waiter ran off, Maud Flynn glanced over towards their table with a smile, signalling she would be there in a moment. She turned back to her niece and continued talking and then glanced their way again. Did something cross her face? A split second of something? What, though? He didn't know. His mind was playing strange tricks with him today.

Maud Flynn and her niece walked over to the table, and the older woman shook hands with Peter and kissed May and then Dorothea on the cheek. And then she came to Eamonn, gripping and holding his hand. 'Mr Cullen, a pleasure to finally meet you.' She beamed. 'Your reputation precedes you.'

'Nice to meet you too, Miss Flynn.' He wasn't sure quite what she meant, but her warm, open smile held no threat.

'A hero of the old country, walking among us. We're honoured.'

Ah, so she knew about his exploits in Ireland. He'd wanted to leave it all behind, but they loved that sort of thing here in America, where they were removed from the cruel reality of it and didn't understand the importance in war of silence and discretion.

'I did nothing, Miss Flynn.'

'Nonsense. You were a hero of the war against the English.'

Dorothea threw him a startled glance. He'd never mentioned being in a war to his fiancé; she was a Quaker and would be horrified. He shot her an apologetic smile and squeezed her hand, wondering how he was going to explain his way out of this one.

'I see you've met my niece, Miss Beatrice Flynn?' Maud asked him as she seated herself beside him; Beatrice was on the other side of her, her head down, fiddling with a lace handkerchief that was embroidered with green shamrocks all around the outside.

'I had the pleasure for the first time just now.' He smiled at the shy, mousy girl, who was definitely not the one who had ordered the men around in the field.

'And are you and your fiancé enjoying yourself here in our little city?'

'We are, we're having a marvellous time. And your hotel is charming.'

'Well, your brother here is being lured back by the leprechauns and the crocks of gold, it would seem. We were charming but not charming enough.' She adopted a look of genuine sadness at the loss of the cabaret. 'I wish you would stay with us, Peter.'

Eamonn was puzzled. He knew that Peter had hoped the summer residency would turn into something else, but it clearly hadn't, yet here was Maud Flynn making out like Peter would be welcome to stay, only he was choosing to go back to Ireland.

'Now, Aunt Maud, you know we have no slot for them. Mr Tibbet has other acts that need to be given a turn,' murmured Beatrice as she twisted her shamrock handkerchief.

'So you keep telling me, my sweet child, and Mr Tibbet is always saying one has to keep things fresh. But now I think about it, Cullen's Celtic Cabaret is so much better than anything else that man has on his books.'

Eamonn glanced at Peter in surprise. His brother was sitting there perplexed, as was May.

'And all your performers are so abstemious, respectful and devout. I'm reminded of Philippians, where we are told that the children of God, who are surrounded by the crooked and corrupt, shine like stars in the world. I know you will bring your cabaret from strength to strength wherever you are – you have the knack of it – but if you could see your way to staying with us a while longer, just until Harp Devereaux is back in the next ten months?'

Peter blinked at her in shock. 'I... I...'

The woman turned to May with a broad smile. 'May, Peter tells me you are the beating heart of the operation?'

May seemed equally stunned by this turn of events. 'I don't know about that, Miss Flynn.'

'Ah, somebody has to run things, May, and someone with a head like yours on her shoulders is what every business needs. So what do you think about staying, May? We would be so sad to see you all go.' The woman was powerful, overbearing and thoroughly charming. 'Enzo, we adore him, swinging upside down from his trapeze, and dear Two-Soups, so hilarious, and Maggie and her singing partner, the one people call the baron, so amusing. And that Spanish fellow and his guitar, and the Indian, and that stunning couple, Aida and Carlos. I'm sure Carlos – I know he's been talking to Mr Tibbet about another show – will be keen to stay with you if the cabaret stays.'

Beatrice was looking at her aunt in horror. 'No... But you said the cabaret was going home to Ireland.'

'Well, I've changed my mind, dear. Now go and fetch the contract on my desk.'

Beatrice went red, then white. 'But that was for Weber and Fields...'

'Well, it's not any more. Be quick!'

With a smothered sob, Beatrice jumped up and fled.

Maud Flynn didn't turn a hair at her niece's distress. She glanced at the ornate clock over the reception desk as they waited and called for more coffee and cakes. When Beatrice came back, red-eyed, with a sheaf of papers, she spread them out on the low table, scratched out and rewrote a few names with a gold fountain pen, then pushed them across towards Peter with the pen.

'Sign here...and here...and here...' she said sweetly. 'Will we increase your share of the profits by fifteen percent? Yes, I think we will.' Taking the pen from Peter's shaking fingers, she corrected a couple of figures, then handed it back. 'Now, I'm sure that must be to your satisfaction, though Mr Tibbet will kill me.'

Peter glanced almost desperately at May, as if he had no idea what to do with this extraordinary good fortune. 'May?'

'Sign it, Peter,' she said quietly. It was hard to tell if she was happy or not, but her chin was determined and she had that light in her eye, the one she had when she knew she was doing things for the best.

Peter relaxed, and his gaze moved to Eamonn, and a huge, joyous smile spread across his boyish face. 'Well, brother, looks like we'll both be in America for a while.' And with a laugh and a flourish, he signed.

Maud Flynn stood up and offered everyone her hand once more; she held Eamonn's for a moment longer than the rest. 'It was lovely to meet you, Mr Cullen. And as a proud daughter of Ireland, I want to thank you for your service to our old country.' Her grip was firm, the eye contact sincere and overt. Then she was gone.

'Well, what was that all about?' May collapsed back in her chair with her hands clapped to her cheeks. 'What on earth possessed her? I wonder did Weber and Fields let her down? Oh, Peter...Peter...' She was almost having to gasp for air. 'It's so, so much money. An extra fifteen percent! Another ten months... What will we do? We'll have to have everyone come and visit, my parents, your mother, Connie, Kathleen... I'm sure Maud can help us with another lodging house to put them all up for a month or more. Nick's twins as well. We'll pay for them all! Peter, we're going to be rich...'

Already her mind was working, planning, making it all come together, while Eamonn's younger brother just sat staring into midspace. Though Eamonn had a feeling his brother was making calculations as well. Perhaps he was thinking about what Maud had said, about Carlos staying...

Dorothea leant in close to Eamonn, whispering, 'What did that woman mean, you were fighting the English?'

'It's a long story. I'll tell you later,' he whispered back.

'Quakers are peaceful people, Edward. We don't fight. Corncrake is a peaceful town.'

'I know that, Dorothea.' He made a mental note to get rid of the knife and the gun that were still hidden in the plain polished writing box, back at the hotel. All he'd brought with him from the box was his wallet, containing his passport and money.

'Will we go and tell everyone, Peter?' May jumped to her feet, beaming, holding out her hand to her husband. 'They'll all be taking their afternoon rest. They'll be over the moon! Oh, and Eamonn, why don't you take Dorothea to the beach? Gertrude must still be there with Remy and Aisling. Don't say anything about staying – I want to see her little face when we tell her.'

He got to his feet at once, even though his fiancé didn't look very happy about it. Of course, this was another wonderful thing about the contract being renewed – Aisling was going to be here in Atlantic City for the foreseeable future, and Corncrake wasn't far, so he'd see plenty of May's brilliant, headstrong little girl.

As the four of them walked out of the hotel, six policemen approached them in a group, guns on their hips.

'Mr Eamonn Cullen?' said the first of the policemen, a dull stolid-looking man with a small moustache, who looked from him to Peter.

Eamonn's heart sickened and his first instinct, well honed over the years, was to make a break for it. But he was there with Dorothea – he couldn't act like he was a gangster. And maybe this was nothing. Peter and May both shot him questioning looks.

'I'm Eamonn Cullen. Is everything all right?'

'They must have found your car, Edward,' twittered Dorothea, clinging to his arm.

The policeman glanced at her blankly and then looked back at Eamonn. 'Can you come with us please, Mr Cullen?'

'I don't understand.' Although he did. He had been fooling himself. Of course it had been Beatrice at the ambush. She had recognised him. He'd gone soft. In the old days, he would have been out of the door at the first sign of something not quite right, but he'd been so determined to settle down, to change his future, to have peace in his life, that he hadn't wanted to believe trouble when it was staring him in the face.

'We have a few questions, Mr Cullen, and we'd like you to come to the station with us.'

Dorothea piped up. 'Is this about my fiancé's car that was stolen a few miles from Corncrake?'

A younger policeman, hardly more than a teenager, answered her.

He seemed to be enjoying himself. 'No, miss, it's not about a car. It's about four dead men, horribly murdered, the lot of them, but they were found a few miles from Corncrake all right.'

'Oh my goodness…' Dorothea dropped Eamonn's arm and staggered back, reeling like she might faint, while Peter went white as a sheet and May shot Eamonn a look of pure horror while taking hold of Dorothea to steady her.

'Sir,' said the more stolid of the policemen, 'it will assist us greatly if you could come with us. Failure to comply will mean we will have no choice but to place you under arrest.' He had Eamonn's elbow now and was leading him away. There were three cars waiting at the kerb, and even more policemen inside them. They weren't taking any chances.

He looked back as he went, his eyes on May and no one else. Her brown eyes held his, her face fierce as she pressed Dorothea against her.

'I didn't kill those men, May. I swear on my life.' He didn't care what anyone else thought, but he needed May Cullen to know the truth.

Within seconds, he was in the back seat of the middle vehicle and was being driven away. And all his dreams of living out the rest of his life in quiet, uneventful Corncrake with a quiet, uneventful wife collapsed around him.

CHAPTER 30

AY

May sat in the waiting area of Trenton State Prison as instructed, until a uniformed guard led her through a door and into another room. Here she was made to turn out her pockets and hand over her hat, coat and handbag. Her body was patted down, and only when the guard was sure she had no weapon or anything else concealed on her person was she told to wait.

The room held no furniture whatsoever; it was just a stone square of ten feet by ten.

Eamonn was being held in this terrifying place, the oldest prison in New Jersey and nearly the oldest in the whole of America.

The prison had said only Eamonn Cullen's fiancé or mother could be granted a visiting order on compassionate grounds, but poor Bridie was in Dublin and knew nothing, and as for that pathetic Dorothea, she'd pulled off her engagement ring and thrown it into the sea and retreated in tears to the peaceful town of Corncrake, where no doubt she'd marry someone as peaceful as herself, as she should have done in the first place, instead of a soldier and a bootlegger.

May was torn between being glad to see the silly woman go and furious at her for abandoning Eamonn in his hour of need. In the end she'd gone to the prison herself and announced she was Dorothea Harticoote of the Corncrake Hotel, Corncrake, near Winslow. She took off her wedding ring while keeping on her cheap silver engagement ring, the one she'd bought herself all those years ago, and she put on a silly, feeble voice and patted her eyes with a hanky a lot. They'd issued her a visiting order for the following Tuesday.

And now she was here, at nine in the morning.

Within minutes the heavy steel door opened and Eamonn, was led in by a middle-aged prison guard. He was in prison garb and hadn't shaved. When he saw her, he blinked, then said calmly, 'Dorothea.'

The door was locked behind them, and the middle-aged guard stood in the corner, gazing straight ahead.

'Edward,' she twittered, and hugged him, with a glance in the direction of the guard; she expected the man to object to physical contact, but he didn't.

'What are you doing here, Dorothea?'

'*As gaeilge.*'

He immediately switched to Irish. '*Cád atá tú ag déanamh?*'

She threw another look at the guard, to see if he minded them switching into a foreign language. He didn't object to this either, just turned to stare out of the barred window into the yard, his broad back to them. 'I'm sorry, but Dorothea refused to use her compassionate pass to visit you – she's gone back to Corncrake. I pretended to be her. Someone had to visit you and find out what's going on. We're sick with worry about you, all of us.'

He ran his hands through his thick black hair, a wild look about him. 'This is all wrong, May. I shouldn't be speaking to you. If I'd known it was you and not her, I wouldn't have come out of me cell.'

'Oh...' She swallowed and tears pricked in her eyes. She was mortified at herself. She'd assumed he wouldn't mind about that silly woman letting him down, but of course Dorothea was his fiancé, so he must love her...

He grabbed her hand. 'No, not like that. I just meant for your own safety. Of course I'd rather see you than her.'

She felt a burst of happiness then, but also guilt, because nothing about this awful situation should make her happy. 'What do you mean, for my own safety? Eamonn, you have to tell me what's going on here.'

'Listen and I will.' Holding her hand, he told her about looking for a job, and an offer of whiskey running, which he was only going to do once, then twice, then maybe five times at the most...and then a fatal, murderous ambush in the sweetcorn fields.

She felt faint as he described it. 'Eamonn, my God.'

He said humbly, 'I'm so sorry, May. I just wanted to try to make enough money to get a start here. I thought it was nothing, honestly.'

'It's not that. You could have died.' A horrible picture had forced its way into her head, of his cold, dead body dumped in the sweetcorn... She recovered herself; this was no time to go to pieces over something that might have been but wasn't. 'Anyway, we'll sort this out as quick as we can. I don't know what the sentences are for whiskey running, but you were hardly a kingpin. We'll get you a lawyer and –'

'It's worse than the bootlegging, May.'

She felt a surge of frustration and fear. 'God's sake, Eamonn, what else?'

'I'm going to trial for the four murders.' He dropped her hand and rubbed his own across his face, hard, like this was a nightmare from which he was trying to wake himself up.

She stood and stared at him, breathing raggedly, hardly able to believe her ears. 'No, but you said you didn't do it...'

'I didn't do it.'

'Then why...'

He shrugged and said bitterly, 'Sure they have to have someone to blame.'

Her breath caught in her throat. 'Eamonn, if they find you guilty of murder, they'll send you to the electric chair.'

He shrugged again, his eyes on the floor.

Why wasn't he trying harder to save himself? She grabbed hold of his arms and shook him; she had to knock some sense into him. 'Why aren't you saying anything? This is ridiculous! You have to tell the police you're innocent!'

He said in a low voice, 'The police are in their pay.'

'Whose pay? What do you mean? Do you know who's behind this?'

He said nothing.

This was extraordinary. 'God's sake, Eamonn, if you won't talk to the police, talk to the FBI!'

'Shh...' He glanced quickly towards the guard, who, hearing raised voices, had twisted to look at them.

She stepped back with a bright smile. 'Everything is fine, officer,' she said in English, and the man nodded and returned to looking out of the window. In Irish again, she hissed fiercely, 'You have to stop this nonsense. If whoever it is that you won't tell me about has got people in here threatening you, ask the FBI to be put in protective custody.'

His blue eyes were full of fear. 'You don't understand. It's not me they're threatening to kill, May. It's you. Maggie. Peter. Aisling. My family here in America.'

'Oh my God...' She was falling into an abyss, a sickening, sinking feeling in the pit of her stomach. She pulled herself together, straightened her shoulders. 'Right, I'll go to the FBI myself.'

'No!' He looked horrified. 'You mustn't do or say anything.'

'That's insane! I have to – you'll go to the chair.'

He shrugged again, with that small half smile that was all his own. 'I've messed up, May. It's all my own fault.'

'You should never have got mixed up in this, that's true, but I can't let you die...'

'You can. You must. For Peter. Maggie. For Aisling. Sure what's left for me in this world anyway? That dream of settling down – it won't work with you always in my mind. What's the point of living when I could do some good dying?'

'No, no, no.' She kept shaking her head. This was insane, ridiculous. She would sort this out, like she always sorted everything out. 'I'll find a way to get you out of this. We'll go back to Ireland right now, and then Aisling will be safe, and then you can tell them, I'll tell them – we'll both talk to the FBI.'

'But you can't leave America. You've signed a contract with Maud Flynn.'

'So what? We'll break it. I'll explain everything to her – she'll understand.'

'Say nothing to that witch!'

He spat the words with such venom, she was shaken. 'I don't understand… She's a good woman…'

'She's not a good woman. Promise me, May, not a word. Don't let her think you're going anywhere. Trust me.'

For a long few seconds, she stood there, trying to get her head around his irrational hatred for Peter's employer, Maud Flynn, the woman who had just given them their big break. 'Eamonn, you have to tell me the reason for this.'

'Just trust me.'

'I do trust you, but that's not the way I do things, Eamonn. You have to tell me something, anything, to help me understand. Why don't you want me to do this?'

He took a deep breath and cast a glance at the man by the window. Even though they were speaking in Irish, he dropped his voice. 'The girl in the sweetcorn field…'

'The one who led the ambush?'

'It was Beatrice.'

May pressed her hands to her head. Her heart thumped loudly in her chest; she seemed to hear water rushing through her ears. Beatrice involved in murder… 'You're telling me Maud's niece was behind this?'

'She's up to her neck in it, and her aunt.'

May felt weak with shock. Maud Flynn, daily Mass-goer, leading light of the temperance movement, owner of the most morally upright hotel and theatre in the entire city, was a crook and a gangster? The upright, squeaky-clean Maud Flynn?

'I can't believe this... I thought she was our benefactor. The new contract...it's worth so much...' And suddenly she understood. The absurdly generous offer was to make sure they stayed here, Eamonn's family, to buy his silence. Until he died.

'Don't say anything, May, please,' he begged.

She said through gritted teeth, 'I won't, and I won't tell her we're going, but I'm taking everyone home. And then I'll write to the FBI from Ireland myself, Eamonn, so you have to talk to them, tell them you're innocent, tell them everything you know.'

In his face, a glimmer of hope. 'But I'd have to know for certain you and Aisling are going to be safe...'

'We will be.'

'I'd die for you, May, without a second thought. And Aisling. I just know in my bones she's my daughter.' His blue eyes held her dark ones.

For a moment she hesitated, then she stepped forwards and threw her arms around him, kissing him, first on the cheek and then on the mouth. 'I love you,' she said.

'Oh, May.' He pressed his lips to hers.

The guard approached them. 'Time's up.'

'A moment.' She clung to him again, kissing him passionately as he kissed her back. Why not? It might be the last time. 'Come back to me, Eamonn, please,' she whispered, resting her forehead against his chest. 'I don't know what we can do about us, I...I just know I need you. It's all such a mess...but please, please, don't die...'

'Come on, miss.'

Eamonn dropped his arms, and she stepped back.

The taciturn guard led her through door after door and then into the yard, and then out through a small gate. As she walked out into the sunshine of New Jersey, she saw the hourly bus already waiting at its stop.

'*Slán*, May Cullen, *turas sábháilte*,' the guard called after her as she ran to catch it.

'*Go raibh maith agat*,' she called back automatically.

And then, as the prison gate slammed behind her, she realised what she'd done.

CHAPTER 31

AY

ALL THE WAY back to Atlantic City, she prayed to God that the guard didn't know what she and Eamonn had been saying.

'Goodbye, safe journey,' he'd said in Irish, and she had thanked him in the same language.

Maybe he was the sort of man who only knew a few phrases of Irish?

She was fooling herself. He'd called her May Cullen; he must have been listening to know she wasn't Dorothea Harticoote. She knew he was on the telephone to the Ocean Diamond right now, telling Maud Flynn that May Cullen secretly planned to get her family out of the country as soon as possible, and that Aisling was Eamonn's daughter, and the man would do anything for her, even go to the chair…

You idiot, you idiot, she raged at herself. And at the same time, she wanted to strangle Eamonn for his stupid recklessness, though her body and lips still burnt from that last passionate kiss.

She shouldn't have kissed him, not that way. But he'd said he was ready to go to the electric chair for her, for Aisling.

At last the bus reached the seafront, she jumped off two stops early and ran and ran.

The scene that greeted her at Atlantic Terrace caused the breath to catch in her throat. Nick and Maggie were sitting on the steps of Number Nine, when they should have been at morning rehearsal, and they were comforting Remy, who was in floods of tears.

'What is it? What's wrong?' she cried as she rushed up.

'May, we're here waiting for you.' Nick's rushed towards her, his eyes were wild with horror. 'Remy came back from the beach alone. He says Gertrude got into a car with Aisling and just left him there.'

May thought she was going to be sick. Nick's words refused to land; she heard them, but her brain would not absorb them.

'What? What are you talking about! They…where did they go?'

'We d-d-don't know.' Nick was distraught as he held his sobbing son. 'It's happened an hour ago. Everyone is trying to find out. Magus and Two-Soups and Ramon are gone to speak to any one on the beach who might have seen what happened, and Aida and Carlos have gone to the police. Peter and Enzo ran to the hotel to see if Maud Flynn knows anything. It was her who recommended Gertrude as Aisling and Remy's nanny. Where did she find her? She can't be a real nanny! How could a real nanny leave Remy unattended like that?'

May opened her mouth to speak but closed it again. No sound would come. Her mouth would not produce saliva. She could barely hear what they were saying to her. Her darling little Aisling, so bright and funny and friendly. She knew not to go off with any stranger, but this was no stranger who had abducted her – it was her own nanny, who worked for Maud Flynn, and Maud Flynn was…

She felt a wave of sickening guilt. She and Peter had brought their daughter into danger by wanting the bright lights of America, wanting to be rich. May's parents were right; they should have left their daughter safe in Dublin, safe in school.

'Aisling didn't want to get in the car!' wailed Remy, clinging to his father. 'She said the men in there were strangers, but Nanny Gertrude dragged her in! We never liked Nanny Gertrude! Aisling said bad words to her in Irish and Spanish and everything. We thought she didn't know, but maybe she knew – maybe she's taken Aisling away to be punished! She pulled Aisling in, and I ran here as fast as I could, and a car nearly knocked me down!'

'Oh, Remy, Remy,' groaned Nick, as Maggie crossed the room and threw her arms around May.

'I'm sure it's all a misunderstanding. They'll be back very soon.'

May sobbed on Maggie's shoulder. 'It's not a misunderstanding…'

'What?'

But before she could explain, a police car pulled up to the kerb, and to her despair, she knew now she would have to waste precious time pretending to know nothing, because she knew every word she spoke would get back to Maud Flynn and somehow that would make things worse.

An officer got out of the car and came over to her; he looked Irish, red hair and pale skin, stocky. Another policeman got out of the car behind him.

'Mrs May Cullen?' asked the first, looking from her to Maggie.

'That's me,' said May, in a voice that didn't sound to her like her own.

'I'm sorry, ma'am,' he said, taking out his notebook, 'but we've had a lady in with us, very insistent, who says your nanny has gone off with your daughter in an unauthorised fashion.'

'Yes, I believe she's been kidnapped.' She fought back panic as she said the word, but her knees weakened.

Maggie tightened her arm around her. 'Come into the house,' she said gently. 'You need to sit down. I'll make you tea – you have to have something. Please, officer, come into the house.'

'Yes…yes…' She let Maggie lead her inside. She did need to sit down or she would faint. Above all, she needed to think. Maud Flynn must have Aisling. She had kidnapped her to buy May's silence, until it was too late for Eamonn.

She couldn't say anything. She had to pretend not to know. She would have to rescue her child without the help of the police.

'Mrs Cullen, you are' – the officer consulted the notebook – 'Ayslynn's mother?'

'Ash-ling,' she said automatically. 'It's pronounced Ash-ling.' She was used to people mispronouncing her daughter's name.

'Yes, Aisling's mother?' He stood over her as she sat in the armchair by the dead fire, where Maggie had placed her before hurrying off to make tea. 'Is there any reason you can think of why your own nanny would want to kidnap your daughter? Have you made any enemies?'

Nick had followed them into the room, and burst out indignantly, 'No…no, of course not. We've only been here a few months. We've been performing at the Ocean Diamond on the Boardwalk.'

'I've seen your show, took the wife for her birthday. She loved it.' The second officer, who did not look old enough to have a wife, spoke for the first time. He couldn't even grow a beard yet, and pimples covered his chin. 'Maud Flynn has such wonderful shows put on, and all so clean. And she's a great woman in the temperance movement. My wife is a great supporter of the League.'

'Thank you, Officer,' said May calmly, digging her fingers into the arms of the chair. She wanted to scratch his face and scream that this was no time for lying pleasantries, that she was sure they knew very well who had taken her daughter. 'Would you like a description of my daughter and the nanny?'

'Your friend Aida Gonzalez already supplied us with the description. Now, I know this is a very puzzling thing to happen, and I assure you we'll do all we can to find them and put your mind at rest, but could you tell me where you were today?'

She didn't bother to lie. They already knew. 'I was visiting my brother-in-law, Eamonn Cullen, in Trenton Prison.'

The officers shared a look, and the first of them closed his notebook and put it in his jacket pocket.

'Is that it?' Nick was astonished. 'The interview is over?'

'I think we've all we need,' said the officer easily. 'We'll use all the resources at our disposal, so try not to worry. We'll make every effort to find the little girl.'

After they had left, Maggie brought her tea with a dash of illicit brandy and then took Remy away for an ice cream to comfort him because the boy was getting hysterical again, leaving Nick with May.

'Will I go and tell Peter you're here?' he asked, hunkering down beside her, his big hand on her knee.

She looked at him, making a decision. 'Yes, fetch Peter and give us a little time together. And while I'm talking to him, gather everyone. The whole of the cabaret. Bring them here.'

'The chorus girls as well?' He looked confused.

'Yes. Peter first, and then the rest. Can you do that? Gather our inner circle, and don't say anything to anyone else. Come back here with them, but tell them no talking.'

'May, do you know something?'

'I just need people we trust now, Nick. Please, gather everyone, and I'll explain everything then.'

As soon as he'd gone, May stood up and walked around the room, her hands cupping her elbows. She kept glancing at the clock, each second ticking by. Aisling would be held by these gangsters until Eamonn was put to death for murder. And her hands were tied. She had no proof of anything, and if she had, she didn't dare tell anyone, for the sake of her daughter. Who Maud now knew was Eamonn's daughter.

After what felt like hours – but it was only fifteen minutes – Peter came in, and he looked like he hadn't slept in days.

He came straight up to her and took her hand, fighting back tears. 'We should never have brought her to America. I'm so sorry, May, so sorry. It's my fault. It was my dream. Maud says...' His throat must have been dry because his voice cracked and broke.

'Yes, what did Maud have to say?' May asked, trying to stay calm, pouring him a glass of water from a jug on the table.

He gulped it down and was able to speak again. 'She feels so guilty for recommending that woman. Gertrude was always saying how much she adored Aisling. Maud thinks maybe she is one of these women desperate for a child of her own – maybe she's just deluded herself into thinking she'd make her a better mother. Maud has promised the police will spare no resources hunting them down – they'll search everywhere, and they'll find her. She called them on the phone while I was there. She gave them instructions...'

May gently disengaged her hand from his and went to the sideboard to put the gramophone on; Vivaldi's 'The Four Seasons' filled the air.

'Music? Now?' Peter looked at her like she was mad.

'Just in case anyone is listening,' she said. She'd learnt her lesson from the guard.

'But...'

'Come and stand by me.'

He did, and under cover of Vivaldi, she explained everything Eamonn had told her. Never mind about Gertrude being some sort of desperate barren woman. She was working for Maud Flynn, and the Flynns had ambushed the convoy, and arranged the murders, and kidnapped Aisling. 'And Peter, it's all my fault. I didn't realise the guard spoke Irish...'

He was reeling, white with shock. 'Ah, May, that's just too outlandish. Maud Flynn, the pioneer of total abstinence, who just made our fortune for us. Maud Flynn is running booze, murdering people, kidnapping... No, this must be wrong.'

May took hold of his shoulders, willing him to believe her. 'The girl who stopped the car was Beatrice, Eamonn is sure of it. The Flynns mean him to die, Peter. He was keeping quiet to protect us. But now they know that he's talked to me, and they've taken our daughter to keep me quiet as well, so Eamonn will go to the chair for murder instead of them.'

He stared at her for a long moment, and she could see her words sinking in. He groaned then. 'We have to go to the police.'

'No. The police are in their pocket, Eamonn says. The only ones that can help us are the FBI. That Federal Agent Joel Kopeck, he's in town still, and I'm going to find him and tell him everything.'

'Joel Kopeck...' The colour came back into his face.

'But not yet.' She put her hand on his arm. 'We have to find Aisling first. She's nearby, Peter, I just know it. She's somewhere in Maud

Flynn's territory. We're going to find her, and as soon as she is safe, I'll tell Kopeck all I know.'

'But why not now...'

'Because if the FBI get involved, Maud's gang will spirit Aisling away, even do worse. Anything to hide the crime. Eamonn as well – they have people in Trenton Prison. They will kill him.'

'How can we find her if the police won't help us?' His face was grey with despair.

May picked up a framed photograph from the sideboard. One of Aisling, taken on the Boardwalk, with a huge smile on her face and a dripping ice cream in her hand.

'I have a plan,' she said simply.

CHAPTER 32

IDA

THEY HAD TO FIND AISLING.

The child was the light of Peter's life; it would kill him if she was lost.

And Aisling was the light of her life as well, she realised. She'd always thought it was just because she was Peter's daughter, but over the years, she had come to love her like her own child. Once, seven years ago, Aida had surrendered herself to torture and possibly death to save Aisling's life before she was even born. Since then she had watched Peter fall in love with his newborn baby, and for that baby's sake, Aida had made sure Peter fixed his marriage and stayed faithful to May. And the little girl was a reward in herself. She was so chatty and pretty and wild, and so clever. She soaked up Spanish from Aida like a sponge, she spoke Cherokee with Magus, she could spin around on a trapeze with Enzo, and she was able to make a perfect dovetail joint courtesy of Two-Soups and his carpentry skills.

The police had been useless, shrugging their shoulders and

asking why a nanny would abduct a child, saying that Gertrude must have taken her somewhere, for an ice cream or something. They clearly thought Aida was making a fuss about nothing, and it had taken ages to persuade them to get off their butts and take it seriously.

After the police had grudgingly taken the details, she and Carlos joined the others on the beach and Boardwalk, asking everyone they could find if they knew anything, had they seen a German nanny pulling an Irish child into a car, had they heard a little girl scream and fight with the woman, did they see a licence plate, did they recognise the men in the car?

The Jewish café owner, the ice cream vendors, the seller of cheeseburgers, the proprietors of various shows and establishments, all shook their heads. It must all have happened so fast.

Though the Jewish man remembered Nick's son running by the Solitary Oyster in hysterics. 'I went after him to see what was the matter,' Albie Fierstein explained. 'The silly boy ran into the road, and I just managed to stop a car that was nearly going to hit him. The driver didn't see the boy, but he saw me, thanks be to God. But then the child disappeared up the road where I know you all live, so I thought, well, he's safe now, and I didn't like to get him in trouble. I just thought to myself, the next time I see him, I'll have a word about traffic – probably he's not very used to it in Ireland. He told me he lives in a very big boring place with fields all around and only one car, but he loves the horses...'

'Silly old fool,' grumbled Carlos as they left the café. 'He never stops talking.'

The Cuban was getting bored; he didn't seem to believe Aisling had been abducted any more than the police.

'I'm sure the nanny just brought her home with her or something, and Remy probably just refused to go with them and ran off – he always wants his own way. You'll see – they'll be back any moment now,' he kept saying, and Aida hoped he was right. Maybe he was. It made more sense than kidnapping a child.

'When she turns up and everyone calms down, you'll talk to Peter about us, yes?' asked Carlos, who always preferred to talk about himself.

Even though the cabaret's contract had been renewed, Carlos was still keen to move on. He didn't like sharing the limelight with the likes of Enzo and Magus; he had hopes for an off-Broadway show of his own, and he wanted Aida to go with him.

She hadn't yet made up her mind, but she was seriously thinking of doing so. If he did get this show, and she didn't go with him, it would say to the world that she'd rather be a satellite in Peter's life than have her own real relationship. And that would mean that May and Peter would never be able to get on with their own lives; she would always be this shadow between them.

And if she was going to have a life partner, as well as a professional one, why not Carlos? She instinctively didn't trust him, but she didn't want to listen to her instincts because they told her to trust no man. Except one, and he was married to another woman.

Aesthetically, she admired her Cuban lover's looks. Physically, she quite enjoyed what they did in bed. Professionally, he was a wonderful dancer. The flamenco had become a huge draw now that Carlos Pérez was dancing with Aida. Before, it had just pleased the men, but now the women too had someone to ogle.

They could speak Spanish together, and she loved that. Ramon seemed to approve of him, which helped. She'd even written to Rafa about him, when she told him all about life in America. She was not sure what the future was for her and Carlos, but she was happy to have someone to write about, to let her father know she wasn't a 'solitary oyster' any more, as Peter once called her. It had made her laugh when they'd first got to Atlantic City and she'd seen Albie Fierstein's café was called the same thing.

In the distance she saw Nick running towards them along the Boardwalk, waving his big arms, and her heart lifted. Carlos said in relief, 'See, I told you, she's back.'

* * *

THE GEM OF IRELAND'S CROWN

They gathered in the living room, everyone from the three houses, Carlos as well, and Peter drew the blinds and shut the door.

For some reason the gramophone was playing Vivaldi.

He asked them to come close, and May stood beside him. 'I want you to know,' he said, looking from one to the other, even at Carlos, 'My wife and I trust each of you with our lives, and in this case, something more precious than our lives – that of our daughter.'

To murmurs of astonishment and horror from everyone, he then told an incredible tale of his brother, and whiskey running, and murders in a forest, and finally the incredible conclusion.

'The crux of the matter is we think Maud Flynn paid Gertrude to kidnap Aisling and is holding our daughter as leverage until Eamonn's trial and execution. She has the local force in her pocket – her own cousin is the chief of police – so we can rely on nobody but ourselves to find my daughter.'

Nick broke the long, stunned silence. 'And you're sure of this?'

'As sure as we can be of anything.' It was May, pale and distressed, who answered him. 'I saw Eamonn today. He told me everything, and we were overheard. It was my fault. We spoke in Irish and I thought we were safe, but the guard understood us. The music is in case someone is listening now. I don't trust anyone except the people in this room. None of you, please, say anything about this that might be overheard. I made a terrible mistake, and as a result, Aisling has been kidnapped…'

She stopped, unable to carry on, and Peter put an arm around his wife's shoulders. 'You weren't to know, May,' he said hoarsely.

'I should have known,' she sobbed.

Maggie was crying, and the other chorus girls, and Magus looked like he was the one bound for the electric chair. Two-Soups had his head in his hands, Enzo and Ramon and Clive had faces like thunder, and for once even Timothy was silent.

May pulled herself together then and turned to Enzo. 'I'm sorry, I know you hate doing this, but…' She held out a framed photograph, the one of Aisling she kept on the sideboard. 'I thought it might help if you can tell us if you see or feel anything.'

Enzo went pale and took a step back.

'What is this?' Carlos muttered in Aida's ear.

She shrugged her slender shoulders. But she knew, because Peter had confided in her how she was only rescued from Dublin Castle because May had brought Aida's photo to Enzo, and just by putting his hand on it, he'd been able to tell May that Harvey Bathhurst had lied about Aida being dead, that she was still alive. Enzo was the seventh son of a seventh son and knew things that nobody had the right to know.

'Please, Enzo,' begged May. 'I'm sorry to ask in front of everyone, but I thought maybe what comes to you, what you say aloud, it might stir some memory in somebody here. For Aisling, Enzo...'

The Londoner stepped forwards and took the picture like it might burn him.

Enzo hated his gift. It was a burden to him, and he didn't know how it worked. When Aida asked how he'd known she was alive, he'd just said he felt what she was feeling. 'I could see bright circles, like gold coins, and that made no sense, but I felt terrible pain, and I was sure you were alive somewhere inside that pain.' She'd walked away from him, trembling, unable to say another word. She knew what he'd seen were the polished brass buttons on Harvey Bathhurst's military uniform as he violated her on the floor of his torture chamber in Dublin Castle.

In the last few months, Enzo had become very tanned from the New Jersey sun, but he was white as a sheet as he turned away from May and sat at the small writing desk in the corner by the door. Taking the photo from the frame, he laid it on the sloping leather surface of the desk, placed his palm over Aisling's smiling face, closed his eyes and became very still. His fingers trembled.

Minutes passed.

Carlos shifted restlessly and whispered to Aida, 'This is all nonsense. Fortune-telling is just show business.'

Then Enzo stirred, and said in a strange voice, 'I can't feel her.'

Peter groaned in horror. 'Does that mean she is...'

'I don't know.'

'Oh.' May collapsed into the armchair, hiding her face.

'See, he's a charlatan,' whispered Carlos, putting his arm around Aida. He'd always been jealous of Enzo because women loved him almost as much as they loved Carlos.

Aida elbowed Carlos sharply away from her and went to stand with her hand on Enzo's shoulder. 'Do you feel anything at all, Enzo?'

He quivered at her touch, like it hurt him. 'Not a little girl.'

'But you're feeling something. What is it?'

'Strength, like steel, like a soldier.'

Aida was flooded with relief. 'Then that's her.'

'No.' His dark eyes opened wide as he looked up at her. 'No, it can't be. She's so young. She must be so scared. What I feel is a soldier, unafraid…'

'Aisling isn't like other little girls. She is a soldier. Do you see anything?'

His eyelids flickered. 'Nothing that makes sense.'

'Say what you see.'

'It is something from a dream.'

'Say it. Maybe someone here might understand it, even if it makes no sense to you.' She was thinking of the brass buttons on Harvey's uniform.

He shook his dark head. 'A woman, floating in the air.'

'In the air?' Her heart sank. Maybe it was just a dream; maybe Aisling was asleep and dreaming.

May sobbed into her hands. 'Is it an angel, Enzo?'

'No, not an angel. A mermaid. A green mermaid, floating in the air. I'm so sorry, May.'

Murmurs of disappointment ran around the room, and Peter stood with his head bowed. Aida glanced towards Carlos, and to her relief, he didn't have an 'I told you so' expression on his face. Instead he was exchanging a shocked glance with the newest member of the chorus, the Cuban American girl, Benita, the one he usually ignored. And Benita seemed to want to say something to him – she came towards him across the room – but the Cuban turned his back on her and said sincerely, 'Peter and May, I haven't been with you long, but I know this is more than a cabaret. This is family. So I know I speak for every one of us, that whatever we need to do to find your daughter, we will do.'

'Thank you, Carlos,' Peter said in a broken voice, and Aida's heart ached for him. She wished she could take Peter in her arms.

'So what do we do?' asked several people at once.

May looked up, wiping her eyes. 'Go back to searching,' she said in a dull, sad voice. 'Spread out around the city, search everywhere, and don't talk about what I have told you here, because if they know I've said anything about this, they might...' She shivered and didn't finish the sentence.

Slowly everyone filed out of the room, leaving only the desolate parents and Enzo, who remained with his elbows on the writing desk and his head in his hands, too exhausted and upset to move.

Aida knew there was nothing she could do or say to make anything any better, so she followed the others. The small crowd of performers were walking away down the street towards the sea, though Benita disappeared into the next house, where all the chorus girls lived, closing the door behind her. She was surprised Benita didn't want to join the search; she'd thought the new chorus girl was very fond of Aisling.

Aida hurried to catch up with the rest, realised Carlos wasn't among them, had a sudden thought and turned and went back. She climbed quietly up the steps of Number Eight and tried the handle. It turned; the door was unbolted. She stepped into the shadowy hall. She heard voices in the kitchen. The door was just a fraction ajar. Aida stood listening, hoping the sound of her heart nervously beating wouldn't give her away.

'You have to tell her, Carlos,' said Benita.

'I'll do no such thing,' said the Cuban coldly.

'Please, Carlos! You know I would but I can't. She'd sack me if she knew where I come from, even though I was only the maid.'

'You weren't just the maid when I was with you,' said Carlos. His voice had a smooth, self-satisfied tone, and Aida felt a sick wave of misgiving.

Benita said angrily, 'Until you set your sights on that Spanish one.'

'Aida is a wonderful woman,' he said, still in that smooth voice.

'A wonderful dancer, you mean, who will make your fortune.'

'We will all three make our fortunes on Broadway. You as well, Benita.'

'I don't want to come with you to Broadway. Maud Flynn has renewed the contract, and I want to stay with the cabaret, and May said I could. This cabaret is the only family I've ever known since my mother died.'

'And they'll pay you a pittance, when you could make good money dancing in my show,' he sneered.

'It's all about the money with you.'

'I seem to remember paying good money for you, Benita.'

Aida felt so sick, she had to lean against the wall. Carlos, who she'd convinced herself to trust and even hoped to love one day, had been a customer of Benita's in that place. Why hadn't she listened to her heart? Why hadn't she kept herself to herself, stayed a solitary oyster? Never would she tell herself to trust another man against all her instincts.

'Don't remind me of that!' Benita snapped. 'That's another life. I've put it behind me now. Carlos, please, don't make me have to tell them I was a maid in Maud Flynn's whorehouse.'

'You were a whore in a whorehouse, Benita,' said Carlos nastily.

'Fine!' snapped the girl. 'A whore.' Then she said in a sad, soft voice, 'You know what Enzo saw, Carlos. And there's only one window in Atlantic City from which it can be seen, now the theatre is built in front of it. Aisling has to be in the attic bedroom of Maud Flynn's brothel, on the very top floor. Please, Carlos, please – you have to tell the Cullens about the mermaid weathervane.'

'Maud Flynn would destroy me if I told on her. I already knew from my Cuban friends, she has her fingers in so much crime, the booze running, the brothels. She couldn't afford to let me live.'

'Then tell Peter to keep your name out of it. I'm sure he'd say nothing to the FBI.'

'Maybe not the FBI. But who do you think he would go gossiping to before the day was out, about me knowing the inside of a whorehouse bedroom?'

'I'm sure he wouldn't say anything to anyone – he would only think of rescuing his daughter.'

'Ha! Aida Gonzalez, that's who he'd go running to. He can't bear it that she prefers me to him.'

There was a long silence in the kitchen, while Aida's whirling brain tried to take it all in. On top of everything else, Maud Flynn ran a whorehouse, and that's where Aisling was being kept. Carlos knew this and refused to help, because he wanted Aida. Well, that was dead now. He would never get to touch her again, not on or off stage. Her flesh crawled at the very idea of it.

Then Benita said in a low, sad voice, 'Fine, I'll tell them and ruin myself. I'll never see Ireland.'

'Do what you want, Benita. But I'll be here in this kitchen, waiting. And if I find you've said anything about me, I'll –'

'You'll what?' she asked, with another flash of anger, and then cried out in pain.

'That's what,' snarled Carlos.

'All right, all right, let go of me...'

She was still sobbing and nursing a bruised wrist when she came out of the kitchen, her eyes so blurred by tears, it took her a moment to see Aida in the shadowy hall. 'Oh...' Her face registered her horror and shame.

Aida put her finger to her lips and took Benita by her good arm. She led the girl out into the sunshine and down the steps. On the pavement she whispered, 'I heard everything. Show me where this house is, Benita. And then I'll tell Peter and May.'

Tears slid down the girl's cheeks, still scarlet with shame. 'Thank you, and please say to Mrs Cullen I'll pack my things and go. She needn't look on me again.'

'You'll do no such thing. I won't even mention your name.'

A look of hope came into Benita's wet brown eyes, but then she flushed red again. 'How can you tell them the view from the attic of a brothel without explaining how you know?'

Aida pulled out her embroidered handkerchief and gave it to the girl to wipe her streaming eyes. 'I'll tell them that Carlos confessed to me, even though he knew it would mean an end to our relationship, because in the end, he was man enough to put Aisling before his own desires.' She took a deep breath, then said with a fierce, proud smile, 'Now, Benita, show me this house.'

CHAPTER 33

AY

'She's in there. She's fine,' whispered Enzo, still breathless, just back from his reconnaissance mission.

Maud Flynn's house of prostitution, which Carlos had confessed to Aida about, was a narrow red-brick building, four storeys high, hidden down a sunless alley behind the theatre. After his act, Enzo had left by the backstage delivery entrance, slipped around the corner and climbed the thin metal drainpipe that ran from the roof of the brothel to the pavement.

May sank onto a chair draped with various fabrics; she was dizzy with relief. 'You're sure? You actually saw her?'

She and Enzo were in the backstage area, among the mess left by the performers, make-up and costumes on every surface, props and bits of scenery resting against every wall, the perfumes of intermingling fragrances hanging in the air. Only a few yards away, on the other side of a wooden backdrop, the last half hour of the show was going ahead.

At first she and Peter had been going to cancel, but then they'd realised the show was the perfect cover, and at her suggestion, and with Nick's reluctant agreement, Peter had asked Maud Flynn to come along to mind Remy in the front row. 'Nick is too afraid of the kidnappers to let his son out of his sight, and Remy worships you, Maud – you're the only person who could make him feel safe.'

Peter was such a good actor. He had Maud convinced he knew nothing and that he still thought she was doing her best to help them, so the devious woman had no choice but to oblige. And Beatrice always came to the show to ogle Carlos.

Though she was going to be disappointed tonight, because for the first time in a long time, it was going to be Peter dancing with Aida. Carlos, after a long shouting match with Aida, had stormed out of Atlantic City without even saying goodbye to the rest of them. It was strange to May how little she cared about the idea of Peter and Aida dancing the tango again. Such small things used to upset her. So stupid, clinging to what she couldn't have.

Enzo sat down on another chair and checked and tightened the laces on his climbing shoes. 'Yes, I saw her. There's a little bed in there, and she was sitting on it.'

'And the window?'

'Was open already, because of the heat. But there's an iron grille over it, locked with a padlock on the inside.'

'Oh God...locked...' Her heart dropped.

'I waved my hand, and she looked up and saw me.'

'Oh, thank God. She must have been so happy to know we've found her!' May could just picture her darling daughter laughing with delight, rushing over to kiss her Uncle Enzo through the locked grille.

'She said nothing. She looked away again immediately.'

'What? Why?'

'Someone else must have been in there with her, and she didn't want to give me away.'

'Oh, how clever of her!' Her brave, resourceful daughter never ceased to amaze her.

On the far side of the backdrop, the music swelled. Nick's and

Maggie's voices rose in song, and there was a rattle of dancing feet on the boards. It was the finale now, with everyone involved. Enzo was usually a part of it, but earlier, when he was doing his trapeze act, he'd pretended to fall and hobbled off bravely to the oohs and aahs of the doting females in the audience, so everyone would think he was resting his twisted ankle.

'I came down pretty quickly then, in case whoever it was came to the window. We can't get her out that way. We're going to have to go to the police, May.'

'No, I've told you, the police are corrupt. They would just go to Maud.'

She had met with the two officers again that afternoon, and they had assured her once more that everything that could be done was being done, that they were leaving no stone unturned. Maud had turned up in her powder-blue Ford, bearing fresh pastries and squeezed orange juice for the actors who were still pretending to search, not to give the game away, as well as a box of 'missing' posters that Beatrice Flynn had printed on her aunt's instructions. It was sickening, the display that woman was putting on, while she knew all along that May realised she was the culprit.

Everyone was so concerned, the shopkeepers, the other mothers who knew Aisling from the playground, the nannies. Everyone was upset and trying to help by putting up the posters. It was lovely that her daughter was already so well known here and loved. May felt a twinge of guilt towards Albie Fierstein in particular, for putting him through the fear that Aisling was injured or worse, when thanks to Enzo and Aida, she knew her child was alive and nearby.

While the fake search continued, May had busied herself packing everything in all three houses into the actors' trunks, ready to go for a fast getaway.

Remy, whom she was minding while Nick and Maggie were out with the rest, watched her anxiously. 'Are we going home without Aisling?'

'We're not going anywhere. I'm just tidying.' She didn't want him letting anything slip to Maud Flynn.

'I thought you were packing.'

'No, we're having the houses deep-cleaned tomorrow, so I need to get everything out of the way.'

'Oh yes, our maids at home do that in the spring.' He seemed satisfied with her answer. 'Is Aisling still with Gertrude and those men?'

May forced a smile. 'Yes, she's most likely having her dinner, and she'll come home after that.'

'I hope Gertrude doesn't leave her alone like she left me. This place isn't all boring and slow like Brockleton – there's fast cars and everything. Albie Fierstein said I had to be careful on the road. He stopped a car from hitting me this morning after Aisling went off with Gertrude.'

'Did he? Thank God for Albie.' She drew Remy in for a long hug and kissed his dark hair. 'I'm sure she'll be fine, but the very best help you can be to me and Aisling now is to be good and sit quietly with that nice Maud Flynn during the show. Can you do that for me?'

'I don't like her. She's creepy.'

'But you don't have to let her know that. You're going to be the seventh baron de Simpré one day, and barons have to be polite.'

'Grandpa isn't polite.'

There was no arguing with that, but eventually she'd persuaded him to sit with Maud.

The other thing she'd done that afternoon, after Nick and Maggie returned to look after Remy, was to meet with Federal Agent Joel Kopeck, who, as she knew from Albie, often ate an early dinner in the Solitary Oyster, out of sight in a discreet booth at the back of the place.

'Is Agent Kopeck here today, Albie?' she'd asked.

The Jewish man nodded and sighed. It was a nuisance how much the FBI agent liked his café; it meant he could never slip champagne into anyone's orange juice. 'Yes, but I'm not allowed to tell anyone. He never wants company. He takes the whole table for himself.'

'I have to speak to him.'

'Is it about the darling girl? I would do anything for that child, even disturb Agent Kopeck.'

'It is about her, Albie.'

He looked around furtively, then pointed May in the direction of the booth.

As she slid into it and sat down at the table, a flash of frustration crossed the agent's face. He lowered his salmon and cheese bagel. 'Please make an appointment at the station if you want to speak to me, Mrs...er...'

'May Cullen, of Cullen's Celtic Cabaret. My daughter has been kidnapped.'

His face showed no sympathy whatsoever. 'I am with the FBI, Mrs Cullen. Please inform the local police.'

'But there's no point in that, because the kidnapper is Maud Flynn.'

He'd been about to take another bite of the bagel, but he put it down altogether, his face without expression. 'Supposing that outlandish statement is true, why does that mean there's no point in telling the police?'

May swallowed. What she was about to say was deeply insulting to the force, but she believed it to be true. He could either take umbrage or believe her; it was a gamble, but one she had to take.

'I don't think the police are entirely trustworthy. The chief of police is her cousin, and I think some of his officers, at some level anyway, are in cahoots with Flynn.'

'You do, do you?' Kopeck leant back, his arms folded.

She could see a raised eyebrow was all she was going to get, so she decided to launch straight into the story. When she finished, she sat waiting for his reply. It was a while coming, and when it did, it astonished her.

'I knew it,' he said, with quiet satisfaction. 'But I thought I would never trap her. She's such a wily old bird...'

A deep sense of relief washed over her. The FBI believed her; they were on her side. 'She's a monster, Mr Kopeck.'

'And your brother-in-law will turn state's evidence against her as part of a plea deal?'

'Yes, he will.' Though she frowned a little at the thought of

Eamonn doing any time at all; she'd have to sort that out when they came to it. 'But not while my daughter is missing.'

'So you want the FBI to rescue your daughter?'

'No.'

The agent took off his heavy-framed spectacles and cleaned them. He had dark hair and a distinct widow's peak. His intelligent but unreadable eyes fixed her with a stare. 'Explain yourself, please, Mrs Cullen.'

'To alert Maud Flynn with an FBI raid would be too dangerous. We know she is unafraid of murder. We have a plan to rescue Aisling ourselves – we have…unusual skills…doing what we do. But once we free her, it is critical we are gone from here at once, where Maud Flynn can't reach us. And you must put Eamonn Cullen in protective custody immediately.'

She had his attention now, she knew it, and she went on to outline exactly what needed to happen next.

* * *

AND NOW HER BRILLIANT, foolproof plan had failed miserably, because even though the room was an attic, the open window was barred by a locked grille. Enzo was right – they would have to bring in Kopeck to rescue her after all, and give everything away, and risk the consequences.

'Go back again, Enzo, and slip this in the window,' said a deep voice from the shadows. It was Magus. How long had the Cherokee been standing there? It was extraordinary how a man that large could be so invisible.

He came forwards, holding out an object that was tiny in his hand, a lady's hair grip. 'Let her see you leave this on the grill, where it can't be seen. And tuck this into the grill as well.' He produced a tiny crumpled slip of paper. 'It has instructions. It tells her to pick the lock if her jailer leaves her alone at all, which surely they will, even to use the bathroom, and then she must wait for you to return in the middle of the night, when everyone is sleeping.'

Enzo looked troubled, his eyes going from Magus to May. 'No, but I can't leave her a note. Her jailer might see it and read it. It would give everything away, and then Fraud Flynn would move her to a different location and then we might never…' He stopped dead, with a quick glance at May.

May shuddered. She knew what he had stopped himself saying. *We might never see her again.* 'Enzo's right. It would put her in too much danger.'

'No, because no one except Aisling would even think these were words,' said Magus softly, unfolding the strip of paper and showing May what looked to her like Chinese or ancient Egyptian or something like that.

The note was in Cherokee.

Enzo took it, and the hair grip, and slipped out into the night again.

* * *

THE SHOW WAS OVER, and as Two-Soups whispered to May, it was the worst performance they'd ever done, as everyone was so upset and worried. But the audience clapped and cheered as usual.

Maud Flynn, who held a gloomy-looking Remy by the hand, appeared backstage in the wake of the other performers. Enzo had just come back in, out of breath again. Seeing Maud, he hastily collapsed on a chair, holding his 'twisted ankle' and groaning.

'Enzo, you should put ice on that. Everyone, please, I want to say how much I appreciate you continuing to be so professional in the face of the worry about the little girl. I honestly was expecting to refund all tonight's tickets, but I'm very grateful to you all for putting the show on. And May, my poor love…' She came over to May, pulling poor Remy along with her. 'My heart is breaking for you.'

The hypocrisy was sickening.

'You're welcome, Miss Flynn,' said May, looking her straight in the eye with a cold smile. 'I know you and the police are doing your level best to find them. We've searched everywhere we can think of. We're going out of our minds honestly, we really are, but it was either do the show or sit in the house staring at the walls and imagining all sorts.'

Fraud Flynn nodded and patted her shoulder. 'If anyone can find Gertrude, my people can. She's packed up and left her lodgings. The landlady doesn't know where she came from – her references were all fake. But through the night, the police will be out. We've people on the highways stopping cars, and I've pulled in contacts in Wilmington, Philadelphia, Newark – not a stone will be left unturned. I give you my word on that.'

'And I appreciate it, I really do, Ms Flynn.'

'Oh, call me Maud – we are such good friends. And it's going to be all right, May. I have been praying all day, and Beatrice is doing the nine-days prayer, never known to fail. And I've Father McAuliffe doing a special Mass tomorrow. It's important not to despair and give up hope, May. Your daughter is under the Lord's protection. We don't always know God's plan.'

May caught Peter's eye over Maud's shoulder. He was red with rage. She knew he would have been happy to dispatch this evil woman at a moment's notice if it could have got Aisling back safely. Instead he was having to play this stupid game of not knowing.

She caught Enzo giving her a quiet thumbs-up from where he was sitting, so it looked like the hairpin and note were safely delivered. Now it was just a matter of waiting until the middle of the night. She would have to call the number Kopeck had given her and tell him to hold off on his part of the plan, which was ready to go into action within the next half an hour.

'May, can you bring me to the toilet?' May suspected Remy was just saying it to get away from Maud, but this was good – it gave her the chance to use the phone in reception.

'Of course, darling.' She held out her hand.

He took it but then dropped it again and rushed off towards the dark back of the theatre. 'Aisling!' he screamed. 'May said you'd come back!'

* * *

'I DID WHAT YOU SAID, MAGUS!' Aisling was delighted with herself. 'I picked the lock, but then I was bored waiting and that silly Gertrude was asleep, so I climbed down the drainpipe myself like Enzo taught me to climb the poles in the tent...'

Peter squeezed their daughter so tight, she giggled.

'Daddy, I can't breathe!'

All around, the entire troupe were in tears, hugging each other in relief and delight, and Maud, who had gone white as a sheet when Aisling walked in through the back of the theatre, declared loudly, 'That dreadful Gertrude! But at least I was right – she didn't harm your daughter.'

All the while she was speaking, her eyes were on May. They were narrow and hard, and May could practically hear the cogs moving in the sly woman's head, trying to figure out her next move.

May met Maud's eyes with an equally hard expression, then gave the evil woman a big bright smile. 'This calls for a drink!' she declared.

Reaching into a crate, she held aloft a bottle of clear liquid marked 'surgical spirits'. It was poitín, the illegal but widely available Irish spirit. The troupe always had a bottle to hand, and everyone knew what 'surgical spirits' meant. It could be used to sterilise a cut, cure a cold, rub sore muscles. But it could also be drunk for pleasure.

The troupe looked confused as May began filling glasses from the several bottles she had stored in the crate, and Maud Flynn seemed frozen in indecision, not knowing what May was playing at.

'Nick, music!' May pulled aside the backdrop, and Nick, puzzled but obedient, went to the piano on the stage. Soon people had had a drink or two and had relaxed, while Maud sat looking stunned on the chair where May had insisted on putting her, with Ramon and Magus standing guard each side of her, stopping her from leaving. And the whole place was a party in full swing as the agents of the FBI burst through the double doors from the alleyway behind.

'This is a raid on behalf of the Federal Bureau of Investigation. Everyone is under arrest. Put down your drinks and make no attempt to escape – the building is surrounded!' Agent Joel Kopeck shouted, his booming voice loud once Nick stopped playing piano.

At least ten agents entered, quickly and efficiently placing handcuffs on everyone.

'Don't worry, darling, this is all part of the escape plan. Just don't tell anyone,' May whispered to a stricken Aisling, who immediately beamed and offered her little hands willingly to the officer, who allowed himself a small smile. 'Just your mom will do, honey,' he said, cuffing May and shepherding her with the rest all out into the waiting armoured vans.

Within ten minutes, the entire cast were being whisked away in one of the prison vans, while Maud Flynn, loudly protesting, was driven off in another, and the third followed the first van down the road.

Aisling was soon snuggled up between May and Peter, playing cat's cradle with Remy with a strand of wool, while Kopeck's assistant, Agent Ernest Barnes, moved around the van taking off everyone's handcuffs and telling them not to worry, that everything would soon be sorted out.

Rubbing her wrists, May sat gazing out the small back window of the van.

The luggage was in the van behind, and they were not being brought in to a police station to be processed for prosecution under the Volstead Act but being delivered to the quayside and escorted aboard the Cunard ship the *RMS Laconia*, bound for Cobh and safety.

Only Eamonn would be left behind. He'd be in protective custody, but in prison nonetheless, waiting to be interviewed by the FBI. What would happen to him? He was so reckless and bad at taking care of himself; he was only good for taking care of other people. If she knew him, he'd be far too honest about how many times he'd gone bootlegging, and probably add some as well; he was the sort of man to confess to loads of stuff to cover up for his old comrade, poor dead Charlie Horgan. He'd been prepared to die for Aisling; he'd think nothing of doing a few years to spare Charlie's family from the shame. Like he'd said, he felt there was nothing left for him anyway in terms of settling down if he couldn't have May.

And here she was, running away, abandoning him to the FBI, who had no interest in him really beyond the use he could be to them. He needed someone like her to manage Federal Agent Joel Kopeck.

She bent to kiss Aisling on the head and tried to imagine being away from her, even for a short time.

'Look, Daddy!' Her daughter was holding up a particularly complicated design to her father, beaming. 'I'm so much better at cat's cradle than Remy. Can Remy stay with us in our caravan? He's so bored at that big boring house of his...'

'Whatever you like, darling,' said Peter, and May inwardly rolled her eyes.

If May did leave Aisling with her father for a month, then he would spoil her horribly, and she'd probably come back to find Bug the real pet rabbit sleeping in the bed with the girl.

Was she really thinking of staying?

Peter's gaze had moved away from his daughter now and was resting on Aida, and he seemed entirely at peace, as if all was right with his world.

He had got his daughter back, and now Aida was back as well, no longer with Carlos, no longer beyond his reach.

May sighed. How she longed to be adored. Not just loved or admired or found indispensable. Adored, the way Peter adored the Spanish woman.

She closed her eyes and thought of that kiss in Trenton Prison.

And felt the heat of Eamonn, and his worship of her...

CHAPTER 34

CORK, TWO MONTHS LATER

ETER

THE LETTER HAD an American stamp and was addressed in May's neat copperplate schoolgirl hand.

When his wife had suddenly announced at the quayside that she was going to stay in America to look after Eamonn, at first he'd been astonished.

'That's pure nonsense, May. Eamonn is a big boy. He can look after himself.'

'But he needs me…'

'May, I'm your husband. I need you. The cabaret needs you.'

'And that's just it, Peter,' she'd burst out suddenly, in the dark, with the light, warm rain falling on her hair. 'It's all need, need, need. With you, all I am is useful to you. I want someone who puts me on a pedestal from time to time, who doesn't just want me because I make their life better and easier, who doesn't even care if I make their life easier because all they want is to make me happy. Someone like Eamonn.'

He'd stared at her in utter bewilderment. 'I'm sorry...what? Are you saying that Eamonn...my brother Eamonn...'

'Yes, I am. I didn't mean to say it right here and now, but yes, that's all he wants, to make me happy. Don't I deserve that, after all these years?'

'But... What... I don't understand...'

'He loves me, Peter! And damn it, I love him!'

It was like one of the trunks being winched up and loaded onto the ship had suddenly dropped on him out of the sky.

She came towards him, the tears on her cheeks mingling with the rain. 'I'm sorry. But it's for the best...'

'Whose best, May?'

'Everyone's best. Tell Aisling I'll write often and I'll be home as soon as I can.'

'Home?'

'I mean to Ireland.'

'Oh my God, May. I don't believe this! You're staying...with my brother... Since when... Don't answer that. This is...' Disbelieving, hurt, furious, he'd stormed off then, leaving her alone on the quayside, and he'd spent the whole voyage pacing the decks, raging, trying to come to terms with the news that his wife had abandoned him for his older brother.

The double betrayal drove him nearly mad.

May's 'as soon as I can' became weeks as Maud Flynn's trial dragged on. Eamonn was still in custody while acting as a witness for the state. Peter knew this, because the whole thing had made the Irish papers; Maud Flynn was Harp Devereaux's employer, and Harp was as famous in Ireland as she was in Atlantic City.

His brother's account of events was the singularly most important piece of the case that Agent Kopeck had spent years building against Maud Flynn, and as the trial continued, every day it made the papers. Not only was this paragon of virtue and temperance supplying illegal alcohol, she was also running brothels and protection rackets. And it seemed the four murdered men in the sweetcorn fields were not her only victims either. The kidnap of Aisling and her daring escape had somehow made the papers too.

The jury found Maud Flynn guilty on the capital offences of murder as well as everything else, and she was sentenced to death by electrocution, the first woman to face that ultimate penalty since 1881. Although the judge then commuted the sentence to life imprisonment, so Maud Flynn would spend the rest of her life in Clinton Farms, the New Jersey State Reformatory for Women, with no possibility of parole.

Gertrude got two years at the same establishment.

Beatrice, found guilty of being her aunt's accomplice, asked to serve her sentence of fifteen years at a different prison to her aunt and was granted her request. A long time ago, Peter had thought Beatrice was a mousy thing, but as the trial progressed, it seemed she had played more than a bit part in her aunt's many deceptions. Evidently she wasn't the innocent she made herself out to be. She was being taught at Fraud Flynn's knee and had been a quick learner by all accounts.

You never could tell with women, he thought to himself bitterly.

While the trial was going on, May wrote to Aisling every week, sending her lots of love and hugs and American chocolate and bright silver dollars. Aisling loved getting the letters, but they upset her a bit as well because she wanted her mammy.

She was so used to being minded by the whole cabaret, though, she never stayed sad for long. She loved her daddy, and Maggie and Magus and everyone else helped take care of her.

Aida Gonzalez was keeping herself to herself, as cool as she had ever been. Peter wanted to go to her, but he was afraid to talk to her, to find out what she was feeling. She must have been so traumatised by Carlos. Both Peter and Aida had been so betrayed. Everything was such a mess.

She hadn't let Peter down, though. She was taking care of the costumes and supervising all the acts so that he didn't have to, and she did it all in her quiet, professional, cool manner. She was calm and helpful when she spoke to him in public, but she didn't come to him privately.

His other friends were doing all they could to keep the show on the road. Two-Soups, he knew, was seeing to the finances, Nick was organising the tent being erected and struck each week, Maggie and Magus were minding Aisling, Clive and Timothy supervised the ticket sales, and Enzo filled in as master of ceremonies when Peter couldn't face it, which was often.

Nick and Enzo had made several attempts to talk to him, but he didn't want to talk. There was only one person he wanted to talk to.

One night he had gone to her caravan after the show, but she'd turned him away. 'I can't let you in, Peter. Look at you – you don't know what you're feeling, you don't know what the future holds or what you want. Nor do I. I may stay, I may go to Spain... I don't understand the world. I need to think, to rest, to heal. And you and May need to sort this out between you.'

She was right. He had to get hold of himself. He had to work out what he wanted.

Now, two months later, he stood outside the post office, looking at the letter in his hands and feeling like he was holding a snake. He knew his wife. She would have a strong fixed notion in her mind how all this should be sorted out 'for the best', as she always put it.

Was May suddenly going to announce that she was taking Aisling away from him to live in America?

Every time he looked at his daughter now, he wondered... No, it wasn't possible. Yes, she looked exactly like Eamonn. But didn't he look like his own uncle, who had died when he was twelve of scarlet fever?

Was this letter going to tell him he wasn't Aisling's real father?

It would kill him.

He walked all the way back to the caravan with the letter in his pocket, passing rapidly through the campsite. Two-Soups was in the middle of fixing Enzo's trampoline, with Nick and Enzo standing around watching him. They waved to him to come over, but he ignored them, went into his own caravan and shut and locked the door.

Then he lay down on the bed. The bed he had shared with May for so long.

After several minutes, he opened the letter.

Dear Peter,
This is a difficult letter to write, so I will begin with the plain facts.

How like May.

I found an excellent lawyer, and Eamonn has been given a very light sentence for his part in the whiskey running. With time served he will be released in two weeks, so after that we will come back to Ireland, and we hope and pray you will see us and forgive us.

He stopped reading and rested the letter against his chest. His heart was pounding, and he could feel the blood rising into his face. With an effort he picked the letter up again.

We will journey from Cork to Dublin and make our home in Dublin, where I mean to build my theatre. Eamonn has many friends in construction who have been underpaid and held back because of the side they took in the Civil War, and they will be glad of an employer who treats them properly, even if we can't pay well at first. At least it will keep them out of trouble.

I think it should be possible for Cullen's Celtic Cabaret to repay me the two thousand pounds with which we started our business, Peter. As traumatic as our time in Atlantic City turned out to be, at least we made a lot of money.

I also think Aisling should go to school, and I know you agree. The easiest way, because you will always be travelling, is if she goes to school in Dublin, and I know my parents are willing to pay her fees.

AGAIN HE RESTED the letter on his chest. He felt sick. He lifted it again.

BUT I WANT you to know, Peter, you are Aisling's father, in the realest sense of the word. You have raised her since she was a baby. She adores you. I will never take her from you. I will never say she isn't yours. She is yours. I want her to spend every holiday with the cabaret – it has made her into the child she is, resourceful and brilliant and brave. She will always be ours, to share.

TEARS CAME INTO HIS EYES. For a moment he could have hugged her, as he'd often hugged her in the past when she'd smoothed difficulties out of his way.

I THINK you should speak to Aida, I really do. Go to her and be honest. Tell her the truth about how you feel about her, the truth we've always known, all of us. And I think she might have some home truths for you too, but that's not my business. And yes, I know, you hate the idea of Maggie being Nick's mistress, and you will hate the idea of Aida being yours. Sometimes, Peter, I think you're the more respectable one of us two.

'MAYBE I AM AT THAT,' he muttered to himself, with a slight smile.

BUT I'M LETTING you go, Peter. In England they have passed a new law making divorce a lot easier, not just for people like Nick. I suggest you go to England and divorce me on the grounds of adultery, and you will be free to remarry over there too.

. . .

'May, a divorce…for goodness' sake…' It was outlandish, immoral maybe, and against both Church and State in Ireland.

I'm willing to be divorced, Peter, and not with bitterness in my heart. I want to free you from your commitment to me.

'So you can marry my brother?' he asked aloud as he ran his hand through his hair. 'Are you actually serious? This isn't some stupid French farce.'

I don't think Eamonn and I will ever marry, Peter. I think we will stay together, but I think we'll play it by our own rules. This is real life in all its messiness, and we are only getting one go at it. And will people be shocked and scandalised? Yes, probably. Our parents will need the smelling salts, that's for sure, but Peter, you know better than most how fragile life can be. And shouldn't we all try to find our happiness?

He shook the letter furiously in front of his face, as if he was shaking her. 'So this is how it's all going to be, is it? May Cullen sorts it out for all of us? Again? Tied up in a neat little bow?'

I don't know what the future holds, but I do know this. I know that you were never really mine. I know that you've always loved me in your own way, and I know that we share our precious Aisling, but we can both raise Aisling together, along with Magus and everyone else.

Peter couldn't help agreeing with that. She was right. Aisling was a child of Cullen's Celtic Cabaret, not just theirs.

. . .

Peter, you deserve to be with Aida. Isn't that what your heart really desires, when you strip everything else away? I manoeuvred you into marriage, and I shouldn't have. I will never regret our time together and what we've built, but it's not enough and I'm trying to fix it before it's too late. And yes, I know it drives you mad when I insist on fixing things 'for the best', but I'm trying to do the right thing for you, so please, take it. I love you as you love me, but not as we feel for other people and that's the truth. Should we spend the rest of our days plodding on, wishing for something else but not daring to risk everything for happiness?

Please take the time to think about this, and talk to Aida, and be happy.

All my love, Peter, and I really mean that, with all my heart.

May

HE PUT THE LETTER ASIDE. And for a very long time, he remained on the bed, staring at the ceiling. Outside, across the field, the music started up. The cabaret had begun without him, and Enzo would be acting as master of ceremonies.

Aisling would be with Magus. His daughter had progressed from doing her little act with her pet rabbit, Bug, in the matinee to helping Magus with his set, letting herself out of cages and disappearing from locked boxes. It gave a light edge to the magician's dark, rather chilling performance, which worked perfectly. After Magus's act, the newest chorus girl, a sweet kid called Lily, who was still in training, would bring Aisling away and put her to bed while Peter finished up the show.

Which he needed to go and do now. It wasn't fair to leave everything to his friends. Hadn't he always said the show must go on?

He got up, washed his face and went to the door, with a last glance around the caravan. Aisling's bunk bed was neatly made, with the velvet rabbit she loved so much poking its head out from under the blankets. Eamonn had bought that rabbit for Aisling a year ago, and every time Peter saw it, he itched to throw it out. But now he just shook his head and thought maybe the more people Aisling had to love her, the better.

Enzo was backstage preparing to dance with Aida when Peter got there. It was dance night, and he was taking down the flamenco outfit from the rack. But Peter put a hand on his shoulder. 'Let me do this tonight,' he said, and the acrobat shrugged and handed him the outfit instead.

'Fits you better, mate,' he said with a wink.

When Peter walked out on stage, he saw the Spanish woman's expression change – a spark of fire and then coolness. He wasn't sure what was in her mind. Always professional, she extended her small hand, and he took it and pulled her towards him. He gazed into her eyes, and she gazed back with the smallest of smiles.

It was the first time he'd had her in his arms since the night of the big bust-up, but nothing had changed between them; they moved as one. Ramon, sitting to the side of the stage, picked out the fast rhythm on his flamenco guitar. The wild music ran through him from head to toe. This was his place, with her. He needed her. He wanted her. He was raw, he was hurt, but having her with him, feeling her – the real Aida, not the mythic creature in his head but a woman of muscles and blood and sinews, a real woman – it was so intense, so passionate, so beautiful.

Out in the auditorium, there wasn't a murmur. It was as if the whole place was empty. He heard only the sound of the guitar and the beat of their feet.

It came to an end. He pressed her against him and felt her heart going wild against his chest. She moved back but still held his hand as they bowed to the ecstatic audience, the whole crowd on their feet, even the children who sat on the benches in front.

LATER THAT EVENING he crossed the field to her caravan, terrified and hopeful, and knocked.

She let him in, and he stood before her.

He'd rehearsed his speech over and over, full of explanations and reasons like in May's letter, and entreaties and coaxing of his own, but in the end, his mind was blank. She was dressed in black, no make-up on her face, her hair in a braid over her shoulder, and she'd never looked more beautiful.

She didn't say a word, and for the longest time, they just stood there, facing each other.

Then he opened his mouth and the words came out. 'I know what I want now. I know my future, and it is you. I love you. I've loved you from that first day in London when you came to the YMCA with your dresses in a bag. If you'll have me, I'd like to be yours, and yours alone.'

She smiled then, tears shining bright in her dark eyes. She nodded, stepped into his arms and kissed him.

As they broke apart, she simply said, 'I will have you.'

CHAPTER 35

AY

SHE DIDN'T TELL him she would be there, but somehow she knew that he knew she would be.

The butterflies danced in her stomach as she stood outside the prison. The bus had driven away almost an hour ago, and she'd been standing here since. It was freezing cold. She'd not been expecting the New Jersey winter when the summer in Atlantic City had been so warm.

She'd dressed this morning in her lodging house in Trenton, though she'd booked a room for that night in the Stacy-Trent Hotel, if that's what he wanted.

He knew that she'd told Peter the truth, she'd written to tell him, but neither of them wanted to make plans for when he was released. It was all too complicated and emotional to discuss by letter, everything they wrote, read by the prison guards. So they kept their correspondence brief and practical. She hoped he still wanted her, it had been all she could think about.

A snowflake whirled down, and she pulled close the fur of her plush dark-green ankle-length velour coat with matching hat. The cuffs and collar were of fox fur. She had been in warm silk underwear since October, since the weather turned cold, but she had sacrificed heat for allure this morning by wearing her American brassiere and French knickers under a silk sheath dress.

Her feet were so cold as she stood outside the prison, she'd lost all feeling in them, but she didn't care. He'd be here soon.

The gate opened, but it was only several guards coming off shift. The sky was an opaque grey, and it began to snow harder.

And then the gate opened again, and it was him, looking down at his feet as he stepped over the lintel.

She moved closer, and as he raised his head, their eyes met, and a slow smile played around his sensuous lips. He looked better than the last time she'd seen him. His hair was cut neatly, he was clean-shaven, and his tall muscular frame was dressed in the very well-cut suit she'd had sent to him for the trial, and over it he wore the dark, heavy overcoat she'd sent him as well.

He came to stand before her, snow settling on his broad shoulders. 'Well then, here you are,' he said, looking down at her.

'Here I am.' She grinned.

He put his calloused fingertip under her chin, tilting her face upwards as the soft flakes fell all around. The question hung between them.

'I'm yours, if you still want me?' She asked in a whisper.

His eyes told her all that his tongue couldn't say.

He bent his head and kissed her, and she slid her hands inside his coat, holding him to her, relishing the feel of him.

'Tell me we have a warm hotel room to go to,' he murmured as they broke apart. 'And I'll show you exactly how much I still want you.'

'Of course we have. You should know by now, Eamonn Cullen, I think of everything. Even the transport, see?'

And she slid her hand in his and led him to the bus, which with perfect timing had just pulled up at the stop.

EPILOGUE

CLARIDGE'S HOTEL, LONDON, JULY 1929

May

'Any luck?' May asked Eamonn as he entered the ornate hotel room.

'I did my best. Peter is trying now. I think she was all right last night but got a fit of nerves again this morning.'

'At least he managed to pack the Narros off for a few days. They'll love the Lake District, and this is going to be fraught enough without throwing a whole family of loud Spaniards in the works.' May applied her lipstick as she sat at the marble dressing table, then checked her hair again. She'd been at the hairdresser's all morning having a finger wave and set.

'Aisling is still with Aida. She said she'll drop her here on the way, but she wanted to practice her dance one last time,' Eamonn said, undressing from his informal shirt and trousers into the morning suit May had hired for him. There was no point in buying one because

Eamonn, unlike his brother, cared nothing whatsoever for clothes and would go out dressed like a tramp, even to his sister's wedding, if she didn't insist. Not that she normally gave a hoot; he was handsome and irresistible no matter what he wore.

He was unaware of her watching him as he dressed, until he caught her eye in the mirror.

'What?' he asked, an eyebrow raised.

'Nothing.' She smiled. 'I'm just admiring you. I'm allowed to now, aren't I?'

Without a word he crossed the room and knelt behind her, allowing his hands to encircle her body and caress her breasts as he planted kisses on her neck, up to her jaw. She'd spent ages getting ready, but somehow that didn't matter, as his passion and urgency were matched by her own. Within moments they were on the bed, the floor scattered with the clothes she'd so carefully selected.

They made love quickly, with an urgency that still took both of them by surprise, even three years on.

'Quick.' She giggled as he rolled off her, his large, muscular body sheened with sweat and his breathing laboured from the exertion. 'Aisling will be back any second.'

He laughed but did as she told him, and as Aida knocked on the door, they were both dressed and May was once again applying her lipstick.

'Mammy, Uncle Eamonn, I can do it!' Aisling was delighted with herself. 'I was using the wrong posture – that's why it wasn't working. You have to use the *quiebro* position of the torso, and one leg crosses the other going from weight shared between both feet to one foot in the finish.'

Eamonn laughed. 'Ah sure, if you'd have asked me, I'd have explained that.'

Aida joined in. Like Eamonn, she laughed a lot more these days.

'*Querida*, you have it now, and it will be spectacular at the wedding party. Go, quickly, get dressed.'

'*Gracias, Aida. Eres la mejor profesora.*'

'*Sólo trabajo con los mejores,*' she replied as Aisling ran to the adjoining room to get ready.

'How is it going with Bridie?' Aida asked then, lowering her voice as she came further into the room.

May grimaced. 'Not good, I think. She was coming around last night. Even getting her here was an achievement – God bless Kathleen – but now that she's here, she's getting cold feet. It will break Maggie's heart if she doesn't come.'

'They're just a different generation, a different way of thinking, I suppose,' Eamonn said, smoothing his ruffled hair in the mirror.

'My father would be the same. He's a very devout Catholic, so no divorce for him either, though having affairs seems to have been all right.' Aida snorted; she didn't sound bitter, though.

Everyone knew Aida and Rafa Narro were close now. He'd repented of his immoral ways. And while nothing could bring her mother back, it was nice to see Aida reconnected with her father and his family. They were all here visiting London, but as much as she loved her father and brothers and sisters, Aida said she didn't want them all around for the wedding, so they helpfully took themselves off sightseeing around the country.

The rapprochement between Aida and her family was due in no small way to Peter, who paved the road of reconciliation on several trips to Spain over the last two years. The fiery senorita would not be told what to do by anyone, but in Peter's hands, she was putty, and the same was true vice versa. Everyone could see it, and they were so happy.

May still thought she and Peter should divorce. Under the new English legislation, she could just check into a hotel with some man who slept in a room down the corridor – she'd never even need to speak to him – the solicitor could arrange it, and the divorce would be granted on the grounds of infidelity. Maybe they would do that one day, but neither Eamonn nor Aida seemed in any hurry. Peter either. They all just seemed happy to finally be with the person they wanted to be with.

'Peter is tryin' again now,' Eamonn said as he tied his shoelaces. 'I did my best, but I think I was makin' her worse. She listens to Peter more than any of us.'

'Poor Bridie,' May said with sympathy. 'We've really asked her to accept a lot these last couple of years. Peter and I separating, then me and Eamonn, then Aida and Peter getting together...'

'I know.' Aida smiled ruefully. 'She's amazing, and she's been so kind to me, and welcoming, even though she thinks we are all terrible sinners.'

'She's trying her best, but this is hard for her. And now Maggie marrying a divorced man in a registry office... Well, it's the last straw, the poor woman.'

'Real love is never a sin,' Eamonn reassured the room as May fixed his tie. 'Our generation has seen enough waste of life, all of us, with all the wars, so we have a duty to be happy and to love and to live the lives we're privileged to have. Ma sees that too, deep down.'

'Look at me!'

They all turned as Aisling arrived back in the room. At almost nine she was growing tall and was as lithe as a panther. Her silky dark hair was pinned back in a bun, and she was dressed in a cream lace dress with burgundy ruffles. Aida had made the dress herself, and they were going to dance the *alegrias* together, a celebratory dance from Cadiz, accompanied in the intricate steps by Ramon on guitar.

'Aw, Aisling, you look lovely, darlin'.' Eamonn beamed; he melted when he saw her. May knew he was sure he was her father, but he had never made that claim and he would never try to take her from Peter. He was happy just to be around her. The truth was they would never truly know.

'Thanks, Uncle Eamonn.' The much-loved child grinned. 'Aida did my hair this morning.'

May fixed a button on the back of her daughter's dress and kissed her cheek. 'You are beautiful.'

'Should we go?' Aisling was so excited. 'Laurent and Pierre said they are going to be giving out drinks, but I don't think they are. They're just saying it because I'm doing a dance and Remy is singing that song in French and they want to be doing something. But only me and Remy are old enough.'

May smiled, Nick and Celine's twins were dismissed regularly by both Remy and Aisling as being 'just babies,' though they were seven.

To the sound of her chatter, they left the room and went downstairs.

Eamonn hailed a taxi, and they all piled into the car. 'Westminster Register Office, please.'

The short trip only took moments, and when they got out, they found Nick, Celine, Millie and the boys waiting outside. Magus and Two-Soups were there, as well as Clive and Timothy in matching top hats and tails. Enzo had Florence Gamminston's arm around him. Lord Gamminston had finally died a few months ago, and it looked like Enzo's days of gallivanting had come to an end, whether he liked it or not, and that he was going to end up as a neighbour of Nick's. All the roustabouts and dancing girls were present as well, including the newest members of the chorus, Benita and Lily, and even Delilah was there with the fishmonger she'd married when she'd realised Two-Soups would never put a ring on her finger. Rosie was looking very happy; Ramon was courting her again now that Enzo was no longer a bad influence.

Up until a week ago, all of the actors had been performing in May's new theatre in Dublin, a two-hundred-seater in Portobello. Although May preferred to put on literary plays, she made an exception for Cullen's Celtic Cabaret at least twice a year. After the wedding, the cabaret would go on a short tour of the United Kingdom and then to Saint-Tropez in August. But in September, May planned to lure Peter away to play Macbeth in her upcoming production.

Peter Cullen had made a good job of playing Lady Macbeth once, in an emergency, at the Gaiety Theatre, and just as well he did, because if that hadn't happened, his father, Kit Cullen, wouldn't have tried to kill him, and then everything would have turned out so differently.

But Peter was a man now, not a slender, beardless boy, and May was going to give him his chance to play the male lead.

'No sign of any Cullens, I see,' Eamonn murmured in her ear as they approached Nick, who was looking around worriedly for any sign of his fiancé and her family.

'It's going to be fine.' She gave Eamonn's arm a squeeze. 'If all else fails, Peter told me he's going to play the Kit Cullen card.'

Eamonn knew what that was. A sure-fire way of having their mother support anything was to point out how much Kit Cullen would have hated it. She delighted in taking the opposing view to her horrible late husband in all things.

'He'll need to use every trick up his sleeve. She was in tears about it all this morning.'

'If anyone can bring her round, Peter can, let's just hope.'

As they reached Nick, she felt the need to reassure him as well. 'It's going to be wonderful, Nick, relax,' she whispered as she kissed his cheek.

Nick just nodded, unable yet to smile, not until the deed was done and Maggie was his lawful wedded wife.

His father was dead, died in his sleep two months ago, and Nick was now the baron. The divorce had gone quickly and smoothly through Parliament. It was minor scandal among the Anglo-Irish for about five minutes, and he knew that what he'd risked in terms of his reputation was nothing compared to Maggie.

The troupe had been delighted for them, of course. Enzo had joked about how he was the one who got all the disapproval for bed-hopping but the carry-on of the top brass left him in the ha'penny place.

The Cullens had taken a bit more convincing. Peter had supported Maggie's marriage to Nick as he promised he would. Connie and Kathleen had come around to the idea, though it took time, because they had been taught from the cradle that divorced people who became involved with other people were adulterers.

Eamonn couldn't care less any more about the so-called sin part, so long as they were happy; he was living in sin himself with May, for God's sake. His initial reservations were to do with the class difference more than divorce. Connie just loved the excitement of it all, but

Kathleen and Mrs Cullen had a real crisis of faith over the whole thing.

Kathleen in the end realised she loved her sister and she liked Nick a lot, so she would be loyal to her even if she didn't necessarily agree with her life choices. And she had tried hard to get Mrs Cullen to agree to the marriage. It had worked, kind of, up to last night.

A car pulled up and Kathleen, Sean and Connie emerged.

Everyone gazed expectantly.

'The bride is on her way.' Kathleen smiled, and Nick looked like he might cry with relief.

'Righto, everyone, let's get this done.' Enzo started shepherding everyone in.

May held Aisling's hand in one of hers and, in the crowd, reached for Eamonn's with the other. He squeezed it and winked at her, and she felt that now familiar sense of peace. No more trying, no more scheming, no more manoeuvring. She was finally happy.

Aida took a seat in front of them, leaving one free at the edge for Peter. The Spaniard was a solitary figure for so long, but seeing her and Peter as a couple felt strangely right. It was how it should have been from the start. May knew that now.

In the front row of seats sat Celine, Millie, Remy, Pierre and Laurent. They were all thrilled about Scotland, which had even more horses than Brockleton, and also a herd of red deer, a boating lake and a school nearby that played rugby and cricket, all of which Remy thought made it a lot more interesting than staying at boring old Brockleton all year round, with his boring tutor. Of course the boys would be back in Ireland for their holidays.

After the honeymoon Nick and Maggie would go back to Brockleton and mind the estate, which was a full-time job. Though, typical Nick, he had already suggested building a theatre on the grounds where the cabaret could settle for the winter if they liked, and which May's theatre company could use when they went on tour. Nothing was ever going to come between Nick and the theatre business.

May gazed around her happily. The room was beautiful, wood panelled, and the seats were all upholstered in powder-blue velvet.

There was a large fireplace filled with silver cones, and elaborate flower arrangements in marble urns four feet tall adorned either side of the registrar's desk. The room was fragranced by sweet pea and lily of the valley. The huge windows, with their silver damask drapes and pelmets, gave the room a serene and elegant feel. It was perfect.

The string quartet that sat in the corner of the room struck up 'Air on the G String' by Bach.

Nick stood at the registrar's desk, looking terrified again at the further delay. Everyone knew Maggie adored him, but her mother's refusal to accept the marriage was something that weighed heavily on her, and he was afraid she would realise at the last minute that he wasn't worth abandoning all she knew and understood.

The small crowd turned, and the sigh of relief was almost audible. There she was, Mrs Cullen, in a lovely primrose yellow hat and coat, a smile on her face.

'Nana!' Aisling called. 'Sit beside me.'

Bridie took one last loving look at her daughter, evidently able to at least accept the marriage, and went to join Aisling. May shot Peter a glance. There passed between them an unspoken conversation. *Well done. You did it. I'm so proud of you.*

All eyes were on the bride, radiant in a white lace wedding gown. Her bouquet was of freesias and peonies. She refused to be done out of her day, she'd declared, and so she was a bride and would dress like one, even if the wedding wasn't in a church.

On her copper curls she wore a straight-edged Juliet cap veil, held in place with organza flowers at each temple, the fabric scattered with seed pearls. She looked like an angel.

Beaming, Peter offered her his arm, and together Peter and Maggie walked to the strains of violins, viola and cello up the short aisle to where Nick stood.

Peter kissed her cheek and shook Nick's hand before retreating to the seat beside Aida.

May leant forwards and whispered to her erstwhile husband, 'The Kit Cullen card?'

He grinned back. 'Works every time.'

THE GEM OF IRELAND'S CROWN

The words flowed soothingly over everyone as the registrar spoke of love and commitment before their friends and family. And in every heart and mind of those gathered, the trials of the past, the losses and loves, the good times and bad, all faded into insignificance.

Then the registrar went on. 'Repeat after me. I do solemnly declare...'

Nick and Maggie repeated the words.

'That I know not of any lawful impediment why I may not be joined in matrimony to this man or this woman.'

There was silence – Clive kept his hand firmly over Timothy's mouth – and then an almost audible exhale of relief as the registrar carried on.

'Do you, Vivian Nicholas Shaw, sixth Baron de Simpré, take this woman, Margaret Bridget Cullen, to be your lawfully wedded wife, to have and to hold, for richer, for poorer, in sickness and in health, as long as you both shall live?'

Nick opened his mouth but shut it again. Everyone knew he'd been practising and practising not to stammer on this short phrase, even though it contained the fatal D. The entire room was holding its breath, the air full of encouragement and silent cheering; it was palpable.

He inhaled slowly through his nose, let it out through his mouth, the way Peter had taught him to relax, then said loudly and deeply, 'I... do.'

Another collective sigh of relief.

'And do you, Margaret Bridget Cullen, take this man, Vivian Nicholas Shaw, sixth Baron de Simpré, to be your lawfully wedded husband, to have and to hold, for richer, for poorer, in sickness and in health, as long as you both shall live?'

Maggie grinned and gazed at Nick. 'I most certainly do.'

A ripple of laughter.

'Then repeat after me. I call upon these persons here present to witness...'

They did as they were instructed, and the registrar announced, 'I now pronounce you man and wife.' And nodding at a beaming Nick, then said, 'You may kiss the bride.'

The string quartet played 'Salut d'Amour' by Elgar as they walked down between their guests, and everyone clapped as Bridie Cullen embraced her daughter.

And Cullen's Celtic Cabaret, the whole company of friends that May and Peter had brought together, walked out into the bright sunshine of another beautiful day.

The End.

I SINCERELY HOPE you enjoyed this series, and like me, you feel a little sad to say goodbye to these characters. If you would like to join my readers club, (100% free and always will be, and I will never use your details for anything or bombard you with nonsense, I promise)

Then pop over to www.jeangrainger.com

If you enjoyed this book, I would really appreciate a review. It makes all the difference. Just click this link to add your review.

https://geni.us/G1HHP

IF YOU ARE ready to start another of my series here is a preview of The Trouble With Secrets. I hope you enjoy it.

THE TROUBLE With Secrets
Kilteegan Bridge Series - Book 1

CHAPTER 1

Kilteegan Bridge, Co Cork, 1948

'Don't leave me, Paudie. Don't leave me. I'll die. I swear, I'll walk into the sea and I'll die.'

'Maria, why are you saying this?' Daddy's voice was strange – it was broken and sad. He was normally stronger sounding or something. 'Of course I'll never leave you.'

'I've seen the way Hannah Berger looks at you, Paudie. *Everyone* sees the way she looks at you, right there in the church in front of the whole parish, in front of her own husband. She wants you for herself. She's heart-set on having you.'

Lena kept very still in her special hiding place behind the carved and painted settle beside the fire. Her brother and sister were in bed, but she'd come down to fetch her doll. She was small for seven, and most days she liked it here behind this long wooden seat with the high back, which could fold down into a bed for visitors. You could hear things, and it was warm near the fire, and nobody gave you a job to do. But now she was listening to things she'd rather not hear, even if she didn't understand any of it. Mrs Berger couldn't have Daddy all to herself, even if she did find him useful around the estate. Daddy belonged to Mammy, and to her, and to Emily and Jack.

'This is all in your mind. I love you, Maria…'

'Then stop going to see her!'

'If we could afford for me to stop working up there, you know I would.'

A wild sob and a crash of crockery. Mammy had thrown something down from the dresser. Lena prayed it wasn't her favourite bowl, the one with the bluebells painted on it that Daddy had brought her from the fair in Bandon. He'd brought Emily a green velvet ribbon at the same time, to tie up her long blond hair. Emily was beautiful, tall like Mammy, and though she was only nine, people always thought she was much older. She could be bossy sometimes, but usually she was nice. Jack was small like Lena. He was only five. Daddy had brought him a small wooden donkey, just like Ned, their donkey that pulled the cart on the farm.

'Maria, Maria, stop now, love…' Daddy's voice was firmer. He was trying to calm Mammy, soothing her like he did with Mrs Berger's stallion up at Kilteegan House when it went wild in the spring. 'I can't stop going to the Bergers'. That's half our income, building stone walls, pruning the orchard, caring for the horses. Hannah Berger's not interested in me as a man. She just needs a strong pair of hands around the place. She's had nobody to do the heavy jobs since her father died.'

'Let her own husband do the work, now he's home from the war!'

'Ah, how can he do that, Maria, and him in a wheelchair?'

'There's that man of his, the Frenchman…'

'He's neither use nor ornament, that fella. All he does is wait on his master hand and foot, and he pays no attention whatsoever to anything that needs to be done around the grounds.'

'You're a fool. You can't see it – she's trying to seduce you, Paudie, with her red hair and her green eyes. I'm scared, Paudie, and if she gets you, then her husband will kill you. He's evil, Paudie. There's something terrifying about him.'

Lena felt a pain in her tummy when Mammy spoke like that, like she believed that evil spirits were in people. She was very superstitious. Sometimes it was fun when she told Lena and Emily and Jack about fairies and things like that, but mostly it was scary because it was a sign that things could be bad for days if Daddy didn't manage to coax her out of it. Lena wanted it not to be like that for Daddy, or for her and Jack and Emily, but when Mammy got into her imaginary world, she often stayed away a long time. It didn't happen often. She hadn't had a bad spell since last summer, when she'd screamed there was a demon on the stairs. Lena had wet her knickers, she got such a fright. Daddy had to tell Lena over and over that these things weren't true, that it was only in Mammy's mind, before she could get to sleep that night.

Daddy's voice was even firmer now, more like his normal self, like a big strong tree in a storm. 'Maria, my love, calm yourself. There's nothing to worry about, honestly. I go up there and do some work, and they pay me well. That's all. I love you.'

Mammy fell silent. She was still breathing harshly, but she let Daddy lead her over to the settle. Lena felt the wood creak as he sat beside her, and she heard the whisper of cloth on cloth as he put his arm around Mammy. He told her all about the wild flower meadow that would be growing between their farmhouse and the sea in the

THE GEM OF IRELAND'S CROWN

spring, in just a few weeks, and how they'd all take a picnic and go to the seaside. Lena could tell from the way his voice was gentle and low and rumbling that she was calming down.

Lena thought her tall, slim mother really was like a selkie, one of those magical tricky mermaids who look like seals in the water but who come to live with human men until they can't stand to be on land any longer and go back to the ocean. There was a picture of a selkie in a book at school, and she had long white hair, same as Mammy's, and it looked a bit like ropes coming down. Mammy tied her hair up most of the time, but sometimes it was loose and reached all the way down her back. She had eyes the same colour as the selkie too, pale as the sea on a winter day, and her eyelashes and eyebrows were so light that it looked like she didn't have any.

Emily and Jack both looked like Mammy, pale-skinned and fair-haired, but everyone said Lena looked just like her father – dark silky hair, brown eyes and skin that only had to see the sun for a day before it went copper.

In the quiet, the fire bubbled in the range and the night wind threw drops of rain against the window. The radio that had been on all this time in the background began playing the popular new song by Al Jolson, 'When You Were Sweet Sixteen'.

Lena's father started singing it softly under his breath. 'I loved you as I've never loved before, since first I saw you on the village green. Come to me, ere my dream of love is o'er. I love you as I loved you, when you were sweet…when you were sweet sixteen…'

And slowly her mother's breathing softened and the pain in Lena's stomach went away. Daddy swept up the bits of broken crockery in silence.

'Dance with me, Maria,' murmured her father.

Mammy still didn't answer, but she let Daddy pull her to her feet. And when Lena peeped out from behind the settle, her parents were swaying together around the kitchen table, her father's big strong farmer's arms around her tall, slim mother, Maria's head on Paudie's shoulder and both of them with their eyes closed. The broken crockery was in a pile in the corner, and it wasn't her favourite bowl –

it was just that cracked yellow and green plate she'd never liked anyway.

Lena crept out of the kitchen, up the stairs of the two-story farmhouse and into the bedroom she shared with her sister. Emily was fast asleep, her long blond hair spread out across the pillow. Lena snuggled in beside her with her doll and lay on her back, gazing up at the sloped ceiling, the beams casting sharp black shadows in the moonlight. She was glad the storm had passed this time.

She hoped Mammy wouldn't spoil things between Daddy and the Bergers, because she liked going up to Kilteegan House with him. He let her bring up a basket of their farm eggs, and Mrs Berger always gave her an extra penny to keep for herself. Sometimes Daddy kept Lena busy, weeding the vegetable garden or picking up the branches he pruned from the trees in the orchard. But other times she played with Malachy, the little boy who was there when he wasn't away at boarding school. He had dark-red hair like his mother, and the same grass-green eyes. They would play hide-and-seek around the garden if it was fine, and if it rained, they'd hide in the tack house, where the saddles and bridles lived, and lay out a clean horse blanket on the stone flags and sit and play cards or draughts.

Chapter 2

Kilteegan Bridge, 1955

Lena sat in the front pew, staring at her black shoes. Her black calico dress was too tight across her chest, threatening to pop a button. Mammy had made it for her for Hannah Berger's funeral six months before, but she was fourteen then and still growing; now that she was fifteen, it was already too tight. The priest was murmuring in Latin, swinging incense around the coffin that lay before the altar. On her left, Jack looked so pale, she thought he might faint. Lena tried to take hold of his hand, but he pulled it away. He was the man of the house now, Mammy had told him, so he thought he wasn't allowed to cry or show emotion any more. On her other side, Emily sat stiffly next to Maria; they looked like sisters, they were so alike. Both of them were in tears. Lena wished she could cry as well, but everything felt so unreal, she couldn't believe any of it was really happening.

Only three days ago, Daddy had been on his way out the door to check on the lambs and saw that the crafty old fox had stolen another one. Daddy and the fox had what he called a 'mutually respectful relationship'. The fox had a job to do, but so did he.

Daddy had trapped lots of foxes in his life. He tried not to kill things if he didn't have to, but this fox must have been especially clever if Daddy decided he needed to shoot it.

She wished he'd just trapped it.

'We're not the owners of this land, Lena,' he would say. 'Nor are we the masters of the animals and plants that live here. We're just minding it. It was minded by my father and his father before him, and now it's for us to care for, and in due time, Jack will take over.'

Daddy loved his farm.

She would never hear his voice again. Never.

Now her father was in that wooden box, and the priest was telling everyone that Paudie O'Sullivan was happier now than he had ever been because he was at the right hand of the Lord. That was a load of rubbish. Daddy would never want to be anywhere except with his family.

It was Jack who had found him. Their father had been lying in his own blood in the top field with his shotgun, which he hadn't used for ages, beside him. Doc came from the village the minute he heard, but he hadn't been able to save his friend. Daddy died in hospital without ever regaining consciousness. It was a terrible accident, Doc told them. He must have fired at the fox, and his ancient shotgun had backfired, killing him instantly. The doctor was nearly as broken by it as the rest of them. He had been Paudie O'Sullivan's best friend since they were children, and he was Lena's godfather, and he always came to see Maria when she was in one of her dangerously low moods.

The Mass was over now, and Doc, Jack and four other men from the village stepped forward to carry the coffin. Paudie O'Sullivan had been an only child, so there were no brothers to carry him, only his son and his best friend and his neighbours. Jack was barely tall enough for the task, but the undertaker put him in the middle and made sure the older men took most of the weight.

Lena's mother rose from the pew to follow the coffin, awkwardly, because she was very pregnant, her stomach huge under her loose black dress. Lena and Emily walked just behind her, holding hands. Emily squeezed Lena's fingers, and their eyes met briefly. Lena knew what her sister was thinking. Both of them had been dreading all morning that Maria would have one of her terrible breakdowns and scream the church down with fear, or else fall into one of her near-catatonic trances of melancholy. But so far, their mother had carried herself with great dignity. Maybe, like Lena, Maria didn't believe this was really happening.

The walk to the cemetery wasn't long, up a pale stony track fringed with wild montbretia under overhanging trees. The graveyard was on a hill overlooking the distant sea, and to Lena's surprise, the priest and coffin bearers headed towards the far corner, away from the O'Sullivan family plot where her father's parents and his two maiden aunts were buried. She touched her mother's arm. 'Is Daddy not going to be buried with Nana and Granda?' she whispered.

Maria said sharply, 'No. That grave is full.'

Lena fell instantly silent. There was an edge to her mother's voice that frightened her.

But then Maria softened and added, 'Anyway, girls, don't you think the plot I chose for him is much nicer?'

She was right. The plot over by the graveyard wall was lovely, shaded by a spreading chestnut tree and with a wide view of the distant bay. If it weren't for the stone weight of her grief, the beauty of the spot would have lifted Lena's heart.

After the graveside prayers and the sad, heavy rattle of earth and stones onto her father's coffin, Lena finally felt the tears come, and wanting to be alone in her grief, she walked a small distance away from the funeral crowd, muffling her sobs and wiping her nose with a scrap of hanky.

Blinded by grief, she nearly walked into Malachy Berger, who stood facing the Fitzgerald grave. She remembered him as the red-headed boy with bright-green eyes she used to play with as a little girl. She hadn't seen him in years except very briefly at his mother's funeral six months ago, and like her, he had grown since then – a couple of inches at least – and his hair was shorter. There were only two months between them in age, she remembered.

The magnificent Fitzgerald family plot was right next to the more modest O'Sullivan family plot, where Lena's grandparents and grandaunts were buried. Hannah's name and dates were the latest to be carved on the massive Fitzgerald headstone.

HANNAH BERGER née FITZGERALD
b.1919 – d.1955
Beloved wife and mother
Gone too soon

Only thirty-six when she died, five years younger than Lena's father.

Lena stopped. It felt rude to just walk on.

Malachy dug in his pocket and handed her a clean handkerchief. 'It's tough, losing a parent, isn't it?'

She nodded, wiping her tears with his handkerchief and handing it back.

'Keep it.' He said sincerely. 'I'm so sorry for your loss.'

Lena thought the words oddly formal for people their age, but she'd never been in this position before. Maybe the whole wretched business had its own language, where young people spoke so formally.

'Thanks,' she managed.

'I remember him kicking a football around with me, back when I was only six or seven years old. My father had only just come back from the war, and he was in a wheelchair, and my mother was lovely but useless at football. Your dad was one of the people I missed most when I went to boarding school.'

Lena smiled through her tears. It was nice to hear this boy remembering her father so fondly. 'I remember your mam as well. She was always smiling and singing. She was full of life, and she always gave me an extra penny for the eggs to keep for my own pocket.'

He looked sad at the memory. 'That's exactly how she was, full of life. She liked you too. She missed you when you and your father stopped coming, but I suppose you were busy on the farm.'

Lena sighed and nodded. 'I missed her as well.'

Still, it had been easier not to go up to the Bergers' big house these past few years. Maria had taken against any of her family having anything to do with them, forbidding her to go, something to do with not liking or trusting Hannah or her husband. Maria took sets against people for slights or insults, a few real but mostly imagined.

For a while, her father had continued going by himself – they needed the extra money. But then Emily, Jack and Lena had all got old enough to help on the farm, and Daddy bought a few more cows, and soon the O'Sullivan homestead was bringing in enough income from milk, eggs and vegetables for Paudie to stop working odd jobs at the big house altogether.

There was a sharp jerk at her elbow, and Emily hissed in her ear, 'Mammy says come back to Daddy's grave.' And Lena stuffed Malachy's hanky in her sleeve and went with her sister without a backwards glance.

The crowd was beginning to thin. Doc had arranged for tea and sandwiches at the Kilteegan Arms, and everyone was moving towards the cemetery gate. Lena and Emily linked Maria on either side, relieved the funeral had passed without their mother making any kind of scene. As they approached the gate, people maintained a respectful distance. Clearly Mrs O'Sullivan was in no fit state to make conversation. Then, as they approached the gate, Lena saw him. Auguste Berger sat in a wheelchair right beside the gate, and he appeared to be waiting for them. As they walked past, he put his hand out.

His English was accented, as he was French. 'My sincere condolences. I know how difficult it is to lose your spouse, the sense of loss, of abandonment.'

Maria stiffened and glared at him, and Lena mentally braced herself. This could be the catalyst for hysterics; that tendency of her mother's was never far below the surface. The risk was made greater because she could no longer take the tablets she used to stabilise her mood for fear of damage to the babies. 'My husband did not "abandon" me,' she said stiffly. 'It was an accident. An accident.'

'Of course.' Auguste Berger tutted sympathetically as he gazed at her hugely swollen belly. 'So sad Monsieur O'Sullivan didn't live to see this child. Or I believe it is *children*? You're expecting twins, *non*? Two new lives to replace the two lives that were lost...' His voice was barely audible.

'Yes, thank you,' Lena responded, not sure what else to say. There was something unsettling about him. Everyone knew Maria was expecting twins because she had to see the doctor in Cork for her pregnancy, whereas everyone else who was expecting just went to Doc.

'Come on, Mammy.' Emily took their trembling mother by the arm and led her gently to the car the undertakers had supplied that was waiting in the autumn sunshine.

Lena glanced over her shoulder at the man in the wheelchair, who raised his hand to her with a charming smile. Auguste Berger, Malachy's father, was now the owner of Kilteegan House. His wife, Hannah, had been found dead of a heart attack in the orchard last spring. The house was her family place, not his. She'd been the Fitzgeralds' only surviving child, one brother dying as an infant and another in a horse-riding accident years ago. So Berger, as her husband, got it all: the big old house, the extensive grounds and a fine farm.

Behind him, holding the handles of the wheelchair, was that strange stocky Frenchman with oily slicked-back hair. He'd arrived with Berger the day he came back from the war and had not left his side since.

As Lena helped her mother into the car, she could feel the pair's eyes on her and her family as they left Paudie in his final resting place.

. . .

Chapter 3

Kilteegan Bridge, 1958

Lena took off her shoes and crept up the moonlit path in her stockinged feet. It was nearly one o'clock in the morning. She'd never been this late home in her life and didn't want to wake anyone. Not her two-year-old twin sisters, Molly and May, who would never go back to sleep, and not Jack, who had to be up in a few hours for the milking, and especially not her mother, who might be in any sort of mood – madly happy or deep in despair or, worst of all, screaming obscenities at her for being up to no good with boys at the dance.

The front of the farmhouse was in darkness, but the moonlight was enough to help her find her way. She glanced up at the bedroom that had been her parents' and was now just her mother's. The light was off. Good – that meant Mammy was getting some sleep instead of wandering the house as she often did, talking to Dad like he was still alive.

It had been a hard few years in the O'Sullivan household since her father died. Lena and Jack had to leave school to run the farm, and it was so difficult – they had been only fifteen and twelve. Luckily, Jack had taken to farming like a duck to water and had learned a lot about old farming methods that were kind to the land. The neighbouring farmers were very good to them and looked out for them; everyone had been very fond of her father. Jack read voraciously about plants and animals and asked the advice of the old Traveller men and women who camped on their land each year about the various properties of flowers and grasses. He refused to use any of the new pesticides or herbicides on the farm, and though it was more labour-intensive, their milk and beef and lamb were always in great demand. He'd told her about the discovery in Switzerland and subsequent use all over the world of DDT – she'd forgotten the long name of it – and according to Jack, it was the worst thing ever dreamed up.

Emily would have helped more, but she had her hands full with the twins. Maria had fallen into such a deep depression after their birth that Doc sent her away to St Catherine's, a kind of nursing home up in

Limerick, where she'd stayed for nearly a year. To be honest, it was easier at home without their mother, especially since Daddy wasn't there to ameliorate her moods. Even when Maria was in a happy frame of mind, it was difficult to deal with her. She might get a figary to redecorate the whole house, pushing all the furniture together in the middle of the rooms and painting all the walls lovely bright colours, until halfway through she got bored and started doing something else altogether, leaving them with half-painted walls. Another time Lena found her planting a rose garden at three o'clock in the morning, or she could decide she was going to make them all gorgeous clothes from bolt ends of cloth she'd picked up in town for next to nothing. Maria was a genius at making clothes; she'd made the dress Lena was wearing right now – a gorgeous fashionable tea dress of yellow silk, with covered buttons. Maria was so creative, but she hardly ever stuck to anything. Lena had finished off the dress herself because her mother had lost interest before it was complete. It was lovely, though.

Probably that's why Malachy had noticed her in the Lilac Ballroom, among all the other girls.

'Malachy Berger.' She said his name in the cool night air. *Lena Berger.* It had a nice ring to it. *A ring.* She giggled. The two glasses of whiskey they'd had in his house after the dance had gone to her head. He was lovely, though. Most other fellas around here would take advantage of a girl who'd had a drink or two, but not Malachy; he was different to other lads. He'd offered her a lift home in his car – imagine, he had his own car, an amazing dark-green Volkswagen Beetle with cream leather interior and a Bosch radio – and on the way, he'd invited her into his house, where he'd introduced her to his father, who hadn't batted an eyelid at his son bringing a girl home at that hour. Lena hadn't seen Auguste Berger since the day of her father's funeral, and though he'd unsettled her then, she decided it was probably that she'd been so upset, because tonight he was very welcoming and friendly.

Auguste Berger was obviously a sophisticated man, and he had an exotic look about him – it was clear he'd spent his life somewhere other than Kilteegan Bridge. The way he sat in his big armchair by the fire, it wasn't obvious he had a disability. That strange manservant brought them whiskies on a silver tray and little sweet cakes called macaroons. It felt very sophisticated, drinking a whiskey and eating a French macaroon in the lovely sitting room, like something in a film. It was surely the best night of her life.

Malachy was as well-mannered as his father. She guessed it helped that he went to Larksbridge, a fancy boarding school up in Dublin, and not the tech in the next town like most of the boys from here did. He never once made any suggestive remarks or tried to grope her; he just spoke to her like she was a normal human being with her own opinions.

He was taller than when she'd last seen him, maybe five foot ten, with broad shoulders. His red hair had darkened to rich chestnut, and he wore it brushed back off his face in an actual style, on purpose, unlike most of the local lads, who looked like they were dragged backwards through a hedge. But it was his green eyes and long dark lashes that captivated her. His lashes would be the envy of any girl. He had white teeth – Lena had a thing about teeth – and a square jaw. He looked like Cary Grant, she thought with a giggle.

When he asked her up to dance in the Lilac, she could hardly believe it. All the other girls were mad jealous, but she loved it. She knew she looked lovely in the yellow silk dress teamed up with her red high heels. She'd saved up for two months to pay for the shoes, but they were worth it even if they killed her feet. Doc had joked that he'd get her wages back from her when he was treating her corns and bunions from wearing shoes like that. She'd retorted that she had no notion of paying him a penny, that working for the local doctor, especially since he was her godfather and her dad's best friend, surely must have some advantages – free corn plasters and bunion paring maybe? She giggled again, feeling silly and carefree.

As she paused on the doorstep, a pang of familiar sadness threatened her happy mood. She glanced skywards, hoping Daddy could see her now. She was sure he would approve of Malachy; he'd always liked him as a little boy. She remembered them playing football together in the orchard of Kilteegan House.

She entered through the kitchen door and hushed Thirteen, her father's beloved Border collie, before creeping up the stairs as quietly as a mouse. Jack was snoring, his bedroom door ajar. Molly and May in the next room had a little bed each but always slept together, and their door was open enough for Lena to see their tousled blond heads and bare feet sticking out from under the blankets. Hopefully they were dreaming of puppies and kittens and ponies; at two years old they were obsessed with animals.

Lena was looking forward to bed herself. She normally shared the room with Emily, but her older sister was doing a course in bookkeeping in Cork and was in digs for the duration. She'd be home in about two months, and while Lena missed her, it was nice to have the bedroom to herself. She needed a few hours sound sleep before she had to get up and give Jack a hand with the milking and then go to her job at the surgery.

She pushed her bedroom door open, and her heart missed a beat.

'Where were you? Were you out dancing?' Her mother's pale eyes were anxious, as if dancing was a terrifying thing to do. Her long hair was loose and unkempt, and she wore her flowing sea-green dressing gown.

'Mammy, I was at the dance in the Lilac – I told you I was going,' Lena whispered, still anxious not to wake her siblings.

'There might have been bad spirits there, evil people, who would do you harm! You can't see them – you're like your father, too trusting. You haven't the ability to see them for what they are...'

'No evil spirits, just normal lads and girls like myself, Mam.' Lena kept her voice low and even; she would not react to this line of conversation. She placed her new shoes in the base of the wardrobe, then took the Pond's cold cream from her dresser and began to clean the make-up off her face.

Mammy had been good for quite a while now, cooking and taking care of them all. When she was happy and well, she was warm and kind and talented at everything she touched. Only yesterday Mammy had been encouraging her to go dancing in her new dress and saying how pretty she was. How Lena reminded her of Maria's own Aunty Betty, who went to America. How her lovely dark hair was so healthy and shiny, and it was because she rinsed it in lemon juice. And how her petite curvy figure was the envy of the parish.

But the downturn always came, and this was clearly it.

Lena knew she should be used to it by now, but it still shocked her every time, how sudden it could be. Poor Daddy put up with it for years. They'd gone to different doctors, and they'd even tried electric shock treatment, but that made Maria so bewildered and forgetful, it was even more terrifying. And in the end, they'd had to accept there was nothing to be done except send her to St Catherine's for periods of time when she was at her worst. They were kind there, and though Maria knew what it meant when she went there, she always spoke of their kindness when she came home. Sometimes it only took a few weeks, other times months and months, but when she came back, it was like the sun had come up again and their mother was back, all the mystery and demons and darkness forgotten.

Lena often wished she could just run away from the whole confusing thing. She was seventeen now, and Doc had given her a job on reception, so if she wanted, she could get a job in one of the nice clinics in Cork, or maybe even Dublin. But she worried about abandoning Molly and May, and Jack was still only fifteen and wouldn't be able to cope by himself – he was a sensitive boy, and Maria frightened him. Lena worried a lot about what their mother's illness had done to her little brother's sweet nature. He was a good-looking boy, fair-haired and tall, the image of his mother, and he had such a gentle disposition. But he had never got the guts up to even speak to a girl, let alone ask one out. He had no real friends – he'd left school early to run the farm, and farming was a solitary activity at the best of times.

Emily was two years older than Lena and had plans to marry Blackie Crean; the two of them planned to run his family's hardware shop in the village. It wasn't much of a dream, Lena thought, but Emily and Blackie had been together since they were in secondary school, and the prospect of a life together forever in Kilteegan Bridge seemed to make them both happy. Blackie's useless, idle, sticky-fingered father, Dick Crean, was gone, skipped to England, but he was no loss whatsoever. Mrs Crean ran the shop now, but she was crippled with arthritis so would be glad to hand it all over. Emily was sweet and would do what she could to help Jack and mind the twins, Lena knew that, but once Emily was married, she'd have the shop and then maybe her own children to look after.

'I'm tired, Mam, so I'll go to bed. Maybe you should too,' she said, trying to keep the sadness out of her voice.

'Not until you tell me who you were dancing with.' Her mother's voice rose a little – anxious, suspicious, angry.

Suddenly Lena felt so tired, bone-weary of it all. She pulled off her dress and slipped on her nightie. 'If you must know, I was dancing with Malachy Berger.'

Her mother paled and her jaw tightened. 'You are forbidden to be near that boy, do you hear me? Forbidden.'

Lena knew that crazed look but wasn't expecting the blow. It knocked her off her feet, and she landed painfully as she put her hand out to save herself.

The sound of her fall and the enraged scream of her mother brought Jack running, his pale hair standing on end as he gazed wild-eyed at them, wearing his pyjama bottoms and a vest. Behind came a confused and tousled May, a terrified Molly behind her.

'Lena, are you all right?' Jack ran to her and helped her up.

'I'm sorry, I'm sorry, I'm sorry...' The words came out in a sob as Maria rushed past her children, making for her own bedroom; she slammed the door so hard it shook the house.

'Awe you awright, Lena? Awe you hurted?' Molly, who couldn't pronounce her R's yet, asked fearfully, and Lena knew she needed to reassure them. Jack lifted her up and carried her to the bed. He was a gentle soul, always finding birds with broken wings or bottle-feeding calves and lambs that had been rejected by their mothers. He knew what that felt like.

'I'm fine, girls. I just had a tumble – it's my silly new shoes.' She tried to laugh through the pain and was rewarded by weak smiles from her little sisters. 'You too, Jack, don't worry. It was an accident. Just go back to bed.' Lena was exhausted and just needed them all to leave her alone.

Chapter 4

When Lena woke, her wrist was so swollen, she was unable to help Jack with the milking. She got the twins breakfast and then brought them across the fields to Deirdre Madden. Mrs Madden and her husband, Bill, had the neighbouring farm, and their daughter, Lucy, was the same age as the twins. Deirdre took care of Molly and May when Maria wasn't able to. Deirdre had always been helpful to the O'Sullivans; she knew the problem they lived with even though they never talked about it. And Bill gave Jack lots of advice about the farm.

Upon returning from the Maddens', Lena stuck her head around the milking parlour door. 'Run me down to the surgery, will you, Jack?'

He looked up from examining a cow whose udder had mastitis. He'd been up since six to get the herd in. 'You're not going to work with that wrist, are you? It's swelled up like a balloon.'

'I'll be grand. Sure, it's my left hand, and I'll get Doc to have a look at it when he gets a minute.'

'You need an X-ray in case it's broken. I could run you to the hospital in Bantry?'

'I'll see what Doc says – you know he's better than any hospital. Stop fussing.'

Doctor Emmet Dolan, whom everyone called Doc, was a big blocky man with brown curls and dark-green eyes. He lived alone over the surgery he'd inherited from his father, who'd been the doctor before him. He wore dark shapeless suits that seemed to be too big even for him, and his leather bag was so scuffed and worn, it was hard to tell what colour it had once been. But the sight of Doc was all the people of Kilteegan Bridge needed to feel safe and cared for. He possessed an innate sense of what might be wrong and was the most compassionate person Lena had ever met.

Doc had bounced her on his knee as a baby, patched up her and her siblings after childhood mishaps and had been a constant, solid presence in their lives. Even so, when he advertised in the post office window for a receptionist and she went for the interview, she told him that she only wanted the job if he thought she'd be good at it, not as a favour to her or her late father.

Doc had smiled at her. 'Trust me, Lena, you'll be good at it – you know how clever you are. My mother, God be good to her, did it for my father back in his day, but I've not had anyone. And honestly, with the health board breathing down my neck for records of patients and the taxman wanting to know more than I can ever tell him, I badly need someone to manage the paperwork and the appointments and that.'

Doc had been dead set against Lena leaving school at fifteen, although he understood that she had to because of the farm. Lena hated leaving school as well; she envied Emily, who was sixteen when Daddy died and so had got her Inter Cert.

Jack looked doubtful at her suggestion. 'Well, I suppose if you have to go to work, a doctor's surgery is the best place. Is she up?' He glanced warily towards the house.

'No. I'd say she'll stay in her room all day. I've taken her up some bread and cheese and an apple and left it outside her door, in case she wants to eat.

'Get all the jobs done as best you can without me, and meet me in the Copper Kettle at five – we'll have a mixed grill and you'll be back for the milking. Maybe Bill can spare one of his young lads to help you. I can collect the twins from Deirdre after tea. She says she doesn't mind having them all day – it keeps little Lucy out of her hair.'

'Righto. Come on so.'

They walked across the yard, and Jack opened the door of Daddy's old Morris Minor. Thirteen bounded out of the hay barn and jumped into the back seat – she loved a spin. Thirteen had been so sad when their father died, but Jack had filled Paudie's place in the dog's affections and now one was never seen without the other.

The car was immaculate and running as well as ever; Jack spent hours tinkering with it. They drove down the hill to the village in silence, both lost in their own thoughts, with Thirteen resting her chin on Lena's shoulder.

'Will we tell Emily?' Jack asked eventually.

Lena knew what he meant – that Maria was bad again, that the spell of happiness was over. Lena suddenly felt so weary of it all. Her wrist was really sore, and the chance of ever escaping this life seemed so unlikely. 'No.' She sighed. 'What's the point? She won't be back till next month anyway, and it will have blown over by then. No point in having her worry. There's nothing anyone can do to set it off or stop it – you know that, Jack. It just has to run its course.'

'I suppose you're right.' He turned into the square. 'Anyway, hopefully this one will be over quickly. Emily would only worry, and we can manage it, can't we? Were the girls all right this morning?'

Lena nodded. 'They seem to be able to block it out. They were on about Dinny O'Regan's dog having pups.'

Jack groaned. 'Oh God, don't let them persuade you to let them have one. We've enough to deal with besides adding a puppy to the chaos. Besides, I don't think Thirteen would take kindly to sharing her space with a puppy.'

The twins were always bringing injured or 'lost' animals home from the fields. Lena smiled. Jack hadn't a leg to stand on complaining about the twins adopting stray animals – he was just as bad – and she knew that he and the girls were too soft for this world.

He pulled up outside the surgery, and Lena leaned back and took her handbag from the back seat with her good hand. 'See you in the Copper Kettle. Thanks for the lift.' She gave Thirteen a pat on the head and the collie licked her hand, and then she left the boy and his dog to their day.

She let herself into the surgery awkwardly with one hand and switched the lights and heat on in the waiting room. The reception desk was neat and tidy, exactly as she'd left it the evening before.

In less than an hour, the waiting room would be full of people with their ailments, real and imagined, and Doc would treat each one as if they were his only patient that day.

The waiting room, surgery, small kitchen and her office were all on the ground floor of the big terraced house in the middle of the main street of Kilteegan Bridge, and apart from sleeping upstairs, Doc spent almost every moment downstairs. Last night, he would have sat in the kitchen at the back of the house behind the surgery, reading a medical paper, and nodded off in his chair over a glass or two – or three – of wine. He had no life really, apart from his patients. He had never married. His brother had emigrated to Australia years ago, and Doc and he had lost touch. And he'd had a sister he loved, Annie, but she died of TB when she was sixteen. Lena knew several women had tried to turn his head over the years, but he was oblivious. It was sad, she always thought. He'd have been a lovely husband and father.

'That you, Lena?' he called down the stairs.

'And who else might it be?' she called up to him, chuckling.

He stood on the top step in his vest and trousers, face covered in shaving soap, his braces dangling down. 'Stick on the kettle there, love,' he said as he retreated to the bathroom on the landing.

Using just her right hand, she made tea for herself and poured it, then added another spoon of tea leaves because Doc liked his strong enough to trot a mouse on, as he said himself.

Moments later he arrived down. 'What happened you?' he asked, immediately seeing her swollen wrist.

'I fell over last night, just as I was getting into bed.'

'Too much lemonade at the dance, was it?' He smiled, bending his curly head to examine it. He smelled of Imperial Leather soap.

'Something like that.' She winced as he pressed on the swelling. 'Is it broken?'

He shook his head. 'No, just a bad sprain, but you'll have to mind it for a few days. Why didn't you just ring and tell me? I can manage here on my own, you know. I did for years when you were a child.'

It was a running joke of his that Lena felt she was indispensable to him. The reality was that she didn't just do all the paperwork but also made sure he took care of himself and protected him from the worst of the local malingers.

'Go on out of that.' She grinned despite the pain in her wrist. 'You'd have keeled over of a heart attack if you'd kept going the way you were. I've taken years off you.'

He eased her sleeve up and sprayed her wrist with something pungent but instantly cooling before strapping it gently in a bandage and making her a sling, which he fixed with a safety pin.

'How's Maria?' he asked. Though he never would say as much, Lena immediately worried that he knew her mother was responsible for her sprained wrist.

She said defensively, 'She's been very happy recently, making lovely dresses and that sort of stuff.'

'But today?' He fixed her with his wise gaze.

She dropped her eyes. 'Well, today she's in bed. She is a bit low.'

'I might call out to her tomorrow.'

'OK.'

He touched her cheek. 'I know she can't help it, Lena. But that doesn't make it any easier to deal with, does it? If she's very low, I'll suggest she go to St Catherine's. She never wants to go, but she always feels better afterwards. Now, can Jack come in for you? Take you home?' He glanced at the clock; surgery would start soon.

'I'll do no such thing. I'll take an aspirin and sit here quietly, and I won't use my left hand at all, I promise. I can still answer the phone and deal with patients.'

'Ah, will you stop it, and have the whole place calling me an awful tyrant altogether?' Doc objected.

'Please, Doc, I'm better here.'

Something in the way she said it gave him pause. 'Is she that bad?' he asked gently.

She stayed silent, not wanting to betray her mother but not wanting to be sent home to her either.

Doc sighed. 'Right, stay. But if I think you're not up to it, I'll make you lie on the kitchen sofa and rest – is that clear?' He was stern now, but she knew he was soft as butter really.

'Crystal.' She grinned.

She unlocked the door, and the day began with coughs and colds and warts and aches and babies with rashes.

Old Seanie Hurley showed up with an infected cut, stinking of dung and with his filthy wellingtons leaving dirt all over the lino. After Doc had thoroughly washed and disinfected the cut, the old man insisted on paying his bill with duck eggs – 'for the baking', even though Doc had never baked in his life. Doc thanked him and told him the eggs were lovely. Sometimes she despaired of Doc's generosity, but he always said the point of being a doctor was to heal the people who needed healing, not to get rich.

The new curate came in, Father Otawe. He was an object of great curiosity because he was a Black man from Uganda, the first ever seen in the town. The schoolchildren loved him because he told them stories about all the wild animals that were to be found around his village back home. They didn't seem to have any difficulty understanding his accent, even though Lena found it hard enough when he was trying to explain to her what was wrong with him – he had a grain of sand or a bit of something in his eye.

Doc had asked Chrissy, who owned the town's only café, the Copper Kettle, to deliver some sandwiches for lunch, which they both ate at their respective desks. Doreen Kiely from the chemist popped in to tell Doc that the new drugs he'd ordered had arrived, and when she saw Lena's wrist, she left and arrived back with two cups of tea and two slices of homemade sponge cake. Living in Kilteegan Bridge drove most young people daft, everyone knowing each other's business, but today Lena had to admit it had some advantages.

The rest of the day passed in the usual flood of ailments, and before she knew it, it was time to go home.

Jack was waiting for her outside the Copper Kettle when she arrived, carrying the box of Seanie Hurley's blue duck eggs, which Doc had insisted she bring home with her. Jack pushed the door of the busy café open and held it for her. 'How was your day?' he asked with a smile.

'Grand, busy, you know yourself.'

Lena smiled at the middle-aged woman with unusually brassy blond hair behind the counter. Chrissy refused to go to the hairdresser's, so her home dye jobs had varying degrees of success. This week she was almost luminous. 'Two mixed grills, please, Chrissy, with tea and bread and butter.'

They took a seat at the back in a booth like they often did, and when their meals arrived, Jack tucked into the sausages, rashers, black pudding and fried potatoes hungrily. He swallowed, then asked, 'What did Doc say about your wrist?'

'It's only sprained. I'm to mind it for a few days, and it'll be grand.'

'So no more dancing for you.' He winked.

'Oh, I don't know – I don't dance on my hands.'

'How was the Lilac last night?'

'Ah, the usual crowd.' Lena shrugged. On the way there, she'd decided not to say anything at all about Malachy to her brother, or about drinking whiskey with Auguste Berger. But in the end, she couldn't help herself – she had to talk to someone, and there was nobody else. 'Do you know why Mammy dislikes the Bergers so much?' she asked, cutting up her bacon.

Jack shrugged. 'I don't know. She never liked Hannah Berger. Didn't she get some notion Hannah had an eye for Daddy or something? And she thought they were a bit high and mighty, looking down at the rest of us from their perch in the big house.'

'The poor man is perched in a wheelchair.'

'Sure he is, but even that fella that works for him, that Phillippe Laurent, when he goes shopping in the town, he acts like he's a cut above, always talking about how the milk and beef and lamb are so much better in France.' Jack sounded aggrieved, and Lena could see how he'd take it personally after all the hard work he did to make sure their meat and milk were pesticide-free.

'Well, I'm sure that's just Phillippe.' Lena knew she sounded ridiculously defensive, but she couldn't help it. 'I'm sure Auguste Berger is very nice and wouldn't say any such thing.'

Jack looked up in surprise from coating his sausages with mustard. 'Why are you so bothered about the Bergers all of a sudden?'

'No reason.'

'Hmm.' Jack raised a sceptical eyebrow.

'Oh, all right.' She felt herself go hot with embarrassment. 'I was dancing with Malachy Berger in the Lilac last night –'

'Ah, that explains it, all right.'

'Stop grinning like an eejit – it doesn't mean anything. But anyway, we went back to his house after the dance, and his father was there, and we drank whiskey and ate macaroons…'

'Ooh la la!' Jack teased. 'Macaroons no less? Did he make you do the washing up?'

'Stop it! He did no such thing. He treated me like a lady and said how much I look like my father, and then Malachy drove me home. He acted the total gentleman, and it was all lovely.'

Jack stuffed in a mouthful of toast, still grinning. 'Just so long as you remember you're my sister and not some posh lady from the big house, Lena O'Sullivan.'

'You don't think I'm a lady?' she teased.

'Of course you're a lady – you're a perfect lady. You're just not a snob, and I wouldn't want you turning into one, even if you do end up being called Lena Berger.'

'Some chance of that.' But even the sound of her name hitched to Malachy's gave her a hot little glow, and she had to hide her face behind her mug of tea. 'Do you want a dessert? My treat.' Anything to get off the subject.

'I certainly do,' he said enthusiastically, and Lena turned to smile and wave at the counter.

Chrissy was busy cooking, so it was Chrissy's fourteen-year-old daughter, Imelda, who sloped over, looking sullen. 'What do ye want?'

'Excuse me?' Lena smiled.

The girl had a full face of make-up and dark hair that could do with a wash. 'What?'

'Oh, I'm sorry. I thought you were speaking to us. Apologies.'

'I was,' Imelda answered, slightly on the back foot now.

'Oh, I must have misheard you. I thought you just said, "What do ye want." But clearly you didn't, because that would be such a strange, rude way to speak to a customer, especially considering your mother is always so friendly and helpful and has worked so hard to build up her business all on her own.'

Lena was very fond of Chrissy, who'd been widowed young, and knew from talking to her that Imelda was a scourge.

The girl coloured beneath the caked-on make-up and was about to say something when the look on Lena's face changed her mind.

'What would ye like to order?' she asked, if not with a smile, at least without the scowl.

'I'll have a piece of apple tart with ice cream, please, Imelda. Jack?'

'Sure, I'll have a bit of apple tart too. It sounds lovely.'

'With ice cream?'

'Cream only, please.'

'OK,' managed the teenager before slinking off back to the counter.

Jack grinned at his sister. 'So, Mrs Malachy Berger, I'm glad you're around to put manners on us natives.'

Lena rolled her eyes at him. 'I wasn't being a snob. That one needs to wake up, or she'll ruin her mother's business. Look at us. We were fifteen and twelve when Daddy died, and we didn't go around looking like the world was against us – at least I hope we didn't – so there's no excuse for sour Imelda.'

Jack sighed. 'I hope not, but I'm not going to lie to you – sometimes I thought it was.'

Lena's heart broke for him, her sensitive little brother, and she reached over and squeezed his hand.

To continue the story you can click this link:
https://geni.us/TheTroublewithSecrets

ACKNOWLEDGMENTS

In researching a book, or indeed a series like this one, it is necessary to cast the net wide in terms of research. I was very fortunate to encounter a wonderful woman called Vikki Jackson, the granddaughter of the famous Vic Loving. Vic was powerhouse behind Ireland's premier travelling theatre, or 'fit-ups' as they were known.

Vikki's charming home is a museum to that theatrical life and a visit there, if you are ever in Bruree, Co. Limerick is something you will never forget.

Vikki was so generous in sharing stories of her grandmother's, and indeed her own life on the road, and that invaluable background gave me a firm foundation on which Cullen's Celtic Cabaret grew. Thank you Vikki, I really appreciate it.

ABOUT THE AUTHOR

Jean Grainger is a USA Today bestselling Irish author. She writes historical and contemporary Irish fiction and her work has very flatteringly been compared to the late great Maeve Binchy.

She lives in a stone cottage in Cork with her lovely husband Diarmuid and the youngest two of her four children. The older two come home for a break when adulting gets too exhausting. There are a variety of animals there too, all led by two cute but clueless microdogs called Scrappy and Scoobi.

ALSO BY JEAN GRAINGER

The Tour Series

The Tour
Safe at the Edge of the World
The Story of Grenville King
The Homecoming of Bubbles O'Leary
Finding Billie Romano
Kayla's Trick

The Carmel Sheehan Story

Letters of Freedom
The Future's Not Ours To See
What Will Be

The Robinswood Story

What Once Was True
Return To Robinswood
Trials and Tribulations

The Star and the Shamrock Series

The Star and the Shamrock
The Emerald Horizon
The Hard Way Home
The World Starts Anew

The Queenstown Series

Last Port of Call
The West's Awake
The Harp and the Rose
Roaring Liberty

Standalone Books

So Much Owed
Shadow of a Century
Under Heaven's Shining Stars
Catriona's War
Sisters of the Southern Cross

The Kilteegan Bridge Series

The Trouble with Secrets
What Divides Us
More Harm Than Good
When Irish Eyes Are Lying
A Silent Understanding

The Mags Munroe Story

The Existential Worries of Mags Munroe
Growing Wild in the Shade
Each to their Own
Closer Than You Think

Cullens Celtic Cabaret

For All The World

A Beautiful Ferocity

Rivers of Wrath

The Gem of Ireland's Crown

Made in the USA
Columbia, SC
04 April 2024

c0152fdb-fc30-406a-92cc-3e6e501091b5R01